D0585661

# The Queen's Secret

www.**transworldbooks**.co.uk

# The Queen's Secret

Victoria Lamb

## BANTAM PRESS

LONDON • TORONTO • SYDNEY • AUCKLAND • JOHANNESBURG

TRANSWORLD PUBLISHERS
61–63 Uxbridge Road, London W5 5SA
A Random House Group Company
www.transworldbooks.co.uk

First published in Great Britain
in 2012 by Bantam Press
an imprint of Transworld Publishers

A CIP catalogue record for this book
is available from the British Library.

ISBNs 9780593067994 (hb)
9780593067987 (tpb)

Addresses for Random House Group Ltd companies outside the UK
can be found at: www.randomhouse.co.uk
The Random House Group Ltd Reg. No. 954009

The Random House Group Limited supports the Forest Stewardship Council
(FSC®), the leading international forest-certification organization. Our books
carrying the FSC label are printed on FSC®-certified paper. FSC is the only
forest-certification scheme endorsed by the leading environmental organizations,
including Greenpeace. Our paper procurement policy can be found at
www.randomhouse.co.uk/environment.

*In memoriam*
*Charlotte Lamb,*
*1937–2000*

# Prologue

## The outskirts of London, May 1575

LUCY MORGAN PEERED OVER THE HIGH WOODEN SIDE OF THE swaying cart. A group of soldiers trotted past, sunlight glinting off their helmets, their dusty blue livery announcing their allegiance to Lord Leicester. Staring back down the road, she could no longer see the distant towers of Richmond Palace, their bright pennants fluttering in the breeze off the River Thames, but only wooded hills and high green hedgerows as the road deepened into countryside.

'I've never been so far outside London before.' She glanced around, but no one in the cart seemed to be listening. Some of the older women were slumped over, asleep in the sunshine, their mouths open. The carts had left London just after dawn and Lucy was tired too, but unwilling to miss anything by closing her eyes. 'Where will we sleep tonight? How will they feed so many of us?'

The woman to her right, plain-faced and soberly dressed in widow's black, tugged irritably at her gown. 'Sit down, girl.' Her voice was sour. 'The cartmen are staring.'

But Lucy did not want to sit down. Even the six months she had spent at court had not prepared her for the activity of the past few days, watching Queen Elizabeth's servants make ready to depart London for the summer months. Wagon after wagon had lumbered off in advance of the Queen's private entourage, creaking with furniture, chests packed with clothes and books, the bric-a-brac of the royal household. Nor had she expected this sweating crush of bodies, jammed in against each other with little more dignity than plague victims flung on a cart. She had seen royal officials and their wives crowded together with their liveried servants, lowly stable boys and gongmen riding the covered wagons of the provisions train, potmen shouting crudely to each other above the grind of wheels, and the women of the Queen's household crammed without ceremony into old wooden carts without seats: seamstresses, laundresses, cooks, serving maids, and court entertainers like herself.

At that moment their cart juddered over a deep yawning rut and Lucy gave a cry, clutching at the side to save herself from falling.

'I told you to sit down,' the woman beside her remarked, and folded her arms as though satisfied that she had been proved right, closing her eyes against the sun's glare.

Lucy had come to court the autumn before, at the age of fourteen, and this was her first summer progress. The court had rarely stayed in any one residence above seven or eight weeks that first autumn. Even once the cold weather had set in, they had been forced to pack up and move to another royal residence as soon as the stink of human refuse grew too powerful to be ignored. It was not always a good thing to be in a new place. In one of the smaller houses, out on the periphery of the city, the female entertainers had slept in a curtained-off corner of the dining hall, and at another place had been herded ten to a chamber, sleeping on filthy rushes through a lack of bedding. The stench had become so bad, it had been almost impossible to breathe some nights, let alone sleep.

Now this: a sweet-smelling wind in her hair, newborn lambs in the fields, eglantine and the white wood anemone shining out from the hedgerows.

The widow tut-tutted as Lucy settled back on the floor of the cart, wriggling to make herself more comfortable on the un-yielding wooden boards. There was little room for them all in the open cart and the boards bristled with splinters, making any sudden movements risky. It did not help that two of the seamstresses were fat-necked, broad-chested peahens, slumped drowsily with clog-heavy feet shoved out in front of them, taking up more than their fair share of space.

'Sorry, mistress,' Lucy offered, more from politeness than genuine concern, having accidentally jabbed the older woman in the ribs as she tried to find a more comfortable position.

'Did your mother never tell you not to fidget, girl?'

'I cannot tell you,' Lucy countered sharply, 'for I never knew my mother.'

She wished she had kept silent as both seamstresses raised their plump, pink-cheeked faces to stare across at her, suddenly no longer asleep. Uncomfortably aware that she was the centre of attention, Lucy added hurriedly, 'My mother died when I was born, you see, God rest her soul.'

The widow crossed herself superstitiously, muttering a quick prayer under her breath. But at least she shifted sideways after that, drawing her cloak a little closer. This gave Lucy room to settle her buttocks squarely on the hard boards, balancing on her palms as the jolting cart rattled on into the countryside.

It was a common enough reaction. A black girl was strange enough in England. But a motherless black girl was bad luck, a curse, someone to be avoided – almost as though Lucy had taken a hand in her own mother's death. Which was true in a way, she supposed, since her mother had died giving birth to her. Or so Master Goodluck had told her.

It was not only the superstitious who shunned her, of course. The kindly gentleman who had employed her at court last autumn had praised her singing, saying with astonishment that she had 'a voice like a skylark'. Yet Lucy had not yet been permitted to do more than sing with the chorus and dance in a few of the set pieces performed each month before the visiting ambassadors and dignitaries. Perhaps old Mistress Hibbert, who supervised the female entertainers, was afraid the Queen would take fright at her African skin and eyes, her unrestrained barley-twists of black hair. So Lucy had been hidden discreetly behind the others every time she sang, hair tamed beneath the smooth white wings of a cap, dark skin concealed by a shawl draped about her shoulders and knotted tight at the throat.

That spring though, the favourite of the troupe, the boastful Peggy, had been found with child and dismissed. Then two of their most experienced singers had come down with the shaking sickness. Even Mistress Hibbert herself, who had hated Lucy from the very first day she arrived at court, had been deemed too old for travel and told to remain behind.

Perhaps this summer, as one of the few sopranos left in the troupe who could sing the full scale, she might at last find herself face to face with Queen Elizabeth – whom she had only ever seen as a pale but beautiful figure above a mass of courtiers' heads.

'When does the court return to London?'

The woman next to her had fallen asleep at last, slumped in her black cloak, but one of the heavy-breasted seamstresses opposite gave her a sympathetic smile. She was yellow-toothed, her cheeks flushed from the sun.

'Summer's end, child,' she soothed her. 'Come September, we'll all be home again.'

Lucy frowned, trying to suppress a flutter of panic. 'But it's only May. Must we stay away so long?'

'Bless your ignorance,' the woman laughed comfortably, 'of course we must, for the Queen herself orders it. Her Majesty won't risk the plague by staying in the city over the summer, and who can blame her with the stench of the palace sewers so bad last week? So we're bound for Grafton House now, then we'll take the road up to Warwickshire and rest a month or so at the castle of Kenilworth, they say – or until the Queen tires of his lordship's attentions.'

The woman chuckled before continuing, as though at some private joke. 'Beyond Kenilworth, I cannot tell you which road the progress will take, though it's rumoured the Queen's to visit some of the grand houses of Staffordshire this year.' She smiled at Lucy's dismayed expression. 'Thirsty, child?'

Lucy nodded thankfully. She accepted a half-full bottle of ale from under the folds of the seamstress's rough white apron. The ale was warm – not surprisingly, given its hiding place – but it refreshed her.

'Thank you. Do you know where we'll stop tonight?'

'Wherever there's a space set aside for us to sleep, my poppet.

And no need of a hedge, either. A grassy field and a hunk of bread and cheese each, that will do me nicely. For there'll be no rain tonight to wet us. Not with this hot sun.'

With another chuckle, the seamstress took a generous swig of ale herself, then tucked the bottle safely away under her apron, shooting a surreptitious glance at the sour-faced woman as though to check she had not seen.

'Best get some sleep now, child. There'll be no stopping again till past noon.'

The open cart rumbled on in the sunshine, mile after mile taking them further away from London and the familiar mud-thick stench of the Thames. Lucy tried not to doze off, watching the trees pass overhead and delighting in the sun on her face. But eventually she too fell asleep, her knees relaxing, her head nodding on to her chest. Her dreams were confused, filled with grinning cartmen chasing her down green country lanes which seemed to go on for ever. In her dream, someone was calling out behind her, reaching out to grab her shoulder.

She woke to urgent cries, finding herself slumped sideways in the cart, her cap askew, her skirts soiled with straw.

'The Queen! Look, child, it's the Queen!'

The whole cart was in uproar. Even the sour-faced widow had struggled to her feet, calling excitedly to the snoring laundress on her other side to wake up, that the Queen's party was bearing down on them and would soon be passing the cart.

Lucy stretched out her limbs, stiff with the tingling cramp of sleeping too long in one position, and immediately felt a very real and pressing need to relieve herself. Except there was nowhere to do so but publicly, in a little tarred quarter-barrel assigned for such needs and then emptied over the side of the cart in full view of the driver and his mate, a thought which dismayed her.

Then she realized belatedly what the others were shouting and lurched to her feet, as eager as everyone else to catch a glimpse of the Queen.

'Look!' someone cried as the first outriders of the Queen's guard came into view, though all she could see was a cloud of dust rising on the road behind them, and the coarse linen hood of the woman in front of her.

The wagon swayed perilously and Lucy was thrown against its rough wooden side, banging her knee. The driver swore an oath she had not heard since her childhood on the streets of London, and called for the 'idiot women' to sit down again before they upset the cart. But none of them paid the man any attention.

The guards came first in their leather jerkins, buckles and mail-coats flashing in the sun. Then she saw the familiar figure of the Earl of Leicester cantering ahead of the royal party, his swift gaze examining the faces of those in each cart he passed. It was almost as if he were looking for someone, Lucy thought curiously, except for the casual turn of that dark head, one gloved fist resting arrogantly on his hip, reins held seemingly slack in the other. She had seen him at court often enough – though he had never noticed her, Lucy was sure of it. And why should he? The earl's feathered cap was pitched at an angle, and he seemed to be controlling the animal with just his knees and booted feet, unconcerned by the speed at which he was travelling.

Reaching the party of foot soldiers, the earl pulled the animal up and spoke softly to them for a moment, then wheeled his sweating black stallion about and rode back towards the Queen.

Lucy turned her head and craned to see the royal entourage as it passed their cart. Her view was impeded by the guards riding in strict formation beside the Queen, their horses almost nose to tail. At first, all she could see was a frilled white-gold canopy supported by four outriders, then the young guard nearest her fell back a pace or two, fumbling with his reins as the horse shied, and she caught a fleeting glimpse of the Queen herself.

Perched on a white horse, Queen Elizabeth sat pale and straight-backed under an elaborate headdress, her glorious red hair coiled high with pearls, a vast ivory ruff fanning out like angel wings on either side of her head. Her face was set, but her eyes seemed fixed on the Earl of Leicester's figure as he saluted her briefly, threw a laughing comment towards one of her immaculately groomed ladies, then brought his dancing stallion round to the rear of the column where the chief courtiers rode.

'God save Her Majesty!' Lucy called out impulsively, if rather too late, as the white-gold canopy swayed out of sight.

The Queen's horse moved on, and Lucy was left feeling a little foolish, leaning out over the side of the cart, gritty dust in her face, with nothing to see but the liveried rumps of the guards' horses.

But someone had heard her. The Earl of Leicester had dropped to a more sedate trot beside one of the courtiers in the Queen's train, a stately old man with a grizzled beard and a heavily ornate gold chain about his neck. Now he paused in his conversation, a courteous smile still on his face, and turned his head in the direction of that shout, swift and alert, like a hound questing for a hare.

His dark eyes found her, and Lucy, forgetting for the briefest of moments to lower her gaze before his as a servant should do, smiled back at the earl.

'Oh now, look you. He's a proper one for the ladies, he is!' The seamstress nodded at Leicester's departing back, then chuckled as her stout companion gasped and nudged her in the ribs. 'These Dudleys. Always one hand on the crown and the other on my lady's crotch. Young Robin Dudley was Master of the Horse when I first came to court. Now he's Lord Robert, if you please, master of the Queen – and father to her children.'

Lucy sat down again in the rocking cart, shocked and staring, appalled by the woman's story. 'Queen Elizabeth has *children* by the Earl of Leicester?'

'Two, so they say,' the seamstress confided, not even bothering to lower her voice, 'and both hidden away safe in the country where the Scots Queen may not find them and murder the poor babes in their beds.'

'Stop peddling your filth to this foolish child, Mistress Cubbon, or I'll report you to the chief steward for speaking treason against the Queen.' The widow shook her head in disgust, her face stiff under the plain black hood as she turned to Lucy. 'Girl, don't endanger yourself by listening to this woman's nonsense. I know her type – little better than a common drunk, for all her skill with a needle. Everyone knows our queen is a chaste, God-fearing virgin and will remain so until her wedding night. And the Earl of

Leicester is a wise and sober gentleman of the court, who has not so much as looked at another lady since his own poor wife died.'

'Aye, and by whose hand did his poor wife die?' the seamstress snorted. But she shrugged uneasily at the widow's furious glare and looked away. 'Well, well, that was long ago. And it may all be nonsense, after all. God save Her Majesty and preserve his lordship.'

Lucy said nothing after this, fearing what might come of such a dangerous conversation, and the women's talk soon died away to bitter murmurs, lost in the creaking sway and judder of the cart.

Desperate now to relieve herself, she sat for the next few miles in an uncomfortable silence, head bowed in her neat white cap, attempting to suck an evil-looking splinter out of her finger. She had decided it was probably best not to mention that the Earl of Leicester had winked at her.

# One

*Kenilworth Castle, Warwickshire, Wednesday*
*6 July, 1575*

EVERY EVENING SINCE HIS ARRIVAL, WALSINGHAM HAD COME DOWN
from his rooms in Caesar's Tower to take his customary walk
along the water's edge before retiring. He tended to keep early
hours in the country, and until the court came to Kenilworth the
Queen's chief secretary had no reason to change his routine.
Three days he had been in residence, having excused himself early
from the progress through Oxfordshire and travelled on ahead to
check that security was in place for the Queen's arrival at
Kenilworth.

The sundial on the mereside wall was in full shadow by the
time Walsingham appeared on the third evening, descending from
the Italian elegance of the keep's arcade into what would be the
Queen's Privy Garden for the duration of her stay. The hem of his
cloak brushed the clipped box hedges as he moved slowly
between the formal beds, pausing to examine a particularly
exotic-looking musk rose entwined with eglantine, or crush
fragrant lavender between his fingertips.

Stretched out on his belly along the gnarled branch of an oak,
concealed by a riot of lusty green foliage, Goodluck watched
Master Walsingham approach, and smiled.

His target was laughably unprotected, considering he was one of the most powerful and influential men in England. His elevated status was not obvious at a glance. Walsingham wore a simple black skullcap and plain ruff, having dined alone that evening, and had brought no company with him. True, there were two guards down at the Watergate and probably half a dozen yawning at their posts beyond the archway into Caesar's Tower. But nobody within earshot.

It was growing dark, the sun's heat had long gone and the cool shadows were lengthening. The gardens would soon be closed.

If Goodluck were to drop down on him now, clap one hand over his mouth and slide a stiletto blade between his ribs, Walsingham would be dead within seconds, and no one any the wiser until the man's body was found in the morning.

Walsingham passed beneath him, humming gently under his breath, adjusting the expensive lace at his wrist. He was so close Goodluck could see the fine gold ring on his finger, and a few grey hairs sprinkled among the black at his temple.

Holding his breath, he swung himself soundlessly down from the oak branch, hung there a second, eyeing the distance to the ground, then dropped. Straightening from his crouch, Goodluck waited for Walsingham's leisurely tread to take him round the corner and behind a massive yew hedge that divided the garden from the castle walls.

Then he followed Walsingham into shadow, silent-footed and intent.

But just as Goodluck came up behind him, poised to spring, Walsingham suddenly whirled about and seized his right arm, twisting it painfully behind his back.

Something cold flashed at his throat. Goodluck focused on the thin blade pressing hard against his skin; there would be a prick-mark there in the morning.

'In general, a man talks more easily without a dagger to his throat,' he said conversationally, and smiled down at the blade. 'Of Florentine design. I know the Italian who makes these. Lightweight, but deadly once you have the knack of them. An excellent assassin's weapon, to be cunningly concealed up a sleeve or down the side of a boot.'

'Well, if you will creep up on people . . .'

The slender blade was withdrawn and once more concealed in Walsingham's generous sleeve.

Goodluck rubbed his neck with a rueful smile. 'I had forgotten your reputation.' Respectfully, he swept him a bow. 'Sir.'

'And I had forgotten your odd sense of humour,' Walsingham replied testily.

With one accord, they moved further into the shadow of the yew hedge, Walsingham almost invisible against the thickening dusk in his sombre black suit and cloak. Cautious as ever, he had not used Goodluck's name.

'I received your note,' he murmured. 'Though your news was slender. Has the code been compromised again?'

'I suspect it must have been. There was an incident when I landed at Dover.' Goodluck shrugged off the memory. 'So we move on.'

'Indeed.'

'The castle is being watched, sir.'

'I expected no less.'

Walsingham had lowered his voice until it was a mere thread of sound, barely audible above the wingbeats of a flock of geese passing overhead. They both fell silent for a moment, watching the white geese disappear into the dusk.

'You've seen those who watch? You know who they are?'

Reluctantly, Goodluck shook his head.

'Then why risk meeting like this?' Walsingham sounded impatient. 'Secrecy is everything. Is it money you want? Because my man in London is the person to see.'

'No, sir.'

Goodluck turned his head and listened, holding up a hand for silence, not much caring if Walsingham found this impertinent. But the sound he had heard was only two of the guards patrolling the entrances to Caesar's Tower; he caught the quiet scrape of a weapon, then a muttered word, and boots going heavily back up the steps. He waited another moment, but there was nothing except a warm, fragrant wind shivering over the knot garden and rustling the yew hedge.

'I came to give you information, sir. Something I did not wish to put in a letter.'

Walsingham's eyes narrowed. 'Go on.'

'Following your orders, I posed as a Catholic and stuck close to the Lorenzo family for almost a year. One night, just after Easter Sunday, a man came secretly to their house. From the way he was treated, I would guess him to be one of the old blood, born of an important family but perhaps not a nobleman. I was not privy to everything that passed between him and Lorenzo, but it was common knowledge the man was in search of money.'

Walsingham frowned, apparently mesmerized by a tiny periwinkle growing wild in the sandy verges of the path. 'To what end?'

'That I was unable to discover. But it's my belief he was seeking Catholic funds for a fresh attempt on the Queen's life.'

Now he had the attention of the Queen's secretary. 'His name?'

'They used no names, which aroused my suspicions at once. But afterwards I heard several mentions of a man they called the "Bear". From what they said, I would guess him to be the assassin they wished to hire. Unfortunately, the man arrived hooded at Lorenzo's, stayed only one night, and left before I was able to get a proper look at him. I remained with the family another fortnight, hoping to glean some useful information from Lorenzo or one of his more zealous followers. You know how these devout, old-family Catholics love to boast of their plans to put a monarch of the true faith back on the throne of England. But no one was talking. Indeed, the more I probed, the more suspicious they became, however much I clowned and acted the fool. I was forced to leave rather abruptly in the end,' Goodluck smiled grimly, 'having outstayed my welcome in Pisa.'

'And his mission to obtain funds?'

'It may have been successful, but I cannot be sure. Before he left, Lorenzo took his guest into town with him, and did not return until the following day. I tried to track their movements all that day and evening, but they kept giving me the slip. With insulting ease, in fact. Either this man was an expert at espionage, or a year playing Eduardo the simpleton had slowed me up.'

Walsingham allowed himself a fleeting smile. 'I should have liked to see you as a simpleton.'

'And a hunchback, no less. From the Pisan countryside. I had to chew grass all day and roll my eyes like an idiot.'

'And now you come to Kenilworth to play . . . what? The courtly hanger-on? The lovesick suitor? You have essayed those roles before, as I recall.'

Goodluck fingered his beard ruefully. 'It took me the last few months to grow back my beard. Some judicious padding, false eyebrows, and I shall be Goodluck once more, master of a troupe of travelling players.'

'In which guise I presume you plan to join the Queen's progress.'

Walsingham began to walk back in the shelter of the yew hedge, and Goodluck fell in silently beside him. The dark gleam of the lake was just visible through the waterside gate. Their footsteps made only a little grating sound on the sandy path.

'Her Majesty should be here in state within a few days. Leicester writes that the court will arrive on Saturday, and the Queen herself some time in the early evening.' Walsingham hesitated, his tone thoughtful. 'If you have brought a troupe, you will need lodgings for yourself and your men.'

'A place to set up a tent near the castle walls, sir, that's all we'll require. It would be prudent not to draw attention to ourselves with any special treatment.' Goodluck produced from his pouch a somewhat dog-eared piece of paper and unfolded it. Inside were a few lines in a distinctive, flowing hand, with a faded cloverleaf stamped underneath: Walsingham's personal device. 'As for introductions, this should see us right.'

Walsingham nodded, turning his head aside to cough. 'Better speak to one of the castle steward's men tomorrow, before it is too late to secure yourself a place close to the castle. And keep your eyes and ears open for the slightest hint of this new Catholic plot. Report back to me at intervals. Discreetly, of course. Your instincts are correct: if our codes have been compromised, we must commit nothing to writing until new ones are established. I shall set that in motion. Watch for the usual signal.'

Goodluck inclined his head. 'Sir.'

They walked another moment in silence, listening to the far-off amorous bellow of a bull in the fields. Stopping just short of the waterside gate, where torchlight could be seen glinting off the helmet of a guard on patrol, Walsingham felt within his cloak and brought out a few gold coins.

'Take them,' he murmured, and pressed them into Goodluck's hand. 'Despite my letter, you will need to produce a bribe for the steward's men, as is customary in these last-minute matters. Otherwise they will be less than helpful.' He glanced at the sundial on the wall as though to check the time, but its gilt face was shrouded in darkness. 'And now I must get myself to bed, for my health is no better this evening, despite the herbal remedies Leicester's physician has prescribed. Ursula joins me tomorrow, and she always knows when I have been staying up too late. I don't believe you ever took a wife, did you?'

'No, sir.' Goodluck laughed softly. 'Nor am I ever likely to marry. I've never felt the need for such a shackle, however attractively disguised.'

They parted with a nod under the gnarled oak tree. Goodluck shinned back up the trunk and settled himself down for another few hours in its uncomfortable branches, arms folded, booted feet tucked up safe out of sight of any passing patrols. He resigned himself to boredom; he would have to wait until the guard was changed on the north gate at midnight before making his exit.

He watched as Walsingham slowly ascended the steps back into the Warwickshire stronghold that was Caesar's Tower, heard the guards' challenge at the entrance to the arcade and the great man's quiet reply. The garden was empty once more. A warm breeze ruffled the oak leaves, wafting a delicious fragrance of thyme and rosemary from the knot garden across his hiding place.

*I don't believe you ever took a wife, did you?*

Unwillingly, Goodluck recalled bright fearful eyes in a dark face, a woman's sweating body as she laboured to bring forth her child, and the long silence that had come after.

If he had ever considered taking a wife, it had been for only the shortest and cruellest of moments, and never again since.

# Two

## *The forest at Long Itchington, Warwickshire*

SHADOWS WAVERED AND SHRANK OUTSIDE THE TENT WALL, HUMAN figures half glimpsed through a ripple of silk. Drowsy, in nothing but her underwear, Elizabeth lay curled on her daybed as though on her royal barge. One hand trailing in imaginary water below, she delighted in the whisper of beech trees above the roof of her tent, sweet country air masking the scent of sweat and unwashed bodies, enjoying the idle warmth of an English summer.

'Is Her Majesty still asleep?' A pause, then another hurried whisper. 'We must move by five, or risk coming to Kenilworth after nightfall.'

Her eyelids flickered, then closed again stubbornly. Elizabeth knew that male voice, would have recognized it anywhere, even heard against the frustrated droning of a bee caught between two folds of the tent.

The guard at the entrance spoke again, and Robert Dudley, Earl of Leicester, made a reply, too low to be heard. But she thought there was a hint of impatience in his tone.

Minded to sit up and call for her favourite, Elizabeth forced herself to remain still on her cushioned daybed, to taste the sweet agony of this self-denial a few moments longer. An old hare tastes better left to stew, she reminded herself, and stretched her arms above her head.

Besides, she could not be private here with Robin, as she liked to call him when they were alone, still using his pet name from when they were young. Her ladies lay about her on the floor of the tent, wilting like caged birds in the heat, their black and white plumage bedraggled after several hours in the saddle. What a glorious hunt it had been! They had eventually brought the panting stag to bay on the wooded banks of a stream, trapped between a line of snarling hounds and Robert's huntsmen armed with sticks and horns.

Turning on to her back, she stared up at the gently billowing tent roof. Robert had been at his most charming this past year, barely leaving her side, his lavish gifts and attentiveness so marked that everyone at court was once more predicting a royal marriage before Christmas. Poor wag-tongued fools, no doubt they thought the Queen would not get to hear their stable-yard gossip. But while darling Robert might be her 'Eyes', she had her 'Ears' at court as well, and those ears were very long indeed.

Despite this, their gossip was not far off the mark. There could be no mistaking the signs. Robert Dudley, Earl of Leicester, intended to make her another proposal of marriage this summer.

Elizabeth closed her eyes. Nothing had changed. She would as soon relinquish her throne to her poisonous cousin Mary as marry and bow to her husband's rule as every good wife must. By Christ, though, she was growing no younger, and the country knew it as well as she. Her chance to make an heir for England would soon be past and forgotten, her womb withered, unused as any prune-faced nun's.

Surely now she must accept her fate and marry, as her own royal physicians had advised her, before it was too late to conceive a child?

But did she truly wish to marry a Dudley, one of her servants – however faithful and desirable – when at the snap of her fingers she could have any unmarried prince in Europe?

Still, the thought of lying with Robert all night in a legitimate bed, waking to him each morning as her sworn husband before God, their union sanctified by the tiresomely disapproving archbishop himself, brought another luxurious smile to her lips. Oh yes, there would be compensations for such an unsuitable match, and not before time.

Robert's low voice came again, outside the tent entrance, enquiring if she was awake. He was right, of course. It was time for her to be out and about, ready for the ride to Kenilworth, although it seemed barely an hour since she had lain down to sleep, drowsy in the afternoon heat after half a day's good hunting and a pavilion lunch under the trees.

Preparing to rise, Elizabeth stirred, but halted at the sight of one of her ladies already on her feet, shaking out a dark crumpled gown before tiptoeing on bare feet to the entrance.

The afternoon sun glinted off a tawny red head, the modest simplicity of her wifely cap removed while she slept, hair arranged in pretty ringlets looped about her ears, her hips swaying with the sharp sensuality of a woman determined to make the most of the man she has caught.

*Lettice.*

Frozen in disbelief, Elizabeth watched as the two shadows – one graceful and full-skirted, the other tall and bowing gallantly at his lady's approach – drew their heads close together outside the tent and conversed in whispers she could no more hope to catch than she could understand the birdsong fluting in the branches above. How many moments passed while she lay still as death and listened, Elizabeth could not be sure. Somewhere nearby a hound began to bark excitedly and was hushed. She could hear the jangle of horses' bits, orders being given, the crack of hooves over the forest floor.

Soon, the other women were stirring, sitting up and talking among themselves. Lady Helena, the sweet girl, fetched a glass of wine, then knelt and held it to her lips.

Elizabeth drank, her face composed, and watched as Lettice, Countess of Essex, re-entered the tent. Lettice's face was flushed, her eyes lively as a young girl's fresh-come from her lover, and she took up her plain white cap with unsteady hands, setting it to cover that tawny tumble of hair as though concealing her shame.

*Too late, too late*, Elizabeth jeered inwardly. But her lips did not form a single word. She allowed Helena to dab her mouth dry with a white damask cloth redolent of lavender water.

With her ladies gathered about her, she stood for the heavy gold-embroidered foreskirt to be fitted. Turning full circle, she raised her arms to allow them to fix and pin the magnificent cloth-of-gold bodice tight about her chest.

*Let Robert and Lettice whisper and play at lovers. I am the Queen and I shall make a triumphal entry into Kenilworth.*

Yes, her people would fall to their knees before her unmatched splendour, and she would raise them up with her hand. She had no time for this courtly art of dalliance, for clandestine meetings and secret looks. She was a Tudor – blunt as a stone in love, but lion-hearted in a fight. As her enemies would soon witness, the Countess of Essex foremost among them.

She stretched out an arm for the heavy jewelled sleeve, releasing her breath very slowly as each ribbon fastened it to her bodice. *Gird me for battle. I shall neither fail nor faint.* Her ladies drew the laces tight, and slipped sturdy riding boots on to her feet. Her wigs were brought forward for her to choose from, her complexion gently rubbed and refreshed with scented oils before the smoothing white paint was applied.

'On to Kenilworth, ladies!'

Her voice rang sharp through the crowded tent, heads turning in her direction, sleepy and surprised. Only her cousin Lettice, still gartering one of her stockings with bowed head and slow, deliberate hands, did not look up at the command.

The women hurriedly cleared a path as Elizabeth left the tent, only Lady Helena having the presence of mind to seize her stiff jewelled train and run behind with it, holding it up out of the dirt.

Outside the sun was beginning to dip into early evening, its thin reddish light burning through the trees. Someone had kicked over their camp fire to quench it, and the drifting smoke left her eyes smarting.

Robert stood waiting like Herne the Hunter under the leafy vastness of an ancient oak, as sturdy as that wood. Age had not diminished his physique, superb in dark red jerkin and doublet, slashed sleeves glinting with gold, his cap feathered and set at an angle. She still thought of him as a young man, so gloriously handsome, his dark eyes bright with ambition and unfulfilled promise. Nonetheless, she did not fail to notice how his face had tightened with the years, the smudges under his eyes gradually deepening, his mouth smiling more warily these days, watching her as much with frustration as desire.

Once, in his youthful pride and arrogance, Robert had only thought to ask her 'When?' Now he knew better than to ask at all, seeming to prefer silence to outright rejection, though even his customary reticence was wearing thin. Whatever would follow it, she was yet to discover.

Her tone was clipped. 'My lord Leicester.'

'Your Majesty,' he replied, bowing low, and Elizabeth felt a stab of satisfaction, glad that he was uncertain of her, remembering perhaps that she was his queen, not some other man's wife whom he must fumble in doorways or under cover of darkness.

She swept past him to where her young page crouched, waiting to help his royal mistress step up into the covered wagon.

'Good lad,' she said with a sudden rush of affection, and tousled the boy's head before setting her foot in his obediently cupped hands. 'May you always serve your queen so well. And *up*!'

# Three

## The Brays, Kenilworth Castle

THE DAY HAD BEEN THE HOTTEST SHE COULD REMEMBER. LUCY'S forehead was damp with sweat. She shook out the crumpled skirts of her gown and swayed, almost too weary to stand, peering down the narrow leafy lane that led towards Long Itchington. That was the direction the Queen's entourage would take, or so everyone seemed to believe.

Furtively, she wiped her face with the torn shred of fabric that had been pressed into her hand an hour before.

'Here,' the man had muttered to each of those waiting at the front of the row. 'Keep one for yourself and pass the rest back. Everyone's to have a flag. As soon as you see the advance party, wave your flags high in the air and don't stop until the Queen has passed through on to the tiltyard.' The man had repeated these instructions in a hoarse yell as he shuffled along the assembled rows. 'Is that understood? Keep waving and cheering until she's out of sight.'

Their carts had been bouncing over rough tracks and through stifling, green-lit woodlands since early morning, and had only reached the vast reddish-brown walls of Kenilworth in the late afternoon. To the south of the castle lay great defensive earthworks, a series of rolling slopes covered in turf. Yet with the gate standing open it became a sun-baked valley through which the

Queen's entourage was to pass, while her people cheered her on from the high banks on either side. On arriving at Kenilworth, they had been herded into this place like cattle, allowed barely a jug of warm, metallic-tasting ale between ten, and a few loaves of bread dipped in gravy. The more senior women had been allowed to rest in the shade, but when Lucy tried to sit down on the grass verge to eat her meagre ration of bread, one of the men in charge had prodded her with the tip of his boot, shouting, 'Get up!'

One of the older women there, a matron in a stiff linen cap, had dared to protest at this treatment, and the man had raised his heavy whip to them both, his thick Warwickshire burr hard to follow. 'There's to be no sitting down. You'll wait in rows like you were told. We have to be ready for when the Queen arrives, see? That's his lordship's orders, good and simple, and any man, woman or child caught out of line will spend the night in the stocks. Is that clear?'

Gradually the sun began to dip below the horizon and the day grew less hot, to everyone's relief.

A hard-faced, yellow-haired man in the now-familiar blue livery of Leicester's staff came riding out along the line of earthworks Lucy had heard called the Brays, slowing to inspect the crowd assembled there on either side of the track.

As he drew level with her, the rider came to a halt. His horse fidgeted as he tightened his grip on the reins.

'You there,' he called down to her, his voice fierce and blunt. 'Give me your name, girl, and tell me what your business is here.'

'Lucy Morgan, sir. I travel with the Queen's household.'

'What position do you hold there?'

'Entertainer, sir.'

'You're an *entertainer*?' His watery blue eyes narrowed as once more he examined her from head to toe. There was a cold, sneering note to his voice. 'What does that mean, I wonder?'

'I sing and dance for the court, sir.'

The man studied her face a moment longer, almost as though suspecting her of insolence, then summoned one of the guards with a jerk of his head. 'You there, move this one to the back. She's to be kept out of sight of the procession.'

When the guard hesitated, obviously puzzled by this order, the rider grew angry.

'Do as you're told, man, and hurry up about it. It's nearly dusk. The Queen's party cannot be far off.' He wheeled his horse about. 'This is a good English stronghold. We can't have Her Majesty frightened out of her wits by a Moorish face in the crowd, can we?'

Two guards seized Lucy and dragged her away from the other women, some of whom muttered rebelliously. Yet nobody dared protest, and Lucy found herself being pulled, without any attempt at gentleness or civility, several hundred feet away from the other entertainers and through a gap in the crowd where a steep, narrow track led to a grass bank and the castle wall behind it.

Forced into this dead end, she spun to face the two guards, breathless and ready to kick out, half expecting them to molest her. But although one shoved her backwards on to the ground, the older man shook his head warningly and pulled the other one away.

'Best stay here, girl, until the Queen's safe inside,' he told her, not unkindly, 'and keep out of sight if you know what's good for you.'

Up on the grass bank, jostling for a clear view of the road, the waiting men were able to look down on her from both sides. Some even laughed as Lucy struggled up, wiping mud from her palms. She tried to ignore the crude comments from above. She was used to such jokes, though they still stung occasionally. It was something she had grown up with in London, the stares, the whispers, and the men on the streets calling after her whenever she dared go out alone.

'If a man ever whistles at you in the street, whistle back until he comes running,' one of her guardian's theatrical friends had once suggested, winking at her across the supper table. 'Then stick a knife to the bastard's groin and take his purse while he stands whimpering.'

Her guardian, Master Goodluck, had been infuriated by this advice. 'Pay no attention to Twist,' he had insisted angrily. 'That kind of behaviour is more likely to get you killed.'

All the same, her guardian had taken her aside later and

painstakingly shown her how to defend herself in a fight: eyeball, throat, groin and kneecap, the weakest parts of a man's anatomy. Especially the groin. 'No need for a knife there,' he had informed her with grim satisfaction.

In the distance, somewhere beyond the trees, a horn sounded three triumphant notes. For a moment there was silence, everyone standing perfectly still in the dim light. Then the blowing of the horn came again, louder, more insistent. 'The Queen!' a woman shouted, half hysterical. 'Good Queen Bess!' The crowd at the front cheered and a few white flags began to wave. The men in charge shouted hoarsely along the lines, then everyone was cheering and waving their flags.

Someone on the grass bank high above had knelt down and was dangling his arm through the sea of legs.

'Here, take my hand,' a voice called, though she could barely hear him over the noise of the crowd. She couldn't see his face but he sounded young and very serious. 'I won't drop you. I'll pull you up on to the bank so you can see.'

She ignored him as she pulled grass from her hair. If those guards were to come back and find that she had vanished . . .

'Hurry, the Queen is almost here!'

The cheering had intensified. Out of the corner of her eye, she could just see an arm waving about in the dim light, searching for her.

'I shall miss her myself if you don't take my hand,' the voice said reproachfully.

Turning to speak sharply, Lucy stopped and stared. For the hand searching for hers was not white and pale as she had expected, but black like her own.

She reached up and placed her hand in his.

Strong and capable, his long fingers curled about hers, and she stared up at them in a trance, memorizing each fingernail and knuckle, the broad sinews of his wrist. Then another hand came down to grip hers and, with a grunt, he lifted her straight off the ground and up the side of the grassy bank.

Gaining a foothold, Lucy released his hand and climbed the rest of the way herself, not caring how dirty she made her gown, clambering up just in time to see the Queen's party approaching.

'Thank you,' she said breathlessly, and looked up into the face of a young man as black as herself and only slightly taller. 'You . . . You're . . .'

'Hush.' He smiled, though seriously, as he pointed down the bank towards the Brays. 'The Queen is here.'

# Four

THE SIBYL, WHO HAD APPEARED TO GREET THE ROYAL ENTOURAGE before the earthworks that marked the entrance to Kenilworth, gave a deep curtsey as her elaborate speech drew to a close. Thin as a cat, hair adorned with flowers and one shoulder bare in the Grecian fashion, scarcely decent in her sheath of white silk, the girl – fourteen, maybe fifteen years of age – peered up at her master the Earl of Leicester with praise-hungry eyes as if to ask, 'So, was my speech performed well enough to please you, my good lord?'

Elizabeth, one gloved hand clenched on the rein of her horse, tried to keep the sting of jealousy from her voice.

'A worthy protégée, my lord.'

At a nod, the girl backed away, her flowered head so low she was almost bent double, a courtesy no doubt hampered by the immodestly tight wrap of her costume. The royal entourage swayed forward once more, the Queen's yeoman guards riding further back than her advisers had suggested. Elizabeth held herself erect in the saddle. She refused to enter Kenilworth as though afraid for her life, despite the usual rumours of plots and threats against her.

By God, she was tired, though. She ached after the long day's ride, and her heavy cloth-of-gold gown, encrusted with jewels from hem to ruff, was stifling on this warm evening. Yet she could see the crowds ahead lining the broad walk and leaning precariously from Kenilworth's battlemented towers, heedless of danger. They had come to see their queen, and she would not disappoint them by sagging in the saddle like an old woman or calling for her chair, to be carried in like her father towards the end of his reign, sick and barely able to walk. Tonight, though, she felt her forty-two years. Her skin hung baggy under her eyes, and no amount of white paint could disguise her pockmarks at close quarters.

Nonetheless, the signs of ageing did not seem to have lessened Robert's desire to marry her. A queen was still a queen, regardless of saggings and wrinkles, and the Dudleys had always been an ambitious family.

As they approached the Gallery Tower, a black shadow loomed out of the dusk and swung low above their heads with a rustle of wings. A mutter ran through the packed mass of people on the grass banks above her, close enough to see what was happening, their white flags glimmering at intervals like will-o'-the-wisps.

'Bats! Bats!'

Pale upturned faces in the crowd turned to watch the path of the creatures as they disappeared into the twilight.

No doubt the people thought it a good omen for the bats to be leaving the castle at her approach, and perhaps it was. John Dee had taught her to watch for such signs of significance in nature, and to use them to her advantage where possible; so here it would be said that her arrival drove out darkness and brought light back to Warwickshire.

Elizabeth gazed up at the tower, craning her neck to see better as Robert brought the court to a halt before its closed gate. High on its battlements stood inhumanly tall figures with vast trumpets – some five or six feet long – glinting in the light of the torches below.

'What's this? A guarded gate and tower, and locked against Your Majesty's arrival? Where is the porter?' Pretending anger, Robert raised his voice. 'You, within! Heave open this gate for your queen, you insolent dogs!'

As though on cue, a door was flung wide and a huge porter appeared, ducking his head to avoid knocking it against the lintel. The man was eight or nine feet in height, a rough club gripped staunchly in one hand and a rattling bunch of keys in the other. Like the Sibyl's before him, his costume was of white silk, wrapped about his paunch and barely concealing the comic bulge of his groin. His cheeks were flushed as though he had been drinking, an impression not denied by his ungainly swaying as he stumbled into the circle of torches.

Was the poor man on stilts?

The mummer played his part well, lurching towards the Queen with such a convincing roar that half the courtiers at her back scattered with undignified haste, leaving the watching crowd in helpless laughter.

'What stir, what coil is here?' he demanded, shaking his vast bunch of keys so violently at the crowd, he himself almost went over backwards.

Again the crowd laughed, partly at the man himself, partly at the old-fashioned language, though the nearest shifted carefully out of his reach. One of her own guards, hurriedly dismounting, took a threatening step towards the porter, but was brought to a halt by Robert's upraised hand.

The porter's voice boomed over their heads, echoing around the outer courtyard. 'Come back, hold, whither now?'

Robert came to stand beside her in the fluttering torchlight. Fleetingly, his hand brushed hers, a taunt in his low voice. 'Afraid, Your Majesty?'

'Of a man on stilts, wrapped up in his own shroud?'

'*A man on stilts?*' His eyes danced, sharing her sense of the ridiculous. 'Why, Your Majesty, this is none other than the great Hercules himself, commanded to guard the castle in my absence.'

'But what dainty darling's here?' Pointing with his club at Elizabeth, sitting still and erect in the saddle, the porter pretended surprise. 'O God, a peerless pearl!'

'I am lost,' she commented to the crowd. 'He has seen me now.'

The crowd laughed and pushed closer, elbowing each other and cursing the guards who held them back, their sturdy pikes crossed. Robert, leaning familiarly against the side of her mount, toyed with his own pearl earring as he listened, the smile on his face that of a satisfied cat, his mouse caught and killed. No doubt he thought her half won already, seeing his popularity with the crowd, knowing how this progress would be memorable chiefly for her visit to Kenilworth.

'This is no worldly woman,' the porter continued, undaunted by the laughter, determined to deliver his lines as written, 'but a sovereign goddess, surely? Her face, her hand, her eye – her features are all come from heaven, and with such majesty!'

'Did you write this nonsense?' Elizabeth asked softly.

'Not I,' Robert protested. 'The author is John Badger, Your Majesty, a most worthy scholar and Oxford man. I could not stop him. He was insistent that he should play his part in this mummery. Indeed, I fear Master Badger has a certain *liking* for Your Majesty. Though no one can blame him for that.'

Master Badger had struggled to his knees in the dust now, requiring the help of another man in this effort at dutiful obeisance, and was holding out his club and keys.

'Come, most perfect paragon,' he proclaimed bravely, 'pass on with joy and bliss. Most worthy, welcome, goddess guest, whose presence gladdens all. Take here, have here, both club and keys. Myself I yield, these gates and all, submit and seek your shield.'

Applause echoed about the outer walls as the porter laid down his club and keys, and ordered the gates to be opened in the name of the Queen. As he knelt before her, the white silk costume, thin as a winding sheet, strained ever more tightly about his groin, its bulge obscene.

Elizabeth looked away while he adjusted himself. One of her ladies-in-waiting sniggered, hurriedly stifling the sound with the back of her hand. It was Lettice, of course.

'We accept your allegiance,' Elizabeth announced. 'Now go and have some cooling ale, Master Badger, for you have earned it.'

The gate swung open in the dusk and the eight-foot-high effigies of trumpeters seemed to raise vast silvery trumpets on the battlements above, beginning an eerie chorus. Robert led her through the Gallery Tower gate at a sedate walk, and the court and her ladies followed them, their horses' hooves clattering across the cobbles, drowning out the sound of trumpets.

Suddenly cold in the gloomy well of the tower, Elizabeth passed under its damp stones and remembered another tower which had housed her once in darkness and despair. She looked down, hoping for reassurance, but could no longer make out Robert's face, just the dark silhouette of his head as they came clear of the gateway.

She shivered. Could the bats have been an ill omen, after all?

# Five

'WOULD YOU LIKE TO SEE THE REST OF THE SHOW?'

Lucy drew her travelling cloak closer about her shoulders, wishing it was thicker. Now that the Queen and her shining entourage had disappeared, and those astonishing spectacles too, the beautiful girl in white silk and the giant porter, had both vanished inside the dark confines of the tower, the breeze from the lake felt suddenly cold on her face. She knew herself to be more tired than she had realized.

'The rest of the show?' she repeated, frowning.

'The porter was only the beginning,' the young man explained. 'Through that gate is the tiltyard – yes, there'll be jousting in a few days – and beyond that the outer courtyard, and then the old keep. At every stop, Lord Leicester has arranged a spectacle for the Queen, and fireworks to follow.' He took her hand without waiting for permission. 'If you wish to see the rest of tonight's entertainments, I can get you through the gate and into the outer courtyard. You won't be allowed through on your own.'

She stared at his blue livery, belatedly remembering what it signified. 'You're one of Lord Leicester's men?'

'And you sing for the Queen?'

Lucy caught her breath at that, taking a quick step backwards as though afraid of what was coming next. It was usually an insult of some kind. 'How did you know I'm an entertainer?' she demanded.

36

'I have ears.' When she continued to stare at him, the young man sighed and gestured to where she had been standing before. 'That oaf who sent you back here asked what you did at court. I was listening.'

Lucy's flush deepened. 'Oh.'

He shrugged, perhaps seeing her embarrassment. 'I work in my lord Leicester's stables here at Kenilworth. There's no shame in honest labour.'

The crowd was beginning to thin as people jumped down from the grass bank and made their way across the Brays to where a makeshift camp had been erected, with tents and rough wooden dwellings and hammocks strung hastily between trees. Numerous small fires had already been lit and the sound of hammering – silenced during the Queen's entry into the castle – had begun again in earnest. Lucy peered into the darkness, at the dozens of tiny flickering lights springing up within the earthwork defences as people set up their campsites for the next few weeks. Now that night had fallen, it seemed everyone wanted a corner to sleep in.

She allowed the young man to lead her down from the bank, instinctively trusting him, even though she felt the touch of his hand was rather impudent considering they did not even know each other's names.

'So you're a horseman,' she said.

She did not ride. It had never been necessary in London, where she had walked everywhere, and certainly not now she was at court.

He jumped down first, then turned to support her as she climbed down more carefully, trying not to dirty her gown again. Until she found the other court entertainers who were sharing a trunk with her, she would not have another gown to wear.

'A stableman,' the young man corrected her. For a moment she thought he was laughing at her, then they passed under the crowded archway on to the tiltyard and out into the light, where his face looked serious again. 'I clean out the stalls, I mend saddles and backcloths, I tend to his lordship's horses and those of his guests.' He paused. 'We have over a hundred horses to feed, water and groom tonight, and that doesn't even touch on the hundreds more running loose in the east pasture, all the horses and ponies that came in with the Queen's household.'

She stared. 'But you should go, then. Won't you get into trouble for not being there?'

'I saw *you*.' His voice was quiet, but the emphasis on *you* was unmistakable. 'I couldn't go back. I had to stay and speak to you.'

Lucy was startled, aware that he must be risking a beating for his absence. But the young man was already leading her through the crowds, past the disapproving guards with a wave of his hand and a muttered word. Whatever she had meant to say in response was lost as she caught sight of the Queen's party again, only a few hundred yards ahead.

Seated on her white horse in a ring of flaming torches, her red hair glowing in coils, her stiff gold and ivory gown so fabulously embroidered and gathered in thick folds, decked with such enormous gemstones that glinted and flashed at her slightest movement, the Queen could almost have been a character from a London pageant, or one of the painted figures Lucy had seen carried through the streets at Easter or Christmastide, surrounded by lights.

'Look!' he whispered in her ear, and she turned reluctantly to see what everyone else was gazing at.

Out across the dark waters of the lake, a floating torchlit island was drawing steadily closer. At its centre stood a woman in white. Nymph-like girls knelt about her as if posed in a tapestry. With their hair streaming loose down their backs, they cast armfuls of what appeared to be rose petals into the water.

'*I am the Lady of this pleasant lake,*' the woman began to recite, '*who, since the time of great King Arthur's reign, has led a lowering life in restless pain.*'

Straight-backed and regal on her white horse, the Queen turned to the Earl of Leicester, amusement clear in her beautiful face. 'The Lady of the Lake?'

'Do you not know, Your Majesty,' Leicester replied, his deep voice echoing about the enclosed tiltyard, 'you are no longer in the wilds of Warwickshire but at Camelot, the court of great King Arthur himself?'

'Then must we resign our throne?'

'Hush, you'll spoil it,' he said, and flicked her gloved hand irreverently as he spoke. 'Be patient. There's more to come.'

Confused, Lucy turned to look at the young man beside her. He seemed curiously intent, his gaze moving from Leicester to the Queen. 'What does he mean?' she asked in a whisper. 'The court of King Arthur?'

'My master is only an earl,' he muttered in her ear, 'but he wishes to marry a queen. If this is Camelot, that makes him Arthur. And what woman would not wish to marry King Arthur?'

'But I thought the Queen had refused him?'

'Many times in private, it's said. But my master does not give up so easily. This is his way of asking her in full view of the court. Everything will be perfect here for a match between them. The clock on the keep tower is to be stopped until the Queen's departure. So we are outside time. Kenilworth becomes Camelot and he becomes Arthur.'

She did not understand, but something in his voice made her wary of asking anything further.

The Lady of the Lake stepped gracefully off her island as it came to land, its bobbing mass anchored on ropes by blue-liveried servants, and passed through a narrow gateway to kneel before the Queen. Her nymphs slipped easily into the water and played beneath the tiltyard mound, gambolling and calling out, their wet silks clinging to their bodies like a shimmering second skin, so that every man present stared and smiled. Now Lucy could see that the Lady was not young, as her nymphs were, but a much older woman, her face lined, grey hair concealed beneath a tight-swathed band of white silk.

'*I will attend while you lodge here, most peerless Queen, and as my love to Arthur did appear, so shall I to you.*'

Speaking these verses, the Lady sank even lower and gestured to the tower's yawning entrance ahead, torchlight glinting off the rings on her fingers:

'*Pass on, madame, you need no longer stand. The lake, the lodge, the lord, are yours to command.*'

'Bravo!' The Queen clapped her hands in applause, and the court hurriedly followed suit. 'I thank you for this poetic welcome. But you say this place has been yours since the days of King Arthur, yet you grant me free access for the duration of my stay?'

The Lady of the Lake seemed to glance uncertainly at Leicester. At his nod, she gave another deep curtsey, the silken folds of her costume shimmering in the torchlight. 'Indeed, O peerless Queen.'

'As Queen of England, we had thought this place was ours by right. And yet you say it's yours? My lord Leicester would do well to remember the old adage that one country cannot suffer two rulers.' The Queen raised her gloved hand and spoke loudly, her voice ringing about the narrow space. 'We thank you for your most gracious welcome, Lady of the Lake, and suggest you return to your watery home, lest we fall out over this matter.'

There was a ripple of uneasy laughter through the court, and Lucy glanced at Leicester, curious to see his reaction to this public snub. But the crowd about the royal party had shifted again, and she could see only the tip of the feather in his cap.

As the brilliant entourage moved on in flashes of gold under the torches, the crowd shuffled forward another few feet, eager to reach the last gate and enter the castle, almost crushing Lucy as they pressed up against her from behind.

Anxiously, she glanced about for the young man but could no longer see him in the close-pressing crowd. The only way was forward, with hundreds of people behind them and a row of guards along the waterside, their pikes levelled. The smell of warm human flesh was overpowering. Lucy felt something push hard into her back, making her cry out in alarm, then somebody's hand touched her, large male fingers fumbling under her cloak at the lacings of her gown.

She tried to turn, to see who was behind her, but at that moment the crowd made a great push for the gate, and everyone staggered forward in the darkness.

Trying not to fall, Lucy grabbed at the woman in front, who, cradling a baby against her exposed breast, dirty yellow hair loose under her cap, half turned to scream abuse at her.

'I'm sorry,' Lucy managed, 'I'm sorry.'

'Here – come this way.'

She felt someone seize her hand, and allowed herself to be jerked sideways out of the crowd and through the row of guards with their menacing pikes. To her relief, it was the young man who had rescued her before. He pulled her aside to a quiet space against the wall where a dying torch guttered in a bracket above them.

'Are you well, mistress?' he asked, watching her as though afraid she might faint.

Too breathless to speak, she straightened her gown and nodded.

'Follow me then,' he instructed her, 'and this time, let us try not to get separated. I must go back to the stables, but I can take you as far as the outer court at least. There'll be fireworks over the lake soon, and musicians, and more of this mummery. Perhaps you'll see one of your friends from the court there, and be able to discover where you're to sleep tonight.'

'Thank you,' she said, but the young man was already threading a path along the wall behind the guards.

Lucy caught up with him as they entered the outer court, the last of the Queen's entourage clattering through the archway on their horses. At least here the way was torchlit and the grumbling crowd from the tiltyard was being held back at pike-point. But she heard one of the guards shout that no one else would be allowed into the castle tonight, and for everyone without a bed to go back to the camp at the Brays. She wondered what would happen if she could not find any of the other entertainers, and tried not to consider the grim likelihood that she would have to sleep rough in that den of thieves beyond the outer walls, with no protection and none of her possessions.

Lucy flattened herself against the wall to allow a body of guards through the gate, and the young man followed suit, though he was clearly impatient to be let through.

'What's your name?' she asked, boldly enough, though she struggled to hold his gaze when the young man turned to look down at her.

'Tom.'

'A short name.'

He smiled then, his teeth very white and strong. 'Thomas Black. Yes, a Christian name, though my parents were both Moors. They were on a slave ship from Morocco that was captured by the English. They chose to convert on landing at Falmouth, and my father accepted the English name of Black.' He studied her, through long black lashes that hid his expression. 'It was either that or face execution.'

'Are you . . .' She hesitated, not wishing to offend him. 'Are you a slave, then?'

'I was born a slave,' he agreed, calmly enough. 'And sold as one when I grew old enough to work. But Lord Leicester gave me my freedom when I came into his service. He will have no slaves in his household. He is a great man.'

'My parents were Africans too. At least, that is what I was told as a child. But I know nothing for sure.'

He nodded, his face sombre again. 'You are like me, little sister. Not meant to be here.'

Lucy looked away, unsure how to respond to such a remark. Her mother had been a runaway slave, it was true, but Master Goodluck had always told Lucy to call herself 'a free Englishwoman', if anyone asked. She had been born in London, just as Goodluck had been. England was her home. She belonged nowhere else.

Then Tom was pulling on her hand again and they were in the outer courtyard, lost at once in a riot of noise and chaos, smoke billowing from a fresh-lit fire to their left, people passing back and forth on foot and on horseback, stinking heaps of muck everywhere so that she had to pull up her skirts and walk with little hops to avoid soiling her gown.

Tom was staring ahead with a frown in his eyes.

'I will have to leave you here,' he said reluctantly, turning to study her face. A lone firework cracked overhead in the darkness, probably set off by accident, and a great 'Ahhh!' went up from the crowd around them as everyone craned their necks to see the streamers of crackling red light. 'They'll be looking for me at the stables. Will you be safe on your own?'

'Of course,' she said doubtfully.

But she did not want him to go. The fear she had felt when the guards grabbed her began to return, and she felt her lips go numb with it.

'Don't be afraid,' Tom said, touching her shoulder.

'I'm not,' she lied, and knew by his expression that she had not convinced him.

She searched the crowds for a recognizable face, then caught a glimpse of little fair-haired Catherine from Norfolk, one of the Queen's tumblers. She waved, relieved at the sight of her familiar white cap and gown. 'Catherine! Over here!'

As the girl began to head in her direction, Lucy dropped Tom a hurried curtsey.

'My friend will show me where I am to sleep tonight. Thank you again for your help, sir.'

'Tom,' he reminded her, still frowning, but Lucy turned away with only the slightest nod of her head.

Linking an arm about Catherine's waist, she walked away, telling her friend all the things she had seen. She did not want Tom to know how much she was beginning to like him.

# Six

AMID CHEERS FROM THE CROWD, AND ACCOMPANIED BY A GANG OF
fluting, green-hosed musicians on hautboys, shawms and cornets,
Elizabeth had ridden through the narrow gateway and on to the
long wooden bridge beyond. The air was thick with smoke from
flaming torches. A series of paired posts awaited her at every few
steps, each post crowned with rare and colourful birds in cages,
luxurious flowers and fruits of the season – a cornucopia of
natural and strange delights which Robert pointed out for her to
admire.

Yet always his eyes scanned the way ahead, sharp and watchful, as though something in the air alerted him to danger.

Catching his mood, Elizabeth stared up at the shadowy rise of
new buildings alongside Kenilworth's ancient keep, stretching
above the old walls with vast candlelit mullion windows and
elegant stonework.

Why would Robert be concerned for her safety here, in his own
stronghold, his home territory of Warwickshire? Well, one jealous
faction or another was always plotting against her crown; she
would not shut herself away like a scared old woman.
No, she would ride it out, as her father would have done, and
see the perpetrators hung, drawn and quartered for their
treason.

Orders were called out hoarsely within the walls. The guards
along the battlements crashed arms in a salute. Shadowy flags and

pennants flew from the high towers, and the crowd cheered once more as she entered the final gate.

The passage into the castle proper was short but gloomy, lit only by the guttering flames of torches set into the wall at intervals, and then she was out in the warm evening air again, surrounded by the crowd, their cheers almost deafening her, some pressing so close that her ladies-in-waiting found themselves hemmed in, one uttering a sharp cry of alarm at the crush.

Everywhere inside the walls was chaos. Only a narrow path ahead had been kept clear for their procession by Robert's men, the sight of their blue livery and gold badges reassuring in the gloom.

When they finally reached the wooden drawbridge into the inner court, Robert threw her horse's reins to a servant and came round to help her dismount. His dark gaze searched her face, then his hands lingered on her waist longer than was necessary as she slipped down from the saddle.

'I can see you're tired,' Robert murmured, his words intended for her ears alone. 'But I haven't forgotten our arrangement. Midnight?'

There was an intimacy to his smile that made Elizabeth itch to slap his handsome face as she remembered his whispered conversation with Lettice that afternoon.

How far had it gone, this dalliance with her married cousin?

'I am not tired,' Elizabeth snapped. She waited until his arms had dropped away before addressing the surrounding courtiers, her voice coldly formal.

'However, the hour is late,' she announced, summoning her ladies with a turn of her head. 'It is the Lord's day tomorrow and we rise early for Mass. Bring torches, and show us and our ladies to the royal apartments.'

'But you will miss the fireworks . . .' Robert began, his voice perplexed and not a little irritated. Then he must have caught the unyielding expression on her face. He smiled and swept her an elegant bow instead. 'I am yours to command, Your Majesty.'

The torches were brought forward, illuminating the darkness of the inner court. To one side, the old keep glowered over them, and to the other, fantastically lit with candles, the large windows of

Robert's new building glittered out across the court, inviting them to enter. Lifting her skirts, conscious that the jewel-encrusted gown was overlong and more suited to riding than walking, Elizabeth made her way through the unruly crowd outside the tower.

Strange faces pressed in on her in the torchlight, their cheers too loud, almost forced.

Roses and lilies were thrown from the crowd. She had not taken more than a few steps when a cannon began to fire over the lake, the booming thud making Elizabeth jerk with its first explosion. Then the sky erupted with fireworks, vast streamers of fire high above the water, reds, oranges, yellows, blinding in their magnificence. The crowd cried out around them, and her ladies paused to look up, clapping their hands excitedly.

For a moment Elizabeth was alone, unsure where she was or who was at her elbow. An old panic flared inside her.

'Hold my hand, Your Majesty,' Robert murmured in that easy, familiar way he had.

It was almost like the first days of her reign, Robert's knowledge and experience on hand to bolster her nervous faltering as she groped her way towards monarchy. But she was no longer that young woman ruling over a court of eyes in the shadows, needing her friend's counsel and companionship at every step.

Chin held high, she ignored his gesture and swept on towards the safety of her apartments, smiling and nodding at the crowd on either side.

'God bless the *Virgin* Queen!' someone shouted with mocking emphasis. The crowd laughed, some a little uneasily, others with undisguised scorn.

Elizabeth bit her lip fiercely, but shook her head at Robert's hasty, furious gesture. The commoners would have their jokes, just as they had joked about her father's tendency to dispatch his wives when they displeased him, and about her sister's 'pregnancies' that had always come to nothing. Yet the vulgar joke still stung, and she looked at the crowd of people more carefully, searching for open disloyalty, for those who would dare laugh in her face.

'Majesty.' Robert's hand came under her arm as he guided her into an echoing passageway beneath an ornate stone entrance. He was angry, she could hear it in his voice. 'I am sorry. My men will—'

'Your men will do nothing. It was *nothing*.'

Waving away his help, she began to ascend the staircase. Robert led the way, feathered cap in hand, his expression un-readable in the flickering light thrown by bracketed torches set into the walls. Once again she remembered entering the Tower of London via the damp, gloomy portal of Traitors' Gate, and once again she fixed her eyes straight ahead, gripping the jewelled skirt of her gown in one locked fist so that it would not drag against the floor.

The heavy wooden door at the head of the stairs stood open. Servants in blue livery bowed almost double on either side as she entered. Her ladies scampered behind them in a rustle of silk and taffeta, Lettice hidden somewhere among them. The richly furnished rooms of the state apartments, lit by a mass of candles reflected in the glass of each tall window, stretched like a glitter-ing prison in front of her. Elizabeth strode to the window and stripped off her gloves, resting her palms on the smooth curved stone. Behind her, her ladies-in-waiting exclaimed in delight as they explored what would be their home for the next three weeks.

'I have made some alterations since your last visit to Kenilworth, Your Majesty. Your own rooms are still on this floor, but your ladies will sleep below you in very comfortable apart-ments.' Several of her ladies giggled behind her back, and Elizabeth guessed that Robert must be smiling at them in his charming way, those dark eyes shining. 'If there is anything amiss, or if that which you desire is not to hand, I or any of my house-hold will be glad to serve you.'

'We thank you, my lord Leicester. Now you and your servants may leave us.'

She did not glance back over her shoulder as Robert bowed and removed himself without another word.

Her knees almost gave way at the sound of the door closing behind him, but she stayed erect, grasping the stone windowsill with her bare hands. It was like some ancient shrine at which she must pray for more strength, for greater patience, as the brilliant cascade of fireworks continued to flash over the lake.

*I shall not bend. I am a queen. I shall not share him with another woman.*

# Seven

LUCY RAN BACK DOWN THE SMOKY ALLEY BETWEEN THE OUTER WALL of the castle and the rickety houses, holding up her skirts to avoid tripping over them. She paused, breathless, at the far end. Smoke from the last of the fireworks lay acrid on the air. Two more alley-ways faced her, both equally narrow and steeped in foggy darkness, warm with the stench of pigs and chickens, and pots slung hastily over the fire.

Once again she cursed the flimsy strap on her shoe, which had broken as she and Catherine had walked towards their lodgings in the Brays. Catherine had gone on ahead, and by the time Lucy had tied up her shoe with the string from her purse, the alley was empty and she had little choice but to retrace her steps.

'Sirs? Masters?' There were two men ahead of her, carrying a long, battered wooden chest between them. From the blue of their liveried coats, she knew they must be the Earl of Leicester's men. 'Beg pardon, but I . . . I'm lost. I'm with the entertainers' troupe. Do you know where I might find Master Payne?'

One of the men eyed her face and then her low-cut gown with a look she found disturbing. 'One of the court entertainers, are you? And what is it you do for those fine ladies and gentlemen, my black beauty?'

The other, an older man with a grizzled beard, laid down his end of the chest with a disapproving grunt. 'Now, Simon Talley, that's quite enough from you.' He wiped his hands on his apron and considered her. The night was warm and airless, and the sound of stamping feet, whistling and a fiddler's rough tune drifted across from makeshift tents under the castle walls. 'Master Payne, is it? He'll be busy housing the Queen's servants tonight.'

'That's why I need to speak to him. I was following my friend in search of our lodgings. But my shoe broke and I fell behind.'

'No need to distress yourself.' The older man smiled, showing broken teeth. 'Did you come down from the outer court? You'd best go back and find a place to sleep. It's a maze in here, with all these tents and what have you, so watch you don't get lost again. Take that lane. Then head through the gate and across the tilt-yard. You'll find Master Payne at his station on the bridge. And if any of the guards ask what your business is, tell them old John Tatter sent you. That'll shut them up.'

'Thank you.'

Calmer now, she followed the old man's instructions and found her way back towards the tall, brooding shadow she guessed to be the inner keep of the castle. The place was still noisy and bustling, despite the lateness of the hour. Passing to and fro between the inner and outer courts, the Queen's servants and Leicester's men lugged bags, trunks and furniture from the unloading carts. Men of office tramped past her in the dark, arguing fiercely, an ancient servant bent almost double behind, laden with books and papers, a secretary's bag slung over his shoulder. Two men lumbered along with a high-backed leather chair. A dog ran barking up the slope and disappeared over the bridge into the inner court, followed a moment later by a heavy young boy in a velvet cap, red-faced, whistling and calling in vain.

Some of the other entertainers were still arriving, loud and colourful in their outrageous costumes, carrying trained animals and exotic birds in cages, looking for a place to set up their tents and hammocks. These were not travelling with the Queen's progress, so had to bribe their way into a place in the castle grounds. Lucy watched as fat purses changed hands on the gate without any attempt at concealment. From their loud discussions, impossible not to overhear, the guards were guiding some of these travellers down to the camp at the Brays. Others were forced to seek their own shelter in the village, or even in the open countryside beyond, depending on their standing with Leicester.

Lucy's attention was caught by one man who seemed unable to come to an arrangement with the guards. Forgetting for a moment that she was supposed to be seeking Master Payne, she stood still, startled by his strangeness. The man was followed by a bear on a stout chain. In a dark robe, rough cap and sturdy black boots, armed with a thick stick, the traveller was arguing with the guards for a place to pitch his tent against the castle wall. He seemed to speak English only haltingly, and kept jerking on the bear's chain.

His bear was black and shaggy, its fur unkempt and missing in patches, its claws almost within reach of the guards. Whenever the creature reared up, which the man often urged it to do with the use of a long stick, one of the guards would level his pike at it and angrily shout an oath.

Eventually, some filthy piece of paper was produced, which the guard pored over dubiously, then shrugged and handed it to his captain. It had the required effect, for soon the man bowed and turned his snarling bear in the direction the guard had pointed. Whatever the paper contained, Lucy had the impression that the guards had allowed the bear-tamer a place near the walls more out of fear than because he belonged there.

So absorbed was she by this exchange, she did not at first notice the large man who came climbing the sloping path towards her, his cloak thrown back over a broad shoulder, his cap set at an angle, his black beard thick as any sailor's.

'How now, Mistress Morgan?' the man remarked, halting before her with a flourish of his cap. 'Why, you've grown so tall, I wouldn't have known you.'

She gave a little cry of astonishment and delight, and threw herself into his arms. 'Master Goodluck!'

'Careful. I bruise easily.'

She laughed and leaned comfortably against his vast chest, wishing that a little of his strength could somehow pass into her own weary body. Master Goodluck was like a bear himself, a great black bear whose sharp claws would never hurt her. She had hoped secretly that her guardian might come to Kenilworth with his travelling troupe of players and acrobats. Before she had gone to court, he had always been there to offer advice or teach her new tricks. But his visits had become less frequent since she had won herself a place at court as a singer and dancer for the Queen. In fact, she'd almost begun to fear that Goodluck had forgotten her.

'I missed you, Goodluck.'

'And I missed you, dearest heart.' His humorous gaze swept the outer court, lingering for a moment on the foreigner and his black bear, which was now rolling on its back, exciting no little interest in the crowd that had gathered. 'But where are you lodged? Here within the castle walls?'

'I don't think so.' She frowned, not wishing to admit her own foolishness. 'I lost my friend, and was told to come back here and speak to a Master Payne. Do you know him?'

'No, but don't fret. I'll help you find him and your lodgings for tonight. But not until we've had a chance to talk. By Mary, you're so tall now, woman, I barely recognized you.' He stuck his cap back on his head and slipped an arm about her waist. 'Shall we walk?'

The bear and its owner had finally disappeared back through the gatehouse, but there was still a steady stream of passing servants in the outer court, and harassed-looking gentlemen with their ladies. Under the trees, a troupe of acrobats in green livery were practising their tumbles, and everywhere was a great hum of activity. Even though the sun had finally set, there could be no privacy while light spilled from every window in the halls of the inner court, though at least there was no Mistress Hibbert here to watch her every step. Now only Mistress Longley remained to guard the women servants of the court. A plump and easy-natured woman, she lacked Mistress Hibbert's dedication to making the lives of her charges a misery.

'Are there gardens here, do you think?' Lucy asked.

'Indeed.' Goodluck smiled. 'Though the best are for the Queen's private use. I came to Kenilworth a few years ago and have always thought it one of the best private homes in the country. But much of this is new.' He indicated the elegant stone buildings at their back. One of Leicester's guards walked past, and Goodluck drew the hood of his cloak over his head with characteristic caution. 'Come under the walls here, where it's quiet and we can talk undisturbed.'

Between the new-built stables and the ancient lookout tower, between shored-up buttresses crowded against the outer defences, they found an alcove cut into the reddish sandstone walls.

Goodluck drew a flask from the folds of his cloak and held it out to her. 'Shall we drink to Her Majesty's health?'

Lucy took a sip and choked. She felt her cheeks redden and her throat sting at the fiery liquid.

'You'll get me into trouble.'

'Too true. You shouldn't be keeping such company, my little innocent, or some might suggest you would not long remain so.'

Goodluck slipped an arm about her waist, drawing her possessively near. He threw back his hood, revealing the full glory of his dark beard again. There had never been a time when she had not known Goodluck, and his mysterious comings and goings had been a constant theme of her childhood. Yet she knew almost nothing about him, beyond his name and the certainty that he would never cause her harm.

'You're not afraid to be alone with me, Lucy?' he asked, half teasingly.

'Not a bit.'

'You break my heart. But it's good to see you again. It must be getting on for a year since I was last in London.'

'More than that. Were you abroad?'

'I can't tell you that. But I shouldn't have left you alone so long, I know. You're well, Lucy?' he asked, observing her from under thick black brows. 'It was a creditable thing to get – and keep – a place at court. But you're not smiling. Are you not happy there?'

She hesitated, glancing cautiously about the castle walls, but they seemed safe from eavesdroppers. 'You remember when I was still a child, Master Goodluck, and could sing and dance whenever I wished, and take pleasure in my skill? At court, we are not so free. There's always work to be done, cleaning or mending or sewing, and we cannot refuse it. I must keep a guard on my tongue too, for fear of drawing attention to myself. And there's another thing,' she added. 'We are *watched*.'

'We?'

'The women, yes. We live surrounded by rules. And they seem far stricter with me than the others. Even looking the wrong way at a man can earn me a whipping.'

'They beat you?' Goodluck's generous, bearded smile did not falter but she heard the anger in his voice.

'Not often. I try to be careful.'

'I'm glad to hear it.' He pinched her chin. 'Though with your mother's looks, I'm not surprised to hear you are watched constantly.'

'You loved my mother, didn't you?'

She had not meant to ask but could not help herself, pouncing on the idea like a hungry bird on a seed. Indeed, there was no one else she could ask about her history, since both her real parents were dead. As she lay dying, her mother had begged Goodluck to look after her baby if it survived. True to his word, he had carried Lucy to his sister's house when she was only a few days old, or so the story went, for he was too often away from home to bring up a child himself. There, she had been taught her trade, for they were a family of entertainers, and she the very youngest of them all, happiest on her hands instead of her feet and gifted from an early age with the voice of a songbird.

'Yes, I loved her, for the short time that I knew her.' His smile dimmed, and he glanced down at her curious face. 'Though we would not have suited. Your mother was a wilful, headstrong piece. Just like her daughter.'

Lucy pretended to pull away in a huff, but laughed when Goodluck's strong hands caught her, one arm soon drawing her back to his side. 'Lucky for you that I am not your father,' he murmured in her ear, his beard tickling her throat. 'For I would make a most stern and cruel parent, and keep you locked up night and day.'

'Then I give thanks that you're my good friend and *not* my father.'

She stiffened, frowning at the sight of Tom Black leading a skittish and sidling piebald into the stables. Tom was stroking the horse's muzzle and whispering in its ear, no doubt seeking to soothe the animal's fears amid all the noise and chaos of the outer court. She stared at him, admiring his broad chest in the plain white shirt and leather jerkin, the muscular turn of his thighs. It was a rare thing to see a man with skin black as her own, and to find one so far from London was strange and wonderful.

'It's bad enough to be under the eye of Mistress Hibbert,' she added, trying not to blush and give her thoughts away. 'Her smiles are sour as lemons. If she could get away with chaining us to the wall, I promise you she would.'

Goodluck had followed her gaze, and his eyes narrowed as Tom disappeared into the huge double-storeyed stable block. 'Mistress Hibbert sounds like a woman after my own heart. Yet where is she, this great scourge of the entertainers? For here you are, a young girl dashing about a strange castle and falling into bad company, and no stout matron in sight to scold you and send you to bed.'

'Oh,' she replied airily, 'we left old Hibbert sick in London. And Mistress Longley lets us younger girls run wild.'

'Not too wild, I hope.'

'Are you jealous?'

'I wish I had time to be jealous. My head's too full of other matters to worry about the comings and goings of pretty young things like yourself.'

She twisted around and looked up into his bearded, weather-beaten face, curious and more than a little concerned. She had known for years that Master Goodluck had a reputation in certain circles as a spy, and it worried her to think of her comfortable old guardian engaged in such a dangerous business, especially when she could not be entirely certain whether he was spying for or against the Queen. She had seen the bloody remains of too many spiked and staring heads on London Bridge to shrug off the possibility that Goodluck might get himself arrested.

'What do you mean by that?' she asked. 'Do you carry news from abroad to the Queen's advisers?'

'Oh, so those dark eyes of yours see more than just goodly young men.' Goodluck shook his head at her questioning look, and took another swig from his flask. 'My work is no great matter for discussion, trust me. My only advice would be to beware of Italians. And that must suffice for now.'

There was a grim look to his eyes that Lucy had never seen

before, a heaviness that made her wish to smooth those lines away. But she knew he would resent such a sisterly gesture, so she pretended not to have noticed. Instead she allowed him to pull her back into his arms.

'For tonight,' Goodluck said, kissing her cheek with a fierce scratch of his beard, 'the Queen is safely tucked up here in Kenilworth, and I am very thankful to see my not so little Lucy again.'

# Eight

LETTICE CARRIED THE QUEEN'S HEAVY, THICKLY JEWELLED FORESKIRT to one of the open travelling chests. With aching arms, she laid it gently alongside the matching sleeves and stiff ivory busk that had kept Elizabeth's torso fashionably flat during the long hot day. She examined the fabric critically, but all the jewels were still attached; there would be no need to note down any lost gems in the wardrobe book. The fragile material of the foreskirt, however, had snagged in several places and would need to be mended before the gown could be worn again, a painstaking task requiring several hours of close, eye-burning needlework. With any luck though, one of Elizabeth's seamstresses would have arrived by now, and she herself would not need to give up an entire evening to the job.

Lady Mary Sidney and Lady Helena Snakenborg were wrestling with the knotted laces of Elizabeth's bum-roll while Elizabeth herself stood in her underwear, tapping her foot, leaning one hand on the wall.

'Damn these hellish contraptions. I can scarce breathe. Where is my wine? One of you, fetch me a glass of wine!'

Lettice saw a wine flagon and glasses laid out on the table – two fluted glasses of rich Venetian ware – and poured Elizabeth a glass of wine. *Two glasses.* She kept her face carefully expressionless, though a savage bitterness filled her heart. So my lord Leicester intended to welcome Elizabeth to his Warwickshire home later that night, no doubt as he had welcomed her previously, with a loving cup and his warm skin against hers in the dark.

Her hand trembled as she handed the wine to Elizabeth, curtseying deep. 'Your Majesty.'

Piercing eyes surveyed her without smiling and Lettice dropped her gaze. Was it possible she knew their secret? Could some spying servant have carried the tale to Elizabeth's ears?

An unexpected flash of rebellion strengthened her. 'Should I fetch you something sweet to eat, Your Majesty?'

Elizabeth looked at her a long moment, her thin lips pursed. 'The Bible. Fetch me the Holy Bible.'

'At once, Your Majesty.'

She searched the assembled luggage in vain, but Elizabeth's small book chest was nowhere in evidence. No doubt it would appear in daylight with the rest of her luggage.

'What's the matter?' Elizabeth demanded irritably as Lettice hunted about the room and the other women continued to ready her for bed. Mary was rubbing a rose-scented lotion into her hands to preserve Elizabeth's skin, as Helena stretched up on tiptoe to remove each slender pin that held her day wig in place. 'Is my order too difficult for you to follow?'

Lettice gave up the search. 'I beg pardon, Your Majesty, but your book chest has not yet arrived.'

'What's that beside the bed?'

Lettice followed the line of Elizabeth's imperious finger and saw, beside the vast gold-canopied bed, a small engraved table in the shape of an octagon on which stood a large leatherbound book with gold clasps and deep gilt lettering to the spine. She took it up and brought it over with an obedient curtsey.

'Open it to the Book of Psalms and read some verses aloud to me,' Elizabeth instructed her, having finally shed her bum-roll. She stood there innocent enough in her simple white shift. By now Helena had placed a wig of straight, well-brushed, flame-red hair on her head and was starting to pin it in place. 'With a clear voice. I am in need of the scriptures tonight.'

Sensing herself to be on trial, Lettice unfastened the gold clasps and turned the gossamer-thin, delicate, gold-tipped leaves to the

Book of Psalms. The bold black lettering in a Gothic font stared up mockingly at her.

She wet her lips nervously. 'It is in Latin, Your Majesty.'

'In Latin?' Elizabeth paused a moment, frowning across at her. 'Then you must translate.'

'I . . . Yes, Your Majesty. Forgive me, Your Majesty.'

Lettice began to translate, her voice faltering, and had not finished three lines before Elizabeth reached across and knocked the Bible from her hands. The holy book fell to the floor with a crash, its gilt-tipped pages flying open. Lady Mary gave a cry of alarm, perhaps fearing such an action was sacrilegious. Nobody else in the room moved.

'Where were you as a girl when your teachers should have sat you down to learn your Latin grammar? With your skirts round your ears in some filthy shrubbery, no doubt.'

Elizabeth strode to the bed in nothing but her shift and knitted silk stockings, Lady Helena running behind with an embroidered silk nightgown draped over her arm. Lady Mary stooped to retrieve the Bible from its ignoble position and replaced it on the bedside table.

'You will have words with the castle steward, Lady Essex, and find my good English Bible in the stores. I will not have this Papist monstrosity in my chambers. You will do this before you sleep tonight. Do I make myself clear?'

'Yes, Your Majesty.'

Fleeing the room before anything sharper than a Bible was thrown at her, Lettice ran from the bedchamber with her head down and her heart pounding.

She stood a moment in the broad torchlit doorway to the Privy Chamber, allowing her breathing to slow and settle. Her abrupt exit had excited a few curious stares from guardsmen and servants still moving Elizabeth's own furniture into her apartments. She straightened her gown, which was soiled and crumpled from travelling, and smoothed the line of her French hood. They might not be in London, but while travelling with the Queen's entourage she was still 'at court' and must behave accordingly.

Calmer now, she made for the stairs. Her legs were trembling though and she had tears in her eyes, like a recalcitrant child scolded by its mother. Except these were tears of rage.

*Where were you as a girl? With your skirts round your ears in some filthy shrubbery?*

Such an ugly accusation to have made. Her Latin schooling had been fair, but she had only engaged with it a few years before being removed from such unnecessary lessons and taught instead to speak French prettily, to dance in the latest courtly fashion, to embroider and make her curtsey. She had not been raised in such royal privilege as Elizabeth, who had needed to know the language of international diplomacy before the lessons of sampler and song. Like Lady Mary Sidney, like most daughters of noblemen, Lettice had been taught to read and write, to know a little history and geography, and had applied herself well to her lessons. But she had been bred to be a courtier's wife, not a great scholar like Elizabeth with a book constantly in her hand – and indeed a wife and mother were all she had ever been.

Elizabeth must know of her renewed affair with Leicester. What else could this violent, unjust temper mean?

Lettice thought of Walter, her husband, the Earl of Essex, of his cold and proudly handsome face. She closed her eyes, sick to her stomach with fear. He had been so angry last time, so aggressive and hard to pacify. If her renewed affair with Robert were to become an open secret, what might Walter do on his return from Ireland?

'Hey, whoa there!'

A strong pair of hands grasped and steadied her, and Lettice realized that she had been running too fast down the staircase, almost tripping in her haste.

'In a hurry, my lady Essex?'

She looked up into Robert's handsome face and knew what she must do, the terrible risk she must take. He alone would know how best to soothe Elizabeth's anger, he who had survived longest at her court.

They were alone on the narrow, dim-lit staircase.

'She knows,' she hissed.

Frowning, Robert laid a warning hand against her mouth. For

a terrifying instant she thought he meant to stifle her. Hurriedly, she kissed his hand instead, savouring the salt tang of his skin, the hint of leather and horses.

He shook his head in silent warning, then removed his hand from her mouth and drew her down a few more steps into the shadows of an unlit landing.

'Not here.'

'Where, then?' she demanded in a whisper.

'In the aviary at the far end of the Queen's Privy Garden. Tomorrow, an hour after we return from church.'

'That will be too late. I tell you, she knows.'

Robert glanced up and down the narrow staircase, then leaned forward to press a swift kiss on her mouth. Unable to help herself, she rubbed her body eagerly against his and felt his instant response, the stiffening at his groin and the possessive curve of his arm about her waist.

*Let her spies catch us*, Lettice thought. *She cannot prevent this. Even the greatest of queens can have no jurisdiction over a man's desire.*

He groaned under his breath. 'Lettice, we must not—'

'Why not? There is no one here to see us.'

Hesitant at first, his hand stroked her throat, then slid down to the deep, pale curve between her breasts. So his desire for her had not been lessened by the fear of discovery, Lettice thought. He tugged at the restraining material of her bodice as though he intended to free her breasts.

'Essex is a fool.' He groaned. 'He should be whipped for neglecting such a wife.'

Hungry as a cat for physical affection, Lettice sank her face into his red and gold jacket with its glorious scent of his body, sweetly spiced, his breath warm on her throat. If only Walter could possess Robert's easy charm, or if he could at least spend more time at home or at court, perhaps she might not feel so starved of love. It was not entirely her fault that she had looked elsewhere.

Arching backwards for more of his kisses, she scratched her cheek on one of his embossed gold buttons and gave a sharp cry.

He caught her shoulders as she jerked away. 'What now?'

'Your finery attacked me,' she complained, rubbing her cheek, then laughed at the expression on his face. 'Wasn't it you who told me love hurts?'

'Yes, I did say that.' He traced her scratched cheek with one finger, his eyes intent. 'But in bed, not on the stairs.'

'Yet one must climb the stairs to reach one's bed.'

He sighed. 'Have a care then, not to fall in the attempt.'

She laid a restraining hand on his arm as he made to turn away. 'You too must be careful, Robert. The Queen suspects us, I'm sure of it. I have not seen her this agitated for months. There was an old Latin Bible at her bedside. She cursed and threw it to the floor when I read to her from it.'

He frowned. 'I thought the Latin would please her.'

'Tonight everything offends her. She called for a plain English Bible, and all but accused you of being a Papist.'

Their eyes met at that, and both laughed. But it was an uncomfortable laughter, and she caught a hint of anger in his face. He had always been so vehemently against the Roman faith, such a groundless accusation must sting hard.

Robert tugged at his jacket as if to straighten it, then paused. Slowly and carefully, he unwound one of her long red hairs from around a gilt button.

His eyes danced as he held up the single hair. 'This could have made for an awkward moment later.'

'I don't see why,' she replied tartly. 'The lady in question might have mistaken it for one of her own.'

He held the hair up to the light from the nearest window slit, examining it mock-critically. 'Hers has not the same rich lustre—'

'For pity's sake, keep your voice down!'

He smiled at her shocked expression, and tucked the reddish hair into some hidden pocket in his jacket. 'There,' he whispered. 'Close to my heart. Now don't look so worried. The Queen will not hurt you, even if she does suspect our affair. You are her cousin and more like Elizabeth than any other woman at court. To harm you would be like cutting off her own right hand.'

'Or her nose to spite her face,' Lettice muttered.

Silently, he moved to step round her, and she caught at his arm.

'Don't bother with her tonight, Robert. She won't let you past the door.'

'I have a prior arrangement. The Queen will honour it.'

'I do not believe she will. Stay with me instead,' she insisted. The sound of carousing drifted up the stairs from the open court-yard below. 'You are master here. We are in your own castle of Kenilworth, not at court where we are constantly watched.'

'Court is where the Queen is.'

She shook her head at his blind submission. 'Find us a place where we can bolt the door and be private together. The Queen won't expect my return tonight. We will not be discovered.'

'Lettice, sweetest, I can't do that.' He kissed her again, once on each cheek and once on her parted lips, then put her gently aside, as no doubt he had once put aside his wife. 'The Queen will be expecting me, and I can't fail to be there. To serve the Queen is what I most desire, even beyond my love for you. It is what keeps a courtier safe and in her good graces. I advise you to cultivate the same desire yourself, unless you wish to find yourself far from court – and me.'

In silence, Lettice watched him step up towards the brightly lit chambers of the royal apartments, leaving her bereft against the cold stone. Was no man ever to show her true love and affection?

She turned and guided herself down into darkness, blinking back angry tears once again. *To serve the Queen is what I most desire, even beyond my love for you.* What further sign did she need of Robert's intentions?

It was July now. If Elizabeth changed her mind and chose to accept him, Robert could be on the throne before the first leaves began to turn.

# Nine

THE TINY SCRATCHING AT HER DOOR SOUNDED MORE LIKE A MOUSE behind the wainscot than someone requesting entry to the Royal Bedchamber. Nonetheless, Elizabeth recognized the sound and halted her restless pacing, turning to the leaded windows of the state apartments. Her ladies stirred but she held them back with a gesture, and they sat back on the floor, attending once more to their embroidery.

Slowly, she tidied her nightgown and robe, then waited another good minute before giving him permission to enter.

'*Veni!*'

The castle grounds had fallen into inky darkness now, all trace of fireworks gone, their burning lights submerged beneath the lake like the village which had once stood there, its people driven out of their homes to make way for the castle's watery defences. High walls, deep water, watchtowers, inner and outer courts, the iron clang of the portcullis being lowered behind her soldiers. She was living in a fortress. Yet such precautions were necessary, it would appear. At their last meeting Walsingham had mentioned another plot against her life, though for once his intelligence was scanty.

Yet she felt safe here at Kenilworth. Her personal bodyguards stood at arms only a few feet away in the Presence Chamber, with orders to admit none but her ladies-in-waiting and her most trusted courtiers, and Robert had posted men at all possible points of entry to the royal apartments.

The door had opened quietly in response to her command. It was her own Robin, of course. She did not need to turn her head to assure herself of that as she followed his reflection across the room in the leaded diamonds of the window. With all the candles in the great chamber, flecks of light swimming in the thick glass, it was like a vision in a cathedral with Elizabeth at the altar, waiting for her prayers to be answered.

Several of her ladies rose in a rustling flurry of skirts and curtseyed low at his entrance. Demurely, they offered him wine and sweetmeats, both of which Robert declined in a smiling voice.

Too impatient to concern herself with the need for discretion, Elizabeth waved the women away.

'Leave us, all of you.'

Nevertheless, she waited until the door had closed behind the last of her attendants before turning to him. He was kneeling with uncharacteristic humility, head bowed. She suspected that someone must have informed him of her mood on his way upstairs. Who else but the faithless Countess of Essex?

Straight-backed in her white nightgown and ermine-trimmed robe, she raised him with an impatient gesture. 'You cannot stay, Robin. Not tonight.'

'As you wish, Your Majesty.'

Elizabeth noticed that Robert's gaze was on the heavy gilt Bible at her bedside, and knew that she was right. Lettice must have spoken to him before he reached her presence.

'I have sent Lady Essex to fetch my own English Bible. That one was not to my taste.'

'Pardon my presumption in providing it, Your Majesty.' He seemed to hesitate, and she knew a moment of curiosity as she wondered how he would deal with his fear of antagonizing her. 'With your love of languages, I thought the Latin would please you.'

She remembered the dancing shadows outside the tent at Long Itchington, and her nails dug into her palms, cutting tiny half-moons in her skin. The memory poisoned her thoughts, left her struggling against the strong desire to scream at him like a common fishwife, to demand the truth about him and Lettice.

'My people are permitted to hear the scriptures in English now. Why should my own Bible be in Latin?'

Robert bowed deep from the waist, seemingly obedient, though his gaze returned rather too swiftly to her face.

'Indeed, Your Majesty.'

Was she a fool to keep refusing his offers of marriage? She had never met a foreign prince she liked better than Robert, however handsome and assiduous in their courtship her various suitors had been, and God knew she had tried hard enough to like some of them. Even gone so far as to allow them to kiss and touch her more privately than she cared to remember. Yet Robert would not be ideal as a husband, a royal consort. He was an ambitious man, and ambitious men made dangerous bedpartners for a queen. Had not her cousin Mary proved that beyond any legitimate doubt?

Even a homely marriage to an English nobleman might silence the doubters though, and perhaps even put a new scion of the house of Tudor into the royal nursery.

The possibility of a child made Elizabeth draw breath. To be married at last, to be a mother!

But to allow a man so close to her throne, and a Dudley no less, that could never be safe.

'Take that Papist book with you when you go,' she instructed him coldly, once more facing the window and the dark countryside beyond.

He came up behind her, a shadow on the glass. His hands were on her shoulders before she realized what he was planning, and she spun, a quick oath on her lips that died at the look in his face. She shook her head, put her hands on his chest. But he would not be stopped, his strength easily superior to her own.

'No,' she insisted.

His arms clasped her tight, pulled her against the rich stuff of his doublet, and Elizabeth felt the old familiar weakening of her limbs, the odd delirious tingling that always seemed to presage a fainting fit yet meant nothing but desire, as she knew now.

'Don't you recall what the common people are saying of me?' she demanded, trying to make him see sense. 'That I am no longer a virgin. That you and I are lovers.'

'And are these things not true?'

'Robin, for God's sake!'

His hands stroked her shoulders through the white ermine-trimmed silk of her night robe. 'The people adore you, Elizabeth, whatever we may do in the privacy of your chamber. Did you not see the men and women kneeling in the road as you left London, begging for your blessing on their heads as you passed? And here tonight, entering Kenilworth ... Didn't you hear the people cheering, or see the flowers they threw in your path?'

'Such things will mean nothing once my reputation is lost.' She shook her head. 'This is not Richmond or Whitehall. We are too public here. If you stay tonight, they will call me a whore.'

His hands seized hers, pressing them urgently against the swell of his body. 'Then marry me, Elizabeth. Make the bastards swallow their words.'

'I cannot.' Her stomach tightened with apprehension. 'England is not yet secure, and many in the Council still wait to see me married off to some stout Protestant prince. No, the times are too dangerous for such a marriage. The country would descend into civil war and tear itself apart, just as it did before my grandfather took the throne.'

'I do not believe it. The people would be happy to see me by your side.'

'Which people?'

'Those who still believe in stability for England.'

'They must be few indeed,' she said drily. 'Besides, if we were wed, you would try to master me. I shall not be mastered by any man, Robert. I have sworn it.'

'And to whom have you sworn this fierce oath?'

'To myself.'

He smiled. 'Bess, my beautiful Bess.'

'Don't call me that. I'm no longer that girl.' Yet the affection behind his childish address pleased her. She found herself turning in to the warmth of his body, her earlier anger almost forgotten. How good it was between them when they were not arguing. 'Robert . . .'

His mouth was at her throat. 'My queen, my lovely beauty.'

Exulting in the heat that sprang between them, the desire still as fervent as when they had been young and nobody had been watching, she let him kiss her, tilting her head back until their mouths met. He spoke against her lips, and she almost pulled back to ask, teasingly, 'What did you say?' Then memory tugged at her again, conjuring two whispering shadows, half glimpsed in sleep, seen through the pale billowing sails of the royal tent, their heads close together. The vision slid back under her ribs with a shock, sharp and demanding.

She wanted to shout the hated name at him, throw it at him in a furious riot of accusation.

*Lettice. What is she to you? How dare you come to me tonight when your eyes would prefer her face to mine?*

But such an outburst could only weaken her position. Besides, to admit jealousy would be to mark her out as her father's daughter, driven beyond reason and diplomacy by the urges of her body.

'Tomorrow,' she said instead, quickly extricating herself with a smile. 'Tomorrow we will celebrate Mass in the village church. Is that the plan?'

Robert straightened. As his arms dropped away from her, he seemed to understand that the moment for embracing was over, that she would not go any further tonight. That was something she had always admired about him. With his innate intelligence and quick grasp of any political situation, Robert Dudley, Earl of Leicester, was the man she turned to first in a crisis. Or when she needed a little wit and light relief. Life at court could be so dull and restrictive that she was constantly in need of distraction. Robert had always made her laugh when no one else could. Surely that must be worth something?

'Tomorrow, everything will be just as you requested.'

Elizabeth managed another smile, but took the precaution of moving swiftly away before he could distract her again with his gaze and his clever hands.

Her ladies already whispered enough behind their idle hands whenever she and Robert danced or walked together or rode out hunting. The court was a stifling prison, its corridors full of watchful shadows. There could be little hope of privacy even at Kenilworth, though knowing that Robert's sleeping quarters were so close at hand was both a comfort and a temptation she could do without.

'Then you may leave me.' She nodded towards the closed door. 'I have other business yet tonight.'

Robert was curious, and not a little irritated; this was clear from the way his dark eyes narrowed on her face. But he swept another extravagant bow, his smile following swiftly. Rather too swiftly, she thought, and held herself aloof, at her most distant, barely acknowledging his departure.

'I bid you goodnight, Your Majesty, and I humbly pray you enjoy better sleep than I expect to.'

As soon as the door had closed behind him, Elizabeth staggered to the bed, no longer able to hold herself erect. The old pain had returned, gripping her belly, her womb. The desire to call him back, to shut her door to the world as she welcomed him into her bed, was powerful. Yet the overriding need to remain silent was like an armoured glove clamped about her heart, its vast metal fingers squeezing her half to death.

Must she never conceive a son to honour and preserve the royal house of Tudor?

She did not have to wait long for her last visitor of the night. The secret knock came a few moments later, as though the old spy-master had been waiting his turn in the shadows while Robert was in her bedchamber.

Elizabeth opened the door herself. 'It's late.'

Francis Walsingham bowed stiffly at her tone, austere as ever in his stern black doublet and hose. His neat white ruff was as high as those of any of the young bucks at court, yet his ornaments were sparing – just one golden link-chain about his neck to proclaim his wealth.

'I would have come earlier but you were otherwise engaged,' he commented without emphasis, his glance searching every corner of her bedchamber with his usual caution. Apparently satisfied, he turned back, observing her ermine-trimmed robe, the silk folds of her nightwear. 'Perhaps I should return tomorrow, Your Majesty, when you are rested?'

But Elizabeth had seen the rolled-up papers in his hand.

Walsingham would not come to her so late at night if it was not a matter of great importance. She sighed, then threw the door wide for him and turned away to her chair, too fatigued to stand any longer. Her eyes stung as though she had been staring too long into the heart of a fire.

'Say what you've come to say, old friend. I'm tired but not yet ready for my bed. As my father would have said, there'll be time enough for sleep when I'm dead.'

Walsingham's smile was dry as he closed the door and limped towards her. 'Your death, Majesty, is the very matter about which I have come.'

# Ten

IT WAS THE UNACCUSTOMED SOUND OF BIRDSONG THAT WOKE LUCY early, not the bells. Bells she heard constantly in London. Her own modest dwelling stood next to old St Mary's, and the black-barred gate down to its crypt terrified her whenever she passed it after nightfall. The church itself had a low crumbling tower with a bell which rang out solemn and rich on the hour. On Sundays and holy feast days, it might be heard to peal all morning, from dawn to afternoon, and sometimes even beyond, with the consequence that she could sleep right through the bells when not summoned to court. There were birds in London too, of course, especially in the grand gardens of the palaces. But birdsong this loud and relentless was alien to her.

Lucy groaned and hid her face in the hard, narrow bolster that passed for her pillow. Had every bird in Warwickshire come to perch on her window ledge?

Rising about an hour later, when the sun was higher, she dressed hurriedly and smoothed her hair back with pins, fastening a white pleated hood over it as she had been shown. At home, she would not have bothered with a hood or cap, for being unmarried she was permitted to wear her hair loose unless at church. She had missed the service this morning, but she knew from experience that it would not do to admit that. The court servants and performers were expected to attend Mass at dawn, long before the court itself was awake. For someone like her, dark-skinned and 'heathen' in her looks, as old Mistress Hibbert loved to point out, the last thing she needed was an accusation of godlessness. So if any should ask why she had not come to church that morning, with her demure white hood in place she could at least pretend to have been there, hidden in the crush at the back.

Lucy emptied her privy bucket out of the narrow window at the back. One of the girls with whom she was sharing the room – long gone, presumably breakfasted and churched by now – had shown her where to empty it, and then told her how to reach the inner court in case she got lost again. The path was easy enough to find by daylight, she had assured Lucy, though she warned her not to attempt it alone after dusk.

She made her way through the smoky, crowded alleyways of the Brays to the tiltyard gate. The guard on duty remembered her from the night before, and as she passed along the dusty tiltyard, skirts raised out of the dirt, Lucy found the place humming with activity. Just as they had done the night before, acrobats practised their tumbles on the rough ground, dogs ran barking between the tents within the outer walls, and she could see her own people returning from the village church.

Worried that she might be seen and her absence at church remarked upon, Lucy made her way hurriedly across the outer court, head down. She was walking so swiftly that she collided with someone and staggered backwards, strong hands catching her before she fell.

'Pardon, mistress!'

It was Tom, her rescuer from the night before. Lucy looked up into his face, shocked to find him so close. His hands were still supporting her, one arm about her waist. She pulled away at once, righting her gown.

Had the others spotted her?

Tom took up the fallen reins of the white horse he had been leading, settling the animal with a muttered word, stroking his hand down its milky neck.

Lucy's hood was askew, her face hot. Quickly she turned her back on the entertainers coming from the gatehouse and tidied her hair, trying not to look at him.

'Thank you.'

'You never told me your name last night.'

'Lucy,' she managed. 'Lucy Morgan.'

'Lucy Morgan,' he repeated slowly and bowed, as though he was a lord and she a lady of the court.

Behind him, the horse stamped impatiently and nudged his shoulder, as though wondering what the hold-up was.

'I ought to go,' she said awkwardly. 'I woke too late for church and missed Mass. The others will be wondering where I am.'

'I didn't think they had any Moors at court,' Tom continued. 'You must be a novelty with your beautiful black skin and eyes. The Queen keeps you to amuse herself, perhaps. I see you wear their court gowns too, and they suit you.' His gaze travelled down over her throat and chest, exposed by the low-cut bodice. She did not find the touch of his gaze unpleasant. 'Do they treat you well, these English lords and ladies?'

Lucy hesitated, unwilling to say anything disloyal about the Queen and her court.

Then the reply died on her lips as a violent roar erupted behind them.

Lucy turned, and saw the bear from last night reared up on its hind legs. Taller than any man there, it clawed at the air with vast hairy paws, its mouth open wide.

Something must have upset the creature – possibly the sound of its owner arguing with the guards on the gate.

The bear-tamer jerked impatiently on the bear's chain, trying to bring the beast back down to the ground. But the bear lunged forward, taking him by surprise. The man's grip on the chain must have loosened, for suddenly the animal was free.

Too terrified to scream, Lucy stood rooted to the spot as the huge creature lumbered across the outer court towards her, its heavy chain trailing uselessly behind it.

While the guards stood gaping, the crowd scattered before its path, women and children screaming in fear, men shouting for a pike or a loaded musket as they ran. Even the horses tied up outside the stable whinnied and reared up in terror at the bear's approach.

'Get behind me!'

Dropping the horse's reins, Tom pulled Lucy into the shelter of his body and shouted into the face of the oncoming bear.

He planted his legs broadly, arms spread out wide to each side, as though trying to make himself the same size as the bear. Now he stood his ground.

Sure that Tom must be killed or maimed, and herself soon after, Lucy hid her face in her hands and prayed.

She burned with shame that she had not gone to hear Mass that morning, not walked to church with the others as she ought to have done and purified her soul of sin. If she died now, in this unconfessed state, the gates of heaven would be closed to her for ever.

Yet the worst did not happen. Nothing happened.

When the bear's hideous grunting stopped and silence followed, Lucy peeped out from between her fingers, shaking, barely able to understand that she was still alive.

The black bear had come to a halt only a few feet from Tom and herself. As she watched in disbelief, it sank back on to its haunches. The animal's mouth yawned wide again and it gave a deep moan.

Within seconds, its long-robed owner came panting up and snatched at the bear's chain, winding it several times about his wrist before berating the animal loudly in his own tongue, whacking its haunches with his stick until Lucy felt almost sorry for the poor beast. Only once he had finished beating the creature did he pay anyone else any attention. He waved away the men armed with muskets, pikes and hard-twigged besoms who had come running up on all sides, eager to destroy the brute.

'No, no!' The bear-tamer stared angrily round at the men surrounding them, his eyes wild. 'No kill bear. No kill.'

There was some commotion at the arched entrance to the stables behind them. Lucy turned with the others, catching her breath as she saw the Earl of Leicester striding towards them, splendid in his rich red doublet and hose, cloak thrown back over his shoulder.

'What's all this?'

The crowd of men fell back at his voice, lowering their weapons. Some threw them down and pulled off their Sunday caps, bowing before their lord. Others muttered beneath their breath as they turned away, clearly disappointed to have lost the opportunity to bait and kill the bear. The long-robed foreigner stayed where he was, looking neither at Leicester nor at Tom but keeping his bear still with a stick held across its huge front legs.

'Tom?'

Tom turned and bowed. 'My lord, it's nothing. I'm sorry you were disturbed. This man's bear got loose.'

'Was anybody hurt?'

'No one, my lord.'

Leicester nodded, surprisingly casual with his servant, and his glance flicked to Lucy. His dark eyes narrowed on her face for a moment. 'Who are you?'

Tom had retrieved the fallen reins of the horse and was comforting the unsettled animal. He did not look up from his task. 'This is Lucy Morgan, my lord,' he said, his voice a little muffled.

Leicester looked from one to the other of them, then gave a lazy grin, clapping Tom on the shoulder. She wondered if he remembered winking at her on the road as the Queen's procession left London. It was unlikely, Lucy told herself, keeping her expression carefully neutral, her eyes lowered. Over a month had passed since that day. Why should a great lord like Leicester remember her?

'Is that the way the wind blows? Well, like attracts like. As no doubt this bear would prefer to have a mate and not be kept on a chain like a disobedient cur. What say you, man?'

Leicester turned his head to regard the man with the bear, his tone less friendly. 'Will your animal be kept chained or must we take this matter before the captain of the guards? He'll know of some place where it can be placed under lock and key. And you with it.'

The bear-tamer's head was bowed, not looking Leicester in the face. 'No, lord. She will be good now. You see.'

'She?'

'Sì lord. Female. Females easier to control.'

Leicester threw back his head and laughed freely. 'By all that's holy, that has never been my experience. Perhaps a female bear may be more docile than a woman. They could not be more fierce, for sure.' He dismissed the man with a wave of his hand. 'Go, take your naughty bear away and keep her chained up from now on. If the beast is allowed to escape again, she will be served to the Queen and her court at high table. Is that clear?'

'*Sì*, lord.'

'Hold a moment there,' Leicester commanded him as the man made his bow. 'You are Italian?'

The man smiled. '*Sì*, lord.'

'And you have the necessary papers to be travelling in England?'

The Italian looked confused, then hurt. '*Sì*, *sì*, great lord. My bear, she is famous. Best bear in all Italy!'

'Very well.'

When the bear-tamer had shuffled away, bowing and dragging his bear after him on her clanking chain, Leicester turned to Lucy again. This time he was smiling, one gloved fist resting lightly on his hip.

'Now, Lucy Morgan, I recall how sweetly you sang at court this Easter, and how the Queen delighted to hear your voice. Will you sing for her again today?'

Her heart hammered and she stared at him like a fool, unsure at first how to reply. 'I . . . I sing with the other ladies. Never alone, my lord.'

'You sang alone at Easter.'

'Yes, my lord. But I took Peggy's part that day.' She hoped she would not be forced to explain why she was never allowed to sing at the front of the troupe. 'She was sick of a fever and could not come to court.'

'And how is Peggy now?'

Her cheeks grew hot. 'She had to leave court, my lord.'

His smile was wry, understanding. 'I see. Yet you are still at the back. Such a pretty voice too. You should be heard by the whole court, not buried in the chorus.'

'But truly, my lord, I am not permitted to sing alone, only with the others. Mistress Hibbert says—'

'Ah, stiff-necked Mistress Hibbert. Well, that sharp-tongued old crow is not here to spoil our sport. This is my castle and I say you shall sing for Her Majesty. The Queen is forever collecting curiosities. And you are a perfect curiosity. You may be just the thing I need.'

Leicester looked her up and down with a shrewd smile. 'Yes, you must walk to church behind the Queen's horse this morning. Mass for the Queen begins in an hour, and I want you among her ladies. Here.' He removed a gold chain from his neck and stepped forward to place it about her own. Lucy bowed her head, feeling the chain weigh heavily about her throat, finer than anything she had ever worn before. 'Now you look more the part. Be especially attentive to the Queen. Smile when she laughs, stay mum when she frowns, follow her every mood like a mirror. And be sure to sing for her on the way back to the castle. She loves a pretty song thrush.'

Lucy curtseyed, but awkwardly, dazzled by the sun, his splendour and the costly gold chain about her neck.

Leicester came closer, his arm on her elbow, his low voice in her ear. 'You were very brave, you know, facing down that bear. Brave or foolish. Most girls at court would have screamed and fainted, or run away. You did none of those things. How much of that was stupidity and how much courage?' He paused, searching her face, his close scrutiny unnerving. 'Courage is a rare quality in a woman, Lucy Morgan. Can you be that brave at the Queen's side?'

'I will try to be, my lord.'

'Do not be afraid to accept what I am offering you. The Queen rewards talent in those close to her, whatever the circumstances of their birth. I am giving you an opportunity here to rise at court, my sweet-throated songbird.'

Lucy stared at him, unsure how to reply, then became aware of Tom standing behind his master as though awaiting further instructions. It hadn't been her intention to look at Tom again, and she hurriedly lowered her gaze to the dusty ground.

But Leicester must have seen the quick flicker of her eyelids or some tell-tale sign in her face, for he smiled, glancing over his shoulder at Tom and then back at her.

'Do you ride, Lucy Morgan?'

'No, my lord.'

'Then you must learn. And swiftly too. Young Tom here will

teach you. The Queen rides everywhere and you shall accompany her, even if it must be on foot for now.' Leicester released her arm with a little shake, his final words meant only for her ears. 'And tell me everything that passes between you.'

# Eleven

GOODLUCK BENT HIS HEAD ON ENTERING THE TENT, AND CAUGHT A distinct whiff of urine mingled with the woodsmoke from outside. Dropping the flap over the entrance, he threw down his cap and kicked a lump sleeping under a cloak. The lump groaned and turned over. 'What?'

'Wake up, Twist!' Goodluck sat down on one of the lidded baskets containing all their props, costumes and play scripts. Not that all of these men could read. In their game, a good memory was more important than being able to read and write. 'Council of war.'

Sos emerged from a damp corner, his hood askew. 'War?' His clever Greek face twitched at the thought. 'We've only just arrived.'

'No time like the present,' Goodluck replied as he bent to remove his boots, tossing each one on to his bed.

'Is that your hose?'

Sos was holding his nose. Goodluck laughed, stretching his cramped toes. 'Talking of smells, we appear to have inherited one of the most scrofulous tents known to man. What happened to the last one?'

'Ned was meant to bring it back with him after patching those holes. Remember the night the cows came through?' Sos shrugged. 'He forgot.'

'This was the best you could do instead?'

Finally abandoning the idea of sleep, the lump that was John

79

Twist threw back his cloak and rolled up into a sitting position. 'My fault,' he admitted, yawning. 'I left it too late to find a replacement. But I don't see what's wrong with this one. Just a few odd smells, and aren't we all used to that? No holes, and it's big enough for all of us too, not like the last one. Better than lying out in the rain.'

'Where *is* Ned?'

'Went out early this morning. Think he might even have combed his beard.' Twist unwrapped a stale-looking piece of bread and began to gnaw on it. 'Church?'

'Or a woman.'

Twist looked at Sos with a sceptical expression. 'Highly unlikely, my friend. Big Ned hasn't had his end away since good Queen Mary was on the throne.'

'*Good* Queen Mary? What was so good about that murdering bitch?'

'She died.'

Sos laughed, and settled himself on a rough stool opposite Goodluck and hooked his feet round the legs. 'So he went to hear Mass. Which must have finished two hours since, unless he went to worship with the court.'

'I don't think he keeps such high company.' Twist spat a piece of bread into his hand, staring down at it in disgust. 'Jesus. Is that grit or dried shit?'

'You'd better hope for the latter,' Goodluck replied. He looked up as Ned came stooping through the entrance flap. 'Shit's less likely to break your teeth. Hey, Ned. We were just debating where you'd vanished to.'

'I was at church.'

'Which finished several hours ago,' Goodluck pointed out.

Ned stopped and looked at their faces, one by one. His frown darkened. 'Aye, and then I dropped into the Castle Arms for a quick stoup of ale. It's a long hot walk up the hill from that church. Why, what's the problem?'

'We thought you were seeing a woman.'

'Yes,' Twist added, his smile unpleasant. 'Name of Mary.'

'Will you stop before you get me strung up? I am not a Catholic!' Ned swore under his breath, and threw a cloth-wrapped parcel down on the basket beside Goodluck. 'Just because I'm not a complete heathen like you three, that doesn't make me a Papist. And I brought back meat and some greens, you ungrateful bastards. We've still half a bag of pulses here. I thought we could knock together a stew.'

'Later,' Goodluck agreed. He sniffed the parcel cautiously before tossing it on to his bed alongside his boots. 'Sit down. We're having a council of war.'

Twist abandoned his bread, his blue eyes narrowed on Goodluck's face. 'Is this where we finally discover why we're out here in the middle of nowhere?'

'Don't tell me you would have preferred to spend the summer in London?' Sos asked, shuffling his stool along to accommodate Ned's outstretched legs.

They called him Big Ned because of his height – he stood about six foot three in stockinged feet, which often proved useful for seeing over hedges or peering in at bedroom windows. Beside him, Sos, who was short and slim, looked like a boy. Except for his beard, which was longer and bushier even than Goodluck's.

'The stench of that place in July,' he continued, pinching his nose expressively. 'Worse even than the fishing boats at Piraeus.'

Goodluck stood and went to the tent flap. He listened a moment, then lifted one corner and peered cautiously around the outer court, but saw nothing out of the ordinary. He dropped the flap and went back to his seat.

'First, many thanks for agreeing to travel up from London,' he said, keeping his voice low out of habit. 'I know you had other plans this summer, Ned. I appreciate your help and will happily give Twist a kicking for you if he can't keep a civil tongue.' He waited until their laughter had died away. 'As for the rest, I don't think it's safe to discuss details here. Too many ears. But if I say we're on the lookout for undesirables of the kind we just discussed, that should be enough for you to be getting along with.'

'Very cryptic,' Twist commented.

'We'll talk about it later. Outside, in the woods beyond the castle walls. Is that understood?'

Sos nodded, his clever face serious. 'And if people ask why we're here?'

'We are here to perform a play before the Queen.'

Twist laughed. 'You liar!'

Goodluck crossed his heart. 'It's the truth. A short piece, to be played before the Queen some time next week, depending on the weather and Her Majesty's mood on the day.'

Ned looked amazed. 'How did you arrange that?'

'Do we get to practise first?'

Goodluck grinned at Twist. 'Every day, if necessary. And as openly as possible. I've chosen *The History of Mad King Canute*.'

'The same piece we played in Banbury?'

'The very same.'

'So we are to perform for the Queen herself?' Sos leapt up on to one of the lidded baskets and strutted along, thrusting an invisible sword back and forth. 'With one eye in the back of our heads for Catholics?'

'Hush, I've told you, it's not safe here.' Goodluck shook his head. 'Twist, I want you on first watch. From dusk tonight until midnight.'

'And what will I be watching?'

'A tent.'

'Our own?' Twist looked surprised.

'No, we'll go out in a moment and I'll show you where it is.' Goodluck threw back the lid of one of the baskets and rummaged for a cloak. 'You'll need something dark to wear. Do you have a hat? Excellent. Keep it low over your face. No one's to notice you watching, or it may be the last mistake you make. Just to be clear, I want to know who goes in and who comes out, and how long they stay.'

'Should I get close enough to listen?'

'No need.' Kicking the lid shut, Goodluck threw him a stained black cloak, floor-length and excellent for disguise. He had used it himself to play a ghost in a tragedy two years before, and very successfully too. 'Even if you could hear every word they said, it would make no difference.'

Twist swung the black cloak about his shoulders and fumbled for the clip. 'Why not?'

'Because, my friend, you don't speak Italian.'

# Twelve

'CAREFUL NOW, DON'T TURN AROUND AND SPOIL IT!' A VOICE WARM in her ear, hands clasped over her eyes. 'Who am I?'

Lettice stumbled and came to a halt on the uneven grass track that led away from the parish church.

The other ladies moved past her, giggling, following the Queen on her white horse. Lettice knew it could not be Robert, who was pacing beside the Queen with a terrified-looking young Moorish girl a few steps behind him. Lettice stood perfectly still. She could see nothing but strips of light between the man's fingers, as though she were blindfolded and about to be led out to the scaffold. She was reminded of a horrible game her husband liked to play with her in their bedchamber. She shivered, recalling the rough hood he used, the fear of a long drop.

The two hands clasped over her eyes tightened, and the male voice asked again, more insistently, 'Come, who am I?'

With relief, she recognized the voice, but played along for a few minutes. Pip Sidney was such an amusing and promising young man, the son of Lady Mary. She had high hopes to see him married one day to her eldest daughter, Penny, whose velvety-dark eyes reminded her so strikingly of Robert.

'Sir, it's not very kind of you to tease me like this. I can't see to walk, and will fall and hurt myself if you don't release me. Do you always treat the Queen's ladies so cruelly?'

'If you fell, I'd catch you.'

'Fine words,' Lettice replied. 'But how can I be expected to trust them, when I don't even know who you are?'

'You can trust me, madam. I am the Queen's servant and a gentleman.'

'Your name?'

'You cannot guess it?'

She heard the hurt and disappointment in the young man's voice, and reluctantly capitulated. 'Well, your voice does remind me of a gentleman of my acquaintance. A fine young man, handsome and a true soldier.'

'Who? Tell me his name.'

His hands dropped away as Lettice turned, smiling up into his eager, high-browed face. 'Why, young Philip Sidney, of course.'

'My lady Essex,' he replied with a grin as he removed his jewelled velvet cap, hair flopping forward over his forehead.

'Oh, Pip. You are such a menace. My heart nearly stopped when you grabbed me.' Laughing, she curtseyed as he bowed with a flourish. Then she embraced him, her affection genuine. 'I did not see you in church.'

'I was late, and thought it best to wait outside.'

'You were right to do so. The Queen is very strict about attending church. She wouldn't have taken your late arrival kindly.'

'Shall we walk on together? Her Majesty is almost out of sight.' He drew a deep breath and let it out slowly. 'I can't get enough of this clean country air. Do you feel the same? After the rich odours of London, all this greenery is like Eden on earth. Though can you imagine what might happen if we were to fall behind and become lost together, my lady? I've heard that these Warwickshire woods are dangerous. I might have to save you from being gored by a wild boar and then carry you back to the castle in my arms, battling savage beasts all the way.'

She patted his cheek. 'Let us catch up with the others. Enchanting though you make that adventure sound, Pip, I have little desire to soil my gown in the woods and none at all to be hoist about by one of my daughter's suitors.'

'One of . . . ?' He seemed embarrassed. 'Penelope is a lovely girl. But I'm nowhere near ready for marriage, my lady, so both you and she are safe from my attentions.'

'*Me?*' Lettice laughed, pretending to look ahead for Elizabeth but in truth watching the tall young man out of the corner of her eye. For the first time, the idea of taking a younger lover struck her, and her cheeks grew warm at the thought. 'You naughty boy. I'm already married, or had you forgotten?'

'True enough, but your husband is safely across the sea in Ireland. And as they say, while the cat's away . . .'

'*Pip!*'

With a nervous laugh, he bowed again, kissing her hand in apology. 'Please forgive me. As you must know, I'm not one for these games of bedposts and secret kisses. My lord Leicester, though . . .' Philip Sidney's clever glance met hers, then slipped away as though confronted by an uncomfortable truth. 'But my uncle is kept busy with the Queen these days, is he not?'

They fell into step together, fitting discreetly back into the throng of lesser courtiers leaving the church. The sun was still hot, the grass dusty, and Lettice was thirsty and tired after the long service.

Several gentlemen tried to catch her eye as they walked, but Lettice kept her head lowered, hands clasped demurely below her chest, employing the stiff white folds of her French hood to conceal her face. She could not grant all the favours she had promised them, least of all an audience with the Queen. But that was not something easily understood by the outer circle of the court, she had found. They seemed to expect a promised audience to mean 'today', rather than 'if I can'. At least she had nothing to fear from Pip, a charming young man and a scholar too, already one of Elizabeth's favourites among the younger generation at court. His boyish good looks had endeared him to many girls his own age too, of course, but at least he had wit enough to keep his flirtations hidden from the Queen.

'You said before, *they say* . . . Are people discussing me and Leicester in the same breath these days?' she asked quietly, careful not to engage his gaze. 'Do they gossip about us in the court?'

'I'm afraid some do, yes,' he agreed, his voice equally low.

'And the Queen?'

'The Queen?'

Raising his eyebrows, Philip glanced at her sideways. At times, she found it hard to remember he was no longer that merry little boy fighting her husband with a wooden sword on the lawns at Chartley, but a grown man of twenty who had served his queen abroad and understood the politics of court life as well as she did.

He fingered his slight beard before answering, as though teasing out the meaning behind her question. 'I would have thought you were better placed to know such a thing, my lady Essex.'

'There are circles within circles at court. Not all overlap with those I frequent. But if you were to hear aught—'

'You would have it straight.'

'I thank you, Pip.'

He smiled, taking her arm in support as the grassy track began to wind back towards the castle, the climb suddenly very steep. Nearer the walls, they passed a row of low cottages. Dirty-faced children came tumbling noisily over the walls to watch the courtiers pass, peasant labourers kneeling in the doorways to their homes with heads bowed and uncovered for their queen, their silence respectful.

'You have always been kind to me, my lady,' Philip pointed out mildly. 'I may be a young man and far beneath your star, but the least I can do is repay your kindness with a little of my own.'

Gently, she pinched his hand. 'Beneath my star? What nonsense!'

'It's the courtly style. You don't like it?'

Smiling up at Philip indulgently, she tried to imagine him married to her Penelope. He would make an excellent son-in-law, that was for certain, if a rather tempting one. How fine their children would look, all bright-eyed and dark-haired, dashing about her house. Though she was not quite ready to be a grand-mother, she told herself ruefully. There was still plenty of life left in her. Time enough for her to grow staid and placid as a cow in a few more years, perhaps, when Penelope was no longer in the care of her tutor. Then there would be nothing better to do than rock a cradle at home while her daughter danced at court and turned men's heads as she had done at that age.

'No, it's rather that I like it too much. But how stupidly steep this hill is. Why must castles always be built on a hill?' She paused for breath on the grassy verge, leaning on his arm. 'Now, young

Sidney, don't dare laugh at me. My shoes pinch horribly and this sun is too bright.'

By the time they reached the castle walls, Elizabeth had dismounted from her horse at the castle gatehouse beside a filthy, hunchbacked old woman to whom she appeared to be talking. Puffed and preened like an exotic bird, the Queen was dressed in silver and white, a thousand tiny pearls stitched painstakingly into the sleeves and rich bodice of her gown, a white-feathered cap set aslant on the riot of her curly red wig. Her careless laughter rang out above the heads of the villagers who had gathered to watch her returning from Mass.

If her older sister Queen Mary had ever visited Kenilworth and gone to hear Mass in the village church, certainly *she* would not have returned laughing so immoderately, dazzling bright in pearls and cloth of silver.

Robert stood apart from Elizabeth, and was holding the reins of her horse while she walked among the commoners. His face revealed nothing but good humour, patient as a rock as he waited for his queen.

Lettice looked at the old woman in her rags. Her lips twitched. Where in God's name did Robert find these people?

She excused herself from Pip's company with a quick curtsey and moved gently up behind Robert, her tread silent on the grass. The Moorish singer who appeared to have attached herself like a shadow to him was still there, a thick gold chain about her neck that Lettice could have sworn belonged to Robert. The singer caught Lettice's warning glance and slipped hurriedly away into the massed crowd of courtiers. As soon as she was out of earshot, Lettice laid a careful hand on Robert's sleeve.

'My lord?'

Robert did not speak nor turn his head, merely indicating with a nod that he had heard. His gaze remained on Elizabeth, steady and watchful.

'I expected to see you last night,' she commented. 'I waited till after three before I slept.'

'I was with the Queen, as you knew I would be.'

'You are not alone in having spies about the Queen, my lord.'

Lettice lowered her voice to a whisper. 'I know you were not with her all night.'

Robert glanced at her then, clearly irritated, and she felt a stab of hurt. 'Yesterday was a long day. We were all tired.'

Lettice drew a quick breath, as she remembered the hours they had spent together in the past, everything sweet and right in each other's arms, the whole world shut out and good riddance. Had Robert lost all memory of that joy now? Was he still blinded by his restless ambition for the throne, the same crazy ambition that had led to the execution of both his father and his older brother?

What fools these Dudleys were! It was through nothing but the simplest fluke of birth that Elizabeth Tudor sat on the throne of England and not Lettice herself. For she was not only cousin to the Queen, but her niece as well.

Everyone knew that her mother Catherine Carey had been Elizabeth's half-sister, fathered by randy old King Henry and passed off at court as Sir William Carey's child. A cuckoo in the nest, they'd called her fiery mother, and Lettice herself was the image of her red-haired cousin. It might be treason to think such things but Lettice had as much right to the English throne as Elizabeth. For King Henry had declared Elizabeth a bastard after her mother's execution, which surely made her no more his rightful heir than Lettice's illegitimate mother.

Of course, such dangerous possibilities could not be voiced, not even to a potential ally like Robert, for this would be the swiftest path to the block.

'Will you visit me tonight, then?' she asked instead, forcing herself to adopt a softer tone, to swallow her impatience and her growing desire for him.

Elizabeth had turned away from the old woman. Now she was bending to bless a sweet-looking child who had fallen to her knees on the grass verge and was holding up a ragged bouquet of pink gillyflowers.

'I cannot. You know how it is.'

'But I must see you privately. Yesterday, you said—'

'I said it was not possible, and that is still the case.' There was a sharp anger to his voice, a clipped tone she did not recognize. 'You must not ask me this again. Not at Kenilworth. We are watched on all sides here. It's too dangerous. The wisest course for us would be to wait until the end of the summer, when we will be safely back in London and can meet without fear of being seen.'

For a moment, Lettice found herself unable to respond. Her hands crushed the fine taffeta of her gown in despair. Was she some lowly servant, like the Moorish girl creeping at his heels all morning, to take this coldness from him, this brusque dismissal? Was she – whose family was as good as his, Boleyns and Dudleys, their fortunes entwined for generations about the throne of England – to be ordered back to kennel like one of his hunting dogs?

Fury burned away her fears. 'I tell you this, Robert,' she whispered. 'If you do not visit me soon, you will never come to my bed again. This I swear by Christ's holy blood.'

His dark eyes sought hers, and she experienced a wave of triumph as she read surprise and uncertainty in that look. Robert Dudley had thought her weak and easily handled – a woman like his dead wife, Amy Robsart, a submissive fool who had never been bidden to court despite her husband's prominence and who, by all accounts, had made little enough trouble wherever he chose to lay his head at night.

Well, he would soon discover his mistake if he could not find more respect in his heart for a prominent member of the Boleyn family.

Elizabeth was nearly upon them, her narrow-chinned face intent, the posy of gillyflowers clutched to her breast.

'Watch for my note,' he whispered at last.

Then he turned and bowed low to Elizabeth, his smile suddenly warm and engaging. 'Will you ride back into the castle, Your Majesty, or walk the rest of the way? It's only a few steps to the inner courtyard. There'll be food and drink served to the whole court there, and a rustic play laid on for your entertainment. Then perhaps a song or two from young Lucy Morgan, and a troupe of Florentine acrobats who can walk on their hands, bent over backwards like crabs.'

Elizabeth looked from his face to Lettice's, as though she knew perfectly well what had passed between them, then gave a smile like a sliver of ice. 'Let my horse be led back to the stables. I shall

walk, as God intended even a queen to do, and enjoy these entertainments you've described. But is all this to be held in the open
air? Will there be shade for myself and my ladies? You know I
cannot bear my skin to be freckled.'

Robert bowed, handing the horse's reins to a squire. 'My men
have put up a canopy for you and your ladies, and there'll be a
goodly amount of shade for those courtiers who sit beneath the
walls.'

'Then let us walk in together.' Elizabeth hesitated, and her gaze
returned to Lettice's face. The malice in her eyes was unmistakable. 'My lady Essex, return to the state apartments and
fetch my silver slippers, would you? You will know better than
anyone else where to find them, for you are always such a help to
me when I am dressing. And how else am I to be comfortable during these entertainments except in slippers?'

Lettice curtseyed deep as the Queen swept past and through the
broad archway of the gatehouse. Her head was lowered dutifully
but her heart burned with an indignation nigh impossible to
conceal.

She, wife to the much-honoured Earl of Essex, sent scurrying
off like a trained lapdog to fetch slippers?

But Robert had capitulated. For all his cold looks and
ambitious plans for the throne, he was afraid to lose her. When
she thought of the love they had shared in secret, the blood rose
to her temples and she felt the old, familiar ache of loneliness and
desolation. If her husband were less cruel, perhaps she would not
have to seek comfort in another man's arms.

*Watch for my note.*

She knew what those words signified. As he had often done
before, he would arrange a private room where they could meet.
Perhaps today. Perhaps this very afternoon, while the Queen
watched the rustic players on the lawns and listened to her
Moorish singer.

Passing unchallenged between the card-playing guards at the
entrance, Lettice smiled secretly to herself as she picked up her
heavy skirts to ascend the stairs to the royal apartments. Oh,
Elizabeth might keep Robert Dudley hard at her heel like the
obedient hound he was, but Lettice Knollys held his heart.

# Thirteen

IT WAS STIFLINGLY HOT, EVEN IN THE SHADE OF THE BROAD, GOLD-fringed canopy. The Queen's ladies, slumped about their mistress on the grass, snored gently throughout the rustic play. Queen Elizabeth herself, having been presented with dish after dish of sweetmeats, nuts and honeyed quince, and having consumed several beakers of the local wine, began to doze on her ornate wooden seat. The rustic players, glancing at one another in surprise and disbelief, continued to act out their play, but in soft, barely audible voices, as though afraid to disturb anyone. Beyond them, the courtiers talked among themselves, the noblemen red-faced and bored, some playing dice on the grass, others sleeping, their ladies fanning themselves frantically in the overwhelming heat, only a few joining in with sporadic applause at each change of scene.

Lucy, standing in the hot sun at the very edge of the Queen's canopy, where Leicester had ordered her to wait over an hour before, was relieved when he finally re-emerged from the buildings behind her. She was beginning to feel a little faint, but revived at the sight of him striding towards her. He had promised that she would sing before the Queen and assembled courtiers that afternoon, and though the very thought of such an honour left her belly cramped with terror, nonetheless she would not shy away from this opportunity.

Her only wish was that Master Goodluck, who had also

slipped away before the play began, would return before she had to sing.

'Lucy Morgan!'

Leicester came towards her and she curtseyed very low in response. Knowing her gown to be a little shabby, she blushed, wishing she could hide. Anything to avoid those dark clever eyes.

'Are you ready to sing for the Queen?'

'As much as I will ever be,' she said boldly, keeping her chin high.

Leicester smiled at her bravado, but she could see that something was troubling him. He drew her aside a little way and spoke softly in her ear, holding her hands. 'If I give you a letter, Lucy, will you carry it to the Countess of Essex? Privately, without a word to anyone?'

Lucy stiffened. This was some courtly intrigue of the kind Goodluck had often warned her about. 'I cannot,' she whispered, and pulled her hands free of his.

'There is no danger,' he promised her.

She flushed. 'Then why not give it to her yourself?'

Leicester hesitated, and glanced cautiously at the sleeping Queen. Then he whispered, 'We are watched on all sides, Lucy. My heart is breaking for this lady, who is so unhappily married. Let me at least write my love to her, and learn whether she feels the same. I know you are not a cruel girl. Will you do me this favour?'

Lucy did not know what to say. Leicester stared into her eyes and she bit her lip, not wanting to deny him anything.

'Lucy?' he coaxed her gently.

'Yes,' she agreed at last. 'But only if you promise it is nothing treasonous.'

He nodded soberly and laid a hand across his heart. 'I promise you most faithfully, Lucy Morgan, that it shall be a love letter and nothing else. I will bring it to you in a few days.'

The players finished their dumbshow and bowed. But they did not disperse. Instead, they looked towards the canopy where the Queen still slept, her head on her hand, snoring quietly. Then they looked at Leicester questioningly, and Lucy realized for the first time how much power he wielded at court.

Leicester gestured to one of the women at the Queen's side. 'Wake her.'

'Your Majesty?' the young woman whispered, her pretty face flushed with the heat.

The Queen snorted, jerking awake. Her flaming red wig was slightly askew.

'Your slippers, Your Majesty.'

Lucy, watching from beyond the deep green shade of the canopy, saw a look of intense suspicion on the Queen's face as the young woman knelt before her, holding out a pair of extravagant silver-toed slippers.

'Where is the Countess of Essex?'

'She has returned to the royal apartments, Your Majesty. Lady Essex was taken sick with a headache. She said the sunlight—'

'Oh, enough.' The Queen looked about her, aware of the court waiting. Impatiently, she accepted a cup of wine from a bowing servant and waved at the young woman before her, still on her knees. 'Just put my slippers on, Helena. My feet ache.'

'Yes, Your Majesty.'

With careful hands, the lady-in-waiting eased off the Queen's riding boots and replaced them with the silver-toed slippers.

'Have the players finished?'

The girl nodded and bore the riding boots away, curtseying low before the Queen as she retreated. Elizabeth sighed and gave the signal for applause. The rustic players bowed reverently before her, then trailed off through the archway, carrying their props.

'Well, what next?'

Robert stepped forward under the canopy, bowing and flourishing his cap. The Queen turned her attention to him at once, oddly girlish, her small eyes widening.

'Lord Robert?'

'The Moorish girl is to sing for you, Your Majesty.'

He beckoned Lucy forward, then took several steps backwards, leaving her alone in front of the seated Queen.

'Ah yes, your young blackbird. Well, she is indeed a handsome girl,' the Queen observed, looking Lucy over. Her voice sharpened. 'And of a marriageable age. Do you ever dream of getting a husband, child?'

Lucy blushed, confused by this intimate and unexpected question. 'No, Your Majesty.'

'Never?'

Lucy swallowed. She felt the eyes of the court upon her and was suddenly unsure what kind of answer she was required to make. 'I . . . I have never turned my mind to marriage, Your Majesty.'

The Queen seemed pleased enough with this reply. She nodded, sitting back with a long sigh. 'But you like to sing, child?'

'I do, Your Majesty.'

Lucy curtseyed as low as she was able, feeling awkward, all arms and legs like a giant spider. Her gown might be clean and serviceable, but she knew it to be plain compared to that of the Queen's ladies – whose stares of amused inspection she could feel on the back of her neck.

'I enjoyed listening to your song as we returned from church this morning. You have a sweet, engaging voice. When I was your age I was often to be found singing, though my sister Mary strongly disapproved and would rather I occupied myself with prayer, especially on the Lord's Day.' She suddenly frowned, leaning forward in her carved chair again as though to see Lucy better. 'What is your birth, child?'

'My parents were Moorish, Your Majesty. But I am a Christian, born and baptized here in England.'

'And your name?'

'Lucy Morgan, Your Majesty.'

'That is a good Christian name. Tell me about your parents.'

'They are dead, Your Majesty. My father was the leader of his tribe in . . . in Africa, I think. When the slaving ships came, they raided our village and took my parents captive. My father died of a fever on the long sea journey. My mother was brought to England with her master, but she . . . she got sick and died in London a few days after I was born.' Lucy's voice wavered and fell away before the searching look in the Queen's face. 'I know nothing else, Your Majesty.'

'If your mother died in childbirth, who told you this fantastical tale of slave ships and fevers?'

'My guardian told me, Your Majesty.'

The Queen waited in silence, her long jewelled fingers tapping the arms of her high-backed seat, as though expecting to hear more. Nervously, Lucy glanced back at Leicester; he merely nodded at her to go on.

'My guardian took my mother in when she was sick, and later paid for my baptism and education. His name is Master Goodluck and he lives in London.'

The Queen raised her eyebrows. 'This man was "good luck" for you, certainly,' she quipped, and those nobles within earshot laughed heartily, a few even clapping their hands at the jest. 'He must be a true Samaritan indeed, to have taken in a sick woman with child and brought up her orphaned babe after she died.'

Lucy met the Queen's gaze frankly, not quite able to believe her own daring. 'Master Goodluck is the best man I know, Your Majesty.'

One of the younger ladies-in-waiting snorted with laughter behind her fan. The Queen shifted in her seat, her pale, heavily ringed hands curled like claws about the ends of the chair arms. She turned her gaze back to Lucy.

'So your father was the leader of his people? That would make him a king, as my own father was.' She stared across at her broodingly. 'Could his throne pass from father to daughter? Or only from father to son?'

Lucy hesitated. Goodluck had spoken about her mother on only a couple of occasions since her childhood, and she had known almost nothing about her father. She could not even be sure that her parents had come from Africa. She stood a moment with her too-long arms hanging loose by her sides, eyes scrunched up against the sun, trying to imagine that hot, distant country.

'I cannot say with any certainty, Your Majesty. Perhaps only from father to son.'

The Queen settled back on her tall wooden seat, silver-toed slippers glittering as they caught the light. Far from being angered by Lucy's awkward replies, she seemed curious and amused.

'I have had enough of rustic plays this afternoon. Shall we hear you sing instead, Lucy Morgan?'

'If it please Your Majesty, yes.'

Lucy sank into another deep curtsey. The heavy silence before a song, once so daunting to her, now felt like a cooling shadow she could step into. She had come on progress to entertain the Queen and her court, and in all the past weeks this was the first time she had been allowed to sing solo. There was no reason to be afraid. She would not hit a wrong note today, nor forget her words in a childish panic. This was why she had been born. What was it Leicester had called her?

*Blackbird.*

Calming an unsteady heart, Lucy clasped her hands before her chest – as she had been taught to do by Mistress Hibbert – and drew breath to sing.

# Fourteen

ELIZABETH SMILED. ONCE AGAIN ROBERT HAD BROUGHT HER A PRIZE worth having at court. She liked this girl's spirit and her respectfulness, and even the innocence which shone from her dark eyes and clean black skin. What use were these shameless young women who were meant to attend her in chastity and obedience night and day, yet could think of nothing but their next sexual conquest? Better to have a true innocent like Lucy Morgan at her side, for at least a virgin would hold her mistress's interests close to her heart, and not be forever panting after some young man with more bulge in his hose than was decent.

The inner court had fallen silent. A refreshing wind threaded the grasses while the people waited for the song, leaning against walls in the blinding sunshine or propped up on their elbows on the grass. There was the briefest of pauses. Then, in her simple gown and chaste white cap, Lucy Morgan opened her mouth and began to sing.

> *Ah, Robin, gentle Robin.*
> *Tell me how your leman doth*
> *And thou shalt know of mine.*
> *My lady is unkind, I wis.*
> *Alas! Why is she so?*
> *She loveth another better than me*
> *And yet she will say no.*

*Ah, Robin, gentle Robin.*
*Tell me how your leman doth*
*And thou shalt know of mine.*
*I cannot think such doubleness*
*For I find women true.*
*In faith my lady loveth me well,*
*She will change for no new.*

*Ah, Robin . . .*

Elizabeth glanced across at her courtiers, surprised by their unaccustomed stillness as they listened to the sweetness of Lucy's voice. Then she looked back at Lucy, and for a moment she too forgot her pain at Robert's disloyalty, the sting of his faithless indiscretion temporarily soothed by this beautiful songbird.

Ah, Robin, indeed.

Then the song finished and Robert was suddenly there, kneeling before her like a knight errant, his hand resting on his sword-hilt in a grand gesture, as though about to draw his blade and battle monsters for her.

'Your Majesty, please accept this gift of a curiosity and forgive my negligence at leaving your side earlier. My business took longer than intended.'

When she did not reply, his gaze touched awkwardly on Lucy, who stood still before the assembled courtiers. Her graceful hands hung loose by her sides as she waited, drinking in the long silence that followed her song.

Robert spoke. 'Does my new find please you, Your Majesty?'

'It does indeed.'

'Will you hear another song from young Lucy Morgan, Your Majesty?' he asked, glancing again at Lucy, who stood silent and unmoving in the midst of all this colour and heat. 'Or would you rather witness the strangeness of a troupe of green crabs disguised as Florentine acrobats?'

'No crabs, I pray you. Let us go inside, where it's cooler, and hear more of this child's heavenly singing while we take lunch,' Elizabeth declared. She saw her ladies' faces lighten with relief.

It was too hot, in truth, to be outside, even in the shade. Nor did she think the temperature would drop until the weather had broken in a storm. Even the breeze from the lake was too warm to be refreshing. No wonder Lettice had gone to bed with a headache. Despite the shade from the canopy and the coolness of the grass underfoot, she herself felt a little faint, the last notes of Lucy's song still ringing in her ears, high and plaintive.

Nonetheless, she managed a sunny smile for Robert as he stood, gallantly holding out a hand to help her rise. 'And you must have a refreshing glass of wine, my lord Leicester. All this rushing about has left you flushed.'

Robert bowed, his eyes lowered. 'I am your humble servant, Your Majesty.'

# Fifteen

GOODLUCK ADJUSTED THE BLACK SKULLCAP ON HIS HEAD, FORCED A little more stoop into his walk, and rapped feebly on the door of Walsingham's secretary. The door opened and Goodluck spoke at once, feeling for the man's shoulder with one trembling hand.

'Your master. I must see . . . your master. The augurs . . .'

Walsingham's man looked down on him with obvious distaste. His lip curled and he held a handkerchief to his nose, leaving Goodluck to wonder if he had applied the duckweed oil too liberally. But the man, who no doubt had seen many odd characters at his master's door over the years, showed neither surprise nor disbelief at this request, merely turning to consult a black ledger lying open on the table.

'Do you have an appointment? What is your name?'

'My name is Malchance. I come bearing a message from . . . from John Dee, the Queen's astrologer. The omens are bad, very bad. Saturn and the Moon are coming into conjunction in the third quadrant. I must be allowed to speak to your master at once.'

'Master Walsingham is much occupied with writing a letter this afternoon,' the man began with a weary air. Suddenly he stopped short, his face intent as he turned his head towards a tiny creaking noise from within.

Over his shoulder, Goodluck saw that the ornate wooden door behind him – presumably to Walsingham's private rooms – had opened a bare crack.

The man nodded as though someone had spoken. He dipped a pen in the inkwell and scratched briefly in the ledger. 'You may go through. My master is expecting you.'

Walsingham was at the window, its plain wooden shutter thrown open, gazing down into the courtyard below. An ethereal voice floated up through the sunlight; it was Lucy, singing a solo for the court. Both men listened in silence for a moment.

'So the Queen has a new plaything. Let's hope she doesn't tire too quickly of this one.' Walsingham closed the shutter and pulled the bar across to secure it. He turned, and smiled at Goodluck's unlikely appearance. 'An astrologer. Whatever next?'

'A Catholic?'

Walsingham seemed to recoil at the suggestion. He shook his head and sat behind his small walnut desk, indicating with a nod that Goodluck should take a seat opposite. 'You have a strong stomach for this work, Goodluck. But not strong enough for that, surely? I received your note. The wording was surprisingly abstruse. It took me a while to follow you correctly.' He rearranged the papers on his desk; Goodluck's note had been written in a code not used between them for many years, but clearly Walsingham had managed to decipher it. 'I take it the man you sought is here?'

'Quite openly, it seems, posing as a travelling entertainer.'

'A knife act?'

'He has a dancing bear. Though it should be a knife act, I agree.' Goodluck allowed himself a quick grin. 'As you've told me in the past, the best assassins play to their strengths.'

'Indeed.' Walsingham glanced at the flagon of ale on the desk. 'I'm afraid I cannot offer you refreshments. These are for a young friend, even now on his way to visit me.'

Goodluck was surprised but schooled his expression not to show it. 'A young friend, sir?'

'A Florentine Italian, one of these younger sons of minor nobility who must make their own way in the world. I doubt that you would know him. His name is Petruccio Massetti, and he was working at the embassy in Paris when I was there in 'seventy-two. I believe he was a junior secretary. He had a fine hand, as I recall, and a gift for languages.'

'And now he comes to visit you in England?'

'His purse is a little light, he tells me, and he hopes England may make it heavy again. You must understand, I owe Massetti a great debt of gratitude. He helped smuggle my wife and daughter out of Paris when those murdering Catholics began to drag the Protestant families out into the street – men, women and children alike – and massacre them in the most bloody fashion imaginable.' Walsingham sighed, then looked across at Goodluck with a twisted smile. 'Massetti comes bearing fresh information against our exiled Catholics in Italy, or so his letter claims, and I am glad to hear him out. A young man of great daring and initiative, and with his heart in the right place.'

'So I have come at a bad time. Should I leave?'

'No, for I would like you to listen to his news and give me your opinion afterwards.' Walsingham regarded Goodluck's outlandish outfit for a moment. 'But out of sight. A man never talks easily before witnesses, in particular those who look and smell as unpleasant as you do. Come, there is a place here with a spyhole. You shouldn't have long to wait.' He stood and pressed a panel above the carved stone mantel; a low door opened in the wall, revealing a dark recess beyond. He gestured for Goodluck to enter. 'A novelty, isn't it? Leicester never ceases to amaze me with his attention to detail.'

Bending lower than his hunchbacked astrologer would have attempted, Goodluck slipped into the recess and stood a moment, allowing his eyes to adjust to the dark. The door was closed behind him and for a moment he felt a sense of rising panic at being incarcerated in the dark, cramped space. Uneasily, he recalled an unpleasant night in a Provençal safe house where he had been required to kneel for some twelve hours in an underground cell somewhat smaller than this hole. He closed his eyes and silently recited a few lines from Dante's *Inferno*. The Italian verses steadied him; after another minute, the queasiness subsided and he was able to turn in the narrow space, locate the spyhole – its sharp pinhole the only source of light – and put an eye to it.

And not a moment too soon. He heard the muted tones of Walsingham's man in the outer office, then the door opened and

Walsingham stood to greet the Italian, his stern black figure entirely blocking Goodluck's view.

Goodluck wondered why Walsingham should wish him to overhear this conversation. Perhaps, accustomed as he was to listening for the holes in every man's story, he did not quite trust his young Italian friend, his 'great debt' notwithstanding. What other reason could there be for asking Goodluck's opinion of the youth?

'Massetti, my dear young man,' Walsingham was saying in perfect Italian. 'I'm so pleased to see you again. I was not able to send out a letter to thank you properly after those dreadful days in Paris. There was such chaos on the streets and we were held under close arrest for our own safety until the bloodshed had ceased.' He turned, still obscuring Goodluck's line of sight. 'Please, sit down. May I offer you a drink? It's not what you will be used to in Italy but it's good English ale, very refreshing in the heat.'

There was a chink of glasses, then Walsingham sat down behind his desk and at last Goodluck had a clear view of the visitor's face.

He was a handsome young man, with a trustworthy face and nut-brown eyes that smiled openly up at his host. He certainly did not have the careful, covert air of an intriguer, nor the shadowy look that dogged those who had tumbled in over their head. Goodluck studied him at length, seeing nothing in Massetti's face but honesty and the warmth of an old friendship renewed.

Was this all he was intended to see? Goodluck settled his back into the recess, and prepared to listen. Only time would tell.

# Sixteen

DUSK WAS FALLING AS LUCY MADE HER WAY ACROSS THE TILTYARD and through the Gallery Tower at the southern end, her throat hoarse from singing. She paused outside the tower gateway and slipped on her wooden pattens, the clogs she wore to protect her best shoes from the earthen mess of the Brays. Then, composing herself again, she struck out across the makeshift camp, unsure of her direction. In the morning it had taken only a few moments to pick her way through the tents and rough wooden huts towards the castle proper. Now though, with the sun's rays failing and half the camp cast into shadow, she had little idea how to reach the quiet sanctuary of her room.

The narrow smoky lanes between makeshift dwellings thronged with life, despite the late hour on a Sunday, for it was here that the vast crowd of commoners that accompanied the Queen on her progress had been allowed to set up camp for the duration of their stay. She saw jugglers and theatricals practising their craft, and acrobats tumbling or climbing on each other's shoulders, much to the amusement of a small crowd of children who had gathered to watch. A scrawny performing dog in a frilled ruff ran past her at the turn of a corner, barking violently, its barefoot owner pursuing it with rude shouts and whistles.

Lucy felt out of place in her new silk gown, procured by Leicester earlier that morning so she would not disgrace the

Queen's presence with her tatty make-do skirts. Lucy did not wish to put herself above her fellows but if his lordship expected her to dress so finely, with this heavy gold chain about her neck and rings on her fingers, she would soon be in danger as she crossed the Brays every night and morning.

'Hey!'

She glanced back over her shoulder, half expecting to see one of the London entertainers, perhaps another lost soul looking for their lodgings.

But the shout had not been directed at her.

A dark-robed man walking a little ahead of her had also turned at the shout. He retraced his steps, passing her as he did so. She could not see his face – it was too deeply in shadow, and a black cloth had been wound about his chin and drawn up almost to the nose – but she caught the glint of dark eyes and looked hurriedly away. There was something about those eyes which unsettled her, a troubling intensity that spoke of the zealot. She had known men like that in London, living and working in the diseased honey-comb of streets near the river.

The hooded man disappeared into a heavily stained and patched tent set back from the rest, a few hundred yards along the lane. Lucy heard a hubbub of furious, unintelligible conversation as the flap fell shut behind him.

She gazed at the tent, her curiosity sparking, and suddenly recalled the Italian and his angry bear. He too had worn long dark robes and had a fanatical look to his eyes. Nor could it be denied that the oddly striped material of the tent, and the green and red ribbons trailing from its central pole, suggested a foreign owner. And whoever lived in the tent was burning some kind of sweet herb, for a little aromatic smoke escaped from the tent flap as it opened and closed.

Were these more Italians? Friends of the bear-tamer, perhaps?

Years of listening through the floorboards to Master Goodluck's stories of adventures overseas gave her the courage to creep a little closer. She knew she ought to mind her own business, but there was no one about in this quiet corner to catch her spy-ing. The entrance to the tent was closed, the dying sun lit up the sloping roof and Lucy stood safe in its shadow, listening to the men inside. The language they spoke did not seem to be French, of which she knew a few common phrases, but the discussion sounded urgent, that much she could tell.

*Beware Italians . . .*

Was that not what Master Goodluck had warned her?

Her instincts told her there was something wrong, that she should fetch someone – one of the guards on the Gallery Tower gate, perhaps, or even Master Goodluck himself. Yet what accusation would she bring against them? She knew no law against being a foreigner.

The sweet smell of smoke from the tent grew stronger. It was seeping out of the tent flap now, thick and heady, leaving her faint. Inside, the men had fallen silent, though she could hear one voice still, intoning a string of foreign words in a hushed, priest-like tone that dropped to a hoarse whisper.

It sounded almost as if they were celebrating Mass, and not a good Protestant one. There was certainly a law against *that*.

Jumping at the dangerousness of such an idea, Lucy hurried away from the tent and began to pick her way back down the lane, telling herself not to be such a fool. Sheer tiredness must have turned her brain tonight, and now the sun had almost fallen below the earthen walls of the Brays. If she did not find her lodging soon, she would be searching for it in the dark.

Suddenly, there was another shout behind her, sharper this time, and Lucy turned to see two men in the entrance to the tent, staring after her through the rising smoke. Both were dressed in dark hooded robes, and she knew from the way the shorter man held himself that he was the one she had seen entering the tent.

Horrified, Lucy picked up her skirts and hurried away without looking where she was going. She tripped over a pile of sticks left at the side of the lane, stumbled back to her feet, and looked anxiously about for someone to call to for help. But everyone seemed to have melted back into their dwellings now the sun had almost gone.

The two men were following her; she heard their footsteps in the gloom behind her.

They must know she had no chance of escape. The tents and wooden huts in this part of the camp were so densely packed, she would not be able to turn off until she reached the wall at the far end – by which time they would easily have caught up with her.

Suddenly, she spotted a narrow opening between two tents and darted through it. Jumping over a still-smouldering bonfire, she headed into the dark. For a moment she felt safer and slowed to look back over her shoulder, but the sight of two hooded figures also vaulting the gap between the tents sent a chill to her heart.

She was going to die. Those men could murder her out here in the Brays, and no one would ever know what had happened.

Panic lent an unexpected speed and power to her legs. Running with her full stride, as she had not run since she was a child, Lucy plunged down the alley with her skirts held high, lurched out of the opening at the far end into another dark lane and began to double back towards the castle. Indeed, she was within sight of the gate when she realized they had almost caught up with her again.

Rounding a corner, she pulled up short, faced with two lanes, both smokily dark and empty of people.

To her right a broad lane led towards the Gallery Tower, but they would catch her before she could reach the safety of the guarded gate. To her left, what looked and smelt like a pigsty stood open, inviting her into its comfortable stench-filled blackness. Outside, a few mud-streaked pigs lay asleep in the gathering dusk.

On impulse, she chose the left-hand lane, ducked inside the low-roofed pigsty and yanked the door shut behind her. Hands flat on the rough wood of the pigsty door, she leaned forward silently and put her eye to a knothole.

At first, she could hear only the last birdsong of dusk as the sky began to darken into night. Then the boots of the two men came thudding across the dried mud, slowing to a halt as they drew level with her hiding place.

So they had not bothered with the right-hand lane either.

What had she done, trapping herself in this disgusting pit? The mud at her feet stank. Glancing down in dismay, she could see it was more than just mud. Pigs' slurry, black and pottage-thick, stuck her to the spot in her high wooden clogs like a scarecrow. She tried to ignore the stench, focusing instead on the bright, uneven disc of light to which her eye was pressed.

The taller man, with a dagger at his belt, had his back to her, and was looking up the lane towards the gatehouse, from where Lucy heard a scrape of iron and shouted commands. The night watch were coming on duty, she realized, and wished there was some way she could attract their attention without revealing her hiding place.

The man with the dagger said something. She could not understand his words, but knew he was angry. His fellow spat into the dirt before replying in the same alien tongue. It sounded as though he was trying to persuade his companion to give up the search and go back to their tent. But the man with the dagger was not so easily deterred. Instead he turned, his dark gaze fixed on the pigsty as though he could see her through the old, gnarled wood of the closed door.

Lucy stood very still, controlling her breathing. She thought of the deer in the forest, its red-freckled body caught into stillness at the crack of a twig, and ignored the truculent rooting of young pigs at her feet. Why were these men so intent on catching her?

She looked again through the knothole. The man with the dagger had disappeared. Then she realized with horror why she could not see him – he was only a few feet away on the other side of the door. She could hear his breathing, the soft creak of his boots as he felt his way slowly across the churned-up earth towards her hiding place. She stood there unmoving, not even daring to blink in case he saw the tiny movement of her eye against the knothole, but her heart was clenched in fear.

What would happen if he caught her? How could she defend herself against his evil-looking dagger?

Lucy considered the terrifying possibility of rape, and it seemed to her worse even than death. To endure such an ordeal—

At that moment, a shout went up beyond the tiltyard and from somewhere in the outer court came the repeated blowing of a horn, a double-noted warning that the castle gates were about to close.

There was a muttered exchange as the man with the dagger left the pigsty, then both men hurried away up the lane towards the castle. Lucy stayed where she was until the sound of their boots had faded away. She looked down. Her skirts were badly muddied and one of the pigs had made a determined attempt to eat the hem, its wet black snout snuffling at her ankle now.

She pushed at the door and blinked at the rush of smoky twilight, her eyes having accustomed themselves to complete darkness. Only then did she allow herself to breathe properly.

Several of the young pigs ran out too, the thin-skinned runt squealing in protest as it was buffeted sideways into the rough frame. Lucy stepped over and around the excited beasts, lifting her ruined skirts as high as she dared, afraid to draw any more male attention to herself that night.

I could have been murdered tonight, raped first, and my throat cut before I could tell of it, she thought, as she stumbled back down the lane in her stinking, mud-coated clogs.

She thought longingly of Master Goodluck. But it was getting dark. Would the guards let her through the gate this late in the evening? She wanted to rest her head against the comfort of his broad chest and tell him what had happened. Goodluck would know what to do. He always knew what to do.

The guards on the gate refused her entrance, but she persuaded one to seek out Master Goodluck and bring him to see her. When he finally arrived, and frowned at her bedraggled appearance, she burst into tears. It was only after he took her in his arms that she began to feel calm enough to tell her tale.

'Where exactly did this happen?' he demanded when she finished. His intense gaze searched the smoky camp at the Brays. She could tell he was very angry. 'Describe these men and their tent. Leave nothing out.'

Lucy did her best, giving him every detail she could remember, then asked if Goodluck would escort her back to her lodgings.

'I do not want to walk through the Brays on my own,' she admitted.

Goodluck nodded, and tucked her hand into his. It was a comfortable feeling. 'Come, Lucy,' he murmured, and his smile reassured her. 'I'll see you safely to your bed tonight, and tomorrow I shall find you new lodgings, away from this den of thieves.'

# Seventeen

Elizabeth nodded, but did not turn away from the window. She had spent the previous evening in the company of her ladies-in-waiting, listening as they took turns to read aloud from a translation of the long French poem *The Romance of the Rose*. It had been a relief not to preside over the feast again, for Walsingham's tales of spies and assassins had left her nervous and on edge when surrounded by the full court. It was not quite noon but already the heat in the Presence Chamber was stifling. She could just see, out on the lake, the blue-green water dazzling, a family of swans making their slow way towards the bank, ducking under the bright surface every few yards in search of food.

The swans' immaculate feathers shone white in the sunlight – as pure and chaste as her own ladies-in-waiting, she thought drily.

Beyond the dusty stretch of the walled tiltyard, she could see the tower they called the Watergate – an unlikely attribution, since the Lesser Pool below it seemed too shallow to reach its base – and beyond it, the ancient earthwork Brays, through which she had passed to enter the castle's outer defences. Smoke rose lazily from the commoners' quarters there, and she heard the distant echo of dogs barking even through the leaded glass in Robert's new windows. She sighed. Sometimes it felt as though she travelled with an army, a warrior queen at the head of her troops, marching into battle each summer against an invisible foe. But then she would remember their poor and ragged state – the soldiers, seamstresses, cooks and artisans who had accompanied her from London – and know the battle for England was only half won if she could not improve the lot of these common people who trailed so loyally about the countryside after her.

There were a dozen lords and gentlemen in attendance today, not to mention their fawning wives and personal servants, all heavily decked out in glittering finery and crammed against the wall of the Presence Chamber to witness her main meal of the day. Yet her own Robin had sent his apologies, and now a deputy with a paunch stood in his place – a red-faced local official whose stammering, countrified explanation of his master's absence she had been unable to follow.

The chamberlain entered, smartly dressed in the blue livery of Robert's household. He presented the first dish, on bended knee, to Lettice Knollys, the most senior of her ladies in attendance that morning.

Lettice took the covered dish and bore it to Elizabeth. She lifted the lid and waited for the Queen's approval before proceeding, with a deep curtsey, through into the Privy Chamber where they would all eat afterwards, out of sight of these lords and ladies, well-dressed burghers and hangers-on. Then Lettice returned for the next dish, an uncovered platter with a beautiful arrangement of summer fruits gathered from Robert's own gardens, unless Elizabeth was mistaken. The apricots in particular were luscious and large, a soft golden yellow that begged for the mouth.

Elizabeth stayed where she was, remaining upright on her feet despite the heat from the sunlit windows. She received every dish with a slight nod of her head. After about the fifteenth dish had been brought forward for her inspection, she signalled one of her ladies to prop open the door to the Presence Chamber. A cool breeze found its way in through the open door, perhaps blowing in from the lake, or wafting across the enclosed inner court and up the warren of stone staircases that punctuated the new building.

The sweetmeats arrived last, borne on large silver platters, with flagons of sweet wine and sugared goblets carried by two almost identical page boys in blue livery. The sunlight beat upon the wooden floorboards, heating the strewn rushes until Elizabeth could feel their warmth through her thin-soled shoes. Someone handed her a goblet of wine and she sipped at it for show, oddly light-headed.

'Your Majesty,' a quiet voice spoke at her elbow.

She turned with some relief to Walsingham, whose absence she had also noted that morning.

Walsingham rose from his bow and stepped aside to introduce a young man of exceptionally handsome appearance. Clad in a stylish red doublet and feathered cap, the young man had olive skin and charming dark eyes that spoke of warmer climes than England. 'May I introduce a young friend of mine, Signor Petruccio Massetti, late of Florence and Paris? He has been an admirer of yours for many years and has come to Kenilworth to meet Your Majesty face to face.'

'Forgive me for staring so rudely, Your Majesty.' The young man knelt humbly before her, his cap in his hand, his dark head bowed. His English was impeccable, almost too good for a foreigner. 'I would be well served now if I were blinded for my impudence. Your beauty, Most High Queen, is far beyond anything I ever saw in Italy. To look directly into your divine face is like a mortal trying to stare at the sun without being dazzled. It cannot be done. It should not even be attempted.'

An Italian, and a practised courtier at that. Elizabeth smiled her pleasure and replied to the young man at length in his own tongue, knowing her grasp of the Italian language to be exemplary. She raised him to his feet and allowed him to stand at her right side while the last of the dishes were served, his flattering exclamations at the elegance of her dining arrangements a secret amusement for both her and her women.

Over the young man's shoulder, she caught Walsingham's dry expression and suspected that her secretary had presented the young man to her as some kind of consolation for Robert's absence.

The thought irked her but she did not dwell on it. Between this extravagantly courteous Italian youth and Philip Sidney's continuing presence at court, she should be assured of Robert's jealousy this summer.

Finally, the ceremony was over, and she and her ladies retired to the Privy Chamber, the nobles bowing and muttering their good wishes for her repast with exaggerated flourishes. Even Walsingham led his young friend away, promising faithfully to bring him to talk to her again soon. Her ladies sighed in the heat, arranging themselves on cushions on the floor of the Privy Chamber while she settled herself alone at the heavily ornate dark wood table, hoping that her appetite might return at the sight of so many dishes.

Just as she was lifting the glazed wing of a duck to her lips, there was a peremptory knock at the door. Elizabeth was annoyed, for it was a rule that no one should interrupt her meal once it had begun. Nonetheless, when the Earl of Leicester was announced, she wiped her fingers on her white damask cloth and nodded grudgingly to the door keeper to allow him entrance.

'Forgive me, Your Majesty.' Leicester removed his cap and knelt respectfully a few feet from her dining table, no doubt sensing her seething mood. 'There was a matter that required my urgent attention. I was under the impression that Sir Thomas Smith would be in attendance here today, but clearly I was mistaken. It grieves me to think you have been without a host this morning. I only hope Your Majesty can forgive my error.'

'What matter was this that required such urgent attention?'

'Once you have taken your repast, Your Majesty, I would be glad to share this business with you. But I see your food is cooling on the table—'

Elizabeth made an impatient gesture. 'Speak! And get up off the floor, I cannot continue to address your head.'

'Your ladies must be hungry too,' Robert pointed out mildly. He rose and brushed down his knee with his feathered cap. 'Though if you prefer to hear this trifling matter first, Your Majesty, I am your humble servant.'

Elizabeth looked about the room, seeing what he saw. Some of her women lay on the warm rushes as though in a faint; others still sat on the floor as ordered, but were fanning themselves against the heat, one or two with caps slightly askew, a fine sheen of perspiration on cheeks and foreheads. She noticed that none of them dared so much as glance in the direction of the table where the food waited, neatly set out for her to examine. Only her official taster stood beside the table, thoughtfully chewing a few morsels of each dish before nodding and moving on, eyes bright in his wizened face.

Robert watched the man with a frown, then turned away, his casual gaze taking in the chamber and its occupants – rather too swiftly, Elizabeth thought, as if he was trying to avoid eye contact with one woman in particular.

'Let us talk and eat at the same time, then!' she said sharply.

She tore a thin sliver of duck from its bed of rosemary sprigs, dipped it in a fragrant bowl of oils and spices, and nodded to Lettice to pass her a selection of the remaining dishes. She hesitated over venison served with green pears in red wine, then turned instead to the baked lapwings, drawn by their delicate aroma.

'Speak,' she commanded him again. Robert took up a position by the carved marble mantelpiece, discreetly not looking at her while she ate. He rested one booted foot on the base of the hearth's marble surround. 'What is this matter that kept you away from your more pressing duty to me all morning?'

Robert glanced at her ladies-in-waiting. But since she had not dismissed them, he merely lowered his voice. 'Your Majesty will be aware, I'm sure, of various threats against your life this summer.'

'Walsingham said something of this the night I arrived at Kenilworth. What of it?'

Her proud chin in the air, Lettice Knollys passed him with the rest of the duck, and Robert watched with undisguised interest as the ladies gathered round the dish to pick hungrily at the remaining meat.

'There may have been a development, Your Majesty.'

She raised her eyebrows, turning her head slightly to gaze at Robert. He looked up and their eyes met for a moment. He nodded, his expression grim.

'There was an attempted attack on a woman out in the Brays last night.' He left the mantel and came to her side, leaning down so he could not be heard by the other women. 'A commoner, but one of your own household, Your Majesty. The woman was unhurt but there may be a link between what happened last night and these threats of which Walsingham spoke. Indeed, we suspect . . .'

She stared at him as Robert's voice died away. 'For the love of God, man, what do you suspect? I am safe enough here, surely?'

Robert spoke in a passionate undertone. 'These walls at Kenilworth are thickly guarded by your most loyal subjects, Your Majesty. But I fear you are not safe anywhere while you remain unmarried. Your enemies' greatest hope is to seize the throne of England and put a Catholic back in power before you can produce an heir to bring stability to this country. And their power grows every year. That audacious creature Ridolfi, who turned Norfolk's hand against you, remains at large in Rome, and may yet have other secret followers at your court. It seems we welcome more foreigners every year into Your Majesty's presence, until we cannot tell Catholic from Protestant, friend from foe.' He drew a shuddering breath, his dark gaze fixed on her face. 'But you know my solution to this problem, and have only to say yes.'

Oh yes, Elizabeth knew his solution. To take his hand in marriage and sign her throne over to an upstart Dudley instead of the noble house of Tudor.

Lettice must have overheard his last remark. She had come with a deep curtsey to remove the untouched venison, but now stood still and white as a carved figure on a tombstone. Then she turned abruptly and carried the heavy platter back to the ladies-in-waiting without so much as a glance in his direction.

Robert flushed and changed the subject. 'The woman who was attacked last night is in need of safe lodgings, here in the inner court. We have cause to believe she may be attacked again. Do I have your permission to house her with some of your own household staff, Your Majesty?'

She frowned at the impropriety of such a request. 'Who is this woman? What is her name?'

'Lucy Morgan. Your Moorish songbird.'

Stunned, Elizabeth stared at him. 'That sweet young girl was nearly . . . ?'

'If Lucy had not had the good sense to run and hide herself

from those pursuing her, I fear she would have lost her life along with her virginity.'

Avoiding Robert's gaze, Elizabeth pretended to examine the bowl of fresh-picked summer fruits that had been set before her. They had looked so tempting outside, clusters of tart red berries nestling artfully against a heap of luscious silken apricots. Now she could barely bring herself to lift a single berry to her lips.

'She may sleep with the household women, if there is a place for her,' she decided, not wishing to have the young girl's death on her conscience. 'You may speak to Mistress Darnley on her behalf. She always knows where there is room for one more. And whoever these men are, I want them found and taken under guard. Even if they turn out to be your own guardsmen.'

Robert grew pale at that deliberate insult but said nothing in retaliation. Instead, he bowed very low, thanked her, and withdrew from her presence, unsmiling.

Elizabeth watched her kinswoman closely throughout the rest of the meal, hoping to see some sign of pain. But if Lettice felt any emotion at having overheard Robert's barely veiled declaration of marriage, her beautiful face reflected nothing but a polite, customary boredom.

# *Eighteen*

TOM LOOKED UP FROM HIS PAINSTAKING ADJUSTMENT OF THE SADDLE girth to where Lucy sat side-saddle on the back of the brown mare. His broad, generous mouth twitched. 'You look terrified.'

'I am terrified.'

He laughed and leaned across her stiff body, rapping her knuckles like a child's. 'Don't grip the reins so tight. You may be scared, but you don't want your mount to know that. Light hands, loose fingers, remember?' He watched her critically as she turned the pony in a painfully slow circle. 'Better.'

'And if I want to go the other way?' She struggled with the reins and the mare skittered sideways. 'How would . . . ?'

'With your knees, if you were a man. A woman needs to use a switch.' He handed a thin-stripped birch rod to her. 'And try to smile. She knows when you're not smiling.'

'The horse knows when I'm not smiling?'

'She's a pony, not a horse,' he reminded her. 'They always know and they don't trust you. So smile.'

Lucy did not believe a word of this, but she forced a reluctant smile, glad to do anything that might help this lesson go a little better. An old man sitting across the green, chewing on a long stalk of grass, smiled back at her, revealing a gappy mouth with only one or two teeth. She stopped smiling and fiddled with the switch.

'What am I to do with this?'

Patiently, Tom showed her how to brush the birch rod across the mare's rump to keep it at a steady pace, or sting it with a smart tap when she wanted the pony to trot. 'You won't need to canter yet, of course. Unless you intend to hunt.' When she giggled, he paused in his explanation and stared. There was a quiet dignity in the dark eyes that searched her face. 'Did I say something amusing, Mistress Morgan?'

'No,' she said quickly, feeling an unexpected heat creep into her cheeks. Had he noticed? To distract him, she practised stroking the pony's sturdy rump with the birch rod, not sure she would ever be able to bring herself to beat the poor animal. 'Though I am plain Lucy, not Mistress Morgan. I was just trying to imagine myself following the hunt like one of the court ladies, with a feather in my cap.'

Frowning, he took her hand and demonstrated again how to flick the crop, jerking her wrist and catching the fleshy part of the rump.

'Do it more sharply. Don't worry about hurting her.'

She thought of the men who had chased her last night, what crimes they might have committed on her body if they had caught her, and snatched her hand away. 'I've got it now.' She saw his offended expression and did not know what to say, how to explain herself without risking shame. 'I should stop now and go back inside. There are duties I was meant to attend to.'

'I was commanded to teach you to ride,' Tom reminded her, drawing her reins forward over the pony's head. 'I'll lead you out to the village green, so you can try it on your own.'

It was cooler and quieter outside the castle walls. On the green that sloped gently towards the church, Lucy was able to concentrate on holding the reins in the correct manner, sitting awkward but upright as he had shown her, and balancing the switch across the bulky skirts of her gown. She wondered if she would ever see her old gown again, or the rest of her meagre possessions left behind in her room in the Brays. But Master Goodluck had promised he would send a man to fetch them before nightfall, and she had never known him to fail her yet.

Left alone on the brown mare, with Tom retreating to what felt too dangerously far away for him to save her, Lucy gathered the reins in her left hand and stroked the pony's rump with the switch. Nothing happened, though the mare did seem to sigh at the contact, its fat belly and back shifting like a mattress being turned under her. She gave a little shriek and clung on, swaying in the saddle. 'What did I do?'

'It's just a touch of wind,' he called back, and she saw his mouth twitch again. 'It happens all the time. Try to sit still.'

'I've forgotten—'

'Smart tap on the rump. Pull the reins to the right.'

Lucy followed his instructions, keeping her hand as light on the reins as possible. This time, to her great delight, the brown mare not only turned in the correct direction but took several steps forward. Unfortunately, it then bent its head to crop the rough grass. Lucy tried to drag its head back up but the mare stoutly refused, ripping the reins free of her too loose grip.

Nearly unseated by this last move, Lucy was secretly relieved when Tom pulled the reins back over the mare's head, and handed them to her with a smile.

'I did it,' Lucy pointed out unnecessarily, trying not to sound triumphant. 'I got her to walk.'

Tom nodded, and she caught a flicker of something in his face which she did not understand. Then he gestured over her shoulder. 'Your friend's here,' he murmured. 'Perhaps I should get back. The hunt will go out soon.'

She turned and saw Master Goodluck heading towards them across the green. 'Goodluck!' Dropping the reins, she tried to get down from the mare's back and found herself falling instead.

Tom caught and steadied her. 'Careful now, Lucy Morgan, it's a long way down for a lady. You must wait to be assisted from a pony, not throw yourself off like that.'

He was right, and she was vaguely aware that she was trembling, as though the fall had frightened her more than she knew. Over Tom's shoulder, she could see that Goodluck had reached them. He held out his broad arms and she ran into them, not caring what Tom thought.

'Master Goodluck!' She closed her eyes, leaning against his striped and slashed doublet. 'I am learning to ride.'

'So I see.' Frowning gently, he held her at arm's length for a moment, examining her face. 'How are you today? Much improved since last night, it seems. Everything has been arranged as I told you it would be. You are to seek out a Mistress Alice Darnley, who is in charge of the court ladies' lodgings. She knows of your situation and will find you a quiet corner somewhere.'

'And my things?'

'A man has already been sent to retrieve them.'

Lucy felt enormous relief. 'I knew you would help me.'

'You did the right thing, coming to me. I have few friends and countless enemies, but those friends I do have are in high places.' All the same, Goodluck continued to frown, stroking his thick beard. 'We were unable to find the tent you described, though. No doubt the men who followed you had packed up and left by the time the camp was searched.'

'But you said you knew who might have been involved.'

'When you told me what your pursuers looked like, I thought the Italian bear-tamer must be behind it. But it can't have been him as he was seen out here at dusk last night, practising tricks with his bear on the green, and came back through the gatehouse at last call. One of my own men was watching him.'

'But surely he and the men who followed me must know each other?'

'It's not enough for us to guess at such a serious matter as conspiracy. We must know it absolutely.' Goodluck shrugged. 'My men will continue to watch the bear-tamer, have no fear of that. But without more conclusive evidence, and only the word of a girl to go on, it will be difficult to do more.'

'But they could have—'

'Hush, don't think of it.' He stroked her hair, which was loose and decorated with a simple yellow ribbon. 'Just promise me not to creep about the camp after dark again, listening outside strange tents.'

'I couldn't help it.' She laughed at his expression, though she knew he was serious. 'I felt drawn to listen. Do you understand?'

'I only understand that I nearly lost you. It was a woman's curiosity and my own foolishness in mentioning my business that led you to spy on a tent full of foreigners. But it ends here. Promise me not to interfere again in my affairs.'

'I promise.'

'On your heart, Lucy.'

She crossed herself soberly, bobbing a curtsey to him as she used to do as a young child.

'Good.' He seemed satisfied by this show of obedience. 'Now, how did your first riding lesson go? And how do you like your teacher?'

Lucy knew he was teasing her and that Tom was listening intently to their exchange, but she refused to look embarrassed. 'I do not like horses. They are too high.'

Goodluck laughed, throwing back his head with amusement. 'That was no horse, but only a pony. You will soon grow used to the saddle. But what of your teacher?' He tickled her under the chin, making her giggle despite herself.

Tom gave a slight bow in their direction and began leading the mare back to the stables. She watched him until he disappeared into the shadows of the gatehouse, then turned back to Goodluck.

'You embarrassed Tom,' she accused him.

Goodluck shrugged, slipping an intimate arm about her waist. 'Then it will be his loss and another man's gain. Indeed, if no one else will claim you, sweet Lucy, perhaps I should make you *my* wife.'

Goodluck was smiling as he said it, teasing her as he had done a hundred times before. But his powerful grip had tightened about her waist and she suspected he was at least partly in earnest.

'A man must seize what is within his grasp, after all,' he said softly. 'If he does not, he is liable to lose his chance at the prize. And to a better man.'

# Nineteen

THE NOTE OF THE HORN CHANGED AND THE PACK OF HOUNDS switched direction, falling over themselves in a heaving, wriggling mass of warm dog-flesh, tails wagging, dozens of throats giving tongue to the chase. The deer had been sighted again and the beaters were out on the wooded hillside, calling to the quarry, driving it towards the hounds with stick and voice. Elizabeth drew rein under an ancient oak, holding up a hand for silence. Behind her she heard the hunt come to a staggered halt, horses whinnying in protest and cracking twigs on the forest floor as they jostled for space. Even her own horse shifted beneath her. Flanks shining with sweat, it nudged towards a stream close by, held back only by her grip on the reins.

Robert's stallion pushed through the hunt and came alongside her own mount. The intimacy of the situation was not lost on Elizabeth, who revelled in the press of his knee against her rich gown. His gaze flashed to her face, and she knew he felt it too. Here they could touch as lovers and no one could raise a word, for every rider was hemmed in by the steaming crush of horses in that leafy space, ladies-in-waiting and gentlemen of the court alike, the Queen and her favourite unregarded.

'You hear that?' she demanded. The horn sounded again, ever more urgent, closer at hand as the hounds yelped and swam past the horses' legs. Their mounts jostled, shoulder to shoulder. Her black gelding threw back its head, the bit and reins jangling, and

Robert seized her bridle as though afraid she would be thrown. Clever, clever. She could not help but admire his daring, the sheer audacity of a man who would take every opportunity to push himself forward, however many times he was rebuked and rejected. 'They've found the stag again. They're driving him downhill.'

'Elizabeth,' he muttered, abandoning all pretence at courtly propriety.

'Robert?'

Not caring that the whole court might see and recognize their intimacy for what it was, she leaned forward to hear him. If she were to accept him this summer, her subjects would have to grow accustomed to seeing their queen alongside her consort, their new king.

Yet how to restrain a man like Robert once he was on the throne? His charming audacity could only grow, given power and influence on that scale, until her own power became diminished.

She had studied history, diplomacy, politics, the classics, and knew how swiftly one prince might oust another from the throne. She had rivals enough already.

The stag burst out of undergrowth to their right, wild-eyed and panting, its majestic antlers trailing ivy, and the hounds started towards it in a triumphant rush, baying for its blood. Elizabeth could see the shock in its eyes – the deer must have thought to have shaken its pursuers off by quitting the open ground for the dense woodland surrounding the castle. Instead it had run from the noisily approaching beaters and found the hounds waiting.

Terrified, the stag leapt forward and made for the river bank, some five or six hundred yards downhill through the tight-clustered trees. The hounds pursued it, their full-throated cries almost deafening, and the sunlit wood echoed to the shouts of beaters further uphill, the throbbing horns of the hunters and the confused jostle of horses.

Robert dropped her bridle, his smile fierce. 'Shall we give chase, Your Majesty?'

For answer, she jabbed her booted foot into the horse's side and followed headlong as stag and hounds plunged down the hill to the stream. At her back, she heard rather than saw the entire hunt catch fire and take horse after her, crashing through the woods.

Elizabeth felt an almost unbearable excitement in the thrill of the chase. She suddenly knew that this must be how Robert felt as he pursued her, as he played the dangerous game of courtly love, his life in the balance, the throne of England his prize.

Like every Dudley before him, Robert played for the highest stakes. Was he really stupid enough to think she would take any affront? Did he not know how closely he was watched? Or perhaps he knew but did not care? Certainly his actions were not those of a rational man. He must realize that to betray her with that she-wolf, the Countess of Essex, was to invite death. Yet still he would not let go, stubborn hound that he was, his jaws locked tight about that forbidden piece of meat while still he sniffed about the Queen's skirts.

He was at her shoulder now, ahead of the hunt, riding one-handed despite the brutal pace, controlling the horse with his knees, his fist on his hip.

*Did he think he was still a young man?*

The arrogance and vanity of such a thought entertained her, yet there was something about her dearest Robert that made such weaknesses desirable. At forty-three he was only a year older than her, and still her soulmate.

'He's making for the water. Shall we let him go, do you think?'

'You advocate clemency?'

'Good sportsmanship, rather. This stag has run a worthy race today. He bested us in the fields, and will soon be in the river. He could be away if we do not allow the hounds to pursue him.'

'So you would sue for mercy, in his position?'

Robert looked at her, perhaps catching something dangerous in her voice. 'When it is a choice between life and death—'

'I forget sometimes that you too have seen the inside of the Tower.'

Below them, the stag had splashed into the thigh-high water. The note of the hunting horn changed, warning the netsmen and beaters ahead to prepare their ambush. The first hounds had already followed it into the river and were swimming eagerly in its wake, their ears floating on the surface like glossy water-lily pads. The rest of the riders came down to the river bank and reined in, hesitating to go any further without permission, watching Elizabeth for the order to kill.

Looking over her shoulder, Elizabeth caught a sudden glimpse of Lettice at the back of the hunt, bold in a lavish black velvet gown, her sleeves slashed and puffed as large as her own, a huge feathered hat tilted provocatively on her head.

She recognized the gown as one she had been given by a visiting French countess some years before. It was a gown she had not worn more than once or twice, for she preferred the more glorious reds and golds. Had her wardrobe mistress gifted it to Lettice? She would have stern words with Mary Scudamore if she had, for Elizabeth was not sure she had ever given her permission to dispose of it.

More importantly, did Lettice really think to put herself above her queen with this extravagance of dress? If so, she must be brought to see the folly of her upstart ways – and swiftly too, before she gained more favour at court than was seemly.

For a few delicious seconds, Elizabeth imagined her beautiful younger cousin on her knees in one of the darkest, dampest cells at the Tower, her pretty hat tumbled off and her expensive gown dirtied in the stinking rushes, while a priest read her the last rites.

Then her head huntsman was before her. Sweating visibly in the early evening heat, he knelt in the muddy soil of the river bank, cap in hand, and begged her royal pardon.

'What is your order, Your Majesty? To spare or to kill?'

She barely glanced at Robert, who was suddenly stiff and cold beside her. Her hand swept up and down in a chopping motion, and the hunt shouted, 'Kill!'

One of the red-faced huntsmen lifted his horn and began to blow the triumphant staccato of the capture. Several men in leather hose and jerkins waded out into the middle of the river, throwing their nets wide. Within minutes, the proud stag was their captive, its eyes rolling wildly, mouth foaming, two fierce hounds clinging to its back. Three huntsmen yanked it by its vast stately antlers to land.

Forced to the muddied bank, the stag grunted and roared, but its efforts were in vain. Two of the men dragged its head backwards and, with an air of quiet deliberation, the chief huntsman drew a long knife from his belt and cut its throat, sidestepping the jet of hot blood.

The watching court applauded, and some of the older men began to sing a traditional song of the hunt, while the rest set to work cracking open the beast's bloody ribs with their sharp tools.

*The hunt is up! The hunt is up!*
*And it is well-nigh day,*
*And Bess our queen is gone hunting*
*To bring her deer to bay.*

Elizabeth smiled to hear her father's favourite hunting song so affectionately adapted to her own name, and clapped her appreciation. Barking and yelping, the dogs milled restlessly about their feet, waiting to be thrown the umbles, the deer's offal.

'The stag's heart, Your Majesty.' The chief huntsman knelt before her horse at the water's edge, respectfully holding up a gory mess of solid flesh wrapped in a swatch of leather for Elizabeth to inspect.

'It was a noble death,' she said to the watching court, waving the man and his grisly prize away. 'Have it sent up to the castle kitchens with my compliments. And let every man here take a cup of ale before he returns. There will be more good hunting tomorrow, if the weather holds.'

She gathered the reins together and turned her weary horse round, glancing over her shoulder at Robert as she did so.

'Asleep, my lord host?'

Robert shook himself, recovering his composure.

'I am at your service, Your Majesty,' he replied promptly, turning his stallion aside to allow her to go first on the trail. His voice was polite, courteous as ever, but all the fierce, pulsing excitement she had sensed in him earlier appeared to have dissolved with the end of the chase. 'A noble death, indeed.'

# Twenty

DISGUISED AS A STOUT RIBBON-SELLER OF UNCERTAIN AGE, GOODLUCK made his way across the ford – at a low ebb, thanks to the recent dry spell – and stopped at every lodging between there and Lower Farm, to make his approach more conspicuous and therefore less likely to arouse suspicion. He was watching for young Massetti, who had been allotted a room in Lower Farm, one of the larger houses beyond the ford in Kenilworth village. It had good grazing land to the rear and a fair prospect to the east where thick woodland had been cleared to make way for a new building.

*Search M's rooms at Lower Farm*, Walsingham's note had ordered him. *To put my mind at rest.*

So Massetti's innocent face and perfectly credible story of falling on hard times were not enough for the Queen's spymaster. Well, it would not be the first time an enemy had presented himself in the guise of a smiling friend, though it seemed to Goodluck that even solid evidence of conspiracy would not condemn this young man to the gallows. For Massetti had done what Walsingham could not. He had conveyed Walsingham's wife and child safely out of Paris at the height of the Protestant massacre. There were some debts that weighed so heavily on a man's conscience, they could never be repaid.

Reaching Lower Farm a little before noon, Goodluck settled himself comfortably on the grassy bank opposite the gated entrance to the farmyard, and unwrapped the bread and cheese he had brought with him. This he ate very slowly, lying back in the sunlight, watching the narrow windows and front door to the farmhouse for signs of movement. Every now and then, someone would pass in front of a window, or go about some business outside in the yard. He observed all this under cover of combing his beard or swatting away the thick-bodied blue flies which had gathered overhead to share his cheese.

Soon, a young girl came trotting along the lane with a basket over her arm. It seemed likely she was heading for Lower Farm.

Coming level with him, she stopped and gave him a curious look. 'Are you another of them visitors from up at the castle?' Her gaze moved down his coarse, shabby clothing to his muddied boots, and then back to his face. 'You're not with the court. Who are you?'

'I'm John,' he told her cheerily, and drew a green silk ribbon from the leather pouch at his belt. 'I'm here to see if any round these parts need fancy ribbons. Go on, take it. Have a good look. I make them myself – me and my son, that is. He's back at home in Warwick. Perhaps I'll bring him with me next time I'm travelling. He's a handsome boy, and he likes girls as pretty as you.'

She took the ribbon admiringly. 'It's beautiful.'

'Though I imagine you wouldn't look at my son while you've got all these foreign lords and who knows what else staying up at the castle,' he mused.

'Not just at the castle,' the girl corrected him, and a smile lit up her face. 'We've four young men quartered here at Lower Farm. But only one foreigner among them. From Italy, he is, though I don't think he's a lord. None of them are here now, of course. They spend every day up at the castle, or out on the hunt.'

'One from Italy?' He winked at her. 'I expect he'll be dark and handsome, that one.'

'Oh,' she laughed, and there was a sudden spiteful look to her fair-skinned face. She handed back the ribbon. 'I don't know about that. He has a handsome servant though. His name's Jack. Or . . . Jacomo. Or some such name. And my elder sister doesn't mind *him*.'

'Taken a shine to the Italian servant, has she?'

She indicated the farmhouse with a petulant jerk of her head. 'She's in there now with him, asked me to go on an errand up to the village while she . . .' She collected herself, and a closed look came over her face. 'Well, I'd best make sure the chickens have been fed.'

With that, she disappeared into the side yard of the farmhouse, clucking with her tongue and calling to the hens in a high, childish voice.

Goodluck followed her through the gated entrance to the farmhouse, then slipped round to the other side and let himself into the back of the property through a narrow barred gate. An extension had been added to the house, with the result that the front was more impressive-looking than the back; here, hidden from passers-by, the precarious slant of the walls and the filthy, crumbling plasterwork were indicative of its age.

Goodluck studied the upper windows briefly, then climbed on to the roof of a lean-to wood store, ignoring its resentful creaks under his feet. From there he swung himself up on to a crumbling ledge below the upper windows, and made his way along it towards one that was open. Several times he had to stop and feel forwards with his foot, his ears straining for any noise inside the house. The last thing he wanted was to disturb the young lovers at their play, but from the low murmurs and occasional giggle he could hear through the wall, he guessed them to be in the room adjoining the one with the open window.

There was a thick curtain in the way. Climbing on to the sill, he pushed it aside and squeezed through into the room. After waiting a moment to allow his eyes to adjust after the brightness of the sunshine outside, he let himself slip down to the floor.

The chamber in which he stood was narrow and gloomy. Goodluck listened for a moment, to be sure his entrance had not been noted, but he could hear nothing but the lovers murmuring through the walls.

There was a sweet, almost sickly scent in the air, which did not appear to emanate from the floor rushes.

Perfume? Or poison?

*To put my mind at rest*, Walsingham's note had said. Or to wreck its peace instead.

At that moment, a sudden breeze lifted the edge of the curtain, and the room shimmered with sunlight. Goodluck glanced swiftly about, taking his bearings in those few seconds before the curtain dropped again.

There was a bed against the wall, draped in a red coverlet, with a cloak thrown across it as though someone had discarded it in a hurry. A shallow curtained alcove stood open near the window holding a few books, a bowl for water and a brush and razor for shaving.

The centre of the room was dominated by an old oak desk, its surface almost entirely covered by papers, some of them spread open and weighted down for reading. A pair of shoes sat beside this desk, along with a large wooden travelling chest that held more shoes and cloaks, various suits of clothing, and two jewelled, golden daggers, their blades blunt, perhaps intended more for ornament than practical use.

Goodluck walked round behind the desk and chair, squinting to read the crabbed hand on the parchment. They were letters, written in Italian. As far as he could make out, they were innocent communications from his family back in Florence. *My dearest Petruccio*, etc. Nothing of a political nature at all. He unrolled a few of the other scrolls but, as he had expected, they were insignificant.

Anything of political importance would be in code – and not left here on the desk, in plain sight, where an intruder might too easily find and decipher it.

Goodluck wondered if Massetti's servant slept here or in another room. Presumably he did not share his master's room, else he would have been tempted to entertain the farmer's daughter here, the bed at least being rather more impressive than a servant's bare mattress.

As he moved around the desk, something crunched under his foot. Stooping, he retrieved a small, misshapen twist of black metal. It looked like part of a ring that had been broken, the kind that might go through a bull's nose. He slipped the metal fragment inside his jacket for later examination.

There was a small locked chest on the desk. It was of dark wood, ornate, intricately carved with human figures, and reminded him of the old holy relic boxes he had seen once or twice in Mary's reign, before such Catholic nonsense was once more banned from churches.

What's in here, he wondered, eyeing the foreign lock. Choosing his slenderest tool from an inner pocket, a mere sliver of iron with a filigree end, he inserted it delicately into the lock and, with eyes closed, bent to listen to the scrape of metal against metal.

The box did not take long to give up its secrets. Smiling with satisfaction, Goodluck laid the pick carefully on the table – he must not forget to lock the box again before leaving – lifted the wooden lid and looked inside.

There were a few tiny scraps of parchment, mostly blank. One bore a list of Italian names, none of which he recognized, though he committed a few to memory before putting it aside. The carved box contained an unmarked bottle with a few fingers of some cloudy liquid left inside – the source of the sickly scent he had smelt on entering the room, he confirmed, sniffing at it cautiously – and a seal with the figure of a bear on it.

Startled, he recalled Leicester's well-known family device, the bear with the ragged staff, then shook the thought aside. He was beginning to look for treachery where none existed.

Did this mean that Massetti could be the 'Bear' of whom he had heard in Pisa? This device showed only the head of a bear, and had no staff or other embellishments – just a few traces of red wax still clinging to its edges. No, it could not be Massetti's personal seal – that lay openly on the desk – but it was a mark he had never seen before.

Examining the desk again, and the floorboards immediately beneath it, Goodluck found more traces of red wax, some not yet fully hardened. So letters had been sent, and recently too, using this private seal. But to whom, and why?

Frowning, he replaced the items and carefully relocked the box. From the room next door, there was a muffled female cry and the creak of a mattress.

Smiling drily, he turned to examine the rest of the room.

So the farmer's daughter had not proved slow at introducing Massetti's man to the pleasures of an English country rose. All to the good. Now he could be sure not to be disturbed for another half-hour at least; these amorous Italians liked to draw out their lovemaking almost as long as their siestas.

But even as he bent to check through one of the letters lying on the desk, there was a shout from outside in the road.

'Massetti!'

Next door, the mattress creaked again, and then the floorboards. The girl started to complain, her voice plaintive, and was roughly shushed, as Massetti's servant jumped out of bed to listen at the door.

Another shout, this time in Italian, and the thud of heavy boots came up the stairs.

'Hey, Massetti! Stop hiding now, come out and face me!'

A coarse oath in Italian issued from next door at this, followed by the sound of a man hurriedly dressing and falling over in his haste.

The owner of the heavy boots was nearly at his door. Goodluck did not bother to make for the curtained window but slipped instead into the covered alcove, knocking the empty water bowl from its stand with a crash. He could only hope that Jacomo's breathless appearance on the landing, and his loud exclamation at the sight of this unexpected visitor, had covered the noise of its falling.

His heart thundering, Goodluck dragged the thin cloth across himself just as the door began to open. Standing rigid behind it, he counted on the dim light in the chamber to keep him hidden.

'So he's not here? Well, you can tell your master,' the other man was saying in Italian, his tone threatening, 'that we want our money. Or we will make sure *his* master knows what Petruccio Massetti involves himself in here in England.'

'You cannot be seen here, Alfonso. It is too dangerous,' the servant hissed, pushing the door shut. 'We are not alone in the house.'

'My people have already acted for your master. This kind of business is expensive. We want more gold, you understand?'

'Get out!' the servant repeated, his voice shaking.

There was a quick rasp of metal, the unmistakable sound of a weapon being unsheathed, and the servant stepped back hurriedly, knocking over one of the chairs.

'Now listen, there is no need for this to become unpleasant,' Alfonso said, his tone deceptively friendly. 'When he comes back, you will tell Massetti that we know where his family is, and where his fine young son has been hidden away. A clever boy, I am told, and handsome too. It would be a shame for such a son to die over a few handfuls of gold.'

The servant made a groaning noise. 'Please, have pity—'

'All we want is the gold we were promised, and before the thing is done. Not after.'

'I will tell him. Now go!'

Hearing the chamber door creak open again, Goodluck seized this chance to peer round the edge of the curtain, but all he saw in the poor light was the servant's back and the hooded figure of Alfonso in the doorway. Left behind was a thick, musty odour of . . . what? The stables? Goodluck could not be sure, and he had no time to consider, for almost at once the servant left the chamber too, locking the door after him and hurrying away down the stairs.

The water bowl Goodluck had knocked to the floor was chipped. Hoping the damage would not be noticed, he replaced it on its stand, tidied the curtain and the various papers he had touched on the desk, then trod silently to the window.

Safely down, he climbed the crumbling wall at the back of the farmhouse and set off across the meadow into woodlands, taking the long way back to the castle to avoid crossing the servant's path. The sunlight fell green through a dazzle of leaves, and Goodluck found himself whistling under his breath. As he walked, he thought of the young couple making love while he searched Massetti's room, the sound of their love-play through the wall, the creak of bedsprings, the whispers and muffled laughter.

*Young love . . .*

It seemed half a lifetime ago since that night Lucy's mother had come running round the corner, crying and with her cheap gown torn, her breasts and rounded belly on show.

Goodluck had pulled her aside into a doorway, laying a hand across her mouth to silence her breathless sobs. He had waited until her pursuer could no longer be seen before taking her home with him, knowing he could not leave a woman pregnant and penniless on the streets.

Shutting away the dazzling memory of her face, Goodluck concentrated instead on Massetti and the furious exchange he had just overheard in the Italian's chamber.

So there was indeed a plot in hand, and Massetti was involved, though not his 'master' – which meant what, exactly? His employer back in Italy, or Francis Walsingham himself?

Whichever it was, it sounded as though Massetti might be an intermediary, bankrolling the Queen's enemies on behalf of a third party. For someone must have supplied the gold to pay the assassins, and it would not have been Massetti, whose impecuniousness had been mentioned by Walsingham. From the threats he had overheard just now, it seemed likely that Massetti was in over his head – and, with his son held hostage, against his will.

*All we want is the gold we were promised, and before the thing is done. Not after.*

But what was this 'thing'?

Finding no easy answers, Goodluck crossed a small clearing in the woods, raising his face to the generous warmth of the sun.

When did the Italians plan to carry out their attack?

*My people have already acted for your master.*

Now this had a sinister ring to it. Yet Goodluck doubted that Walsingham could act on this information, for they still did not know what was being planned, nor who to arrest.

Goodluck sighed, his heart heavy with foreboding. He knew only too well that if a high-ranking English nobleman was behind this latest plot to assassinate the Queen, Walsingham would wish to discover that individual's name before making his move, even if it meant baiting a trap with the Queen herself.

# Twenty-one

HIDDEN AWAY AT THE REAR OF THE HUNT WITH THE OTHER LADIES-in-waiting, Lettice sat sore and limp, exhausted by many tedious hours of jolting side-saddle over rough terrain, following Kenilworth's hounds up and down steep banks and even through briar patches. Her hands trembled with fury on the reins, but she kept a smile pinned to her face. Robert Dudley, Earl of Leicester – her lover, the man she would call husband if she were not already shackled to the unspeakable Essex – had not so much as glanced in her direction the whole afternoon.

And why? Because Elizabeth, with her wrinkled face and false red hair, had been monopolizing him for hours. Indeed so deep had her talons been buried in his flesh that Robert had been unable to leave her side for even a moment. Powerless, Lettice had been forced to watch as Elizabeth, the bastard daughter of an adulterous whore, had ridden in state with the leaders of the hunt, laughing and shouting out to the huntsmen on foot, her voice loud and coarse as that of the commonest fishwife.

Lettice was not even sure that Robert had noticed her, despite her extravagant, low-cut gown – the furthest she could push Elizabeth's peevish injunction that none of her ladies should wear anything but black or white. This, she had claimed, was to preserve their chastity and protect them from vanity. Chastity! Elizabeth was, Lettice knew, no more a virgin than she was. And as for vanity – it was plain to Lettice that Elizabeth wanted to be certain that none of her ladies-in-waiting outshone her at court.

Even little Kitty, with her mousy brown hair and simple smile, could outshine a woman so clearly past her prime. For all her gorgeous silks and jewels, her fantastical gowns and hair dressings, Elizabeth Tudor was old enough to be a grandmother – had she served her country with proper female submissiveness, that is, and married some virile prince while still young enough to bear him heirs to the throne of England.

Lettice bent to avoid a low-hanging branch. It turned her stomach to think of her own darling Robert having to touch Elizabeth's wrinkled breasts and kiss her sharp red lips, while her ladies-in-waiting sat scarlet-faced over their embroidery in the Privy Chamber, pretending not to know what was going on inside their mistress's bedchamber.

Of course, she knew Robert performed such services for advancement only, that he felt no physical desire for the Queen – and never had done.

It was growing dark among the trees, and torches had been lit ahead of the hunt to show the way back to the castle. The woods shone with their smoking light. Lettice looked up and shivered. In the strange billowing glow, the leaves on the trees looked as though they were made of metal, a thousand glinting spear tips above her head.

'My lady, at the back again? This is too modest for a countess. Surely you should be riding at the head of the hunt, alongside Her Majesty and my uncle?'

It was young Philip Sidney, his smiling wink conspiratorial as he reined in his horse alongside hers.

She smiled at him wanly, careful not to give any impression of discontent or unhappiness that could be taken back to Elizabeth. For all she knew, he had been sent to spy on her.

'I am happy enough here with the other ladies,' she murmured.

'Have you come to a decision yet? Will you accompany the court to Chartley when we leave Kenilworth? I have written to my Penelope, to let her know you may be among the Queen's party. She is eager to see you again. And grown so tall, you will not recognize her. She is almost a woman now.'

'I have spoken to my uncle on the subject, my lady, and he sees no reason why I should not stay on with the court a little longer. There is some business in London I will need to attend to, but nothing so pressing it won't wait until the end of the summer.'

He bowed his head, but she saw the flicker of deception in his eyes. She was disappointed, but not surprised. Few could live at court more than a few months and not become corrupted by its dazzle, however pure they had begun.

'So add me to your list of guests at Chartley, my lady Essex. And let me know if there is any other way I can serve you.'

Dear sweet Pip. But what was he hiding from her? She continued to smile while her mind ran through the possibilities. Had Elizabeth drawn him into her service already?

She lowered her voice, conspiratorial. 'Serve me?'

Philip looked startled but swiftly recovered. 'In any way you desire, madam. Just say the word.'

'Would you spy for me?' she asked lightly.

Philip's face seemed to pale in the gloom, and his eyes widened in shock. 'Spy? My lady, I cannot countenance—'

'Don't look so alarmed. I only mean for you to spy on your uncle Robert for me. He and I—'

She checked herself and looked about again, but it seemed safe enough. One of the huntsmen had begun to sing and some of the women were humming along with his tune, their faces lightening as the hunting party approached the end of the Chase. Already they could see the torches, set on the castle's outer defences to guide them home, flaming ahead on the hill.

'He and I have an understanding,' she continued more softly, 'as I'm sure you must be aware. Yet your uncle still looks elsewhere, even though he can have no hope of success. You are an intelligent man – I don't need to speak the name aloud – but it grieves me to watch their intimacy, just as it grieves others.'

He seemed to choose his reply carefully as he looked along the mane of his horse.

'My lady, I'm honoured that you should confide in me with so delicate a matter, but I cannot help you. No – let me explain: more influential men than I have tried and failed to stop this *intimacy*, as you put it. Unless it directly affects the succession, as a courtier, what happens behind closed doors is none of my business and I shall not interfere, though I see how it must grieve you to witness such hurts at first hand. But you are a married woman, my lady Essex, and your husband has his own spies here at court. Nor have you been entirely discreet since your arrival.' He raised his head to look at her, and she was shaken by the frown in his eyes. 'To be blunt, I would strongly urge you to drop this matter – unless you are not afraid for Essex to discover it.'

'And is this your only answer? That I should give up what little I have and cede it to *her*?'

'It must be so. I'm sorry.'

Her face flushed with anger. 'What do I care if my husband learns of this?' She did not expect a response, for to tell the truth her heart was thudding at the thought of Essex's reaction to the news that she and Robert were lovers. She felt a wave of nausea but kept her head high, her back straight in the saddle despite her weariness. 'My husband does not love me. I am merely a brood mare for his stable. He will not care what I have done.'

'You are mistaken, my lady, and I advise you to be cautious what you say. There are those who might overhear you and mistake your meaning.' Philip's voice had dropped to a stern whisper.

Lettice looked behind her and saw a rider in black and silver nudge past, as though he had only now caught up with the rest of the party. She did not recognize him at first, then caught the glint of his gold chain as his head turned, the curling black hair under his feathered cap. Massetti, the young Italian who had only recently come to court and now seemed to be working for Walsingham. Could he have overheard their conversation? Handsome and charming he might seem, but Massetti would no doubt repeat every word to his master as soon as the hunt returned to the castle, and then she would have to answer for her disloyalty.

At her side, Philip leaned towards her, looking grim. 'You must be aware of how things stand with the Queen. Her life is in constant danger.' He gathered his reins. 'Until she agrees to marry, she will be the target of every crazed Catholic assassin and mercenary in Europe. Her stubborn insistence on clinging to a virgin state destabilizes England as surely as if we were at war.

And if the man who has the honour of sharing her throne should be my uncle . . .' He shook his head. 'In truth, I cannot think of a better husband for our queen than Robert Dudley.'

Lettice drew breath to respond but Philip pressed her hand warningly.

'Remember what happened to poor Amy Dudley, my lady, and have a care what you say,' he muttered in her ear, then set spurs to his horse and rode to the head of the hunting party, leaving Lettice on her own in the dark.

# Twenty-two

'COME, BESS, LET US RACE FOR HOME!'

Elizabeth had not ridden so recklessly since she was a child. Branches whipped at her face under the low-hanging trees, her cap tumbling off as they raced back to the castle. Bent low along her horse's neck, with only Robert ahead and two of his men riding behind, she thrilled at this sudden, unexpected burst of freedom. All that mattered was this wild gallop across rising ground to the safety of his fortress. Its dark towers loomed ahead, and she could see some kind of commotion along the walls: men were pouring out from the gatehouse, the guard dogs were being brought forward, and a long row of Warwickshire bowmen had already assembled on the battlements in their distinctive green and black livery, their vast yew bows drawn back and trained on the woods. Why the display of force, she wondered.

As they approached the gate the guard barked out a warning, and pikes flashed down to bar their way into the castle. Then Robert shouted the password, swiftly the pikes were withdrawn, and their horses clattered noisily under the sombre archway lit only by wavering torches, their smoke thick and acrid.

A boy ran forward to help them dismount, but Robert waved him away. 'We're riding on,' he seemed to be saying, his voice muffled by the stone walls all around them. 'Tell those who follow that the Queen is safe inside.'

He turned in the saddle to look at Elizabeth, and she caught his excitement. He spoke without his usual deference, his tone as direct and intimate as it had been in the days before her sister Mary died, before she had come to the throne of England. There was a boyish exhilaration to his voice that she had not heard for many years.

'Bess, do you trust me?'

'With my life.'

'Then follow me, and keep low on the horse. Whatever happens, look at no one and stop for nothing.'

Dismissing the two guards who had followed them from the woods, Robert spurred his horse across the outer court, where tents and hammocks hung among the ancient oaks. Elizabeth kept close by his side, bending low as he had instructed her. Men scattered before them, and curious faces peered out from under tent flaps as they passed. One or two shouted after them, but none dared get in their way. A moment later they were thundering across the narrow wooden bridge into the inner court.

Again, the guards on the entrance raised their pikes in surprised obedience to Robert's staccato command, clearly taken aback by the sight of their lord and queen entering on horseback unaccompanied.

'Allow no one to pass until the entire hunting party has returned,' he called out, and the men saluted.

The inner courtyard was deserted.

Dismounting from his sweating horse with uncharacteristic carelessness, Robert turned to help Elizabeth. 'Come.' He pulled off his feathered cap and handed it to her. 'Cover your hair, and follow me. Draw your cloak tight. Not a word, understand?'

Elizabeth nodded, sensing no fear in him, only urgency.

There was a low door at the base of one of the towers. He took a key from his pocket and unlocked it, then gestured her inside. It was suffocatingly dark. With no torches to light the way, she was able to make out only a stone staircase in the tiny space before the door swung shut behind them.

Quickly, he locked the door and checked it was secure. 'Up there,' he told her, urging her towards the spiral staircase, his voice echoing eerily. 'Keep climbing.'

'Where are you taking me?'

'Hush, I'll explain when you're safe.' Robert ran lightly up the stairs, soon catching her up. 'Don't stop.'

He was close behind her in the darkness; she felt his hand in the small of her back, guiding her upwards with a gentle but insistent pressure.

For the first time, Elizabeth felt a flicker of fear. What could Robert be planning?

'What is it?' he asked, reading her thoughts.

Instinctively, she lied. 'Nothing,' she whispered. She stripped off her gloves, suddenly needing to feel the tower wall under her fingertips. 'Where are you taking me? What is this place?'

His hand touched her cheek and she flinched. Robert laughed under his breath. 'Coward.'

At his laughter, her temper, brought to the edge of her control by fear, snapped. She gasped at his impudence, batting his hand from her face as she might knock away a wasp. 'God's blood, don't tease me! I am your queen, or had you forgotten?' Her voice resonated about the stone walls, deep and furious with command.

Robert took a quick step backwards, perhaps surprised by her anger, and she pressed home her advantage.

'Why did you bring me here, and why isn't there a single torch on the wall of this godforsaken tower? Must we stand about in darkness all night like dumb beasts in a stable, or will you take me to some properly furnished chamber?'

Huskily, Robert whispered her name and caught her by the waist. 'Elizabeth, my love.' One hand dragged her close to his body, the other cupping her cheek. It was not the reaction she had expected. Pressed against the rich fabric of his doublet, her head was almost on a level with his, and she stared into his face in dismay.

'Let me go or I shall scream.'

'Not without a kiss, sweet Bess.' He was smiling again, she could tell from his voice. 'Besides, there is no one to hear. This tower is empty except for us, and the walls are thick enough to withstand a siege – or muffle a woman's scream.'

She struggled against his hold. 'This is treason!'

'If it's an act of treason to kiss you, to lie with you and touch you, why is this wicked head still on my shoulders?'

Elizabeth felt the heat rise in her cheeks. Several times, Robert had crept into her bed and lain beside her for a secret hour, kissing and touching her with feverish need, their half-clothed bodies pressed up against each other like a young couple before their wedding night.

Oh yes, she burned for Robert Dudley, and she had never concealed her desire from him or the court. But her fear of becoming pregnant was greater than her fear of assassination.

'I do not like this dark,' she said decisively.

Robert hesitated, then released her. 'Very well,' he said unsteadily, and Elizabeth realized with a sudden spasm of sympathy that he was not her enemy, merely a man in the grip of the same helpless desire as herself. 'There's a private chamber above. You will be both safe and comfortable there until I have sent out to make sure there is no assassin loose in my castle.'

'Surely we are beyond the reach of our enemies here?'

'Someone fired a crossbow at you in the woods, Elizabeth. The bolt missed but could have killed you.' She heard the strain in his voice. 'When will you learn to take your safety more seriously? It would be hard to rule England if you were dead.'

All argument defeated, she followed him up the winding stairs. Her heavy riding gown gripped in one hand, she felt for the tower wall with the other.

There was a lit torch guttering in the room above. Elizabeth stood uncertain by the door while Robert carried its smoking remains to two freshly trimmed torches set into brackets in the wall, which flooded the chamber with light. It was a small room but comfortably furnished, just as he had promised. A large bed, strewn with silks and furs, stood in the centre, and beside it a table with two straight-backed chairs and an intricately carved chessboard. It spoke of the most intimate of meetings, a secret assignation. Like a good host, Robert lit a large cylindrical candle from one of the torches and set it on the table, where it glowed with a gentle light.

Was this the scene for a seduction?

He drew back one of the chairs and bowed in her direction. 'Your Majesty?' She came forward, noting a flagon of wine on the table and two smokily patterned cups of the most exquisite Venetian design. 'Shall I pour you a drink?'

She nodded, not trusting herself to speak, and watched as he served her.

Robert passed her the wine. 'Excuse me a moment,' he murmured. He left the room via a narrow doorway she had not noticed before, closing it behind him with a quiet click. Another means of escape, should that prove necessary.

Elizabeth sat in a tense silence, sipping at the strong Rhenish wine, willing it to revive her. Her thoughts tumbled about like the pack of hounds they had followed, excitable, chasing their own tails, waiting for some definitive scent or sign from the wild. *Someone fired a crossbow at you in the woods. The bolt missed but could have killed you.* She understood now their headlong flight back to the castle, and Robert's urgency. But for what purpose had he brought her here, vulnerable and alone, without even the watchful company of her ladies? Did he intend to force her to accept his offer of marriage at last, perhaps by means of a rape?

Elizabeth smiled and rearranged the full skirts of her riding gown. It would not be a rape. Nor would it sway her mind either way. Not while that she-wolf Lettice still stood between them, ambitious, hoping perhaps to be elevated to the throne herself.

She gulped at the fragrant red wine. My sweet cousin, she thought wretchedly, whose neck might yet taste the loving edge of an axe. Yet what could she do to part them forcibly that would not have the court and the whole of England itself in an uproar? It was one thing to have power, and quite another to wield it. Every action had its consequence, and she did not want the people to think of her as too much her father's daughter.

Robert came back after a few minutes, his face grim. 'The hunt has returned. It may have been a false alarm. I've ordered a full search of the woods though.'

'I must return to my rooms.'

'No hurry.' He perched on the edge of the table, looking down at her. 'I gave out that you are resting from the day's exertions.'

Anger flared in her heart. 'I am not so frail, my lord. You had no business to tell such lies about your queen.'

He smiled. 'Not frail, no. Yet still a woman.'

'There will be talk.'

'There would be talk even if we never saw each other again. That is the way of the court.'

Elizabeth had to acknowledge the truth of that. She placed her wine carefully on the table, glancing at the board there. 'Chess?'

'Would you like a game?'

She thought about it, then shrugged. 'Why not?'

Robert slipped off the table, still as light on his feet as he had been when they were young. He pulled out the high-backed chair opposite, settling himself in it loosely, and leaned on the table, one booted foot swung over his knee. Elizabeth smiled, watching as her favourite dragged the heavy chessboard to a more central position, turning the board so that the white pieces were towards her. Robert had never been able to sit still for any length of time. She supposed such restlessness must be common in men of an active temperament. She too loved to be active, yet as a child it had become second nature to sit still as a stone and attempt not to be noticed, for those who were noticed might not live to learn the lesson.

'You'll wish to play white, I imagine.' His smile was crooked. 'Unless you had rather keep to my story and go to bed?'

Their eyes met and she knew he was serious. 'Oh,' she said lightly, though she could not quite control the tremor in her voice, 'I will not give you what you can get so easily elsewhere.'

'Explain?'

She sent a pawn forward two paces. 'My lady Essex.'

Robert considered the board, frowning. He moved a pawn to counter hers. 'A married woman. She cannot give me what I desire.'

'Which is?'

'Marriage, of course.'

She smiled. 'You had a wife once before, my lord. Matrimony did not seem to suit you, as I recall.'

'I married too young and unwisely.' He watched her deliberations with apparent fascination. 'Amy was the wrong wife for a man like me, God rest her soul. She had no fire, no spark. She was nothing like you, Elizabeth. Nor could she give me the joy of a son or daughter.'

A sharp physical pain pierced her belly, like a red-hot skewer suddenly forced into her innards by some relentless enemy. She knew what it meant. Elizabeth bit her lip, not wishing to cry out, though she felt her cheeks go pale and cold. 'I too . . .' She hesitated, the intricately carved piece still in her hand. 'To be able to have children . . .'

'Then marry me.'

She shook her head, her hand trembling over the board. 'I would no longer be queen. You would be king in my place. My father—'

'You are nothing like your father. You must not allow that fear to haunt you. You are a great prince, Elizabeth, and you know the constitution of this country sideways and backwards. No marriage could ever take away your right to hold the throne and govern England.'

'But when my cousin Mary married—'

He interrupted her again. 'Mary is a fool and a Stuart. You are a Tudor and the most intelligent woman I have ever known. Marriage to an English nobleman would strengthen your position on the throne, not weaken it. It would prevent all possibility of good Tudor blood being tainted by that of foreigners. The English have had their fill of Spanish and French overlords.'

He leaned forward, laying his warm hand across hers. Again she became aware of how alone they were in the tower chamber, not even one of her ladies-in-waiting in attendance. 'Marry me, Elizabeth. I'm not only the ideal candidate but your preferred man. We both know how it lies between us, this heat. Why settle for a stranger when you could have a love match? Marry me before it is too late to bear a son and grant the people their wish for a true English succession.'

'It's already too late!'

He shook his head, denying her bitter outburst. 'That is not what the physicians' reports have told us. You know as well as I that some English women have been able to bear children even up to their fiftieth year.'

'I could not hope to. My health will not permit it.'

'This is nonsense, Elizabeth. Look at yourself. You are as fit and able to have children as any woman I know.'

Her lip trembled. Either Robert was an excellent liar or he genuinely did not know how difficult she had always found her monthly flow of blood, how rarely it came these days, and the pain when it did come, which sometimes left her weak and barely able to stand.

She pulled her hand away from his, consumed with jealousy and helpless fury. 'What, even Lettice Knollys?'

His smile froze. 'Lettice? Have I not sworn—?'

'You lied.'

'What?'

'Come, you have been sleeping with Lettice behind my back. Yes, even here in this very castle. Or do you think my spies earn their keep for nothing?'

It was a lie, but a bold one.

He looked at her directly then, his eyes very dark. 'Very well, I lied. But I have needs, Elizabeth, as any man has. Being so close to you every day, granted so much intimacy, yet unable to touch you . . .' His voice became strained. 'And Lettice is so very like you in looks. If you will not marry me, you cannot blame me for turning to her for my relief.'

His face was deeply flushed. She recognized it as shame, and found it hard to breathe. Suddenly she did not want to hear of his infidelities.

Elizabeth reached for her gloves, knocking over the flagon of wine in her haste. It spilled across the table, the chessboard bloodied with its rich stain.

'I am ready to return to my rooms now,' she said coldly, making for the narrow door he had used before. 'Unlock the door.'

'It was never locked.'

Her hand trembled on the heavy iron handle, her vision blurred. She wrenched open the door and stumbled out into a deserted, torchlit corridor.

*Lettice is so very like you in looks.*

'Wait.'

Robert was behind her in the corridor, buckling on his gold-encrusted sword-belt, his face unreadable.

'It's not safe for you to go about the place unaccompanied.' His voice was neutral, his anger laid to one side. 'I'll instruct my guards to double their watch. And I must speak to Walsingham tonight, even if I have to rouse him from his bed. If they can get to you out in the Chase, they may be able to get to you within the castle too.'

# Twenty-three

LUCY HESITATED IN THE DOORWAY, HOLDING UP HER CANDLE. SHE peered into the warm, dark chamber at rows of sleeping bodies on mattresses. One woman snorted in her sleep and turned over, breathing heavily.

'You may store your things here,' Mistress Darnley said. Her pale blue gaze flickered over the straw bag Lucy clutched against her chest. 'Hurry, I have other duties to attend to. No one will touch your pack, girl. We are not common thieves.'

Uncomfortably aware of several pairs of female eyes studying her balefully, Lucy dropped her bag behind the screen and straightened up.

'Where should I . . . ?'

'There is space for another mattress under the window,' Mistress Darnley conceded, indicating a narrow strip beneath the leaded panes. The rushes were thin there, and even by candlelight the wall showed signs of rain damage. Damp and draughty then, Lucy thought, but she managed a polite smile and a curtsey. A draught would be welcome in the heat, at least, and she would not have to worry about the other women envying her place.

She would almost rather have slept outside under the stars, or begged a place in one of the communal tents, than share this cramped room that stank of bodies and perfume. She knew herself to be an object of hatred here. Being allowed to share this space would elevate her status, but lower theirs.

'Get yourself ready for bed then, and quick about it. I do not allow any of the women under my care to wander about in the night, so keep to your corner until dawn. As last in tonight, you will be in charge of emptying the privy pot, behind the screen there, first thing in the morning. Is that understood?'

'Yes, Mistress Darnley,' Lucy muttered, her eyes discreetly lowered. The woman bustled away, the keys on her belt-ring jangling.

Lucy found an ancient mattress cover in the cupboard, and a handful of straw and discarded rags, and hurriedly made herself some kind of bed for the night. The mattress was damp to the touch and smelt of urine, but if she wrapped herself in her cloak it might be possible to get some sleep.

She unlaced her shoes and fumbled out of her gown, wishing her shift was not so threadbare. Lucy accidentally knocked against a sleeping woman and blushed at the vicious curse thrown in her direction. She had not realized court women knew such back-alley words, they looked so respectable from a distance, with their fashionable gowns and starched white aprons and bibs.

Bending to scatter the rushes more evenly, she caught the shiny gleam of eyes watching her from across the chamber and recognized one of the plump, heavy-jowled seamstresses from Richmond Palace. Lucy smiled hesitantly. The woman sighed and heaved herself about, turning her face to the wall, and Lucy knew that she had been snubbed.

That one tiny gesture pricked her more than any of their muttered insults could have done. Her lower lip began to tremble and quick tears sprang to her eyes.

*Don't let them see you cry.*

Raising the candle before it guttered into extinction, Lucy stepped barefoot between the sleeping women, the tattered hem of her shift held clear of their bodies. She had to get out of that place, even if it meant wandering about the corridor shoeless and in an embarrassingly thin shift. Ignoring a few hissed protests at the draught, she jerked the door open and escaped into the corridor.

It was so dark outside the women's chamber, and the candle gave little useful light. Which way should she go, east or west?

Anywhere would be better than that airless, barb-filled prison. She took a few steps to her right, then retraced them to her left, trying to remember the direction Mistress Darnley had taken from the inner courtyard.

The candle stump spilt hot tallow on her fingers. She dropped it with a cry, and was plunged at once into darkness.

Sucking her burned fingers, and no longer sure where to find the doorway to her room, Lucy crept further along the corridor until she had located the only source of light and air, an open slit in the stone where the wind blew in sweet and cool from the mere. She could see the orange glow of firelight in the distance and caught the sounds of continuing revelry from the camps, an hautboy being blown to the steady beat of a drum and people clapping.

Lucy leaned her forehead against the stone, enjoying the feel of the breeze on her hot skin. She grew calm, almost happy again, able to see that while it was not exactly a comfortable position to be in, she had improved her situation by moving from the smoky encampment at the Brays to a stately room off the inner courtyard.

Suddenly, she heard the echo of booted feet coming along the corridor towards her. It had to be the castle guards making a regular patrol of the stairways.

She could already guess the response of the other women in the bedchamber if she were dragged back in disgrace, caught out of bed by the leering castle guards. What further evidence would they need that the Moorish singer was a whore, unfit for their company?

Lucy scrambled backwards in the darkness, feeling for a door through which she could escape. She fumbled her way along the rough stone wall, while the sound of the boots grew louder and more insistent. She fled round a shadowy corner and suddenly the floor disappeared beneath her feet. With both hands out to save herself, she fell sideways, cracking her head against the stone.

*Stairs.*

Not seeing them in the dark, she had fallen down a steep stairway. Painfully, Lucy dragged herself to a sitting position and hugged one hurt knee to her chest, forcing herself to be silent as she listened for sounds of pursuit.

None came, and after a few moments she began to breathe more easily. The guards in their noisy boots must not have heard her fall.

She stood up and limped slowly towards the torch flickering at the far end of the corridor. There was nobody about. If she could find an empty storeroom, she could sleep there until dawn and then creep back to the upper level.

Suddenly, a door was flung open and she found herself face to face with a middle-aged man dressed in black, with a stiff white ruff. A gold chain hung about his neck, and he wore the largest gold ring she had ever seen.

She stared at him in consternation and the man stared back, showing very little surprise at discovering a scantily clad girl outside his door in the dead of night.

Nonetheless, his eyebrows arched slightly upwards. There was the hint of a smile on his lips as he took in her unbound hair, the thin fabric of her shift, and her bare feet.

'I thought I heard something.' He stepped aside, gesturing her to enter the room. 'You must be cold.'

'I thank you, sir, but—'

'Come inside and don't be a fool,' he said shortly, though not without another smile to temper his words. 'You can't wander about the castle at night. Unless you were looking for someone? Some young man, perhaps?'

'No, sir. I was trying to find my way back to the women's rooms above when I heard something and panicked. I fell down the stairs.'

'Let me see.'

Obediently, she held out her hands.

The man took them in a cool grasp and turned them over, examining the grazes on her palms. His own hands were immaculately clean, each fingernail filed to a neat half-moon curve, his pale skin showing no signs of hard toil, the only mark a slight ink stain to his right thumb and index finger, as though he had recently been writing.

'You'll survive,' he said drily, pointing her to a water bowl and folded cloth on a washstand in the corner. As she bent to clean her grazes, marvelling at the softness of the cloth, the man returned to his desk and began shuffling papers as though he had forgotten about her. Outside his window, which stood slightly ajar, she could hear boots again, and the scraping of arms, and guessed that the guard was changing in the courtyard. 'I've heard about you, Lucy Morgan. Who would have thought the orphaned daughter of a Moorish slave could find such favour at the English court?'

She had dropped the cloth at the sound of her own name, turning to gape at the man in astonishment. He met her stare without smiling.

'Do you know who I am, Lucy?'

'No, sir.'

'My name is Walsingham. I am the Queen's servant, and my entire life is spent attempting to protect her, to stay one step ahead of those who would harm her and this country.'

He sat down in his scroll-armed chair, watching with apparent interest as she folded the soiled cloth and laid it gingerly to one side. Lucy turned to face him and tried not to stare, but it was difficult to keep her eyes off his face.

She had heard of Walsingham. He was the Queen's spymaster and one of the most dangerous men at court. Some said he had strangled men with his bare hands and could sniff out a lie at a thousand paces. She could well believe his reputation. He had thin, papery eyelids that barely seemed to move, his dark gaze steady and unblinking, like that of a watchful snake. She lowered her own eyes, focusing instead on his immaculate hands resting on the parchment-strewn desk, the vast gold ring glinting on his finger. She could imagine those hands about her neck, squeezing the life out of her.

'And what of you, Lucy Morgan? Are you a good servant to the Queen? Or are you her enemy? You are not wearing shoes, I see. Was that to muffle the sound of your footsteps?'

'No indeed, my lord,' she stammered, suddenly terrified that he thought her a traitor. 'I am the Queen's servant too, my lord.'

By the Lord, it must seem suspicious though, her wandering the castle at night with no light and no shoes, especially after the rumours about a fresh plot against the Queen's life. The gates had been closed early, leaving the unwary outside for the night, and the guards had been doubled on the entrance to the inner court-yard and the state apartments. Small wonder that this man – who spent his life, as he had just confirmed, rooting out traitors to the throne – should be questioning her loyalty, having discovered her sneaking around near the royal apartments. She stood before his desk with her eyes wide, not knowing how to convince him of her innocence.

'I believe you.'

'Master Goodluck will vouch for me,' she added, then blushed as she realized what he had said. 'Thank you, sir.'

His cold stare seemed to turn elsewhere, abruptly losing interest in her. Walsingham picked up a knife and began sharpening his quill with quick, expert strokes.

'Master Goodluck is your guardian, is that not so? He knew your mother. Did she die in childbirth with you?' When she nodded, surprised at how much he knew about her, he looked down at his pen again, his tone quiet, contemplative. 'I'm glad to have come across you like this, Lucy Morgan. I had been intend-ing to engineer a meeting between us. But this is rather better – a chance encounter late at night, no one to overhear or witness our conversation. One might almost see the hand of God at work here. Tell me, what have you to say about those men who fol-lowed you?'

Once more, she was astonished, both at the abruptness of his question and at his knowledge of things she had thought secret.

'I'm not sure what you mean, sir.'

'The men who pursued you through the Brays. Though one can hardly blame them, considering they caught you spying.'

The flush in her cheeks deepened. 'I was not spying, I swear it. There was something odd about one of the men. He . . .' She tailed off lamely. 'I was curious about the language they were speaking. I just wanted to listen for a moment, that was all.'

'Listen at a foreigner's tent in the dusk?' Walsingham smiled. He tested the sharpened quill against his finger. 'That sounds like spying to me, Lucy Morgan.'

Lucy stared at him, speechless.

He gestured her to sit in the carved wooden chair opposite him. She was appalled, clutching at her shift with anxious hands – a nobody, a mere court entertainer, sitting down in the middle of the night to talk to one of the greatest men in the land; no, it was not right, and no good could come of it. Walsingham sighed, and snapped his fingers at her to obey.

'Sit down, child. You are far too tall, did no one ever tell you? I'm getting a crick in my neck looking up at you. And barefoot too.' Walsingham gave a hoarse bark of a laugh, settling back in his chair, rearranging the thick, dark folds of his cloak about himself. 'I imagine you may be taller even than Her Majesty within a twelvemonth. That will not please her. You were best advised to stoop in the Queen's presence from now on. She does not easily forgive height in a woman.'

Wishing herself anywhere but here, even back in that stifling room with the women who thought her little better than a whore, Lucy perched like a bird on the very edge of the seat. She was so tired that her legs trembled, and after a moment it was hard even to think of standing again.

He had tricked her, she thought. Gripping the arms of her chair, Lucy stared at Walsingham.

'You said there was something *odd* about one of them,' he went on calmly, leaning forward to pour himself a glass of wine. She watched his careful, precise movements, just as she had watched him sharpen his pen earlier. She had the feeling Walsingham did these things to distract her, to make her forget she was being interrogated. 'What exactly did you mean by *odd*? Can you remember? Was it the man's face? The way he walked? Or something about his behaviour? Would you say his behaviour was furtive, for instance, like a man with something to hide? Or did he seem confident, sure that he was safe and unobserved?'

For the next hour, she answered the spymaster's questions as best she could, struggling at times to remember or understand what she had seen. She was nudged back into the past by his voice, that haunting intonation, and her responses grew more certain as he guided her through the various possibilities. She became numb with it though, answering in a daze towards the end, struggling and failing to explain something that was, after all, merely a woman's instinct.

Afterwards, when Walsingham had stopped questioning her, she could barely recall what they had discussed. Her mind was as exhausted as her body. She slumped in the chair and accepted a glass of wine from him as though he were a servant, quite forgetting his rank.

He left the room for a while, and Lucy almost slept, jerking awake with a start as he returned. A small man with a wizened face stood behind him, his expression impassive, holding a candle.

'John will show you to a place where you can sleep tonight,' Walsingham told her, 'and tomorrow we shall try to find you quarters apart from the other women.'

Lucy stumbled obediently to her feet, following the servant's glowing candle along the corridor and down another flight of stairs to a small room, more like a privy than a bedchamber, with a truckle bed hidden by a wooden screen. It was a cramped, narrow space, but she curled up in it gratefully, barely able to nod her thanks before darkness and sleep engulfed her.

# Twenty-four

LETTICE CRANED HER NECK OUT OF THE WINDOW TO SEE THE CLOCK on the high tower. That was when she remembered that it had been stopped, on Robert's orders, on the evening they arrived. One of his more fanciful ideas, that time should stop for the duration of Elizabeth's stay. 'Let us halt the forward motion of time and return instead to the merry England of King Arthur's reign,' he had proclaimed.

Now she had no idea what the time was.

She squinted at the sky. From the downward slant of the sun and the shadows cast across the inner courtyard, Lettice guessed it to be about six in the evening. Too late to go hunting, but not so late that she needed to be dancing attendance on the Queen yet. Another hour or so and Elizabeth would become restless again, no doubt asking to change her gown or her hair, and wishing to go out somewhere before it was night. She had left the Queen resting in her state rooms, a crowd of overdressed courtiers hovering dutifully about her, listening with apparent fascination as Pip read out some intolerably lengthy tale from Chaucer of honourable knights and weeping ladies imprisoned in towers. Or had it been the other way round?

Lettice did not much care for poetry and stories, though she had enjoyed them as a girl. Her own life was turbulent enough without indulging in these ancient tales of courtly love.

She tugged impatiently at the bodice of her gown, loosening the stiff fabric another inch until her breasts swelled out of the top, full and ripe, her dusky pink nipples almost visible. The gown itself was a triumph, such full white skirts, pure as a nun's wimple, but with a hint of scarlet beneath whenever she raised the hem. Turning, she caught a ghostly, bubbled reflection of herself in the window's leaded glass. She looked like a whore now, with her breasts hanging out, ready for a long night's trade, except that her reddish hair was still tucked away under her cap, in deference to the Queen's spiteful demand that it be kept hidden.

Laughing, Lettice jerked the wife's cap from her head and pulled out the pins until her hair tumbled to her shoulders, loose and in wild riot, as though she had been in bed for hours already.

Let him ignore her now, she thought. Let him turn away, un-interested, and go back to his mewling queen with her pockmarked face and long, skinny thighs that barely knew how to hold a man between them. Robert would not do it. He could not, faced with this invitation to bed.

'Where are you?' she whispered, staring out of the window again, watching the shadows lengthen across the inner court.

Next moment, the door was flung open and Robert stood there, resplendent in a red and black doublet, black feathered cap, tight hose to match, and a slim Italian sword by his side. Looking up at him eagerly, Lettice knew she had already forgiven Robert for being late, for trailing about after the Queen like a lovesick puppy, now that he had kept his word and come to her.

'I couldn't get away,' he said at once, as though anticipating some burst of temper. He shut the door behind him, drawing the bolt across with a jerk. 'There's been some trouble. No doubt you've heard.'

'Another failed assassination?'

He frowned, tossing his cap on to the chair by the bed. 'Don't make a joke of it. This country's safety depends on her staying alive.'

'If she would name an heir—'

'But it's not as simple as that, is it?'

Robert looked at her properly at last, and she saw his eyes widen, taking in the loosened bodice, unbound hair, and the shocking red hem of her petticoat as she swirled the white skirts about her ankles, approaching him on light feet. He licked his lips, watching her greedily, one hand on the embossed hilt of his sword, standing with his legs slightly apart.

'By Christ, you look . . .'

'My lord?'

'Like the perfect woman,' he finished, though the compliment seemed reluctantly given.

'Is that so?' Lettice allowed him a tiny smile, secretly delighted by his response. Men were always wary of giving a woman credit for her natural skills. She laid a hand on his chest, choosing her words carefully. 'I thought my royal cousin was the perfect woman.'

'Who?'

She gurgled with laughter at his humour, suddenly breathless. Under her fingers, she could feel the rapid jolt of his heart. 'Are you still on the hunt?'

'Yes, and in sight of my prey now.'

He grabbed her, kissing her roughly. Lettice pushed him away and pretended to be offended. She twisted in his arms and arched her back until her nipples popped over the top of her loosened bodice, her little cry of despair fooling neither of them. He gave an exultant groan and pulled her close again. His hands dragged at the stiff fabric to free her breasts, ripping the seams, and she hissed then, genuinely annoyed by his carelessness.

'Sorry,' he muttered.

'Let me,' she insisted, swiftly removing her gown with practised fingers, allowing him to help her where necessary. It might not be very modest for a lady of the court to look so keen, yet why shouldn't she undress herself? Her need for this coupling was as urgent as his. 'You like what's underneath?'

'Scarlet is your colour,' he whispered in her ear. 'Though I prefer you naked.'

Dropping the silken shift to the floor and kicking it aside, Lettice stood shameless before him without a stitch to her body. Although she had borne the Earl of Essex several children, she was still trim enough to pass for an unmarried woman in her tightest gowns, her breasts high and pleasingly full. She had often seen Elizabeth undressed and knew herself to be not only a match for her pale, virginal looks but to surpass her in curving hips and breasts, the marks of a woman who knew how to please a man.

The darkness in Robert's eyes told her more than he could have expressed in words. If he *had* lain with Elizabeth last night, his hunger had not been satisfied. Her nipples stiffened with excitement at the thought. Glancing down, she saw his groin swollen with desire.

'How long do we have?' she asked, licking her lips.

'Less than an hour.'

'Then let us get on,' she said bluntly, dropping to her knees before him, her hands reaching for the lacings without hesitation.

He helped her, breathing hard, and stiffened as she freed him, feeding his swollen length into her mouth, her long fingers squeezing and stroking just as her husband had taught her.

Her husband had learned the trick of fellatio from a whore in Italy, where such outrages were apparently common even between man and wife, and brought it back to England with him. Lettice had always disliked performing this act with him though, finding it beneath her dignity to kneel and suckle on her husband like some soot-smeared serving girl pleasuring the cook. But with Robert, fellatio had taken on symbolic importance, as though by granting him something he would never receive from the Queen, she had somehow triumphed, stolen some of Elizabeth's power.

'Yes.' His hand came down, heavy and urgent, pressing her head into his groin.

She ought to have been angered by such a gesture. Instead, she closed her eyes, imagining him as king and she his queen, her husband and the hated Elizabeth dead, and the way open for them to rule England together. Once they were married, Robert would never need to stray from her side, not while her mouth offered him such delights, her complete submission to his desire a token of her adoration. It would be a love match such as the English throne had never seen before, and she would bear him heirs, strong sons like her own darling boy.

He nudged her away, clearly impatient for more. 'On the bed,' he muttered, tearing at his doublet and hose, barely able to wait until she had arranged herself on the covers before kneeling between her thighs.

She stared at him hungrily. Leicester might no longer be a young man but he was still powerfully built. Most of the male courtiers of his age were overfed fools, their bodies soft with inactivity. But Robert had kept himself fit. He spent so much time outdoors, riding and hunting, or down in the training yard with his soldiers, practising swordplay, the muscles in his arms stood out like ridges on an oak tree.

Robert bent over her, his mouth finding hers in a deep kiss. His chest brushed her breasts, the tingle of his hair causing her to gasp as she instinctively drew up her knees on either side of his buttocks, signalling her willingness to be entered. But she had forgotten that Robert was not like her husband, to take what he wanted and think nothing of a woman's needs. His fingers still stroked tiny circles between her thighs, teasing her, gently but purposefully, as though intending to wait for her climax before mounting her. Lettice was on fire though, moving beneath him like a cat on heat, undulating and rubbing herself against his nakedness. She did not want to wait, even for her own pleasure.

Shameless in desire, her voice shaking, Lettice took him in hand, guiding him inside her.

Robert laughed at her urgency, then closed his eyes. Why did he never look at her? Was he thinking of Elizabeth?

Lettice cried out angrily, pushing at his chest. He ignored her and kept moving, his head thrown back.

Outside, the sun had dipped below the buildings, but it was still warm enough in the dark little room for sweat to spring out on their bodies. Lettice wrapped her legs about his back, closing her own eyes and accepting his strength inside her, bitterly aware she could never entirely exorcize Elizabeth from their bed. Robert must have sensed her mood because he began to move carefully and with purpose, trying to satisfy her, but she refused to give way.

After a while, he groaned and buried his face in her throat, his movements slowing.

'Turn over.'

Lettice obeyed, wordlessly burying her face in the coverlet. His hands arranged her, no longer gentle; he pushed her thighs apart, and then he was inside her again, his thrusts suddenly urgent, reminding her of her husband on his brief visits home. Enjoying his unexpected roughness, Lettice smiled as she imagined how 'virginal' Elizabeth would scream and tear her white-painted face to see her and Robert in such gloriously mortal sin.

Just before he finished, Robert pulled out and rolled on to his back beside her, groaning with pleasure. Lettice turned, still on her elbows, bottom up in the air, and stared at him a moment in disbelief.

'Why did you do that?'

He sat up and reached for his undershirt, draped over the arm of the chair, his tone coldly matter-of-fact. 'We can't risk another pregnancy, Lettice. Not with your husband still in Ireland. He would not stay there long, that's for sure, should the news reach him that you're with child again.'

Lettice leapt out of bed and began to dress again too, her fingers fumbling angrily with the fastenings. 'Did you do that with *her*? Or are you happy to risk a child with the Queen?'

It was not the first time they had argued over this, for Lettice knew that with every secret child of Robert's she carried she would bind him closer to her heart. He let her temper burn out a little before replying, then came up behind her and kissed her neck as she pinned her hair back into some semblance of order. His hands stroked her shoulders, light and reassuring.

'I love you,' he said simply, and turned her to face him.

'And Elizabeth?'

He shrugged the name off, as though it were of no importance, but she knew he was lying.

She closed her eyes, breathing in the scent of him, his doublet still unfastened, the warm, animalistic reek of sex. 'I shall not wait for ever, Robert. Let my husband come back from Ireland. There are ways and means for us to be together. Why shouldn't we seize a little happiness for ourselves, when so many others take it freely and without deserving?'

His hands stilled. 'What do you mean?'

'You *know*.'

'I will not be a party to your husband's murder,' Robert muttered under his breath. He took a cautious step back from her, one eye on the door as though afraid someone might be listening.

'Of course not, my lord, how could you even suggest such a terrible thing?' She laughed, and tidied her hair with exaggerated care, hiding her glinting tresses once more beneath the neat wifely cap. 'Though while we're on the subject, you never did tell me how your wife died.'

His face was pale. 'You know how she died, Lettice. It was an accident. She fell down the stairs at Cumnor Place, as everyone knows. It was decided by a jury. I was not even there that day, but in London.'

'The right man may do such work for pay,' she commented idly, wincing as his hands bit into her arm, whirling her round. 'Let me go!'

'Don't say that. You must never say such things.'

'Or what?' Her eyes dared him. 'Will you have me toppled from the head of the stairs, my lord, or stifled in my bed? But you must forgive my womanly stupidity. I see now your ambition knows no checks or bounds, and our love-play here this evening was nothing but an amusement on the way to greater things. It was wrong of me to mention my husband, for I cannot advance you by marriage. Not like Elizabeth.'

His eyes had narrowed on her face. 'You've been speaking to someone,' he declared, releasing her arm. Calm settled back around him. She had given him a problem and he was worrying at it like a dog in the undergrowth. 'Who?'

She rubbed at her arm through the sleeve of her gown, and knew she would have to be careful when undressing tonight. There would soon be bruises for sharp eyes to see.

Robert straightened the feather on his cap, his gaze speculative. 'I can always call in my spies if you will not tell me yourself.'

'Do you have *everyone* watched?'

'Only those who can harm me.'

She sat down in the chair and slipped her shoes back on, not caring if he knew or not. The boy was Robert's own nephew, after all, and a great favourite of his. There could be no hurt in telling him the truth.

'Very well,' she shrugged easily. 'It was Pip.'

Robert frowned. 'I don't believe you.'

'Then wait for your spies to tell you,' she spat irritably, and was a little shocked and even frightened by his expression, though she hid it well. 'What? Did you think your nephew a saint, never to discuss his uncle's business?'

'I thought him loyal, yes.'

'Oh, I doubt he would drop such heavy hints to anyone who was not sleeping with you, my lord.' Lettice smiled at his muttered oath but kept a careful eye on him as he prowled the small room, knowing how quickly a squall could blow up in those dark eyes. 'Pip was being a friend. He wanted to warn me about you . . . and what happens to the women who surround you. As if the whole world did not already know you had your wife killed, leaving you free to marry Elizabeth. Though the Queen has been strangely slow in taking you up on that offer. Perhaps she is afraid a similar fate awaits her once you tire of her companionship.'

'Perhaps,' he said drily, stopping by her chair. His voice was clipped, unpleasant, but he was back in control. 'I am surprised that, thinking me a wife-murderer, you should so ardently wish to have me to yourself.'

'My husband is a wife-beater who hates me. Yet I've borne him children and kept his bed warm for years. We are not so very different, you and I, whatever Pip may say. I can understand your desire to be free of your wife,' she said, looking up into his eyes, 'if you can understand mine to be free of my husband.'

His hand dropped from her shoulder. 'I must go.'

'Of course you must.'

'I am the host and will be missed.' He pulled on his leather boots. 'I'll send word when we can meet privately again. I may have found us a new go-between, by the way. Someone who is not also being paid to report back to Walsingham.'

Lettice frowned. 'Who?'

He seemed amused, but shook his head. 'If it works out, you'll see soon enough. Now I really must leave. There will be music tonight, out on the lake, and I have to speak to one Master Goodluck before I go to the Queen.'

She looked askance. 'One of your men?'

'Walsingham's. But Goodluck is a sensible man, thank God. He'll work wherever the pay is good. I believe he has some plan to catch these conspirators we've been looking for.'

She raised her eyebrows mockingly. 'So you didn't engineer that little alarm last night yourself, my lord, in order to get the Queen into bed? Rather a dangerous gamble, I'd say. Imagine if she had fallen from her galloping horse and been killed.'

A dark red flared in his face and he strode to the door, not looking back. 'Some days I wonder why I still bother with you, Lettice Knollys,' he threw over his shoulder.

Unbolting the door, he flung it wide and left it open behind him, not caring who should look in and see Lady Essex sitting in a torn gown, a clutch of livid bruises on her arm, more like a whore than a countess.

# Twenty-five

'WHERE IS HE?' ELIZABETH SCREAMED, HURLING A WOODEN STOOL AT the vast velvet-curtained painting on the wall. The picture crashed to the floor, the curtain pole rolling away to reveal Leicester in full armour, one fist resting on his hip, at his most regal as he posed for his Italian painter. Elizabeth jerked away from the portrait in fury, knowing every face in the room to be turned towards her in fear and astonishment. 'Don't just stand there. Fetch him, you fools. Wherever he is, find Leicester and bring him to me.'

'Your Majesty,' someone said soothingly. She spun round to find Francis Walsingham bowing his head, neat in his customary black suit. 'You are not well and must sit down. Pray take my arm, allow me to guide you to a seat.' He turned his head and spoke softly to one of her young ladies-in-waiting. 'Some wine for Her Majesty, and be quick about it.'

'He is with *her*,' Elizabeth muttered savagely.

But Walsingham's look silenced her, and she sat down heavily at the table.

In truth, her legs were trembling so hard she could barely stand. Robert had been gone for hours and she knew, she *knew*, where he was. She knew she ought to control herself, that it was not the first nor the last time he would absent himself from her side without leave. Yet the restless fury inside her refused to abate.

Suddenly, she saw the Moorish girl staring at her wide-eyed from a corner and remembered that she had come to sing.

Robert's absence had put all thought of entertainment out of her head.

'Come hither, child,' she demanded shrilly. Her eyes narrowed on the girl's innocent face. 'Are you still a virgin?'

'Yes, Your Majesty,' Lucy stammered in response, clearly terrified.

'See you stay one, then, and never marry,' she hissed, glancing contemptuously at the other unmarried women in the room. Not a virgin among them if rumour was to be believed. 'For no man is to be trusted in affairs of the heart, not even the most loyal, the most loving—'

Elizabeth broke off hoarsely and sank her head into her hands, only stirring when Walsingham touched her arm. He had pushed a glass of wine across the table, but she waved it away with a grimace.

'You need to drink something,' Walsingham told her frankly. He waited until she had taken several sips before continuing, his voice discreetly low. 'Leicester is on his way. I have seen to it that he knows of your concern over his whereabouts. When he arrives, Your Majesty, for the sake of your reputation with the foreign ambassadors, you could perhaps attempt not to scream and throw things at him. At least, not until you can be private with the gentleman.'

'Am I such a fishwife?'

He hesitated. 'You are a woman, Your Majesty.'

'And your queen,' she reminded him sharply, throwing him back the same stern look that had silenced her earlier.

Nevertheless, she straightened her spine and glanced about the chamber, daring anyone to meet her gaze. Her ladies-in-waiting had scattered to the four corners of the room, some sewing feverishly with their heads lowered, others pretending to play at dice while covertly listening to the Queen's conversation. Even Lucy had found a large, silver-tasselled cushion to lie on, and was staring up out of the closed window as though wishing herself far away from the stifling confines of the state apartments. Only Mary Sidney dared to watch without pretence, and she lowered her head to her book when she caught Elizabeth's glance.

'They mock me with these public absences,' Elizabeth

volunteered, turning back to her adviser, 'flaunting their illicit affair before me.'

'What do you intend, Your Majesty?'

Elizabeth looked at him directly, biting her lip. She was still hopeful that something could be done to separate them, and swiftly. She could not pretend otherwise, even though she knew others to be listening. At that moment she would have listened to anyone who could promise her that Lettice would be gone and Robert's affections restored.

'What can I do?'

Walsingham spread his hands sympathetically. 'Nothing that will not earn you the disapproval of the people, Your Majesty,' he murmured, careful not to be overheard by the others. He saw her look of dislike and shrugged. 'You would be within your rights to send my lady Essex to the Tower for adultery. But there is not a man, woman or child in this kingdom who would not see a darker purpose behind that.'

'What if I were to recall Essex from Ireland?'

'You mean to tell him?'

'Nothing so unsubtle.' Elizabeth took another cautious sip of wine. She did not want to lose control again. Her ears were still ringing slightly and she felt faint. 'Bring the earl home to England, and it must come to his ears sooner or later that his wife has been sleeping with another man. They have not been *discreet*.'

'Then let us pray they have been careful, at least.'

She stared, feeling her face go red, her hand suddenly trembling. She pushed the wine aside.

'A child?'

'Popular rumour has it she has already been brought to bed of one, though it was stillborn and the body disposed of before even a priest could be called.' He frowned. 'But you must have heard this nonsensical tale before, Your Majesty.'

'Something,' she agreed, breathless, struggling to keep her voice to a whisper. 'This is not a new thing, then? They have been lovers a long while?'

'Robert renewed his attentions early last year, or so I was told. While her husband was away and she was summoned to court without him.'

'You think me cruel, separating two lovers?'

'By no means,' Walsingham asserted. 'It is only judicious that we keep this affair from blowing up in our faces. A rift between noblemen at the heart of the English court could have dire consequences, as we have discovered in the past. Such a division must be avoided at all costs.'

Elizabeth sighed, forcing herself to think like a prince and a statesman instead of a deceived woman. 'I know you are right. But I still *hate* them.'

The chamber door was thrown open with a crash. Robert, his face dark with fury, stood in the doorway with one fist on the hilt of his sword, clenching and unclenching his fingers as though he longed to pull it from its scabbard and use it against her. His furious gaze sought hers across the room. Elizabeth met it unflinchingly, and for one brief moment it was as though no one else was there, just her and Robert, his rage beating between them like a black tide.

Several of the ladies giggled, then bent hurriedly to their work. Elizabeth rose from the table, her hands clasped tight in front of her skirts, her voice as icy and controlled as she could manage.

'What is the meaning of this theatrical entrance, my lord?'

'You summoned me, Your Majesty,' he responded, quite unsmiling, and gave her a deep, exaggerated bow. 'And I am here.'

'So I see.' Her voice rang throughout the chamber and beyond, delivering a deliberate and very public snub. 'We missed you this afternoon and evening. Your duties as host at Kenilworth do not extend, it would appear, to keeping your queen company.'

Robert straightened, and for a moment she saw genuine hurt and anger in his eyes. But he swallowed it, removing his hand from the hilt of his sword.

'I most humbly beg your pardon, Your Majesty, if you have been left at a loose end during my absence. I was engaged with preparing your entertainment for this evening.' He bowed. 'If you would do me the honour of descending to the inner court, I shall be pleased to accompany you and your ladies to the water's edge where a cushioned barge awaits your pleasure.'

'Walsingham will accompany me,' she declared coldly, glancing at her women. 'Come, ladies, put aside your work. His lordship has prepared an entertainment for us this evening.' She noticed the young Moorish girl hiding at the back and crooked her finger, summoning the child as well. 'Lucy Morgan, you will walk behind me and carry my train.'

She brushed past Robert in her dark red silk, her embroidered bodice seeded with tiny pearls, knowing how well her pale skin showed against such a gown. She had almost made her mind up to forgive him if he could show true penitence. But then, in passing, she caught a hint of female scent on his clothes, and her back stiffened.

'Your Majesty,' Walsingham murmured, 'you should wait for your bodyguards.'

She remembered last night's scare and frowned. 'No one would dare come at me here, my Ears,' she replied, lingering on Walsingham's pet name so that Robert might dance in an even greater fever of uncertainty, 'not in Leicester's own stronghold.'

'But last night—'

'Fiddlesticks!' She signalled Lucy to pick up the bulky train of her gown, and began to negotiate the stairs. 'The whole episode was nothing more than Lord Robert's over-wild imagination.'

Robert made an angry noise under his breath but said nothing in his defence. He walked a few steps behind their awkward little party, Elizabeth leading, Walsingham attempting to keep up, and the Moorish girl fumbling with the train as though she had never carried such a thing in her life. Never before had Elizabeth missed her wise old friend and councillor William Cecil so much. He would have known how to advise her. She wished he had been able to stay the whole three weeks in Warwickshire, but it had seemed churlish to refuse her treasurer a few days' leave when his wife was unwell.

'When will Cecil return?' she asked, her voice a little petulant even though she knew he had only just left. 'I miss him when he is not at court.'

'I believe Lord Burghley plans to return here soon with his son, whom you are knighting on Monday next,' Walsingham murmured, smiling as they passed out of the shady arcade into the covered walkway along the top of the Privy Garden. 'The Council will have to manage without him until then. It is not too difficult for us to reach decisions in his absence, I believe, Your Majesty. But I must applaud the skill of your gardeners, my lord Leicester. Such glorious scents! Such a harmony of colours!'

Such unlikely compliments, Elizabeth thought cattily, but she paused to clap her hands as though in agreement.

Two butterflies flew past her head in a flickering dance, and she stared longingly after them.

'Robert, it is true. You have surpassed yourself here at Kenilworth. This is a garden of the senses indeed and I shall walk here with my ladies every morning at dawn.'

They had reached the water's edge, the walkway cool and shaded now as evening fell across the lake, her ladies trailing behind in a whispering rustle of taffeta and silk. A small, rugged-looking fellow with a thin moustache stepped forward, dragging off his cap and giving her a shaky bow.

'Your barge awaits, Your Majesty, if it please you.'

Elizabeth pulled her heavy skirts to her ankles and stepped into the rocking barge, shaking off Robert's steadying hand at her elbow. 'Lucy Morgan, you will travel with us and sing us across the water.'

Leaning back in the barge and settling her skirts about her, Elizabeth patted the huge velvet cushions at her side. She saw one or two of her noblewomen shoot disgusted looks at Lucy from under their chaste white caps. Elizabeth almost smiled, knowing how much it must gall these lofty bitches to see a nobody, a mere court entertainer, granted such distinction by the Queen. But her sternest look was reserved for her favourite.

'Help the girl aboard, Robert. And you may come too. For you will only get yourself into trouble if I leave you alone.'

# Twenty-six

THE GREAT HALL HAD BEEN DECKED WITH LIGHT FOR TONIGHT'S feast, its dark corners illuminated by what seemed like a thousand table-top candles and torches thrust into high sconces. Their massed flames glittered between the tapestries, reflecting off the vast leaded windows as though Christmastide had come half a year early. Despite the lack of a fire, it was suffocatingly hot. So hot, indeed, that country dignitaries and their wives who had stupidly chosen fur-trimmed gowns and mantles for this grand occasion were now wilting at the lower tables, fanning their flushed faces in a sea of waving, ring-encrusted hands. Servants hovered among them, pouring sack and Rhenish wine and serving lavishly dressed dishes of wild boar, baked lark, partridge and quail. At the top table, two men were elaborately carving a roast swan for Queen Elizabeth's own plate. Just as a page boy came to the Queen's side, bearing a vast silver salt cellar shaped like a galleon in full sail, a parcel of live wrens was released from the swan and flew up into the rafters with a great flutter of wings, to deafening applause from the courtiers.

Lucy Morgan was singing again, and everyone was supposed to be listening. But of course nobody was. They were watching the Queen instead, for all day a mischievous rumour had been making the rounds that Leicester had offered for the Queen and she had refused him, or else that the Queen was pregnant by the earl and still would not have him to husband.

As delicately as possible, given her hunger, Lettice mopped up the last of the goose fat swimming on her platter with a fragrant wedge torn from the manchet bread. Then she too lifted her head to stare across at the Queen's table.

Robert had seated himself at Elizabeth's right side, as was his custom at these public affairs. He still loved to push his suit as royal consort, despite a lack of any official status. Splendid in a jewelled doublet of red and gold, his broad sleeves puffed out like a peacock's tail, Robert was watching the Queen pick at her food with spindly white fingers. Lettice thought she looked more like a spider than a woman, barely eating anything, her white-painted face a mask of disdain. Robert began to talk, his head bent to whisper in her ear. Elizabeth, however, made no indication that she was listening. Rather, her gaze was fixed on her new court favourite, whose high, soaring voice was beginning to make Lettice's head hurt.

This feast was supposed to be a celebration, not a wake, Lettice thought. Could they not have cheerful songs to accompany such an occasion, instead of all these dirges, laments and tedious madrigals?

Elizabeth had turned her head at last, responding sharply to something Robert had said. It was clearly not what she had wished to hear. Robert sat back, a sulky look on his weathered face, and stabbed at the remains of his goose meat as though it were Elizabeth's own heart.

For a moment, Lettice imagined herself there beside him – seated in Elizabeth's high-backed and ornately carved seat, Robert adoring her as his wife and queen, the mistress of Kenilworth and England. At the daring of such a vision, the room began to spin. Yet still Lettice continued to stare, her mouth slightly open, the dripping bread forgotten in her hand. Branches of flickering candles on the tables dazzled her, like sunlight glimpsed at noon through a high window, until she had to squeeze her eyes shut.

'Are you quite well, my lady Essex?' a solicitous voice asked at her side. 'You do not seem yourself.'

Recovering her senses, Lettice turned and managed a curt nod. With no little effort, she forced herself to smile and unclench her fists. She must be careful, for it was Robert's sister at her elbow. Sharp-eyed Lady Mary Sidney, who saw everything and said nothing. Poor bitch, marked for life by the pox that had struck her down while she nursed Elizabeth back from the brink of death, and for what? Barely a word of thanks from her royal mistress for the loss of her good looks. Yet still she served the Queen, and still she was faithful. These Dudleys, Lettice thought, suddenly angry, never knew when to stop begging and shivering like whipped curs at the foot of the throne.

'A moment of dizziness, Lady Mary, that is all. I must have taken too much sun again today. It has been a hot summer.'

'And a mercy we are not in London during this heat,' Mary Sidney agreed smoothly, and signalled a servant to refill their wine cups.

Lettice muttered some banal agreement, and turned back to her perusal of Robert and Elizabeth.

Lucy Morgan had finished her song at last and everyone was applauding while the wretched girl attempted a curtsey, her black hair so coarse and unmanageable it looked like a wild pony's. Lettice watched Lucy with a sudden dislike. The child was growing uncomfortably close to the Queen; it had been short-sighted of Robert to use her as a messenger the other night. If Lucy chose to tell the Queen that they were exchanging messages, even if most of them were in code, their lives could be in danger.

She frowned, glancing at Mary. 'What did you say?'

'I said, my brother is looking well this summer.' Lady Mary was also watching the Queen's table, an indulgent smile on her pock-marked face. 'This heat suits him, and the outdoor life. He was always a tremendous horseman, even as a young boy. That is one of the interests he and Her Majesty have always shared, of course, their love of hunting and riding.' She sipped reflectively at her wine. 'You do not care much for horses, I believe, my lady Essex?'

'I cannot be blamed for that this summer. Not even the hardiest of our ladies have managed this progress entirely on horseback. I cannot even recall when we left London, it was so many weeks ago.'

'This past week at Kenilworth has proved a comfortable rest from travelling,' Mary agreed, though her eyes still searched

Lettice's face. The woman would find no incriminating evidence there, however closely she looked. Yet her careful voice continued to probe. 'We move next to your own house at Chartley, is that not the case? You'll be glad to be home again, I'm sure, among your own people.'

'I am looking forward to sleeping in my own bed,' Lettice admitted grudgingly. 'Though it will be hard, entertaining the Queen and court. Chartley is a fine country seat, but it cannot compare with the size and splendour of Kenilworth.'

'Does Lord Essex plan to return from Ireland in time for the Queen's visit?'

'No,' Lettice replied shortly. 'My husband will not be home this summer.'

'I see.' Mary Sidney glanced again at her brother, who was still speaking to the Queen. There was a stubborn, passionate look on Robert's face that Lettice recognized only too well, and the Queen's head was turned away while her long white fingers drummed the table. It seemed today's rumours might hold an element of truth, for Robert was clearly not in favour tonight. But Mary had not finished with her meddling. 'The earl's long absences must be difficult for you to bear. If I can be of any assistance, you have only to ask.'

'Thank you, my lady.' Lettice pretended a gratitude she did not feel. She only just managed not to bare her teeth at the woman's patronizing interference. 'You are very kind, but I have every confidence in my steward's ability to manage the Queen's visit, even without my husband.'

Mary smiled, but Lettice knew she was annoyed at the rejection of her offer. Not that she cared a straw if Mary Sidney's nose was pushed out of joint. Mary had no influence whatsoever over her brother, and Robert was all Lettice cared about.

Those at the Queen's table had risen, and Lettice realized belatedly that music for dancing had begun. All eyes had turned once more to the Queen as Robert led her with slow ceremony to the newly cleared space before the unlit fireplace. Massetti, the charming young Italian, scraped back his chair to make room for the Queen's jewelled gown, bowing low as she brushed past him with a laugh and a rapid exchange in his own language. Servants had hurriedly pushed back emptied tables and benches, and were now sweeping away the rushes soiled by grease and spilt food. The local gentry of Warwickshire stood about the torchlit walls to watch their queen and Leicester, clapping and laughing as though they had never seen a dance before, their faces bright with wine and heat.

Then the Queen said something and Robert half turned to glance over his shoulder. The rhythm of his footsteps faltered.

What had they seen?

A bearded and barrel-chested man appeared at the side of the dancers, the gold chain and other badges of office proclaiming him a man of some standing in the County of Warwickshire. It was clear from his bearing and the amused glances of those about him that he had taken too much drink and was making a nuisance of himself.

Staggering forward, the local drunkard watched the Queen and Robert dance for a few minutes more, a look almost of disgust on his red-cheeked face.

Then he seemed to throw off his restraint, unable to contain his impatience any longer, and called out slurringly to Robert, 'My lord Leicester!'

Heads turned across the hall, astonished at the man's insolence.

The man ignored their gasps, continuing loudly, 'You summoned me here tonight, my lord, and I must come as a good servant of the crown. But I shall not wear the suit of blue livery you so kindly sent me, my lord. No, not even if it means a spell in the Tower of London!'

The music had come to an abrupt halt, Robert waving the pipers to silence with an angry gesture.

'Arden,' he addressed the man stiffly, 'you may be Sheriff of Warwickshire, but you hold that office only through the good grace of the Queen, your sovereign. How dare you interrupt her entertainments in this manner?' Robert took a step away from the Queen, whom he had been protecting with his body. His question echoed Lettice's thought. 'Have you run mad?'

'No, my lord,' the sheriff replied ebulliently, his hand moving to his sword-hilt in response, 'I have come to my good senses. I will not accept the blue livery you sent over for me to wear tonight, nor will any of the men serving under me in Warwick.'

'What's wrong, Arden?' one of the courtiers called out lazily from a side table. 'Is blue not your colour? Would green suit you better, perchance?'

The great hall, held silent and astonished by the exchange so far, burst into ripples of nervous laughter. One of Arden's young followers stepped hurriedly forward and whispered in his ear, knocking the drunkard's hand away from his sword-hilt. If the fool had drawn, he would have found himself under sentence to lose his head, for to draw a sword in the Queen's presence except in her protection was an act of treason and punishable by death.

Elizabeth ignored Robert and came around him to face the man. She looked down at him with disdain as he bent his head. 'What is the meaning of this outburst, Sheriff? Speak up at once and make your grievance plain, or I shall have you removed from this castle and thrown into your own prison.'

'Your Majesty,' Arden responded, bowing so low that his bloated doublet seemed almost to creak, 'my grievance is that I cannot wear the livery of a man without honour and not lose my own. I shall not submit to it, Your Majesty. Nor should any man here.'

The silence that followed this unexpected statement nearly undid Lettice. She could not breathe properly. She felt like a bird trapped in a cage, her gaze moving distractedly from the sheriff to the Queen's face.

*Without honour.* She repeated his words feverishly in her mind, trying to understand them. *Without honour.*

What did this vile, outspoken man know?

'And what,' Elizabeth asked clearly into the silence, 'would force a man of your standing into making such a dangerous accusation against the Earl of Leicester?'

The man swallowed. His fear was suddenly apparent. A sheen of sweat formed on his forehead and his hands shook. But he was not ready to back down, even if he could not quite bring himself to make his accusation specific.

'There is a lady at this court who is married, Your Majesty, and yet who has become too . . . who is known to his lordship . . .'

The sheriff stumbled over his tale as the whispers grew again, then he came to an uncertain halt. His eyes flickered nervously to Leicester, no doubt realizing that the lady in question was not without a male protector here. Nonetheless, he managed to draw breath to deliver his final indictment.

'I shall not wear the livery of a whoremaster, begging Your Majesty's pardon. That's all I've come to say tonight.'

'And you will die for it!' Robert swore.

Elizabeth snapped a hasty command. Robert, his eyes burning, had lunged forward with his sword half drawn before the Queen's guards stopped him. The sheriff also swayed forward as though keen to fight and was held back by half a dozen of his own guards, the two men glaring at each other across the narrow space, their chests heaving, each one utterly furious and ready to kill.

Lettice sat and bore this public humiliation in silence, her eyes fixed on the high candlelit windows, determined not to utter a single word that might shame her family.

'This lady's name?'

The sheriff stared at the Queen for a moment without replying. Again, his gaze shifted to Robert's outraged face and his half-drawn sword. He wiped his damp brow with the back of his hand. 'I have forgotten, Your Majesty.'

'Forgotten?'

'No, I . . . I never knew it. I heard the story from . . . from . . .'

The man faltered, looking about the silent hall as though seeing it properly for the first time, his gaze slipping hurriedly over the bench where Lettice sat, her face unmoved. There was panic in his voice now, a trembling note of fear, but Lettice knew it was too late. He could not put the cat back into the bag.

'Perhaps I was mistaken, Your Majesty. I most humbly and reverently beg your pardon.'

'You deserve a public whipping, sir. But I must take your rank and your drunkenness into account.' Elizabeth looked at him a long moment, then nodded to her guards. 'Release my lord Leicester, who is under pain of death not to unsheathe his sword in this hall, and escort the Sheriff of Warwickshire to some room set apart for prisoners. Let him remain there under guard until he sees the arrant folly of publicly accusing one of the greatest men in England of *nothing* and makes due recompense to the Earl of Leicester for these drunken slurs.'

At the Queen's command, the music began again and the sheriff was dragged away, bellowing his apologies. Elizabeth retired to her seat, not even glancing in Robert's direction. Dancers took to the floor, the swell of conversation rose again in the hall, and the moment of danger seemed to be past. Yet it was another half-hour before Lettice found an excuse to slip away from the Queen's party and fumble her way to a low door at the back of the great hall, from where she knew a staircase would lead her to the state apartments.

Head bowed, Lettice hurried back towards the cramped room that she shared with the other ladies-in-waiting when the Queen did not require their presence in her bedchamber. She tried not to show any fear at what had been said out loud in the great hall, nor consider how her hot-headed husband would react when he heard the scandalous tale, but her heart was beating so loud it sounded like a tambour in her head.

'My lady!'

A hoarse whisper drew her to a standstill. Lettice turned, unsure what to expect.

It was Lucy Morgan. The Queen's new singer stood behind her in the shadowy corridor, out of breath. She must have run from the great hall in order to catch her.

'What is it, girl?' Lettice demanded, unnerved by this meeting. Had the Queen sent her? 'Speak.'

Hurriedly, Lucy thrust a sealed letter into her hands and backed away, her eyes very wide.

'From Lord Leicester,' she whispered, then turned and was quickly swallowed up by the shadows.

Lettice hid the letter cautiously in the folds of her gown. Her hands were shaking but she was exhilarated, nonetheless. A message from Robert? He must have given it to Lucy before the feast began. She could not open it here but would wait until she was safely alone in the ladies' chamber.

Reaching the base of the new building where the Queen and her ladies were housed, Lettice was surprised to find the stairs unguarded. She stumbled upstairs in a daze, wishing she had not drunk quite so much wine at table tonight.

She met one of the young guards hurrying down the stairs. 'Why were you not at the door below?' she demanded.

'Her Majesty's at the feast—' he began, but Lettice interrupted him.

'That is no good reason to desert your post,' she replied sharply. 'What if a thief had entered? Or an assassin, wishing to hide himself before the Queen's return?'

The man glanced nervously back over his shoulder, and Lettice thought she caught a movement on the stairs above them, a black-eyed girl wrapped in a dark cloak whisking out of sight as she looked up. So that was his 'reason' for deserting his post, taking a sly moment to tumble some serving girl in the Queen's apartments.

'It won't happen again, my lady. I swear it.'

'And where is the other guard?'

'He needed . . .' The man swallowed, not meeting her eyes. 'The privy, my lady.'

Lettice dismissed the young fool with a stern warning for his negligence and continued up to the room reserved for the Queen's ladies, concentrating hard on each step. She guessed the girl must be one of Leicester's own staff, for she had never noticed that dark, slant-eyed face at court before. She prepared a stern reprimand for her too. Yet when she reached the first landing, she found the maids' room empty, as was the ladies' cramped and dark bedchamber, and the door to the Queen's apartments was still shut, just as it had been when they left it.

All she could think of was the scene she had witnessed in the great hall, the whispering courtiers, the suspicious glances of the Queen.

She had come so close to the Tower tonight, she could almost taste the filth and darkness of it on her wine-stained lips. She had a stitch in her side from running up the stairs. Breathless, she clutched at it, only allowing herself the luxury of a few tears now that she was alone.

This courtly game was too dangerous, she dared not play it much longer. Not while her husband still lived.

In the darkness of the ladies' chamber, Lettice fumbled with the laces to her French gown, kicking off her shoes. She lit a candle and read Robert's letter. It contained nothing of interest beyond another time and place for them to meet. Lettice bared her teeth in frustration. Robert would have written this letter before Arden destroyed everything tonight with his drunken accusations. Now he was unlikely to meet her privately again while they were at Kenilworth, for the Queen's eye would be upon them constantly.

Lettice held Robert's letter to the candle flame and waited until it was nothing but ashes.

She was sure now that she had imagined that face on the stairs. For the dark-eyed girl had not been here when she reached the top, and there was no other way out – unless she was able to fly.

# Twenty-seven

'UP, YOU LAZY LOT!'

If there was one thing folk would find suspicious, it was a troupe of travelling players who never rehearsed their pieces. Bearing this in mind, Goodluck roused his team early on Saturday and, ignoring their sleepy protests, forced them out of the tent for a few hours' rehearsal. It had rained during the night, and the grass was slippery and wet. The wind still blustered from time to time, slapping the tent walls and catching violently at their cloaks, but a patch of blue sky eventually appeared and the sun came out. Such weather did not bring a halt to their rehearsal though. Most of Goodluck's agents were veterans of stage and street pageant, so it was not long before they had gathered a respectable audience and were playing it for laughs, keen to make the odd copper when the hat was passed round.

'Whoops!' cried John Twist, as Goodluck, playing King Canute, tripped over his outstretched foot. 'Allow me to help you up, sire. Heading for the seaside, Your Majesty? Hope you don't get your feet wet.'

A roar of appreciative laughter greeted this sally as Goodluck, righting himself with Twist's help, strode about the circle of spectators with his arms flung wide, a long grey beard stuck over his real one and a painted wooden crown perched on his head. He slipped several times on the damp grass, which made his frown grow even more ferocious.

'Argh!' he roared, and the children in the audience shrank back, giggling but uncertain. 'The sea shall obey me for I am Canute, lord of this isle, and of its waves too.'

'So where's your trident?' a heckler demanded from the back. 'Did it get swept away in all that rain last night?'

Goodluck roared again, shaking his fist at the man, and the crowd applauded his bravado. Swaggering, he made another noisy circuit.

But his attention was only half on the play, for a few hundred feet away he had seen the bearded Italian with his bear, chained and now muzzled. The man, apparently entertaining those who had gathered to watch, used his long stick to coax the vast black bear up on to its hind legs and made it take a few staggering steps forward.

Finishing his foot-stamping circuit, Goodluck feigned exhaustion and sank down on to his 'throne', tossing aside his crown and hiding his face beneath his cloak. As Twist took up the slack with his usual cautionary speech about the arrogance of kings, Goodluck watched the man and his performing bear from beneath the folds of his cloak, frowning in puzzlement.

If this was the skilled assassin he had heard about in Italy, the man they called the 'Bear', how did he plan to get close enough to the Queen to kill her? And what role, if any, would the great lumbering beast play in it?

The bear-tamer had a long face and an oddly mournful expression, though even at that distance his black eyes gleamed with intensity. The intensity of the assassin, perhaps. A dangerous man, then. And a cautious one too. Goodluck trusted his instinct that this man was one of the conspirators they sought, if not their leader.

But where did the smooth-tongued Massetti fit in? He was a clever young man, well educated and accustomed to the workings of foreign embassies. Had he forged their travel documents, per-haps, allowing this man and his fellows to move freely between countries? Goodluck was now convinced that more than one or two people must be involved in this plot. Even with Massetti's help on the inside, this bear-tamer – however talented an assassin – could not hope to extinguish the Queen's life on his own.

Elizabeth was too well guarded at Kenilworth, too protected on all sides for any lone assassin to reach her and perform his deadly task unchecked.

But perhaps on the open road . . .

'Goodluck, that's your cue!'

Sos, the little Greek, kicked his 'throne' from behind, and Goodluck sprang up with a cry as though roused from a deep sleep. He staggered about groggily, shouting for his crown and a fresh pair of boots, 'for these are soaked through!'

The spectators roared with laughter at these antics. Ned took up his battered lute and began to pluck out a country dance at double speed, while Goodluck attempted to keep up with the steps. He jerked wildly about the circle like a madman, with his wooden crown – handed to him by a small boy from the crowd – slipped down over one eye, giving him an even more crazed look.

Meanwhile, John Twist strolled about the circle with his hand held out for offerings, flirting with all the women, regardless of their looks or the menacing stares of their husbands and brothers, and bowed low as each coin chinked into the hat.

Stumbling in and out of the crowd, Goodluck reeled about with mock-drunkenness, pretending to fall over and swearing 'God's holy cockles!' each time at the top of his voice, much to every-one's amusement. At his next tumble, a pair of strong hands steadied him and he looked up, expecting to see a man, but found a thin, unsmiling girl with painted eyebrows, dark aslant eyes staring into his, black-kohled as an Egyptian queen's.

'Take care,' she warned him in slow, deliberate English, 'that you do not hurt yourself in this, master.'

By way of reply, Goodluck whirled his old cloak about and roared back into the centre of the circle like a madman. When he turned, the girl with the strong hands was gone, as were the Italian and his black bear.

The crowd slowly dispersed once their rehearsal – or improvised performance, in truth – was over. Still in costume, Ned knelt to make up a fire between their tent and the oak tree. Once the flames were high enough, he put a stewpot on to boil and slung in a skinned and jointed rabbit. Goodluck smiled, sitting with his back to the oak trunk, whittling a rough new pipe – the old one was cracked across, all but unplayable. So that was where Ned had got to early that morning, leaving their tent even before first light. Goodluck, who had spent a sleepless night, had seen him go through one half-open eye. He had been wondering whether to doubt Ned's loyalty, a question he disliked having to ponder, but the rabbit was explanation enough.

'Did I miss the play?'

It was about an hour later when Lucy Morgan came stealing up behind them, peeping round the oak trunk at him as though she were still a child, a mischievous look on her face. Grinning broadly, Goodluck rose from the grass and tucked the half-finished pipe into his belt pouch.

'Why, if it isn't the Queen's songbird!'

He kissed her on the cheek, laying his hand a moment on her simple white coif. Such a beautiful girl, so honest, so natural and vibrant. The thought of those men watching her, pursuing her with evil intent, still had the power to fill him with shaking fury. But now was not the time to be angry. With an effort, he pushed the memory to the back of his mind, smiling down at his ward.

'You only missed the rehearsal. Though I was good. Very good, truth be told. Far better than the others.' He ducked a leafy twig thrown at him by Twist, turning his back on the fire. 'So, how is your new life in the bosom of the court, Lucy? Are the great lords and ladies treating you well? It's been days since—'

'Don't let's talk of it,' she whispered, raising her eyes to his face. Goodluck nodded silently, though he did not like what he saw there.

Then Lucy smiled, her whole face changing, like a player putting on a new role as he steps out from behind the curtain. She moved past him to the fire where Ned was stirring the pot, almost as though she were eager to put some distance between them. Goodluck did not like to consider what that meant either.

'What's this?' she demanded, sniffing the steam. 'Rabbit? It smells delicious, Ned. No, I've already eaten. But I'll stay and take a drink with you, gladly. And a dance?'

So it went on, her nervous chatter, her defensive smile. And only Goodluck, who had known her longest, could not smile back, though he pretended to. Sos threw a rope up into the oak, then pulled himself up, quick as a squirrel, into the broad branches of the tree, his lute strapped to his back. There, he balanced the lute on his knee and strummed out a tune for them to dance to.

In the sunshine, Lucy whirled about the circle of flattened grass with John Twist, light on her feet. She laughed so merrily, Goodluck could almost have supposed he had imagined those shadows in her eyes. But he knew he had not, and he blamed himself for leading her into danger. All her young life, he had striven to keep Lucy away from the perilous work he undertook as one of Walsingham's agents. Now their two worlds had begun to cross, and his fear was that the men who had frightened Lucy out in the Brays had done so as a warning to *him* – a warning to keep his nose out of their business.

'Goodluck?'

'Yes?'

He turned away, glad of an excuse not to dance with her himself. Lucy had changed since he had left England for Italy, had grown up in a few brief years, become a woman. Now that he was back on English soil, he found her different, far more of a challenge. The jokes and rough bear-hugs they had shared when she was a girl seemed to fetch only a wan smile now, and nothing had taken their place.

Ned was suddenly at his elbow, an odd look on his face.

'What's on your mind, Ned?'

Ned cleared his throat. He had always been nervous around young women, and Goodluck could see that Lucy's presence today had unsettled him. Not that Ned could be blamed for that. Lucy was indeed unsettling, especially in this wild, sparkling mood.

'You never said what you found the other day when you searched Massetti's room. Anything of significance?'

'Perhaps,' Goodluck muttered. 'Perhaps not.'

Lucy gave a shriek of laughter as John Twist spun her wildly about, and Goodluck glanced over his shoulder at his young charge, then checked the rest of the field, reassuring himself that no danger threatened. But why did he still do this? Lucy was grown now, fledged and gone from his guardianship. She had her own friends and a good life at court. It weakened him, this continuing fear for her welfare. He needed to let her go.

'Well, I found this.' Goodluck fished in his pouch, past the rough pipe and his knife, and brought out the small, misshapen half-circle of metal. 'It was on the floor under the desk, almost as though someone had dropped it without noticing. What do you make of it?'

Ned weighed the curved metal piece in his palm. 'Part of a ring of some kind? Do you think it's important?'

'I'm not sure. It could be.'

Handing it back to him, Ned shrugged. He glanced over to where Lucy and John Twist were still dancing. 'Those men who were after her in the Brays, were they connected to this plot? Will they try again, do you think?'

'Yes to both, I suspect,' Goodluck admitted heavily. 'Though as long as Lucy stays close to the court, there should be little danger.'

'Why Lucy though?'

Goodluck considered the question for a moment, then reluctantly shook his head. However often he thought about it, the pattern on the loom was no clearer. 'I'm not sure yet. Perhaps she saw or heard something that evening that she ought not to have done, something which might disturb the course of their plot. Or that is what they fear, and wish to guard against.'

'Have you questioned her? She might remember something.'

'That's the first thing I did when she came to me. Nor was I the only one who questioned her. If she saw anything that night that bears directly on this latest plot against the Queen, either she has forgotten it or she has already told us what we need to know, and we have not realized the significance of her testimony.'

'I don't understand.'

'What may provide evidence against them may look like nothing to us. Often it is only with hindsight that we see the importance of something that has lain in plain sight the whole time.'

'You suspect the Italian with the bear, do you not? Why not simply arrest the man and have done with it? Then we could get paid and go home early.' Ned looked away, his mouth twisting.

He was not a man to discuss his private life much, so his next words came as a surprise. 'My wife is due to be brought to bed with another child next month. Our fifth. Her last lying-in was . . . difficult.'

Goodluck laid a hand on Ned's shoulder. 'I understand your anxiety to be back in London, my friend. But I promise you, this affair will reach its natural end here at Kenilworth. Which is why we must tread carefully. It's clear that this castle is where they intend to strike, and we must not leap in like fools but hold steady a few days yet. To make arrests now would be to capture only the assassins, and not those minds – and purses – that have shaped this attempt on the Queen's life. You understand?'

Ned gave a brief nod. 'There's sense in that,' he began. Then he fell silent, looking at someone over Goodluck's shoulder.

Lucy had come up behind them. 'Dance with me, Goodluck?'

Goodluck turned, unable to resist the charm of her girlish voice. She put her hands in his and tugged. He allowed her to lead him back out into the grass circle, smiling despite himself. Innocence shone from her face – and God grant it should long remain so. At least until she was safely married off to some worthy man and no longer his responsibility. Goodluck could not help thinking what a remarkable wife Lucy would make. Yet the thought of seeing her married, the daily charge on his conscience lifted for ever, left his spirits oddly depressed.

'No, no!' Lucy laughed as Goodluck stumbled over a tree root, losing his step; she turned and gestured to Sos, still seated up in the tree with the lute in his arms, to start the tune again. 'Do you not know this dance? It is all the fashion at court. We cross hands here – see? Then you must bow and I make my curtsey. Oh, pay no attention to Master Twist. He didn't know the steps either.'

She led Goodluck about the grass circle they had marked out earlier for their rehearsal, patiently teaching him the steps of the dance. It was warm now and Goodluck was soon sweating, uncomfortable in his player's costume. Lucy kicked off her shoes and unlaced her white coif, letting her shining black hair hang down loose over the shoulders of her gown. He made his bow as shown, wishing he could be at court more often and watch her dance before the Queen, so boldly graceful, almost a woman with her figure rounding out at breast and hip in the tight-fitted gown. The steps became subtler and more complicated, ever harder to remember, and Goodluck shook his head, pulling away.

'I'm done!' he muttered, his voice hoarse. 'You'd be better off dancing with John.'

Under the shelter of the oak tree, Goodluck threw off Canute's cloak and took a swig of ale from the jug. Even Sos seemed to have had enough. He had stopped playing and was scrambling down from his perch in the branches with a broad grin on his face. The sound of applause drifted over the lush, waving acres of grass. Goodluck turned and saw, in the furthest reaches of the field, a troupe of acrobats in green livery rehearsing for a small crowd of onlookers, tumbling and jumping through hoops. He took another warm swig of ale and looked back at the girl he had long ceased to consider his 'daughter'.

Lucy, left without music or a partner, turned silently on her own in the grass circle, arms spread wide. She was at her most natural there, barefoot, her hair uncovered, raising her face blindly to the sun. John Twist spoke to her in passing and Lucy laughed, but did not open her eyes.

Taking them all by surprise, Sos suddenly darted out and caught Lucy about the waist, whirling her round a couple of times, then tickled her sides before squirming back up his rope into the broad oak branches above.

'You can't catch me!' he called down triumphantly.

With mock outrage in her flushed face, Lucy stared up at the little Greek hidden among the green leaves. She was laughing again now, a mischievous look in her eyes. It seemed the terrors of her night adventure out in the Brays had been well and truly forgotten, a thought which pleased Goodluck and at the same time disturbed him. If Lucy was able to forget the threat of danger so easily, she would soon find herself back at the point of a knife.

She jerked twice on the knotted end of the rope that dangled beside her. 'Oh, can I not?'

'You're a woman. And everyone knows that women can't climb.'

She gurgled with laughter, and shot a naughty look at Goodluck. 'Did you hear that? Alas, your friend does not remember the household in which I was so delicately raised. He has forgotten who tutored me and taught me his trade. Not the quiet art of embroidery, or cooking, or how to clean a house from top to bottom. But how to listen at doors, and how to puzzle out a coded message . . . *and how to climb a rope!*'

With a defiant gesture, Lucy swung herself up on the rope, took two firm pulls to raise herself above the ground, then fixed her bare feet to the knotted end and used the rope to help her climb more swiftly. Her cumbersome skirts billowed out as she climbed, revealing a flash of strong black thighs to the men below.

Sos gave a great shout of surprised laughter and scrambled back along the branch, away from his pursuer. More concerned than amused, Goodluck stood beneath the rope, tense and watchful, on guard to catch her if she fell. Reaching the branch above, Lucy hoisted herself on to it with all the clumsy grace of a sailor climbing back on board a ship, then began to crawl after Sos, laughing all the while.

'Lucy, you hoyden, be careful!' Goodluck called up after her, but she and Sos were already lost to his sight in the thick foliage.

'You taught her how to read a coded message?'

Goodluck lowered his gaze to Ned's disapproving face. 'Once, that's all,' he explained defensively. 'It was raining and my sister had left her in my care for the afternoon.'

Ned managed one of his rare smiles, though his voice was heavy with irony. 'I'm surprised you never married, Goodluck. You would have done well with a parcel of strapping young sons to teach, all fine spies in the making.'

'I have not taught Lucy how to be a spy,' he said impatiently. 'Drop it, would you?'

'Very well.' Ned shrugged, without any heat. He had never been one to pry into another man's business, just as he preferred not to discuss his own. 'So what's our next move?'

Goodluck stoppered the ale jug and tossed it to John Twist, who had come up behind them, listening to their conversation. 'The plan is simple. We watch the Italian bear-tamer and keep an account of his movements. By day as well as night from now on. Rumour is that the Queen's furious with Leicester for making too free with the Earl of Essex's wife. They say she may leave

Kenilworth at any moment and head north instead. So it's fair to assume that any conspirators will be looking to make good on their plan in the next few days, rather than lose this opportunity.'

Twist passed the ale jug to Ned. 'We've been watching two men so far, the bear-tamer and this Massetti character. But you suspect there are more conspirators in this business, is that right?'

'There are certainly others, yes. But since we don't know how many are involved, or who those might be, we should concentrate our watch on the bear-tamer. If I am right, and our luck turns for the better, he will lead us to these other plotters.' Goodluck looked at the men's faces and, sensing their hesitation, knew some further explanation would be necessary before he had their full trust. 'Massetti seems to be here in no other capacity than as a source of payment for the assassins, and he has kept to his room when not paying court to the Queen. No doubt he fears for his life.'

Sos had swung down out of the branches and was helping Lucy down too. Landing light on her feet as always, the girl trod softly into their little circle, her dancer's grace attracting all their gazes. No longer smiling, she accepted the jug of ale from Ned and drank a long draught.

'This man with the bear,' Lucy ventured, wiping her wet mouth with her hand. 'You think he may be the Italian you've been chasing all summer?'

Goodluck glanced carefully about, checking nobody was close enough to overhear their conversation. But although the path through the field was filling up with people again after the damp start to the day, nobody seemed interested enough in their motley gang to stop and listen. Even the troupe of acrobats in the far corner of the field seemed to have finished their rehearsal and were talking together earnestly, head to head.

'There's a chance this is the man himself, yes,' he admitted reluctantly, not keen to draw Lucy any further into this business than she already was. 'Though if he is indeed the Italian I've been seeking, he is bolder than I gave him credit for. He has paraded himself and his men before us ever since the night he arrived, almost daring us to make our move.'

Ned, who had turned silent, leaning against the oak with his arms folded, stirred again at this. 'But why would he take such a risk?'

'Why indeed?'

'Perhaps,' Sos speculated slowly, 'this man is a distraction, a game to make us look the wrong way. Perhaps we are supposed to notice the shiny coin in this hand, while the other hand wields a long knife.'

Lucy stared at Sos with widened eyes and lips pressed tightly together.

Wishing to reassure his young charge, Goodluck added lightly, 'That's a possibility. But let us not forget that all this is guesswork, nothing more. The man may be what he appears. An Italian bear-tamer with a bad temper.'

'And a beard to rival your own,' Twist murmured.

# Twenty-eight

THE CURTAIN ABOVE HER MATTRESS RATTLED ON ITS POLE AND LUCY
sat up in shock, roused from a sleep so deep her dreams still
possessed her. It was dark in the corridor, but the man who was
leaning over her makeshift bed was carrying a lantern, as though
he had come from outside. Lucy thought she recognized him; one
of the Queen's aides, a stocky man with greying hair. The flame
flickered dimly inside the lantern, illuminating the man's face.

'You're to get up at once. The Queen wants you.'

Lucy stared, still groggy with sleep, not quite understanding the
order. 'The Queen? But . . . But it is not yet dawn.'

'You have three minutes to make yourself ready and follow
me,' he told her sourly. He hoisted up his lantern to illuminate her
cloak, hanging beside her cap on a hook above her bed. 'Don't
bother to dress. You must come without delay.'

The man stood discreetly aside while Lucy swung herself out of
bed, sought for her shoes and pulled her cloak around her. There
was not time to dress her hair properly; instead, she dampened it
with a splash of water from her bedside bowl, dragged a long-
toothed comb through its unruly length, and tried to press it
down under the collar of her cloak. The Queen's aide coughed,
clearly impatient.

'I'm ready,' Lucy announced, pulling the curtain shut behind
her. She followed the eerie swinging glow of his lantern along the
corridor and down one of the narrow stone stairways of the keep.

There were window slits at every turn of the stairs. Lucy shivered in the draught, and dragged her cloak closer at the throat. Outside, a ragged light along the horizon signalled that day was breaking. No other souls appeared to be stirring in this part of the keep.

The low wooden door at the base of the stairs led out into the keep's arcade, a paved area decorated with white fluted columns and miniature citrus trees in large wooden planters. The man gestured her to keep up, quickening his pace through the arcade, the air fragrant at this early hour, everything still fresh from last night's dewfall. His lantern was barely necessary now, a ghostly flicker as the sky began to flush with light above them. He led her down a short flight of steps and through a rose-covered archway on to a narrow walkway. Lucy recognized the neat herb beds and clipped hedges of the Privy Garden reserved for the Queen and her ladies, the great marble fountain at its centre spilling an endless cascade of water, the only sound to break the silence.

The Queen was waiting at the end of the lime-tree walk, pacing back and forth as though unable to keep still. Her ladies, wrapped in cloaks, their heads close together, stood huddled by the gated entrance, within sight of their mistress but evidently forbidden to approach any closer. One or two of the women raised pale, resentful faces as Lucy entered the garden, surveying her undressed hair and shabby cloak with disdain.

'Lucy Morgan!' the Queen exclaimed, seeing her approach, her eyes keen and bright. 'Well done, Fenlon. You will wait with my ladies and escort Mistress Morgan back once I am finished with her. No, take the lantern. We shall not need it, it is almost dawn.'

Once the man had retired to the gate with the others, the Queen signalled Lucy to walk alongside her.

Clad in a floor-length hooded cloak that hid an intricately embroidered nightgown, its hem peeping out from beneath the dark woollen folds, the Queen walked in silence along the path under the lime trees again, shooting occasional glances over her shoulder at her women.

Her face was more flushed and agitated than Lucy had seen it before, except perhaps when she had been screaming for the lord Leicester the evening of their barge ride. But her voice was low and urgent this time, almost a whisper.

'I cannot trust them, you understand, not a single one of my women, or I should never have summoned you like this. When my dearest Kat was alive . . . but now, I cannot be sure. Times have changed since I was first queen. You, though, can have no secrets to conceal, Lucy Morgan, my blackbird, my lovely song thrush.'

Unexpectedly the Queen halted, and whirled in a rich rustle of material to fix Lucy with a sudden, terrifying stare.

'Has anyone come at you these past few weeks? Asked questions about me? Given you gold or jewellery, perhaps, to carry them word of what I do or say?'

'No, Your Majesty,' Lucy replied, though to her dismay she heard her voice shake – more from fear of what such questions might mean than from any hidden guilt. She tried to suppress the memory of Leicester throwing his gold chain about her neck and asking her to report back to him whatever Her Majesty said or did, for she was sure his motive was love, not intrigue. Luckily the Queen did not appear to have noticed.

'I had to ask.' The Queen began to walk again, biting her lip. 'Even after all these years, there are still those in this country who would seek to harm me, to topple me from my throne. It is imperative that I keep my private affairs secret and give such men no weapon to be used against me. You understand? Not a word of what I say here must pass your lips. Not even on your deathbed, though it might cost you your life under torture to stay silent. You understand?'

Lucy nodded, feeling a rush of pride at the Queen's faith in her discretion, even as her knees weakened at the word 'torture'.

'You must know that I have a special place in my heart for Lord Leicester. It is no great secret.'

'Yes, Your Majesty.'

'Then you will understand why I must ask you to spy on him for me. And on Lady Essex too.' The Queen jerked to a halt again, her eyes flashing under the shadowy hood. Her tone became accusing. 'Tell me truthfully now, has Leicester asked you to carry messages to the Countess of Essex?'

Lucy did not dare to lie. 'Yes, Your Majesty.'

'To what purpose?'

'I . . .' She twisted her hands, then let them fall to her sides, knowing that any attempt to protect the Earl of Leicester would be futile. The Queen had her own spies, she must want only confirmation of her own part in the deception. 'Forgive me, Your Majesty. I cannot say what was in that message.'

'I thought you could read.'

'I can, Your Majesty. My guardian saw to my tutoring as a child. But the letter the Lord Leicester gave me was sealed.'

The Queen stared. 'You did not think to open it?'

'I am no spy, Your Majesty. I would not open any letter not directed to me.'

'Highly commendable.' But the sharp flicker of her gaze over Lucy's face showed how unconvinced the Queen was by this explanation. 'But you think they met?'

Struggling against her desire to stay silent, Lucy glanced beyond the Queen to the small knot of women huddled near the gate. To betray a trust would be an unspeakable act of treachery. Yet to refuse to answer the Queen would be treason, surely?

'The Earl of Leicester asked me to carry a letter to the countess, Your Majesty, and that is all. I do not know what was in it. I took no letter back to his lordship from the countess, and I never saw them together.'

'Not once?'

'Never, Your Majesty.'

'You swear this on your life?'

'I . . . I swear it on my life,' she managed, nodding, and at last the Queen seemed satisfied, turning away and so not seeing how Lucy's hands wrenched at each other in anguish.

It was not a lie, she told herself feverishly. But she had not admitted the whole affair to the Queen. She knew, after all, even if she had not seen it with her own eyes, that the two must be lovers. There could be no other explanation for their secretive behaviour.

Elizabeth sat on a bench at the end of the walk, and gestured Lucy to join her. Although her cheeks were still pale under the hooded cloak, she seemed calmer now. The light was growing stronger, and the early mist that had swirled about her ankles on entering the garden had begun to melt away.

'I had the most horrible dream this morning, just before first light. It was only a dream but it felt like truth, like a premonition. Do you believe in such mysteries?' Staring down at her hands, lying still and white in her lap, the Queen did not wait for an answer but continued, speaking almost to herself. 'In the dream, I was in prison again, back in the Tower – I was imprisoned there as a girl, did you know? I had been deposed and my throne seized. I lay on the floor, face down on the filthy stone, too weak even to stand and confront my accusers. I had no champion left, no one to fight for my cause. They had all turned their faces away from me. I had to lie there and await my execution as the false Queen of England.'

'It could not happen!' Lucy burst out, forgetting for a moment to be quiet and respectful. 'You are the rightful heir. Who would dare seize the throne from the lawful daughter of King Henry?'

Queen Elizabeth's gaze lifted, a flash of anger in those eyes, and Lucy realized that she was looking directly at the Countess of Essex, a tall, cloaked figure waiting with the other ladies. 'There are some,' she explained slowly, 'who feel the legality of my birth to be still in doubt and their own claim to the throne as strong as mine. You are too young and innocent, my songbird, to under-stand the greed and envy of the court, and how swiftly a prince may lose his crown through courtly guile and trickery. Yet trust me when I say that it can happen overnight – especially if that prince is deaf to the whispers and manoeuvres of the ambitious.'

'Your Majesty, there is no one at your court who does not love and honour you as their true queen. You have many loyal followers who would never allow such a calamity to happen,' Lucy declared hotly.

'And my dream? This premonition?'

'Don't listen to it, I beg you. I've had nightmares too, when I've eaten too much or the moon is full, and they mean nothing.' She cast about for some comfort to offer the Queen, whose face seemed so downcast. 'Master Goodluck says a bad dream is nothing but a bad dinner that returns to haunt the eater.'

The Queen laughed at that and pinched her cheek. 'In truth, your guardian seems a very wise and learned man.'

Lucy blushed, and looked away as she remembered her earlier lie. What would Master Goodluck say if he knew what she had just done, how she had protected his lordship rather than tell the Queen the truth? She felt sure he would be very angry, and consider her a traitor to the throne.

'Come now,' the Queen said, rising to her feet and shaking out her cloak with a wry smile, 'it is dawn. The cock is crowing. The castle will soon be awake and here I am, still in my nightgown and cloak, like a child caught out of bed. You too had better return and dress yourself. For we have another busy day of entertainments ahead, and the delight of your voice may be required again once I have breakfasted. But promise me one thing before you go, Lucy Morgan. For I felt a kinship with you as soon as you spoke before the court of your mother's death and your lonely upbringing, and I know you will want to help me because of this. Next time his lordship hands you a letter to bear to the Countess of Essex, or indeed to any other lady of the court, you must bring it to me instead.'

Lucy stared, unable to speak properly. 'Your Majesty?'

'And you shall be well rewarded. Do you understand?'

'Yes,' she whispered, 'yes, Your Majesty.'

The light around them had grown stronger, almost blinding now as it winked off the white marble fountain at the centre of the Privy Garden. It was indeed late, and unseemly for a young maid like herself to be standing about in only a cloak, with her hair all undressed and her face untended. Yet long after the Queen had swept away down the herb-scented path towards her ladies-in-waiting, Lucy found she still could not move, her legs unsteady and her whole body shaking as if with a fever.

Carry Lord Robert's messages direct to the Queen instead of to the Countess of Essex?

She felt sick and it hurt her chest to breathe. She had had no choice but to agree; Elizabeth was the Queen and Lucy was nothing, a mere servant of the court.

How could she obey both, and yet betray neither?

# Twenty-nine

BEAR-BAITING WAS HORRIBLE, AND LUCY WISHED SHE HAD NOT stayed to see it. The Queen called out to the castle steward to allow the dogs into the arena, and after that no sound could be heard but the barking and yelping of the hounds and the furious roaring of bears. From her position at the side of the dais, Lucy could see how the bears had been chained to stakes that ran down the centre of the tiltyard so they could not escape. At the signal from the steward, the slavering hounds were let loose on them. The dogs leapt up at the bears, and were knocked back by blows from their great paws. The tethered animals roared at their attackers, rearing up on their hind legs, almost twice the height of a man. Cuffed dogs flew backwards from the posts, yelping in pain, some of them bleeding, others quicker and able to rush in under a bear's paws, attacking an undefended hind leg with their vicious jaws. The crowd called out and stamped their feet, some of them having bet on particular bears. Through all this, the bear-tamers stood at a distance, their sticks ready to strike any bear that seemed to be flagging, their hoarse voices exhorting the animals to 'Fight! Fight!'

Lucy covered her face with her hands. She felt sorry for the poor bears, unable to escape their attackers. Some of them even had their claws filed down so they could not fight off the dogs properly.

The Italian and his bear were not there, she noticed with an odd sense of relief. But perhaps because his animal was a dancing bear, a performer, it was not forced to fight. It would not have been fair to see a dancing bear torn to pieces by these half-starved hounds, however frightening the bear had seemed when it charged her in the outer court.

Lucy pushed to the back of the crowd, her hands clapped over her ears, and waited there until the bear-baiting seemed to be over.

The sun beat down on her head. It was intolerably hot in the white, sandy enclosure of the tiltyard; no wonder the Queen and her chief courtiers had chosen to watch today's entertainments from beneath the cool shade of a canopy.

Three of the bears lay dead on the sandy ground, still chained to their stakes. A few others looked badly hurt; their owners stood over them, shouting and striking them with sticks, attempting to get them back on their feet. One brownish bear seemed to have survived with only a few crimson gashes to its vast belly. Several dogs lay dead or dying near where it had been staked and Lucy witnessed a heated altercation between the bear's master and the furious owner of one of the dogs. He seemed to be claiming that the bear's claws had not been properly clipped before the contest.

Belatedly, Lucy realized that the Queen had already risen and left the arena. Now the crowd of commoners had begun to follow the court back inside the castle walls and Lucy found herself being jostled forward by the force of people pressing towards the tilt-yard gate. She cried out, trying to fight her way back to the safety of the dais, but no one was listening.

Then a hand plucked at her sleeve, dragging her aside out of the crush of people.

'Lucy!'

It was the Countess of Essex, her pretty face flushed and nervous. She drew Lucy against the wall of the tiltyard and whispered in her ear. To Lucy's surprise, Lady Essex spoke with a frank, soft-voiced intimacy – as though they were sisters or close friends, not noblewoman and servant.

'Will you come with me tonight, Lucy?' The countess's smile seemed forced, her gaze restless. 'I have a plan, if you are willing

to help me. Bring a hooded cloak for me and tell the guards I am
your friend. They would let a servant out of the inner court. But
I dare not walk out alone, not so late at night, not beyond the
state apartments. If I were to be caught—'

'Go with you?' Lucy repeated stupidly, still in a daze. She
looked about, suddenly afraid again, but no one was listening;
they were standing alone under the wall of the tiltyard, the passing crowd too noisy to overhear their whispers. 'To meet Lord
Leicester, you mean?'

The countess nodded, watching her. 'And wait for me in the
stables until we have . . .' She hesitated. 'Until we are finished.'

'Wait on my own?'

'It will not be above an hour, I swear it.' She squeezed Lucy's
hand, her muttered words frantic. 'Please, say you will help me. I
cannot do this alone.' Her gaze searched the crowd as though
looking for someone in particular. 'They watch us every minute of
every day. Even to speak to you like this is dangerous.'

'Perhaps you should not visit his lordship then,' Lucy dared to
suggest, and saw a flash of anger in the countess's eyes, swiftly
hidden. She thought of the Queen's request that she should spy on
these two lovers, and knew she could not go through with it,
could not betray them. But perhaps she could steer them away
from the danger of discovery. She might not be the only one the
Queen had asked to watch and listen. 'You could write a letter. A
letter without any names would be safe enough.'

'No, I must see him. I must speak to Robert *in person*.'

'But the danger—'

'You do not understand!' The countess looked half insane, her
cheeks suddenly blotchy with heat. Her eyes filled with tears. 'I
have no choice in the matter. Not any longer. I have received a
letter from my husband in Ireland. It was delivered to me only
a few moments ago. The courier brought sealed letters from Lord
Essex for the Queen and some of her councillors too. I'm afraid
what may be in them. I must speak to Lord Leicester tonight, and
somewhere we cannot be overheard.'

Lucy felt almost sorry for the lady, seeing the genuine fear in
her face. Although she could not condone what Lady Essex had
done, she knew such arrangements were common at court. And

his lordship was a handsome man, and charming too. The countess must be very much in love with Lord Leicester, to countenance committing the sin of adultery. Though perhaps it had not gone so far yet between them?

'Please, will you help me?' Lady Essex begged her once more, and Lucy, looking into the woman's flushed, terrified face, could see no way out.

Reluctantly, she nodded, and agreed to meet her ladyship on the stairs below the state apartments later that night, with a hooded cloak. Lady Essex would bring a bribe for the guard, in case that should prove necessary.

When the countess had gone, Lucy stood a moment in the heat of the afternoon sun. Her hands were trembling. She wished she had not agreed to something so dangerous. Leaving the inner court at midnight, waiting alone in the dark stables, no one there to protect her. Goodluck would be furious if he knew the risk she was about to take. But seeing Lady Essex so very afraid, how could she have refused?

She turned back towards the gate, and bumped into a boy. He had the freckled, sunburned face of a commoner, and a triangular patch on his tunic where the cheap material had torn and been mended. But what caught her attention were his eyes. They were red-rimmed and damp, and from the streak of dirt along his cheek she guessed he had been trying to wipe away tears.

'What's the matter?' Lucy asked gently. The boy tried to run past her, but she caught him by the shoulders and turned him to face her. 'Hey, not so fast! What is it? Are you lost?'

He stared up at her without speaking, his dark eyes still swimming, his lip trembling, and she knew he was trying to decide whether or not to trust her.

'What's your name, little brother?'

'I'm not your brother,' he managed in a whisper, wrenching free of her hands.

She realized then that he could have run away at any second, but stayed to stare at her, taking in the richly dark skin of her hands and face, her coarse black hair. She watched, half expecting to see fear or distrust in his face – that was the usual reaction from commoners who had never seen a Moor – but instead the boy looked her over in unconcealed admiration, his dark eyes intent and his tears forgotten.

'But my name is Will,' he continued, and a slight flush entered his cheeks. 'Will Shakespeare.'

'Well, Master Shakespeare, my name is Lucy Morgan. And please don't run away, I'd like to talk to you for a moment. If you don't mind, of course. But what are you doing wandering about here on your own? Do you live in the village, perhaps?'

He shook his head. His accent was countrified, but not as thickly rural as she had imagined it would be. Perhaps the boy came from a good family. Though a family, she thought, glancing at his patched tunic, that had fallen on hard times. 'My father brought me here to see the Queen. We live in Stratford.'

'Is Stratford a long way from here?'

'Far enough. We left before dawn, but it still took most of the morning to get here. We have a good cart, but the horse is slow.' He was frowning now, his head on one side. 'Do you not know Warwickshire?'

'Not a bit,' she admitted cheerfully. 'I am from London.'

'London?'

There was a touch of awe in his tone, which amused her, and a little longing too. No doubt life in Warwickshire could be dull at times for a boy with a restless mind. His gaze dropped over her once again. Daringly, he touched her hand, brushing her knuckles and up towards her wrist.

'So why do you have black skin?'

'Because my parents were Moors,' she explained carefully. 'They came from a burning hot country called Africa, many thousands of miles away over the sea. That is why I have dark skin. But I was born in London.'

He thought about that for a moment, then his face cleared. 'So you are English. I heard one of the men say you are a dancer,' he added, thrusting his hands behind his back and not meeting her eyes. 'Is that true?'

'I dance and sing for the Queen, little brother.' She smiled as Will's dark gaze lifted to her face again, a certain resentment in his eyes. 'Sorry, I forgot. We are not brother and sister. But you said you came here today with your father? Have you lost him?'

His head jerked in a nod. 'There were so many people . . .'

'Don't worry, I'll help you find him. What does he look like?' She smiled down at him, holding out her hand. 'Like you, only taller?' Will slipped his hand into hers and she shivered, feeling the cool skin of his palm against hers. 'How can you be cold in this heat? Come on, let's try down towards the Brays. Where did you last see him?'

They found Will's father searching for his son through the narrow, smoky alleys, stooping to question an old woman sitting at the entrance to a makeshift dwelling. Master Shakespeare was a broad-shouldered man, muscular where his son was still thin as a birch twig. His clothes spoke of some prominence in society, though they were too plain for him to be gentry. Lucy caught the same restlessness on his face as on his son's and a sharp intelligence about his eyes and mouth.

'Father!'

The man straightened as they rounded the corner, and Lucy saw relief flash across his face at the sight of his son, and a touch of anger too. He held out his arms and Will ran into them.

'Where have you been the past two hours?' his father demanded, and held him out at arm's length. He looked over the boy's head at Lucy, taking in her appearance with one swift assessing stare. 'I've been half mad with worry, boy. I ought to take a rod to you for this new piece of idiocy. Master Lunt took the cart down the road to see if you'd started for home without us. He's been gone a while too. We'll have to hope he comes back, or we'll be walking home to Stratford. And who's this with you?'

'This is Lucy Morgan,' Will stammered. 'One of the Queen's own ladies. She's from London and lives at the court. She found me in the tiltyard and helped me look for you. I . . . I was lost.'

'One of the Queen's ladies, eh? It seems I owe you my thanks, Mistress Morgan.'

Master Shakespeare seemed a polite and well-spoken citizen. She was glad for Will's sake that his father's anger appeared more bluff than anything else, as she did not like the idea that the boy might be beaten.

'Lucy, please,' she corrected him, smiling. 'And your son has given me honour I don't deserve. I'm only a court entertainer, not a lady.'

'Well, whatever you are,' he said, and she saw his eyes move cautiously over her face again, 'I thank you for finding my errant son and bringing him back to me. Be a shame to lose the boy now, after the cost of feeding and clothing him for eleven summers.'

Will blushed and protested under his breath, as though embarrassed to have his age mentioned.

Master Shakespeare ruffled his son's hair. 'But all's well that ends well, as they say. We'd best head on back towards the Stratford road, see if our neighbour has waited for us.' He hesitated. 'Did you get to see the Queen in the end, boy?'

'Yes, sir.'

'That's one thing, at any rate. Now we must get on home. And on a Sunday, when we should be at rest.' Master Shakespeare shook his head, looking at her. 'I'm sorry if he chattered on to you. The boy's got nothing in his head but London these days.' He flicked Will's ear, but his son did not protest this time, staring back at Lucy with a sudden intensity, as though imprinting her face on his memory. 'See? We're too dull and slow in Warwickshire for the likes of my Will. Give you good day, mistress.'

He bowed, and she curtseyed in return. Then they were gone, the man leading his son away through the smoky alley. Lucy stood and watched them go, aware of a few curious stares from the poorer people here. When she had last walked through the Brays, her gown had not been so rich. But she would not show them any fear. Goodluck had taught her that. To show fear was to invite violence, or so he believed. So she stood straight-backed, with her head held high, and ignored the nervous hammering of her heart.

At the end of the meandering alley through the Brays, just before it curved out of sight, she saw Will look back and lift a hand in salute. She waved merrily, and then they were gone, two shadowy figures lost in the drifting smoke.

She stood another minute in the rutted dust of the Brays, then turned and made her way back into the castle, wishing she had not weakened and agreed to help Lady Essex sneak out of the women's quarters and meet Lord Leicester tonight.

There was only one way such a dangerous adventure could end, and that was in disgrace for all of them.

# Thirty

SLOWLY, NOT WISHING TO RUIN HER LUCK BY SUPPOSING THEM SAFE too soon, Lettice let out her breath. Lucy Morgan, with an air of surprising confidence, had demanded passage into the outer court and the young guard, hardly old enough to hold his pike steady, had waved them through the gate without a second glance.

Nevertheless, Lettice remained silent until they had reached the far side of the wooden bridge that separated the outer and inner courts, and were safely out of earshot. For a moment there, as she was approaching the guard post in her disguise, the dangerous nature of her adventure suddenly dawned on her, and she shrank back into her hood, as far from the guard's lantern as possible. But the four men on duty had seemed more interested in their dice game than in two serving women at the gate, barking at the youngest to 'Let them through!' without pausing to demand their names or their business in the castle at this late hour.

Perhaps the guards thought them whores, returning from an hour or two of paid pleasure with some dissolute courtier. Or perhaps they simply did not care who came and went within the castle's stoutly defended walls.

'He didn't even look at us,' she whispered to Lucy, unable to hide the exultation in her voice. 'Did you see?'

'Yes, my lady.'

Shoulder to shoulder, they crossed the outer court in silence with their skirts held up above the dew-damp grass, taking care not to draw attention to themselves.

The main stables lay in darkness, except for a lantern hanging mistily under a gable roof at the far end, where one of the tall double doors had been left open a crack. As they approached, hurrying now towards safety, the door creaked another few inches and Lettice could just make out a male figure in the shadows, waiting for them. It was the Moor who worked for Robert.

'Tom!' Lucy exclaimed, then thrust a hand over her mouth as though to snatch back the name.

Lettice stared at her. The foolish girl seemed to be trembling.

The young Moor ushered them through the entrance to the stables, taking an oil lantern from a high shelf and lighting Lettice's way with it. The horses nearest to the doors moved restlessly in their stalls, one or two whinnying at their presence. Lettice shuddered at the smell of the stables, and lifted a fine linen handkerchief to her nose.

'His lordship awaits you upstairs, my lady,' the young man whispered, indicating a steep ladder. 'Once at the top, keep to the left.'

She stared at the ladder in horror. 'I am to climb that? In this gown?'

The young man hesitated, clearly surprised. 'Well . . . yes, my lady. There's no other way up.'

Lettice pursed her lips at the steepness of the ladder and gestured him to lift the lamp so she could see her way more clearly. 'Lucy, you are to remain here until I return. Is that understood?'

Lucy nodded, though she looked wide-eyed and uncertain under her dark hood. Lettice only hoped the silly young thing would not take fright and disappear before she and Robert had finished their business. Then she remembered Lucy's startled reaction at seeing the young Moor in the doorway. Looking from one to the other, she saw their faces properly by the light of the raised lantern. *Well, well.* The Queen's shiny new favourite, already in love and looking fit to lose her precious virginity before the night was out.

'Enjoy yourselves,' she said more softly, then drew up her heavy skirts and set her slippered foot on the lowest rung of the ladder. 'Young man, avert your eyes!'

At the top of her precarious climb, Lettice stood a moment, adjusting to the dark, her heart thudding under the tight bodice of her gown. Then she heard Robert whisper her name. To her left, a door creaked slowly open and a light shone out of a room at the gable end. The fear came to her that it might be a trap, but then he appeared, blocking the light in the doorway, and her eyes devoured him hungrily.

'Robert!'

Without a word, he drew her inside the room and shut the door. The place was dimly lit and low-roofed, a straw mattress to one side and a table with a lantern flickering dully. She took a few quick paces to the window, examining the room with the careful eyes of a conspirator. He had covered the narrow casement with an old horse blanket so they could not be seen from the courtyard below, and had spread his cloak over the straw mattress. So his sense of chivalry was not entirely dead, she noted with a surge of sudden, almost unwelcome desire.

'I am glad you asked to see me,' she began, turning to face him. She felt under her cloak for the letter. 'This arrived today. Yes, you may well stare. It's from my husband. A letter in which he all but accuses me of being your lover, and threatens to tell the Queen.'

Robert held out his hand for the letter, his face a mask. 'I heard of the courier's arrival, of course, and knew he brought letters from Ireland. But I hadn't expected this. Has he told the Queen?'

'I presume not, or we would have heard by now.'

'Have been arrested, you mean,' Robert corrected her drily, and unrolled the letter, reading down it swiftly. His eyebrows rose at several points, then he swore under his breath as he reached the end. 'The bastard. After the sheriff's public accusation, this letter alone is enough to condemn us. What have you replied?'

'I haven't, as yet,' she admitted, stepping closer. 'I've been waiting to speak with you first, to see what you advise. The courier will take back my reply with the Queen's own letters tomorrow or the next day.'

'Tell him it is a lie,' he said flatly, thrusting the letter back at her as though it burned his fingers.

She stared at him. Her breath caught in her throat. 'Robert, it's too late to tell him this is a lie. I have not bled for nearly ten weeks now.' She saw his eyes darken and narrow on her face.

Lettice held her head high and did not blush. It was nothing but the truth. And the earl must know it was his child, after all. There had been no one else, and Essex had been in Ireland too long for it to be his. She had held back from telling Robert for weeks, hoping that matters might resolve themselves on their own, nature being a fickle mistress. But now that her husband had learned of their affair, and the blasted child seemed to be taking root inside her, what else could she do but admit everything?

'Mine?' he demanded. He swore again when she raised her eyebrows at the insolence of the question.

'It's time you settled this score anyway,' she pointed out, watching Leicester's face carefully, his expression still under control, no doubt fooling himself that something could still be salvaged from this mess. Her tone became acid. 'Unless, that is, you are content to see Essex cast me out on to the street as a whore and an adulteress. Which he will do, on his return from Ireland, if he finds me with a belly as big as a whale.'

Still Robert said nothing.

She shook her head at his lack of response. 'Robert, he knows about us.'

'And what would you have me do, exactly?'

'*Kill him!*'

Robert's eyes widened in shock and for a moment she wondered if she had gone too far, or as far as it was possible to go before he crumbled and ran back to the Queen, a beaten hound with its tail between its legs. She stared back, meeting his gaze, willing him to be strong, to do what was right for her and their unborn child.

He strode to the door, throwing it open and staring back along the unlit corridor as though expecting to see some spy loitering there, some listener in the shadows. But there was no one; the stables below were silent, except for the restless stirring of the horses. Slowly, he shut the door and turned to face her.

'I am no assassin, my lady. Whatever you may have heard . . . I would never . . .' He drew a harsh, uneven breath. 'My wife's death was an accident.'

'When he returns from Ireland, then,' she said softly, deciding to sidestep what he had said in case it led to further trouble between them, 'seek out my husband, put some quarrel on him, and kill the man. Then we can be legally wed.'

'It seems I won't have to seek him out,' he replied bitterly, gesturing to the letter in her hand. 'If Essex comes back to find you with child, we'll both be locked up in the Tower for adultery before I have time to quarrel with anyone, let alone pull out a sword and fight for your honour.'

'Are you afraid to die, my lord?'

Her voice had been a little shrill. Robert straightened, looking at her angrily. She thought he might strike her, as her husband had been known to do during their quarrels, but Robert's hand never moved from his side.

'Yes,' he agreed calmly, without any sign of shame. 'And so should you be, my lady. The Tower is a grim place. No one who has ever been there would wish to return.'

Lettice walked back to the covered window and stood there a moment. Her mind worked feverishly. It would do no good to make him angry. She was pregnant, of that she was sure. All the early signs were there, and she knew how much he wanted a son and heir. Surely she could convince him that Essex must die? What other solution was there? Somehow she had to turn the quarrel aside, remind Robert that she was not his enemy, that he loved her, that she was to be the mother of his child.

Besides, it would be a disaster to lose him now, with her husband aware of their secret meetings and her body ready to betray her to the Queen and court.

She let her shoulders bow slightly, and felt her eyes fill with hot tears. 'But I am,' she whispered to herself, though she knew he was still there, listening. 'I am afraid. And alone in this.'

Robert hesitated, and the sound of his silence filled the low-roofed room, then he came forward. His hand was light on her shoulder, as though waiting to see if she would shrug him off.

Then he reached round and unfastened her borrowed cloak. It fell to the floor in a rustle of cheap cloth.

'My lady,' he whispered, bending his head to kiss the nape of her neck. 'Lettice, you are not alone. But these are not easy things to discuss – our child, your husband's return, what must be done to make this right. And I admit, my mind has been elsewhere these past few weeks. Though that's hardly a surprise.' He kissed her neck again, his voice muffled, though she could hear the stress behind it. 'I've had the Queen's visit to plan, with all her entourage . . . several hundred servants, their horses and carts. And you know the danger, this fresh plot against her—'

'There are always plots against the Queen!'

He laughed then, and she knew he was still hers. 'If I did not know better, I would think you almost glad of such a thing. Your cousin Elizabeth is forever watching her back, looking for spies and assassins at every corner. She can never be herself, but must submit to the will of her councillors. That is no life.'

'Elizabeth is the Queen,' Lettice pointed out, no sympathy in her heart for her cold-faced cousin, who had always made her life at court as unpleasant as possible. 'These troubles come with the crown.'

Robert nodded soberly. 'So you ought to pity her. If you were in her position—'

'Yes?' Lettice turned and looked up into his face, suddenly eager, her cheeks flushing. 'If I were queen?'

He drew in a sharp breath, staring back at her. 'Lettice, my love, you must be careful. You have no idea how dangerous it is even to think such a thing, let alone voice it.' His tone softened and his hand slipped down to her belly, stroking the fine material of her gown. 'For the sake of our unborn child, promise me you will never attempt to put yourself above Elizabeth. She will not stand it, trust me.'

Triumph flickered inside her and she had to bite back a smile, force herself to conceal that glorious, lit-up reaction. *He had thought it! He had imagined her on the throne instead of her cousin, too old now to bear him a son!* The realization made her reach for his face, stroke his cheek fondly. She would give herself to him again tonight, though she had sworn to do so no more until Essex was dead and Robert in her marriage bed instead.

'Dearest,' she murmured, kissing him slowly. She felt him harden against her belly. 'Are we to talk all night?'

# Thirty-one

LUCY WHISPERED 'NO!' AGAIN, BUT HER URGENT REFUSALS DID NOT seem to be having any effect on Tom.

Instead, he had pushed back her hood to reveal her thick black hair, combed back and held in place with a single white ribbon. Then he loosened the cloak about her shoulders, ignoring her protests that someone might come in and disturb them.

Now, holding her gently by the shoulders, he lowered his head and kissed her. The feel of his lips against hers was a shock. Even more so was the knowledge that they were quite alone, hidden in the shadows of Lord Leicester's stables, the door closed and the lantern dimmed.

'Hush,' he murmured, burying his face in her hair. 'There's no one to see us. And my lord will be a good hour above, you'll see. What else should we do to pass the time?'

'Not this,' she hissed, feeling a sudden flare of panic as Tom dragged aside her bodice to reveal her breast. 'You must not!'

His voice sounded thick. 'But your body is like an angel's. And your hair . . . Lucy, Lucy . . .'

'Tom, no!'

Struggling against him for an undignified moment, Lucy soon managed to fight free of his hold. It was not so difficult to escape after all, she realized with a faint surprise, feeling his hands drop away without protest. Tidying her gown, Lucy took a few hurried steps backwards, and saw him follow. She turned, fleeing the intimacy that had sprung up so unexpectedly between them, and nearly slipped on the uneven cobbles, damp and strewn with foul-smelling straw, that paved the stable entrance.

Tom caught her by the arm, his dark eyes concerned. 'Careful, you'll hurt yourself.'

He was only trying to protect her, her instincts told her that. Nonetheless Lucy pulled free, forcing herself to look as cold and disdainful as Lady Essex had done when Tom had told her to climb the ladder. It felt strange, stiffening her face into such a mask. But she could not allow him to get close again, knowing now what he intended.

Maybe she would never make a good marriage. Maybe this was the best she could hope for, whatever Master Goodluck might say. A stable worker, yes, but one of her own people, a man who would never judge her for the colour of her skin. There would be some honour in such a union. But she was not married yet, nor likely to be if she allowed Tom his way tonight.

Besides, she had promised the Queen she would remain a virgin, and a stable was hardly the place to lose her much-prized innocence, lying on her back in some filthy stall, listening to the sighing of horses in the darkness.

'I'm sorry,' he muttered, and she believed him.

'It doesn't matter,' she said, brushing the apology aside, though in truth she was glad he was not as crude as she had feared, wanting only one thing from her. 'But perhaps I should wait here alone for my lady to come back.'

'His lordship instructed me to wait with you, and that's exactly what I'm going to do,' Tom insisted, a stubborn note in his voice. 'And don't you bother arguing with me, Lucy Morgan, because it will make little difference. You've already had your life threatened once. I'd lose my hide if I were to leave you here alone at night – and I'll not risk a whipping on account of a girl.'

'A girl? You thought me enough of a woman a moment ago,' she snapped back. Then she saw the confusion on his face and was sorry for her sharp tongue. She was uneasy herself, waiting in the dark for the countess to return from a forbidden meeting.

Tom held back whatever it was he had been intending to say,

and laid a hand on her arm. 'Lucy,' he said, her name echoing about the stalls. He frowned, lowering his voice. 'I shouldn't have spoken so harshly just now. We won't have to wait too long. Come back under the light.'

She acquiesced, mollified by his apology, and allowed him to draw her close against the wall. Tom meant her no harm, after all. And he was handsome. She dared to look up into his face, every feature sharpened, lit up by the lantern on the wall.

'Forgive me, I still want to kiss you,' he said simply, stroking her cheek with his forefinger.

It was an intimate gesture, and one she ought not to have allowed. Yet she did not move away.

'Is that so wrong?' Tom asked, interrupting her thoughts. His eyes searched hers, almost hungrily. 'Lucy?'

She thought again of the Queen, her stern white countenance hovering spectre-like over his shoulder, like an owl in the night, and realized with a guilty start that she did not wish to end up like Her Majesty – chill and alone in her bed, hanging like the last leaf on a barren tree, waiting only for the fall.

'No.'

'No?' he repeated, and the word seemed to fall oddly, testing the rustling silence of the stable.

Lucy shivered and closed her eyes against the misty halo of the lantern. He kissed her then, and instead of pushing him away as she ought to have done, she slid her arms about his neck.

They stood together like that for a few moments, lost in a thick, suffocating silence, while she imagined herself drowning without any fear, the warm, seductive water creeping into her lungs. His hands circled her waist, slipped lower, cupping the swell of her buttocks, pulling her close against his groin, and she moaned at his daring, vaguely aware that she should resist yet finding no immediate reason to do so.

From above their heads, a woman's sharp cry split the silence. Lucy dragged a hand over her face, abruptly remembering who was in the room above them. The danger she was in struck her like a cold slap across the face, and her desire fell away in that instant. She had brought the Countess of Essex here tonight to commit adultery with the Queen's favourite. If they were discovered, there was no doubt that her life would be forfeit. The countess might only be imprisoned, but she . . .

Lucy felt her throat constrict, as though the hangman's noose was already around it. It was hard to think her way clear, she was suddenly so afraid. The countess had tricked her. Or told her less than the truth about why she wanted this meeting, and Lucy had behaved like a wanton fool, allowing herself to be manipulated into accompanying Lady Essex here tonight. And now she had almost risked losing her virginity, the only thing she possessed of any value – except for her voice.

Tom did not seem aware of the danger, though. He was already reaching for her again, still openly aroused, a half-smile on his lips. 'You hear that? It seems we're not the only ones enjoying ourselves.'

'Tom, we mustn't. The Queen said—'

He looked startled, even a little impatient. 'The *Queen*? What are you talking about?' He tugged her towards the nearest stall. 'Hush, Lucy sweetest, we don't have time for a discussion. Her ladyship will come down soon and we'll have lost our chance.'

She shook her head, dragging her feet, and faced his irritation with a growing sense of sadness. He did not understand. Queen Elizabeth had no more significance for Tom than the midday sun in the sky – too huge and far above him to be of any consequence. Above *them*, she corrected herself, slowly realizing that Tom saw her as no more nor less than himself, a mere servant of the court.

But what was she telling herself? That she was, in some way, more important than Tom, more than just another servant?

The breathtaking arrogance of such a belief shook her, and she jerked her hands free of his. She had been so glad to come to court last year, so happy to watch the fine lords and ladies from the back of the chorus, only occasionally aching to push herself forward, to be allowed to sing before the Queen on her own because she had sensed, had *known* deep in her heart, that her voice was good enough for such an honour.

But to put herself above Tom, to see herself as somehow better than another servant, that was an abuse of the intimacy in which the Queen held her.

'I need some air,' she whispered, turning away from him. Tight-chested, she fled into the outer court.

As soon as Lucy was outside, she realized her mistake. It was dark and still, and there was no moon that night to light the path back to the gatehouse, only a few lights flickering in the high windows of the state apartments.

The memory of those hooded men following her in the Brays came back to haunt her, and she stood a moment, unsure whether to turn back inside or make a run for the gatehouse and the inner court. At least there she would be safe from those who sought to harm her, if not from her own conscience.

Turning, Lucy frowned and peered through the darkness. What was that?

No, she had not imagined it. There was a man on the far side of the outer court, standing in the shadows near the base of the Watergate Tower. He was a big man and stood unmoving against the wall, his face hidden in the shadows, though even at this distance she could see the pale glimmer of his eyes.

Then she caught a movement out of the corner of her eye, and froze, staring through the darkness. Closer at hand, someone was walking along the base of the castle wall, towards the Watergate Tower. One of Leicester's guards? Or someone on their way to meet the man waiting there?

A horrible feeling of dread came over her and she shrank back against the stable, not caring if the rough wall ruined her cloak. Surely that odd way of walking, the hooded cloak he was wearing . . .

The man glanced over his shoulder, perhaps sensing somebody's gaze on his back, and in a flash she recognized the face under the hood. Swarthy, bearded, with a cruel unsmiling mouth. It was the Italian bear-tamer, and he was staring straight at her.

Next thing she knew, she was lying on the dew-damp ground with Tom kneeling over her and the countess behind him, her white face a mask of disdain.

'Is she awake yet? I can't stay any longer.'

Seeing Lucy staring back at him, Tom straightened and stood

up, a look of relief on his face. He gave a grim little smile as he helped her to her feet. 'You fainted.'

He supported her, one arm about her waist, as she stumbled, her legs still unsteady.

'Careful now. Are you able to walk?'

'Of course she is,' Lady Essex hissed, pulling the hood of her cloak further forward to conceal her face. 'We must get back to the women's quarters. Hurry, before we are seen.'

Lucy stared at the hood in a daze, then gasped, suddenly remembering what she had seen.

'The bear-tamer!'

Tom frowned. 'The what?'

But it was no use trying to explain. Both the bear-tamer and the other man were gone, and the outer court was dark and silent.

Lady Essex turned on her heel, making an angry noise under her breath. 'Come,' she threw out sharply, lifting her skirts free of the damp grass. She began to climb the slope back to the sturdy wooden gatehouse. 'If you have put me in danger by this, Lucy Morgan, I swear I'll have the skin off your back for it. And your lover's, too.'

# Thirty-two

THE BODY HAD BEEN BROUGHT TO SHORE AND DROPPED IN AN ungainly fashion by the watermen – still in the shallow skiffs from which they plied their trade, bleary-eyed from the earliness of the hour but staying to keep guard over their strange catch. The coming dawn was a thick reddish-grey, the clouds to the north-east of the castle heavy and brooding, a warning of rain to come. It seemed the prolonged dry weather was finally about to break.

Beside the reedy edges of the lake, the dark-haired Welshman named Caradoc who had come to rouse Goodluck from his bed prodded the corpse with his foot and glanced back at his companion curiously.

'Are you a Queen's man?'

'Why do you ask?'

The Welshman looked Goodluck up and down, presumably noting that his patched and rain-stained hood had seen better days and that his coat was a dull buff rather than blue.

'You're not one of Leicester's men,' the man sniffed.

'I serve England,' Goodluck replied shortly, then found himself baulking at such a reply. 'Lord Leicester sent you to fetch me, did he not?'

Caradoc nodded.

'Then let us get on. I'm missing breakfast for this.'

Goodluck crouched to examine the body the watermen had dragged out of the lake. It was a portly man with heavy thighs and a decided paunch, somewhere in his early thirties. His sodden blue tunic, pulled in by a large leather belt, and blue hose proclaimed him one of Leicester's household. His muddied yellow hair had been razor-cut, short to the ears, and his beard – a strand of weed caught in it now – had been recently trimmed as well. A self-indulgent man then, his paunch speaking of late nights on the castle ale, but one who nonetheless liked to take care of himself, perhaps with an eye to the ladies?

Lifting the dead man's left hand, Goodluck examined it closely. Tough, callused fingers spoke of daily labour but not hard, menial work, and his fingernails were short but unbroken. On his right hand he wore a broad gold ring inset with a small agate. His nose was slightly crooked – a fight in his past? – and above the mud smears to his cheeks, his bulging blue eyes were wide and staring.

Goodluck reached forward and gently pulled the lids over his eyes. It was all he could do to repress a shudder. To kill a man and dispose of his body afterwards was one thing. To deal with a sodden corpse first thing in the morning was enough to make the bile rise in any man's throat.

He leaned closer, and prised the man's stiff lips apart. There was an odd yellowish tinge to his mouth, and a sickly odour in the air. The unpleasant smell reminded him of something, but he could not place what it was.

'The watermen found him, you said?'

'Yes,' Caradoc agreed, straightening up at his questioning glance. He had bent almost double to see what Goodluck was doing, clearly fascinated by his examination of the dead man. 'They went out on the mere just before first light, as is their habit. The boat ran up against the body – with a right bump, they said – over there, nearly under the tiltyard wall. They pulled him into the boat, rowed back to the jetty, and the boy there ran to fetch help. That's when I was informed. I'm assistant to the castle steward, see? It's my duty to inform the coroner and the dead man's next of kin, and see that the body's properly taken care of.'

'His next of kin? So you knew this man?' Goodluck was startled. 'Why didn't you say so when I first came down here?'

Caradoc shrugged. 'You didn't ask. Besides, I didn't know

myself until I seen him close up. But soon as we turned him over, I knew it were Malcolm.'

'Malcolm?'

'That there is Malcolm Drury. He worked for the steward too. Though he didn't want to stay on at Kenilworth after this summer. Said he was going to London, to make his fortune there.' The man laughed, almost contemptuous. 'Dreams!'

Goodluck said nothing. He had found it was often more useful to observe unpleasant behaviour than to comment on it. Besides, a pale sun was rising out of the mists along the lakeside, and the castle above them was beginning to bustle with life. He did not wish to draw more attention to himself than he already had. It was evident that Lord Leicester had wanted him to see the body and to report back to Walsingham on his findings. But in doing so, Goodluck ran the risk of being identified by those who constantly watched the goings-on at court and took reports back to their masters. Or by the Italians, who might even now be watching him.

'Why did his lordship want you to see the body?' Caradoc asked, still worrying away at the question in his head.

'We've been missing a man since we arrived,' Goodluck lied blithely, hoping he would not be curious enough to make his own enquiries and discover this was not true. 'Lord Leicester may have thought this was him.'

'Oh no,' Caradoc said at once, shaking his head with the air of one who knew more than was common knowledge. 'Couldn't have been. This is his lordship's man. Besides, this one,' he said, and prodded the drowned man again with his shoe, 'hasn't been in the water that long. Well, I know that because I saw him two days ago with my own eyes. But a man who's been in the mere a week or more, he'd look a good deal greyer than Malcolm here.'

'I take it you didn't like Master Drury much?' Goodluck asked wryly, squatting back on his haunches. His stomach rumbled but he ignored it, not feeling too hungry now that he'd started the day with a sodden corpse.

'We shouldn't speak ill of the dead.'

'He can't hear you. What was it that made you dislike him?' He glanced at the body. 'Did he like to show off? That ring would have cost a year's wages at least. Malcolm must have come from a wealthy family: he couldn't have bought such a trinket with his own money.'

The man's lips tightened. 'No, that he couldn't. But he wasn't a wealthy man's son. Old Master Drury kept a few acres west of here. Long dead now, his wife Goody too, and nothing to show for his sweat.'

Goodluck considered that for a moment. 'So where do you think he got the money from?'

'His new friends, I'd say.'

'Who would they be, then?' But the man seemed to feel he had already said too much, shaking his head and backing away. Goodluck had to press further, trying his luck with other ideas. 'From the court, you mean? Those travelling with the Queen?'

'He had no friends at court,' Caradoc muttered scornfully.

'The others, then? The drinkers, the hangers-on, or perhaps those who came here this week to make money by their wits?'

Glancing back at the dead man, Goodluck frowned. His attention had been caught by something. A mere cat's whisker, it seemed, standing upright and tickling the edge of one bluish-white finger. He leaned forward again, and turned the man's stiffening right hand upwards. Sure enough, something was trapped under the broad gold band of his ring.

Slowly, Goodluck extracted the whisker and held it up to the strengthening light of day – a long, coarse, black hair, such as might be yanked from a man's head or beard in the throes of a struggle. It certainly had not come from the dead man's own head, since he had been fair.

'What's that?'

Goodluck tucked it into the leather pouch on his belt. 'Nothing. Go on, you were saying?'

But Caradoc had clearly decided that one drowned man was enough and he would not put himself in danger. He volunteered a comment about being late for his rounds, looked sideways down at the body and made the sign of the cross. Rather late for piety, Goodluck thought with a touch of asperity.

'Remember, nothing's to be said about this business,' he added, giving the man a shilling for his silence and bidding him be on his way.

But Goodluck knew the watermen would not keep quiet, nor the boy who had run for help, nor the handful of commoners now gawking over the tiltyard wall.

At least in this hood he could be anyone. Well, anyone with a beard, he realized, fingering it ruefully.

So, Goodluck reasoned, Malcolm Drury had found some new friends this past week, friends who were prepared to dig into their pockets in exchange for information. For who better to tell them the secret ways into the castle than one of the steward's men? A man with no pressing urgency to remain loyal to his lord when tempted by more gold than he had ever seen before.

Goodluck ordered the two waiting groundsmen to carry the body discreetly up to the castle, wrapped in sacking so as to disguise who it was. He dropped a few 'indiscreet' comments as he gave his orders, then walked back up the narrow path to the Watergate, secure in the knowledge that by the time the news of the death crept out, it would be claimed that Malcolm Drury had consumed a yard or two of ale, tripped over his own feet on the way home and ended up drowning in the mere. No one, it seemed, would mourn him. Least of all those who had arranged for the greedy and foolish Drury to meet his fate in this manner.

'You there!'

The boy walking ahead of him stopped and looked round, fear in his thin, pale face.

'Don't worry,' Goodluck said, giving him a smile. 'I won't bite. You were on the boat this morning when the watermen found him, weren't you?'

The boy nodded. He looked to be maybe eight or nine years old, barely grown enough to be working on the boats. It was, however, a demanding trade and best learned early.

'Tell me, were there any keys on his belt or about his person when your masters pulled him from the water?'

Warily, the boy shook his head.

'Perhaps one of the watermen took the keys – not to steal them but fearing lest they fall into the water,' Goodluck persisted. Still the boy shook his head. He tried another tack. 'Perhaps the other man took them, then. The one who came down to see the body before me, the chief steward's assistant. He wouldn't have allowed the castle keys to just lie there, on a dead man's belt, so he would have taken them away with him. That must be it, mustn't it?'

'There weren't no keys on that one, master. Nor when we pull him out, nor when the other man come down.'

Goodluck frowned, pretending to be confused. 'But . . . But he was working for the steward. He would have been wearing his belt of keys when he fell into the water.'

'There weren't no keys on his belt,' the boy repeated stubbornly. 'We would ha' heard tha jangle.'

Flipping the boy a coin, Goodluck smiled grimly to himself in the shadow of his hood and carried on up the damp slope.

A dead man, a missing set of keys, and a heavy gold ring on the wrong sort of finger: the mystery of how the Italian conspirators intended to enter the castle was becoming clear at last. Yet one thing still bothered him. Even if they had the key to every chamber in the royal apartments, how in God's name did they plan to get past the guards and into the inner court?

# Thirty-three

THE MIRROR IN ELIZABETH'S HAND SHOWED A PALE, POCKMARKED face, stripped now of her whitening paint, the short spiked hair on her head like that of a demented baby. She stared down at herself, her dry lips trembling, her eyes wide – still alert, with the watchful gaze of the young woman she remembered. Without her bright wigs, her potions, her jewelled gowns, the trappings of princedom, what was she but an ageing hag, a foul-breathed creature any man would pass by in the marketplace and shudder to imagine beside him at night?

Hating what the cruel light revealed, she threw down the gilt mirror so sharply that it cracked. She blew out the candle. Two candles remained lit, one by her curtained bed and another at the high window, flickering against lead-marked glass like a malevolent star. At least that one was far enough away not to be a threat to her beauty.

'Leave me,' Elizabeth said hoarsely, watching as her women curtseyed and filed out of the room. All except Mary, who was turning down the covers and preparing to rest on the narrow truckle bed that stood at the foot of the Queen's bed. 'You too, Lady Mary. Go sleep with your husband. I swear, you will be more comfort to Henry tonight than to me.'

'But it is my turn to watch over you, Your Majesty.'

'In God's name, I do not need someone to "watch over me" as though I were a child and might hurt myself in my sleep,'

Elizabeth snapped, pointing rigidly at the door. It was important not to appear too excitable, lest one of them suspect. Though of all her ladies-in-waiting, Lady Mary was the least likely to betray her. 'Now leave me, I pray you, and bid the others not to enter this chamber until morning, under pain of death. I wish to be *alone* tonight, and wholly *undisturbed*. Do I make myself plain, madam, or must I go out there and repeat that to every fool in the outer room?'

Lady Sidney curtseyed low and withdrew at once, though her face was troubled. 'I understand, Your Majesty,' she murmured, closing the door behind her. Its loud click seemed deafening in the silence which followed.

*I understand?*

How was that to be taken, pray?

From the busy Privy Chamber next door, Elizabeth heard urgent whispers that eventually died to nothing, leaving the night quieter and more still than any she had known since her arrival here. She turned away from the door and took a few paces towards the uncurtained window, stopping just short of the glass. She did not wish to be seen from outside.

My ladies will have gone down to their own sleeping quarters on the floor below, she thought, and Mary to her loving husband Henry. Only the guards would be left now, standing at arms in the dark and empty antechamber. It must be after midnight, she realized.

Her body ached with tiredness, though her mind was still racing, turning over the day's events with pleasing alacrity. Her brain at least was still as young and fresh as ever. Her arms trembled though from being stretched out for so long while the women disrobed her, and her legs ached too.

Elizabeth took up her night wig, the one reserved for when she expected visitors, and placed it carefully on her head, smoothing down the straight red tresses as best she could without the aid of her women.

She tidied her French lace nightgown, rearranging its white ruffles to be more revealing, climbed into bed, and leaned across to blow out the candle on her bedside cabinet. The one still burning in the window threw a pale light across the chamber. Sitting up in her high curtained bed, with the embroidered drapery pulled back to the far edges of the poles, she set herself to watch the furthest corner of the room where the shadows lay darkest. Then she waited, white hands folded neatly in her lap like the coyest of virgins.

Time passed slowly. Elizabeth sat upright with a jerk, realizing that she had dozed off. Staring hard at the shadows, she knew that she was no longer alone.

'Robert?'

A panic possessed her when her visitor did not reply. Her eyelids flickered as a man stepped forward.

She was ready to cry out, to summon help from those sleeping in the outer chamber and her personal bodyguards in the room beyond.

But it was him. She saw the outline of his broad shoulders, and knew at once the light, dancerly grace with which he walked, the sense of purpose. Sexual excitement caught at her breath, made her heart thud loudly. It had been nearly three years since he had visited her at night – it was always such a risk; the scandal of the Virgin Queen discovered *in flagrante delicto* would rock her throne – and the possibility that her favourite had come to make love to her, to make *sure* of her, left her both flushed and light-headed.

'You know who I am,' he said softly enough, but with a strange tension in his voice. 'Unless you did not receive my note?'

'I received a note from one of my more impertinent subjects,' she replied coldly, keeping control, refusing to rise to his bait, 'letting me know I could expect the intrusion of his presence in my bedchamber long after a time when such visits could be deemed acceptable.'

Robert had stopped at the foot of the bed, and was looking down at her. She thought his eyes quite wild, hooded in darkness, with a tiny reflection of the candle flame burning in each of them, hot and staring.

God's death, was she in danger from him?

For one terrifying moment she caught the glint of what looked to be a weapon in his fist. She sat bolt upright against the pillows, groping beneath the coverlet for the little jewelled dagger which

Walsingham had advised her to keep always at hand in her chamber. Her heart juddered violently.

Could her darling Robert be the unknown courtier-assassin Walsingham had warned her of?

Then he tossed a golden locket on to the bed. 'Take it back!' he said sharply, and Elizabeth realized with a shudder of relief that he was merely angry, not there to plunge a knife into her heart.

She did not reach for the locket, nor even look at it. There was no need. She knew what it contained. Her miniature and his, facing each other like husband and wife in their tiny gold frames. She held herself stiffly, meeting the anger in his face with some of her own.

'How dare you speak to me like that? Have you forgotten that I am your queen?'

'As queen, how could you stoop to such a petty act? And put the life of one of your own ladies in danger, to boot?'

She cradled her cold hands together in her lap, hiding the fact they were trembling, and silently thanked God for the darkness of the night.

'I have no idea what you mean.'

'Don't lie to me, Elizabeth. I know you too well for your politic deceptions to work.' His bitterness rang out like sparks from flint. 'You had Essex informed of his wife's *indiscretion*, did you not?'

'Oh, that.'

'Yes, that.' He was suddenly next to her on the bed, grabbing at her thin hands, pressing them into his chest. 'I never believed you capable of such a terrible deed, Elizabeth. You of all people. You know Essex will kill her for this, don't you? The man is a sadistic bastard. After what your father did to your mother—'

'Silence!'

'How can I remain silent? You have all but condemned that poor woman to death, and for what? Some paltry act of revenge – because I've looked at her sideways a few times, instead of crawling after you on my knees as I ought to have done, scraping up whatever crumbs you deign to throw down for me.'

'Let me go,' she insisted, trying to pull her hands away, but without any real conviction.

The heat came and went in her face. She must remain in control, whatever happened. She could not allow this man to bully her over her decision to send a secret envoy to Lord Essex. What was she meant to have done, after all? Allowed the two of them to continue their affair right under her nose, making her the laughing stock of the court? No, by God, not as long as she had breath in her body and the strength to do what was right.

She tried to sound stern and chaste but the touch of his hands, and the secret isolation in which they finally found themselves, were weakening her resolve.

'Get out of my bedchamber, my lord Leicester, or I shall call my guards and have you arrested!'

'No, you won't,' he replied icily, and she knew that he was right.

With an oath, Robert leaned forward, seized her painfully by the shoulders and ground his mouth against hers.

She felt the man's fury and resentment, and responded with an almost instinctive female submission, lips opening to admit his tongue, hands trying to placate him with caresses. He ignored those acts of surrender and continued to kiss her with a ruthless lack of regard for her rank, hurting her and leaving her in no doubt of his anger.

Elizabeth gasped under his mouth when he jerked her white nightgown down to her waist, tearing the fine laced garment at the seams. He told her brusquely to 'Be quiet!' and bent to slide his mouth hotly over her shoulder, then across the swell of her breasts. She realized that Robert intended to take her like a whore, without any attempt to woo her or excite her senses first. That would be a fitting revenge for her cousin's exposure as an adultress.

'Why?' he was muttering under his breath. 'Why do such a thing? What has Lettice ever done to harm you?'

He thrust her back against the pillows, and for a moment she delighted in his brute force, the wrench of his hands on her bare skin. To be free of the restrictions of princedom at last, to do what other women did in the darkened privacy of their bedchambers ... The pleasure of such a freedom was worth twice the pain he would inflict on her.

'Is this how it started with Amy?' he demanded suddenly, dragging her wrists above her head. He stared down at her naked breasts as they rose with the action, the stretch of her skin over her ribs, then he slowly raised his gaze to hers. 'Tell me truthfully, will the Countess of Essex be next to meet with an unfortunate *accident*?'

Elizabeth gasped, deeply shocked by the insinuation. 'What do you mean by that?'

'You have denied it and denied it,' he continued raggedly, 'but I know you were behind her death. The evidence is irrefutable, Elizabeth. Did you think I wouldn't pay for a copy of the coroner's report? Two deep puncture wounds to her head, made by a sharp instrument, and then her cap replaced to hide the marks from her servants. Oh yes, you may well stare. It's been over ten years and still I think of her, my poor wife, her body broken at the foot of those stairs, her murder unavenged. And Amy's *fault*?' He gasped on the word, his eyes cold and hard as an executioner's. 'She loved her faithless husband too much.'

'You truly believe that I would—'

'It was lucky for you that I was not nearer to home at the time, and that a good friend of mine was foreman of the jury, or you might have lost your would-be husband to the axe. I know it all, I have spent years speaking to those who were there, piecing the puzzle together. You arranged for it to be covered up, didn't you? For Amy's death to be reported as an accident, and the jury paid off in my favour.'

She could not deny that part of it. 'For you,' she managed in a whisper. 'I did it for you, Robert. Cecil told me . . . that is, he believed you had . . . that you had ordered her murder yourself. I could not bear to see you brought to trial and executed. Not when I knew you must have done it for me. So we could be married.'

'Murder my wife so I could marry the Queen?'

He threw back his head and laughed, and she was suddenly afraid for her safety again, seeing the ugly look on his face. Not that she could summon her bodyguards, for to draw attention to Leicester's presence in her chamber at this hour would be tantamount to admitting to the entire court – and the rest of Europe – that they were lovers.

'Even if that were truth,' Robert continued, 'her murder won me nothing but another ten years of waiting at your chamber door.'

'I gave no order, Robert. Your wife's death was none of my doing.'

'Then whose?'

Elizabeth licked her dry lips, not knowing how to placate him. Perhaps it would be better not to try? Even a headstrong horse might be brought to stand again with a spur and whip.

'I do not know.'

She wrenched her hands free of his grasp before he understood her intention. She pushed herself to a sitting position, not bothering to cover her nakedness.

'But you must understand, Robert, that you have done nothing to make yourself liked at this court. Lesser men both hate and fear you, and there are still those among your peers who would rejoice to see you fall. Not merely from influence, but under the axe itself. And much of that unpopularity you brought on yourself by hanging too close about me and denying power to other men who offended you in some way.' She raised a cold, level gaze to his face, hoping he would see the innocence in her expression, hear it in the steadiness of her voice. 'Yes, I knew your wife had been murdered. But until this moment I suspected you to have had a hand in that terrible business yourself. Now that you swear you are not guilty of Amy's murder, I can only assume it was one of your enemies who ended her life. Someone who would benefit from seeing you discredited in my eyes.'

'One of *our* enemies,' he corrected her, but the fierce light in his eyes had died away. He said softly, almost to himself, 'Poor Amy.'

Jealousy bit into her like a whiplash and she leaned back on her pillows again. Her movements were slow and deliberate, and she triumphed to see how his gaze was drawn instinctively to the sway of her naked breasts. Why suffer under the sting of jealousy? His wife Amy Robsart was long dead and buried. Lettice Knollys was an adulterous whore who could offer Robert nothing but her already well-used body. Lettice could not provide him with a throne, nor even the comfort and stability of the marriage bed.

These were the things Robert hungered for. Yet she, Elizabeth, was Queen of England, and her chosen consort would be king.

'Poor me,' she murmured in response, gazing directly at the firm, sensual line of his mouth.

His attention snagged and held like a fisherman's line. Robert drew a shuddering breath and placed his hand on her breast. 'You are so very beautiful.'

'You like what you see?'

'I am dazzled.'

'Still my keen Master of the Horse, ready to break even the most wayward mare to bit and bridle?' Her smile tightened as he stroked her nipple with one callused thumb; she could not help the cattiness of her taunt. 'Unless, that is, you are too exhausted from your travails elsewhere, my lord?'

He lifted his gaze to her face then. There was a hard flush along his cheekbones. 'Travails?'

'Lettice Knollys,' she whispered.

His eyelids flickered, but Robert said nothing. Instead, he leaned forward and touched the tip of his tongue to her nipple, a tingling shock which ran through her. Then he began to lick and tease her nipples so slowly and delicately, moving from one to the other, that she had to bite her lips to prevent herself moaning aloud with frustration.

'You mean the Countess of Essex?'

'She changes lovers so frequently, I forget which name . . .' Elizabeth clutched at his dark head. 'Oh, Robin!'

The candle at the window flickered, about to go out. He kissed her slowly, caressing her breasts, her belly, leaving her dizzy and trembling.

'Lettice means nothing to me. She is a distraction, nothing more. A game I play, while I wait for you to say yes. The countess is a married woman, you have said it yourself.' He seemed to hesitate. 'I will not miss her if she leaves court.'

His hand sought the apex of her thighs, too bold, too headstrong, and she slapped him away.

'You think I should dismiss her?'

'I think you should let me make love to you.'

She laughed into his shoulder at that, and grew bolder herself, stroking down his own body. 'You forget the etiquette due to your prince, my lord.'

'If you were a prince, my love, I would not be here.'

'Your queen, then.'

'Oh, we are too familiar to stand on such stately ceremony. How many years has it been since first I kissed you?'

'Do not speak of it,' she hissed, hating to think of the lines on her face and hands, her sagging breasts, how she could not even wear her own hair in bed with this man. 'We are young and this is spring, our May flower, our cuckoo-time.'

'You have only to wish it for it to be true. The clock on the tower has been stopped for you.'

Soon, he climbed on to the bed and lay beside her in the glimmering darkness, dragging away the covers to reveal the rest of her body. She ought to have been afraid of her women hearing them and coming to find out what the noise was, but there was room for nothing in her mind but desire. She saw the flattering bulge at his groin and reached for his lacings, impatient to stroke and kiss him as he had done with her. Robert helped her at first, laughing at her clumsy eagerness. Then he fell silent as she wrapped her fingers about him, squeezing his swollen shaft like a hen's neck at Christmas, just as he had taught her last time.

She wanted to lower her mouth to him too, but did not quite dare, in case he thought her shameless and pushed her away.

His eyes lingered on her face a moment, then surveyed her breasts, the slender curves of belly and hips, and her sex, sparsely covered with reddish curls.

'I love you,' he said thickly.

His passion thrilled her, a flush mounting in her cheeks as she looked back at him with equal intensity. 'Robin, Robin . . . my lover, my true oak.'

Their eyes met, then she allowed her thighs to slip open and part, her acquiescence unspoken. This time, unlike every other time they had lain together like husband and wife, there was no talk of protections against a pregnancy, and Elizabeth found she did not even care.

The lightning realization crossed her mind: if he got her with child, who would dare delay their marriage?

Then he was on top of her, fumbling between her thighs for the entrance, not even bothering to undress himself or her, urgent as a boy at his first mounting, eyes closed, his breathing fast and shallow.

'Elizabeth,' he groaned, and in response she gave a sharp cry, half in fear, half excitement, for suddenly he was there, nudging between her damp thighs, pushing his length inside her. His hand came forcefully across her mouth to stifle her cry and too late she remembered the women sleeping on the floor below, the men on guard in the antechamber.

She bit down hard on her lip. To be disturbed now . . .

'Yes,' he muttered, as though she had spoken, and removed the gag of his hand. 'My sweet obedient queen.'

'My only master,' she whispered back, her arms linked about his neck. She whimpered with satisfaction as he began to thrust, the bed creaking and rocking beneath them.

Afterwards, lying together in heavy-limbed torpor, he kissed her throat, her mouth, stroking down the line of her belly to between her relaxed thighs.

His deep voice rumbled in her ear, slow with sated pleasure. 'My love, what if there should be a child from this?'

'Then we shall marry.'

'You swear it?'

'On my life.' She felt him sigh beside her, and stretched luxuriously, her voice tailing off into sleep, unable to keep her eyelids open an instant longer. 'You are the only man I have ever wanted, Robin. The only . . .'

# Thirty-four

'YOUR MAJESTY, THE PHYSICIAN IS HERE.'

Elizabeth turned her head on the pillow, and felt another flush of fury at her own weakness. To be reduced to this feeble state by a few hours of physical pleasure was nothing less than a humiliation, a divine punishment for her lasciviousness that she could stomach no longer. For surely this pain and bleeding must be a sign from God that such activities were forbidden? Yes, the message was clear: the body of an unwed queen was sacrosanct and not to be invaded by any man, even he to whom she had all but promised herself.

She groaned, closing her eyes at the thought of what she had told Robert as they lay together in pleasure – the foolish, impossible promises she had made the man.

'Send him in.' Her fury lent a much-needed strength to her voice. 'Then everyone else, out. Except for you, Lady Mary. You will remain and see to my comfort.'

'Yes, Your Majesty.'

The man who approached her bed in a plain brown doublet and hose was unknown to her. When he saw her awake and gazing on him, he bowed so low, his nose almost brushed the floor.

'Your Royal Majesty, I am honoured to be called to your bedside. Whatever I can do to alleviate—'

'Where is *my* physician?'

236

Lady Mary stepped forward. 'He is unwell, Your Majesty. Both he and his assistant. They had fish for dinner last night which may have been unfit to eat.'

'Fools!'

'This man is Master Boden. He is Leicester's own physician here in Warwickshire. He serves both Kenilworth and Warwick, where I am told he administers to the Dudley family. He comes very highly recommended, Your Majesty.'

The local physician bowed again, wringing his simple cap in his hand.

'I will not be attended by a stranger!'

'Your Majesty,' Lady Mary murmured in her ear, 'you are not well and must be seen.'

'It is beneath the dignity of a prince to . . .' Elizabeth began to protest, then groaned between her teeth, unable to suppress the sound entirely, racked by another violent spasm in her belly. 'Very well, he may attend me. But first he must swear to secrecy.'

'Your Majesty, I have already sworn never to reveal—'

'You will swear again, in my presence.' She motioned Mary to fetch the English Bible from her bedside table. 'Place your hand on this Bible, sir, and swear by all that is holy not to speak of the matters we discuss to any living soul, now nor in years to come, on pain of your death.'

He swore the oath exactly as she had told it to him, repeating its terms in a shaky voice. When he lifted his hand from the Bible, a sweaty imprint of his fingers was left behind.

'Now, sir,' she muttered, 'you may examine me.'

He hesitated. 'Your ladies . . .'

'Lady Mary here will attend me. I need no other.'

Master Boden laid down his cap meekly enough and stood at the bedside, looking over her with careful, watery blue eyes. He was a tall man with a pronounced stoop, perhaps from years of bending in just such a manner over the bedsides of his patients.

His hands trembled as he folded back the edge of her rich coverlet. He hesitated, hardly daring to lift his gaze to her face.

'What ails Your Majesty?' He must have caught her sudden uncertainty, for he added hurriedly, 'I cannot treat that of which I know not.'

She gave a stiff nod. 'I bleed. From below.'

'I see.' The physician seemed to need a moment to digest this information, glancing from her to Lady Mary Sidney. 'Is it not merely your monthly courses?'

'They are not due for another ten days.'

'I see,' he repeated, licking his lips. 'In that case, I have no choice but to examine you. Do I have your consent, Your Majesty, to . . . to make a proper physical examination?'

She nearly baulked at that, not wishing to have any man, and in particular a stranger, examine her in such an intimate manner. Though perhaps it was as well not to involve her own physicians, who would be believed if they spoke out of turn. This man was just humble enough to have his word doubted.

Determined to get through this unpleasant trial as quickly as possible, Elizabeth nodded her consent.

Heavy-handed, the physician signalled Lady Mary to help him pull back the thick embroidered coverlet. The two of them folded it down to the foot of the bed but did not comment on her exposed bedsheets, crumpled and stained from last night's passion. Lady Mary moved silently to Elizabeth's left-hand side, as though to protect her from the sight of anyone who might dare to walk unannounced through the door to the Royal Bedchamber.

The physician asked Elizabeth a series of delicate questions about her symptoms, which she answered in a monotone, keeping her replies short and evasive. Then he begged her pardon most humbly and asked if Mary could pull up the Queen's nightgown so he might examine her more thoroughly.

This request she denied, her cheeks flushed with anger, finding herself unable to agree to such a humiliation.

'Forgive me, Your Majesty,' he muttered, bowing his head to examine the bloodied sheets instead.

'Oh, hurry up!'

'As you wish, Your Majesty. This was not . . .' Master Boden paused, looking up at her awkwardly. 'This was not your first . . . *occasion?*'

She did not look at Lady Mary, though she heard the woman's shocked intake of breath. Robert's sister might be quiet and placid about court but she was no fool and must have grasped by now to what the physician was so obliquely referring.

'No,' she admitted flatly.

'I see.' No doubt sensing her anger, he straightened and nodded to Lady Mary to replace her bedcovers. 'That is all I require, Your Majesty. Tell me, have you experienced bleeding on previous occasions?'

'To some degree, yes.'

He considered this response for a moment, washing his hands in the gilt-edged bowl Lady Mary held out to him. He dried his long fingers on a white damask cloth which he then dropped carelessly on to the coverlet, the sight of its reddish-brown stains leaving her light-headed.

'It is not unknown for some women to suffer in this way, though it is always unfortunate in . . .' He glanced at her and then away, and again she felt some covert insolence in those watery blue eyes. 'In a *married* woman, who must endure copious blood loss in order to conceive. Was there any discomfort or bleeding at the time?'

'Not that I noticed.'

'And how long does this blood loss and physical weakness endure?'

'A few days, sometimes more.'

He began to ask another question, but Elizabeth brushed it impatiently aside.

'What is it that I am suffering? Can you treat it?'

'From the symptoms you have described, Your Majesty, and my own rather cursory examination today, the only possible treatment is abstinence.'

*Abstinence?*

Elizabeth had not missed the sternness and disapproval in his voice, and knew the physician was judging her. Guilt at her own deceit and wanton lasciviousness warred inside her with the violent desire to have this little man, this nobody, imprisoned for his insolence in presuming to judge *her*, Elizabeth Regina, the anointed Queen of England.

'You will give me nothing for the bleeding? I must get up, I cannot lie about here all day so uselessly.'

'Your women can bind you about with cloths, just as they would for your monthly flow of blood, so that you may rise from your bed. And I can bleed you. Though in my experience, this has little good effect on a woman in your state.' He shrugged. 'There are also some purgatives I can prescribe, that my apothecary will make up for you before I leave. But as for the pain and weakness you describe, they clearly derive from some problem of the female anatomy.'

Master Boden coughed delicately and looked away, as though Elizabeth had been found to have some terrible deformity.

'I can do nothing for that condition, Your Majesty, which must be borne as the Lord intended. But in the meantime,' he added, turning to his medicine chest, 'I have to hand a powerful infusion of my own devising, of wormwood and other cleansing plants, which will balance the humours and instill such a feeling of well-being that Your Majesty may go about your duties unremarked.'

'Very well,' she muttered, determined to regain her composure. She gestured Lady Mary to remove the unpleasant physician from her sight. She had heard enough of his gloomy prognostications. 'Leave a bottle of it with Lady Sidney. She will give you the proper remuneration for your pains. And do not forget your oath of silence, Master Boden, on pain of death. You will be watched.'

Later, standing by her window watching rain spatter against the thick leaded glass, Elizabeth heard Robert's voice raised in enquiry outside in the Privy Chamber. The chamberers were bustling about behind her, changing the soiled sheets and laying fresh rushes.

At the sound of his voice, her heart began to beat as rapidly as a girl's in the first flush of love, and she put a hand to the stone sill to steady herself.

But there was also fear in the pounding of her heart – a deep nagging fear that gripped her like an iron glove and refused to let go. *He must not know.* She dreaded the thought that Robert might come to hear of this abnormality, these horrific bouts of bleeding and pain, that he might discover she was *unfit* for proper relations between husband and wife.

The very idea of talking to him of such matters mortified her almost to the point of death.

No, Robert must *never* know.

The door to her bedchamber opened a crack, and through that tiny gap she caught a glimpse of a crowded Privy Chamber, the whisper and rumble of subdued voices as the courtiers outside waited for her to emerge. Then Lady Mary Sidney slipped back into the room, her white-capped head demurely bent, her silk skirts rustling. Lady Mary ignored the busy chamberers gathered about the bed and came straight to Elizabeth's side. Her curtsey was low and respectful as ever, but Elizabeth was irritated to catch a flicker of something else in her placid face as she straightened.

Excitement? Pity?

Lady Mary had always been one of the most priggish, self-righteous women at court, though she could not fault Mary's loyalty to the throne nor her devotion to duty.

'My brother, Lord Robert, is outside in the Privy Chamber and would speak with you urgently, Your Majesty.'

'Urgently?'

'So he says, Your Majesty.' Lady Mary lifted cool, dark eyes to Elizabeth's face, eyes which reminded her strikingly of her own darling Robert's – though far less knowing and ambitious. 'I have informed him that you are indisposed and will not see anyone until tonight, including him.'

'And what did your brother say to that?'

She gave a little smile. 'Lord Robert was not pleased, Your Majesty. Not pleased at all.'

Turning her face into the pillow, Elizabeth closed her eyes in defeat. Robert would not comprehend her refusal to see him, yet she could not allow him to know of this physical weakness, to witness it for himself and know that he had caused it. The physician was right to suggest she was malformed in some way; she had feared as much herself since she had first begun to bleed, however much her dear nurse Kat had told her not to concern herself, that all women suffered in the same way. Now this pain and lethargy – no, she could not countenance such a life, having to staunch the bleeding each time she lay with her new husband

and consort, to lie abed for days when the business of state required her to be up and seen about the court.

'Where is Lady Essex?' Elizabeth remembered to ask a while later.

She had sat up at Mary's insistence, strangely restless, with a dull ache in her belly, to take half a cup of the physician's foul-tasting herbal infusion. The curtains had been drawn about her bed to block out the light, and she had to remind herself that it must be nearing the middle of the day, though the continuing rain made the room dark and chill.

'Is she in the Privy Chamber with the other women?'

She disliked not knowing what was happening beyond the closed doors of her bedchamber. Now that Robert had removed himself from her apartments, his repeated demands for admittance ignored, she could not help but worry that he and Lettice must now be closeted somewhere privately.

Mary tilted the infusion to her lips once more, her face unreadable in the dim light. 'Lady Lettice is unwell, Your Majesty.'

'Unwell?'

'She too did not rise from her bed this morning, I am told, and cannot keep anything down.'

Elizabeth stared, her heart tightening with an inexorable agony. *Cannot keep anything down?* The terrible possibility that Lettice was with child by Robert came back to haunt her.

Abruptly, she remembered a brief private letter sent to her from Ireland: Lord Essex's terse request had been that his wife should be sent home from court to tend his younger children in his absence. Elizabeth had ignored his letter, for she disliked being told how to order her own ladies, however much she might relish the thought of banishing Lettice to the depths of the country. Besides, it had seemed politic to keep her red-haired cousin close by, where her spies might more easily watch both her and Robert. It was not beyond the bounds of belief, after all, that Lettice could make a play for the throne, given the right allies about her.

But now she wondered if it was not too late, if her favourite had not already visited Lettice's bed – and carelessly made a child on the vile woman.

'Send her to me at once,' she told Mary.

'But, Your Majesty—'

'Do as I bid you.' Elizabeth knocked aside the cup with its few remaining drops of herbal infusion. 'And get this stinking privy water away from me. I will see the Countess of Essex this very day, even if she must be carried to my chambers on a litter.'

# Thirty-five

THE OLD WINE STORE HAD NOT BEEN USED IN SOME YEARS. 'EIGHT, AT least,' the steward's assistant, Caradoc, had told Goodluck, no doubt hoping it would make him less interested to see inside the old place. Instead, Goodluck's curiosity had grown and he nodded for the Welshman to show it to him. At the door, Caradoc fumbled for the correct key on his belt, muttering under his breath, shoving one after another aside with a jangle before coming to an ancient-looking copper key with a lozenge-shaped head and a flattened shaft. It reminded Goodluck of one he had seen for an old church crypt in London, the lock dating back several centuries.

'How long since this cellar was built?' Goodluck asked, looking at the squat, heavily studded door. 'Is it one of the oldest parts of the castle?'

'Not this, no,' the Welshman replied, his tone contemptuous. 'Though you'd have to ask the master steward for the dates. He'd know.'

Caradoc fitted the key in the lock and attempted to turn it. It would not budge. He removed the key, spat on it several times, then pushed it back into the lock.

Goodluck stepped back, angled his neck and peered up the sheer stone face of the castle proper. Small wonder Leicester had not expressed too much concern over this latest conspiracy. He could see from here how difficult it would be to effect an entry into the state apartments: the stones fitted so smoothly together, there were no gaps left for foot- or handholds, nor were the windows on this side wide enough to admit a man, even if a rope could be let down.

But if the conspirators were to enter the castle by some other means . . .

The door to the old wine store sat low in the wall, midway between the old building and the new. The old part of the wall was lichened and crumbling in places, and the fresher sandstone of Leicester's new construction stood gleaming in the sunlight, still bearing scoremarks from the builders' instruments. Someone's initials had been chiselled into the soft stone above a doorway and, rather higher up, a rude message about one of the labourers' wives.

'Ah, that's it now,' the Welshman grunted and, putting his shoulder to the door, got it open at last.

A waft of dank air blew out past their faces. They both stood and stared into the unpromising darkness.

Caradoc looked at Goodluck. 'What is it you think you're looking for, anyway?'

'I don't know.'

Caradoc gave a shrug and a shake of his head, as if to indicate that if Goodluck didn't know, he didn't know either.

'You'd best go in, then. Take a look around.'

Goodluck ducked his head and entered the chamber. There was a step down to a floor that was part stone, part sand and mud. The place leaked, clearly. Several stacks of old crates stood to the left of the doorway. He did not see them in the darkness, his eyes not yet adjusted after the bright sunshine outside, and he knocked some over with a clatter. Caradoc said nothing, but stepped over the fallen crates and pointed significantly up at the ceiling.

In the dim light from the open doorway, Goodluck could just make out a wooden hatch of some kind in the roof. There were no windows in the store, and he wondered if it had been intended for ventilation.

He asked Caradoc if he knew the reason, but the Welshman shook his head.

'Though I did hear that in the old steward's day,' he offered up as an afterthought, 'barrels were sometimes hoist up on a pulley into the room above, to save the men rolling them round to the back of the great hall. It's a steep slope out there, as you'll have seen. But that stopped about eight years back. They sealed up this old place and used the stores by the kitchens instead for keeping the lord's wine cool. Though why the hatch was put there in the first place, I couldn't say.'

'How would it have been opened?'

'From above, though there'd be nothing to stop it being pushed open from this side.'

'And is there any direct access to the state apartments through that hatch?'

Caradoc scratched his head, considering the matter. 'There's another storage room right above us, though it's just full of clutter these days. There's a corridor, then another storage room. And that leads into the new apartments. So yes, I suppose it would be possible to reach the state rooms from here.'

'Is the hatch kept locked?'

'I don't think so. But this door is.'

With his eye, Goodluck measured the distance between the ground and the unlocked hatch. It was not a high-ceilinged room, but was not low enough for the hatch to be reached without the aid of a ladder.

'The gate in the mereside wall,' he asked. 'Is it always guarded?'

'Only now, while the court is in residence,' Caradoc replied. 'The Queen's storeroom is in the base of the new building, holding all manner of precious goods and furniture, and must be guarded night and day. We passed the entrance on the way up here.'

His deep voice echoed in the empty wine store, rumbling about the walls. So the gate in the wall was kept guarded, to protect the Queen's storeroom just beyond it. This whole business was giving Goodluck a headache. It was one mystery after another, and none of the pieces fitted together. There was something he wasn't seeing, some piece of the puzzle he had missed. He thought of the odd loop of metal in Massetti's room, which he now took out of his pocket and showed to the steward.

'What do you make of this?'

The man frowned, taking a closer look. 'Could be a belt-ring. For attaching keys to a belt, like the one I'm wearing.'

He loosened the sturdy leather belt from around his middle. Hanging down from an iron ring was a thick, stubby chain, at the end of which dangled various keys to the castle. He held the broken piece of iron next to his own belt-ring. It seemed a likely match – or likely enough to satisfy Goodluck that the odd twist of metal was linked to Master Drury's missing keys. Caradoc seemed struck by this discovery, and a little suspicious too. He handed back the broken ring reluctantly.

'I'd lay a wager that's come from Malcolm's key-belt. Where did you find it?'

'Nowhere in particular.'

Caradoc looked at him sideways, bleary eyes narrowed. 'What's all this about, if you don't mind me asking?'

'I do mind you asking,' Goodluck replied tersely, as he stooped through the low opening again into the sunlight. He had seen enough of that dank hole.

Goodluck stood a moment on the steep grassy slope under the castle wall, staring over the bright waters of the mere towards the encampment at the Brays. Behind him, Caradoc swore and wrestled again with the recalcitrant lock.

Another dead end, or so it seemed to him. Even if they had murdered one of the steward's men to obtain the key to this door, the conspirators would soon find themselves out of luck if they tried to use it. For a start, they would need a ladder to reach the hatch. Then, there was a constant guard on the wall-gate down yonder, a gate designed to block folk from penetrating the inner defences of the castle where the Queen's most precious possessions were kept under lock and key. And while the newly rebuilt wall between the courts might be just about scaleable, the idea of an assassin struggling over a fifteen-foot wall with a ladder in his hand was laughable.

'Is that all you need to see?' Caradoc demanded, no longer bothering to be polite.

Goodluck followed him down the slope, unable to enjoy the feel of the warm sun on his face. For all he knew, time was running out, and yet he seemed no nearer solving this puzzle. Nor did he have any inkling which nobles at Queen Elizabeth's court might have instigated this latest plot, though he felt sure one or two at least must be involved.

'A good day to you then,' Caradoc grunted, letting him out of the narrow wall-gate. He gave the guard there a significant look, as though to indicate that Goodluck was not entirely to be trusted.

'Thank you for your help,' Goodluck murmured in polite reply. He doffed his cap and wandered off in search of some refreshing ale, the Welshman's suspicious gaze burning a hole in his back.

# Thirty-six

A MILE OR SO FURTHER ON FROM THE CHASE, THE BROAD PATH
through the woodland began to narrow, and soon the horses had
to trot close together under the fresh damp green of the trees.
Lucy kept her reins light, as Tom had shown her, and was glad
when he stopped pointing out her faults, riding stiff-backed
beside her instead. The breeze shook the branches above them,
sending raindrops scattering across the woodland track.

The first wild flowers of the summer had begun to wilt, Lucy
noted with a touch of sadness, and a few tattered beech leaves lay
on the grassy path, brought down by the sudden wind and rain of
the past night. It was the first sign she had seen that the summer
was more than halfway through. Soon they would be moving on
to Chartley, the Countess of Essex's stately residence – a beautiful
mansion by all accounts, though nothing like the vast expanses of
Kenilworth Castle. Not long after that, the progress would turn
and begin to make its way back to London, stopping at other
great houses along the way. Lucy did not think they were due to
return until September, by which time half these green leaves
would be sere and fallen.

Every few moments, Tom's knee knocked against hers on the
narrow track, though his face remained averted, his surly
apologies barely audible.

Her soft-mouthed mare, good-natured but greedy, nudged her
way towards a clump of rain-dewed grasses and yellow-flowered

plants at the side of the track. It was becoming warm again this deep into the forest, and they had been drilling outside the stables a good hour before setting off. No doubt her mare was tired and thirsty, as indeed she was too.

Out of sympathy, Lucy dropped her hands and let her mount bend to tear off a good mouthful of the damp yellow-topped stems and grasses.

'No!' Furious, Tom grabbed at her reins and dragged the mare's head away. 'What do you think you're doing?'

'The poor thing only wanted some grass!'

'That's not just grass.' He sounded exasperated. 'Do you want to kill your horse?'

She was stunned, staring down at the slim, yellow-flowered plants waving appealingly in the breeze. They looked innocent enough.

'*Kill* her?'

'Ragwort. It's deadly to livestock.'

He shook his head at her expression, and kicked his horse into a fast trot, still holding both their reins. Her mare was forced to keep up with his sturdy bay gelding, her tossing head and back-ward-flicked ears an indication of her annoyance at this unfriendly treatment.

Lucy held on to the saddle and jolted about uncomfortably. She looked dubiously at the horse beneath her. 'Will she die? I mean, she must have taken a good mouthful of the horrid stuff. Would that be enough to kill her?'

His smile was tight, almost contemptuous. 'No.'

'Oh look, can we stop?'

She had almost tumbled off as the mare stumbled over a stone.

By way of reply, Tom slowed his gelding with his knees and her mare followed its example. He handed back her reins only when they were walking sedately again, his face still surly.

'Why are you so angry with me?' she demanded.

He had the grace to look uncomfortable at least, a slight frown knitting his dark brows together. But he did not admit that he knew what she was talking about. Perhaps he tried to seduce young servants every day of the week, she thought with a sudden burst of fury. In which case, it was as well she had rejected him.

'We'd better get back,' he muttered instead, and made a great show of examining the patch of sky just visible above the tree-tops, as though trying to guess the time. 'I was told to have a number of horses groomed and saddled, ready for the Queen to ride out after lunch today. But no one came down from the state rooms this morning to let me know how many and which horses. So perhaps they are no longer needed.'

'Perhaps,' Lucy said airily, noting that he had not even attempted to answer her question. If Tom could ignore her so easily, she could ignore him.

They rode in awkward silence for a few moments, then Tom spoke again. His voice sounded troubled, quite different from the sharp tone he had used before. 'Did you hear about the man who drowned? Malcolm Drury, his name was. They're saying he got drunk and fell into the mere.'

She looked at him, surprised. 'I did hear something. Was he a friend of yours?'

'Malcolm?' He seemed shocked for a moment. 'Not at all. I don't think the man ever spoke to me. No – but it's not true.'

'What isn't?'

He steered her mare absent-mindedly round a young tree grow-ing in the middle of the track, then relaxed his hold on her reins, allowing the animal to pick her own way back across the uneven grassy verge.

'What they're saying about the way he died. You see, I happened to overhear my master talking to your guardian about it last night.'

'You mean Master Goodluck?'

He nodded. 'I should not have been eavesdropping, I know. But it was in the stables and they did not know anyone else was there, so I just kept quiet and listened. Your guardian told Lord Leicester that the man was drowned on purpose. Because of something he knew. But after I'd heard them talking about it, I remembered what you'd seen outside the stables. You said, "*The bear-tamer!*" '

Lucy shivered, despite the growing warmth of the afternoon sun. 'I know, I saw him in the distance. Or I thought I saw him. It was so dark.'

'Should we tell the earl, do you think?'

She stared, taken aback by his sudden interest. 'About me seeing the bear-tamer?'

'It might be significant.'

'And then again, I *might* have imagined the whole thing,' she pointed out, and added spiritedly, 'considering how rattled my nerves were at the time.'

He frowned and looked away, his back very straight, his mouth stiff. So that blow had hit home, she thought with satisfaction, and could not understand why she felt so tearful.

They were nearing the end of the track; through the trees ahead she caught a glimpse of high towers and the reddish stone teeth of the battlements. Soon they would be back inside the castle, and she would have to return to her duties. Her heart ached at the thought.

She had to be wary where Tom was concerned. He did not see why her virginity needed to be so carefully guarded; he merely desired her, and expected her to feel the same. What Tom did not know was that it had taken a huge effort of will not to give in to him that night – and finally discover why the other servant girls of her age enjoyed cavorting naked with men, shameless as cats in heat. But she had promised the Queen faithfully that she would keep her virginity safe – at least until she was respectably married, if ever that should happen – and Lucy intended to keep her promise.

As they neared the castle entrance, a servant stood waiting for them under the impressive archway of Leicester's new gatehouse, his pride and joy, just finished in time for the Queen's visit. He had even had Her Majesty's initials carved into the stone supports on one side and his own on the columns opposite, an impertinence which some said had left the Queen and her ladies gasping.

The servant ran to grasp Lucy's bridle. 'His lordship wants to see you,' he told her flatly. 'Now, in the music room.'

'Lord Leicester wishes to see *me*?'

Her voice was high with surprise, coming out almost as a squeak, and she felt heat in her cheeks as Tom reined in at her side and stared across at her resentfully. What was wrong with him now? Did he think she had engineered this excuse to escape her riding lesson early?

'Now,' the servant repeated sourly, without further explanation. No doubt he had been kicking his heels at the gatehouse a long while, waiting for them to return from their ride.

'When should I come back for my next lesson?' she asked Tom, slipping down out of the saddle as gracefully as she could manage, glad of the servant's helping hand at her back.

'You don't need any more lessons,' Tom growled.

She looked at him. Managing a lighter tone, Tom asked the servant to walk Lucy's mount back to the stables, then swung out of the saddle, landing lightly on his toes beside her.

'That is, you'll learn best now from just riding. We haven't had time to go over jumping, but it's unlikely you'll need to ride to hunt. And if you do, just remember to sit well back in the saddle and keep a short rein.' He fiddled with his horse's bit, seeming distracted, his face unreadable. 'Some follow the Spanish method and say it's easier if you lean forward on the jump, but if you follow that advice on an English saddle it won't be long before you're unseated.'

'Well, thank you for teaching me to ride,' she stammered, and heard the words fall hollow and empty in the echoing archway of the gatehouse.

*You don't need any more lessons . . .*

Her heart hurt as Tom cleared his throat and grimaced, not looking at her, though he inclined his head in acknowledgement. It seemed neither of them wanted to meet the other's eyes.

'It was nothing. Now you'd better run along and find out what my master wants.'

'Where is the . . . What was it again?'

'The music room.'

She looked blankly in the direction of his pointing finger, and he sighed, his voice hard and impatient. 'Through the first archway in the inner court. Now hurry. Every minute you delay, you are keeping the Earl of Leicester waiting.'

As if she wasn't already aware of that!

Picking up the heavy skirt of her riding gown, she fled through the puddles of the gatehouse, up the crowded slope of tents and makeshift camps, and over the bridge into the inner court. A small boy called out her name from the branches of a great oak, and she turned to look, almost tripping over a twisted root in the grass.

'Will?' She recognized the sweet, dark-haired boy who had lost his father that day in the tiltyard, and managed a quick smile despite her panic at being late. 'I'm sorry, I cannot stop and play this time. Is your father here?'

Will pointed across at a broad-shouldered man helping to right a tent which had fallen over, and she saw Master Shakespeare. Satisfied that Will was not alone this time, she waved a cheery farewell as she ran on.

Breathless, her hair trailing loose from under her white cap, Lucy burst through the door into the music room. The astonished lute player, a small man in a black velvet suit with very little hair and a black skullcap, immediately stopped playing.

'I'm sorry to be so very late, your lordship,' she gasped, hot-faced, closing the door behind her and forcing herself further into the chamber, 'but I was out in the woods on a riding lesson and the servant you sent to find me did not know where we had gone and—'

'Hush now, come and meet Master Oldham, who is going to teach you to sing a song which I have written for the Queen.' The earl took her by the arm and positioned her next to the lute stand. She had expected him to be angry at the delay, but there was a smile in his dark eyes. 'Master Oldham, this is Lucy Morgan, the singer I was telling you about.'

'Yes, my lord.' The man turned and looked her over with small, bright eyes in a wizened face. 'Stand straight, girl. Belly in. Chest out. And the head – no, don't tilt it backwards. You are not look-ing up at an angel!' He reached out and adjusted the set of her chin with long, parchment-dry fingers. 'Just so.'

He began to play and sing, teaching her the song Lord Robert had written, in a thin, reedy voice which still held power. Lucy listened and nodded, accustomed to committing new musical arrangements to memory in a short space of time. Master Oldham seemed pleased that she knew how to read music, and they progressed swiftly to her singing while he accompanied her on the lute.

The earl left them alone to finish the work. He returned to the music room about an hour later, and smiled at the sound of her voice soaring through the higher notes of the song. It was a beautiful little melody, poignant but strong too, a song of love and faith tested and still found good. Lucy thought Lord Robert must possess an excellent ear to have written such an intricate piece for the Queen, and wondered why he did not compose more often.

'Well done!' Leicester exclaimed as the song came to a close. He clapped his hands in praise. 'Will you be ready to perform it on Tuesday?'

'Tuesday?' She flushed, seeing both men looking at her expectantly, as though her opinion was somehow important. 'I . . . Yes, my lord, I think so.'

Leicester drew her aside as Master Oldham gathered his music sheets together. There was a look on his face she had never seen before, a sort of wild exultancy in his eyes, and his voice, though kept low, was not as discreetly quiet as she had grown to expect from him.

'I hear the Queen summoned you to her presence recently. Very early in the morning, so the matter must have been urgent. What did Her Majesty want? What did she ask you?'

'I . . .' She stared at him, unsure how to answer without betraying the Queen. 'My lord, please forgive me, but it is not right for me to repeat what the Queen has said to me in private.'

She expected the earl to be angered by her refusal, which – coming from such a lowly servant of the court – must seem the height of impertinence to a man of his power and influence. But to her astonishment, Leicester threw back his head and laughed.

'You women and your secrets!' the earl exclaimed, and the loudness of his voice made Master Oldham turn and stare, his look disapproving.

Leicester seemed oblivious to the impropriety of his behaviour. Instead, he compounded it by kissing her on the cheek, an unexpectedly intimate contact which left Lucy flushed and unsettled.

'Keep mum, then,' he said, dismissively. 'I can guess at Her Majesty's wishes. She has so few friends at court. Yet she is growing to trust you, Lucy Morgan, for you are so different from everyone else here. When she called you to her side, the Queen will have asked if I had spoken of her, if I had confided in you how much I love her.' He met her wide-eyed gaze. 'Is that not the case?'

Lucy bit her lip, knowing how very far he was from guessing the truth. Leicester seemed to take her hesitancy as a sign that he was right. He pulled at her white cap with playful fingers and laughed uproariously when she gasped and straightened it, backing into a rack of hautboys and knocking them to the floor with a clatter. His mood today was bright as a flame, warming the room and making it impossible for her not to laugh too as she bent to set the instruments upright again.

Master Oldham bowed low and left the room, his music sheets safely encased in a leather folder under his arm.

With a shy smile, Lucy fixed her cap over her unruly locks and looked wonderingly at the earl. 'You seem very merry today, my lord.'

'I am merry, it's true. But I have good reason to be. The best of reasons.' He paused, looking at her. 'Can you keep a secret, Lucy Morgan?'

She blushed at the deep note in his voice, then experienced the full force of the earl's attractiveness as he leaned closer, his smile so provocative, his dark gaze bent on her face.

She grasped at the lute stand for support, suddenly light-headed as though she had not eaten for days. She heard herself stammer, 'Of course, my lord.'

'Though you need not keep it long, for soon everyone will know.' Leicester came so close their bodies were almost touching. He lowered his face to her neck, his warm breath fanning her skin. 'The Queen and I are to be married, you see, before the year is out. We are in love and secretly betrothed.' His whispering voice shook, it was so thick with triumph and excitement. 'What do you say to that, my little songbird?'

Her heart hammered against her chest at the immensity of his secret, and for a few deathly moments she could not find her voice.

Unbidden, she remembered how Tom had touched her in the stables, the hunger in his eyes that had both frightened and

aroused her, and could not imagine the pale, stately Queen sub-
mitting to such caresses from a man. Not even from this man, as
handsome and powerful as he was.

But his lordship was waiting for an answer, so she smiled and
drew a trembling breath.

'I wish both you and the Queen happy, my lord,' she managed
at last, her eyes discreetly downcast so he could not see the doubt
in them. 'Very happy indeed.'

# Thirty-seven

STARING DOWN FROM THE WINDOW OF THE WOMEN'S APARTMENTS, Lettice shuddered at the Queen's shouts from above. She had been summoned to the royal presence, and had little choice but to dress herself and make her way upstairs to face Her Majesty, though her blood chilled at the thought of what might await her there. Lady Mary Sidney had sent a note down with a serving girl; brusque and to the point, it demanded that she wait on the Queen within the hour. The serving girl, shy and pretty in her clogs and neat white apron, had waited by the door while Lettice roused herself from bed, threw a light over-gown on top of her shift, and composed herself to answer.

'You may tell her ladyship,' she said calmly, 'that I shall attend Her Majesty as soon as I am well enough to rise.'

Fine words. But they meant nothing. She would be expected to go upstairs to the Privy Chamber and face the Queen whether she was fit to leave her bed or not.

When the girl had vanished back up the stairs to deliver her brave message and the door closed once more against the bustle of the outside world, Lettice went to the window. Outside the day was pale and rainy, an occasional breeze shaking the treetops. She could hear music through the floorboards. Someone in the royal chambers above was singing to the accompaniment of a lute. The high, ethereal notes drifted down through wood and stone, casting her out of herself for a few moments, letting her forget who she was and how precarious her position at court had become.

By God, but it had been so hot this July, until these recent rains. Now the weather seemed to be closing in again, making the days unbearable and the nights . . .

She ran a trembling hand across her forehead, which was running with perspiration. This room, which held nearly ten women at night, was high-ceilinged and not ungenerous in its proportions. But with so much flesh crammed together in one space, the mattresses lying almost end to end, it was no place for a sick woman. Not a sick woman of her rank, that was for certain.

Her lips tightened with anger. In her own home at Chartley she would be comfortable, with her own large bed, her sitting rooms and servants, and the extensive grounds where she loved to ride and play with her dogs and children. It was a place where, in her husband's continuing absence, she gave the orders and was obeyed. She would not be a servant in her own home, as she was at court. While Elizabeth remained on the throne, she would be forever taunting her with her power – and her influence over Robert.

The door creaked open. She turned to see Robert in the doorway, a strange look on his face.

'I heard you were sick.'

She perched on the broad stone lip of the window seat, trying to control the pitch and swell of her nausea with shallow breaths. It must be a girl she was carrying, she was always more sick with a girl.

'You know what causes it.'

His glance lingered on her belly a moment, hidden beneath the loose folds of the over-gown, then it rose to her face. He seemed pale, unsure of himself, and she suddenly realized what he had come to say. 'Lettice,' he began, as he came into the women's bed-chamber and half closed the door behind him, clearly keen not to be overheard. 'I need to speak to you.'

Lettice folded her hands in her lap, sitting as erect as she could with a sick belly. Her heart ached with a dull, nagging rage as she watched her lover thread his way gingerly between the scattered bags of possessions and the lumpy, straw-filled mattresses draped in white linen for the court ladies. Showing his age for once, Robert heavily went down on one knee to address her. With any other man, she might have thought he was about to propose marriage.

But his was not the face of a man who intended to honour his promises.

'Yes?' she prompted him.

Better to get this betrayal over quickly, she thought, wishing she could be elsewhere. A place where this bad news could not reach her. Her own cheeks must be pale too; they felt as chill to the touch as an alabaster tomb, and her heart had slowed to a distant, muffled thud, as though she were soon to die.

For a brief moment, Lettice considered the possibility of tears. Then she forced her trembling lips to be still, her gaze to reveal nothing. What use was emotion when it was powerless to turn this man's mind to her advantage?

'This child,' he muttered, and again his glance moved across her belly, 'I cannot acknowledge it. Nor will I challenge Essex for you on his return. To do so would be to risk a divided court.'

'A divided court,' Lettice repeated, restraining the sudden impulse to laugh at the feebleness of such an excuse.

'We are not yet safe,' he continued, head bent, speaking under his breath as though to justify his actions to himself. 'The country is riddled with spies and turncoats. Even at court we are surrounded by traitors to the crown – those who would seize any opportunity to destroy the peace we have built here in England since Elizabeth came to the throne.'

'And for this I am thrown aside?'

Robert made a helpless gesture. Yet he seemed genuinely torn by the choice he had to make, seizing her hand and carrying it to his lips.

'I love you, Lettice. I have sworn to it. But you are already married, and to a man whose power at court might rival mine in a fight. For us to quarrel openly – and that is what it will come to, if knowledge of this bastard you carry gets out – the court will have to choose sides. And once that happens, with the court split asunder, the country itself will be lost.'

'So my royal cousin has nothing to do with your decision to abandon me?' she demanded. 'It is all over politics?'

She thought he hesitated rather too long before answering. 'The Queen would not see me. I went to her bedchamber, to lay everything before her and beg her forgiveness, and she refused me admittance.'

'One of the women told me the Queen is sick.'

'A ruse, nothing more. To keep me out of her rooms. What else could it be?'

Lettice frowned, suddenly wondering if Elizabeth could be confined to her bed for the same reason she was sick this morning. The idea struck her in the belly like a dagger. A child? Had he managed to catch a child on that pale-faced weakling Elizabeth, whose monthly courses were more often absent than not? The past seemed to rush in on her and Lettice knew, with a terrible certainty, that what she had feared when they first came to Kenilworth this summer had occurred: Robert and the Queen had lain together once again, and made their lovers' vows in the darkness. And she had not had enough of a hold over Robert to prevent it.

Henceforth she would be out in the cold, a disgraced wife, an adulteress, bearing another man's child and without even the protection of a roof over her head, for as such her estate would be forfeit. Though without a doubt she would find a new home in the Tower soon enough.

Lettice stared down at the man before her, hating him suddenly, his bent head, his lame excuses. 'You get me with child, and then run back to Elizabeth like a schoolboy to his mother.'

'Hush!' He released her hand angrily, his dark eyes on the half-open door. She had spoken too loudly. 'This is nonsense, madam. You're unwell. You don't know what you're saying.'

'Does she promise to make you her lawful consort?' she hissed, lowering her voice again so only he could hear. 'Are you to be king now and rule over us?'

The earl rose and stared down from the leaded window at her back. 'You are a married woman. She is not. She is still available. God grant me strength in this, my love, but what would you have me do? Turn down her offer of marriage?' His voice broke. 'Do you know how many years I've waited, the prizes and desires I have given up in order to try my luck at her side?'

'She will never go through with it.'

He looked down at her. 'Yes, she will,' he muttered, and Lettice saw with another stab of horror how his glance dropped almost unwillingly to the hidden curves of her belly.

The Queen must be with child, she thought wildly. Her mind panicked, unable to come to any coherent idea without stumbling over the image of Elizabeth, married to Robert and dandling a newborn infant all wrapped in cloth of gold, a new Tudor prince for England.

She would never come within an inch of the throne if Elizabeth were to have a child.

Her despair at this horrific thought was so overwhelming, Lettice clutched her own belly and groaned.

'Should I fetch a servant?' Robert asked, staring at her in consternation. 'Or would you prefer the physician? There is a local man, Master Boden, wandering about the castle somewhere. I spoke to him earlier. Let me send him to you.'

'No!' She gave him her hand, and gestured him to help her stand up. 'I must see the Queen. She has sent for me, and if I do not attend she will take it amiss.'

'Your gown?'

'There, on the bed.'

He passed her the demure, dark-ribboned gown and helped her on with it, surprisingly adept at the task.

'Let me at least assist you up the stairs.'

Lettice straightened her gown and reached for her best slippers.

'No, my lord,' she told him straitly, making her way to the door. 'It is not seemly that you should help me. Not if you are soon to be my king. Tell me, has a date been set for the wedding?'

'Lettice, for the love of Christ—'

But she turned in the doorway, and was pleased with how coolly she spoke. 'Pray do not follow me, your lordship. The Queen's Majesty would not thank me for arriving with her own intended on my arm, however secret your betrothal.'

\*

The curtains about the royal bed had been drawn back, allowing a little light to fall across the red and gold coverlet and white embroidered pillows. The dark wooden headboard, ornately carved by some skilled artisan, featured woodland scenes that matched the elegant mantelpiece surrounding the hearth, with stags and foxes sniffing the air, and tall ivy-clad trees dripping with autumnal fruits. Someone had set a bowl of sweetmeats at the Queen's elbow and a twisted glass flagon of pale wine stood waiting on a side table, yet both remained untouched. On her way into the Royal Bedchamber, Lettice glanced at them discreetly. Perhaps Elizabeth was sick, after all?

The Queen was sitting up in bed when she arrived, the red and gold covers turned down, a fine gilt net stretched over her hair, her face in shadow.

Curtseying low to the floor, Lettice was forced to remain in that ignominious position until she heard Elizabeth say, 'Rise.'

Bent over, staring with a suitably humble gaze at the exquisite hand-woven rug by Elizabeth's bedside, she felt more nauseous than ever. But she hoped this act of submission would emphasize her obedience – even if it had taken nearly an hour for her to respond to the Queen's summons.

'I have been told that you are unwell, Lady Essex.'

The Queen snapped her fingers and one of the younger ladies passed her a gold-handled ostrich-feather fan, no doubt one of Robert's more lavish gifts to her on their arrival at Kenilworth.

Wafting the fan to and fro, she regarded Lettice from under thin, pale lids. The anger Lettice had heard from below – the shouting and the footstamps of fury – seemed to have passed, but a malicious fire still burned in Elizabeth's eyes. She reminded Lettice of an adder in the long grass, waiting to strike.

'I am very much recovered, Your Majesty,' Lettice murmured in reply, bending her head again. 'I fear some of the fish we enjoyed yesterday was unfit to eat.' Daringly, she raised her gaze to Elizabeth's face and added, 'You yourself have been in bed with a touch of sickness, I hear. Perhaps Your Majesty had the misfortune to take a little of the bad fish as well?'

Elizabeth's eyelids flickered but she said nothing, still watchful and unmoving in her high bed, though the feathery twitch of her fan was a constant irritation to the nerves.

'I am glad you are recovered,' the Queen said at last, as though finally reaching a decision, 'for I have some good news to impart to you.'

'Your Majesty?'

Whatever she had expected, 'good news' had not been on the list. Threats, fury, insults, even the order for her to be arrested and thrown into prison . . . All these Lettice had anticipated at this meeting. And indeed she would have accepted any punishment but the last as part of the price any lady at court must pay for playing so deep against the Queen herself. But this was something different, something she had not predicted, and Lettice stared up at her royal cousin with open unease and did not care who saw it.

'I have seen how much you miss your beloved husband, and now read from his letters that Lord Essex misses you too, his wife and the mother to his many charming children.' The Queen's smile was spiteful. 'So I have sent for him to return to England this very autumn. No doubt when we visit Chartley House you will wish to give your household orders to prepare for their master's return from Ireland.'

Barely able to stand, Lettice heard a rushing in her ears. Numb, she could no longer feel her feet. She swayed. But she must not fall. Not here, in the Queen's presence.

'Thank you, Your Majesty.'

'I knew you would be pleased at this news,' Elizabeth told her, leaning forward to allow her pillows to be rearranged. In the sunlight Lettice saw a cold satisfaction in the Queen's face. 'I have insisted in my letter that your husband should be back on English soil before the end of the autumn – indeed, as soon as he may be excused from his duties.'

'You are too kind to your humble servant, Your Majesty.'

'It is nothing.'

'Nonetheless, Your Majesty does us too much honour,' Lettice murmured, her voice lacking all emotion. She sank once more to the floorboards in a deep curtsey, wondering with a final flicker of hatred if her cousin was indeed pregnant by Robert, and how that state of affairs would be managed by the Council. It would certainly be open knowledge by the time they came to be married. 'I should like to write this good news at once to my daughter Penelope. The poor girl quite pines for her father. If Your Majesty would consent to excuse me?'

'As you wish.' The Queen nodded her permission, but added, from behind the languidly flickering ostrich fan, 'Pray do not remove yourself too long from our presence, though. I would watch you carefully, Lady Essex, to be sure that you are recovered from this mysterious "sickness" of yours. I will not have it said that we neglect the ladies of our court.'

'I am quite well now, I assure Your Majesty.'

'And I have said I am glad to hear it.' Elizabeth's smile did not reach her eyes. 'But you will stay within the royal apartments, if you please, where you will find most comfort. What would your husband Essex say if he were to come back from Ireland to find you confined to your bed?'

Lettice swallowed, hearing the sharp double meaning behind her cousin's question. She bowed her head. 'I will not leave, Your Majesty. Indeed, I am most grateful for Your Majesty's solicitude.'

Curtseying herself backwards from the Royal Bedchamber, Lettice made her way through the crowded Privy Chamber with as much dignity as she could muster, feeling unfriendly eyes upon her the entire way. Many at court must now suspect the dangerous lie of the land between her and the Queen, and would be drawing away from Lettice for fear of being seen in the wrong company. Robert himself, of course, was nowhere in evidence.

If only she were not so light-headed. This heat . . .

'Your ladyship?' The servant she had summoned bowed to hear her bidding.

'Fetch me pen, ink and paper.' She raised her voice for the benefit of the courtiers nearby, indicating a table near the window. 'Bring them to me there, and a cup of strong wine. Do not delay. I have good news from the Queen to send to my daughter.'

Then, slipping calmly out of the door, she passed through the guards unchallenged and hurried down to the women's quarters on the floor below. There was no one in the sunlit chamber.

Searching swiftly through her travelling chest, Lettice found the glass vial she had been keeping for just such a terrible moment. She pulled out the stopper with only the briefest of hesitations.

The vile stink of the slimy black liquid made her gag, but she put the tiny bottle to her lips and tilted back her head to receive the contents. Tears were running freely down her cheeks. She swallowed and nearly retched, controlling the impulse with an effort. It had to be held down.

Lettice hid the empty glass vial in her chest and closed the lid. Dizziness struck her as she straightened, and she stood a moment, sick and swaying. One hand at her belly, she gave a wild little sob. His unborn child! Yet what choice did she have?

# Thirty-eight

'WHAT'S THIS?' ELIZABETH ASKED, PEERING OVER THE BLACK-MASKED heads of the morris dancers as they lunged and leapt with their thick, ribboned poles.

The Queen had come back from divine service that Sunday the long way, stopping to speak to cottagers along the road and promising to lay on hands tomorrow, for those afflicted with a wasting palsy. The people called it the king's evil. She was not convinced, however, that the laying on of her hands would make any difference to those unfortunate souls. The commoners seemed to relish the ceremony though, and since Cecil had finally returned from home she knew that he would make her go through with it. Well, let them have their superstitions. There were some she held to herself, after all – though astrology had been proven a science now, not a superstition.

'A bridal, Your Majesty,' Robert said, stepping on to the dais.

The court had been herded into the narrow tiltyard after church, where a high-backed, richly cushioned seat had been set for her, and cushions strewn for her ladies to sit at her feet. Above their heads the gold canopy had been erected once again, its fringed shade welcome now that the dull weather of the past few days had broken once more into sunshine and deep summer heat.

He bent to her ear. 'This is a local bride and bridegroom, Jack and Bess, who were married in the village church earlier today and wish to celebrate their bridal before you and the court. Will you permit them to approach?'

This was better than laying on hands for the sick. Elizabeth beckoned to those leading the bridal procession, addressing the court. 'There is nothing pleasanter than a summer bridal. Let the wedding guests come before us and make their bows to the court. I shall speak to the bride myself. For though I have never been a wife, I understand a woman's duty to her husband, which is not unlike a prince's duty to his country.'

A party of groomsmen and bridesmaids came first, the men dragging off their caps at the sight of Queen and court, the girls pretty enough, their hair dressed simply with flowers, giggling as they led the bride forward to the dais.

The bride herself seemed oddly reluctant to be presented to the Queen. She came shuffling forward, whispering fervent denials to her new husband. She even held up a posy of rosebuds and sweet williams to hide her face. Perhaps she was worried that her wedding gown, clean but of a rough, green-dyed cloth, and plain except for the festive ribbons they had attached to her sleeves and waist, was not expensive enough to be worn before the Queen and court.

'Don't be shy, Bess,' the Queen encouraged her, leaning forward, her tone as reassuring as she could make it. 'You are my namesake and so are doubly welcome. Have a little courage, there's no need to hang your head. Bring your husband with you and let me bless your marriage before the court.'

What was wrong with the foolish girl? She was a little on the dumpy side, it was true, and perhaps older than Elizabeth had thought at first, but that was nothing to be ashamed of.

Then the bride straightened, flushed and anxious, a nervous smile on her lips, and her face was plainly seen. Elizabeth sat back with a stifled gasp, not knowing where to look. She felt every eye in the court must be turned towards her, watching for her reaction.

This local bride was no girl, but a woman of some thirty-five years – maybe older. Her face showed wrinkles, deep set about her mouth and brow, her nose plain as a pickle, her jaw sturdy and overlong, more like that of a horse than a woman, and as she smiled, it was clear she had lost most of her teeth. Facing her directly now, Elizabeth could see how thick-set this bride was, with no neck to speak of but a squat trunk on short legs, no waist for her new husband to grasp but hips broad as a doorway, and breasts so large she might almost have been ready to suckle her firstborn.

It would not have surprised Elizabeth to learn that this creature had given birth to several brats already, born out of wedlock, and each to a different man.

And her name was *Bess*?

Seeing the Queen's gaze upon her, the matron-like bride simpered and smiled, lips drawn back to display her few remaining teeth, for all the world like a mare cropping at a thistle.

Struggling to hide her fury at this affront, though her hands trembled and her face felt as stiff as a mask, Elizabeth signalled Robert to bend closer.

'Is this one of your ill-devised jests?'

'Your Majesty?'

'This creature is named Bess?' she hissed, for his ears only. 'This ancient, toothless bride is named for your queen, and presented in front of the whole court . . . ?'

Elizabeth could not finish her thought but swore viciously under her breath, her vision a dark red haze.

'By God, I shall not stand for such mockery!'

Robert was staring at her, his smile fading as he realized the extent of her fury. Behind her, Throckmorton cleared his throat and looked pointedly in the opposite direction, while Lord Burghley appeared bemused, as though he did not understand what the problem was. Some of the other courtiers were smiling behind raised hands and fans, none of them quite daring to laugh out loud but whispering to their neighbours instead.

Elizabeth stiffened. 'Remove her at once!'

Robert glanced swiftly across at Cecil, one of the few courtiers not smiling at this public humiliation of his queen, and a look passed between them.

Elizabeth waited, tapping her fingers on the arms of her high-backed seat. The court was eager to see which path Robert would take, the easy or the hard. The Queen was probably the only one there to understand what nerve it took for Robert not to obey her at once.

He bent again to her ear, his whisper urgent. 'Your Majesty has promised to bless their union. If it is not done—'

'Enough!'

He was right. Of course he was right. But now that he had spoken, it was vital that it must seem like her decision, not one her favourite had prompted. She waved him aside and raised a gloved hand, sketching the sign of the cross swiftly in the air before they could see she was shaking.

'May your union be blessed with good health, a long life and many children, God willing.'

Robert snapped his fingers as Elizabeth subsided into her seat, her face rigid, and the bridal procession moved on with a flurry of pipes and drums. The bride and groom glanced uncertainly at each other, but the young bridesmaids laughed again, flushed and excited at having been presented before the Queen.

Cecil was suddenly on her other side, sombre in his neat black suit and modest ruff. Elizabeth would have given much to know if he agreed with her on this public humiliation, but his face remained carefully neutral as ever.

'Will you stay to watch the bridal games, Your Majesty? There will be tilting between the groomsmen, I am led to understand, and a country dance to follow. And later the Coventry players will present a tragedy to the court. Or possibly a history.' He paused, looking carefully over her head at Robert. 'My lord Leicester will be able to correct me on this point, I imagine, for it is he who engaged the troupe.'

'I cannot recall—' Robert began in a ragged tone, but Elizabeth interrupted him, raising her hand.

'I shall stay to watch the tilt and the country dancing. Then the court will retire indoors to eat. Afterwards, the players may still perform their piece, but I shall watch from my window. For it is too hot to be outside in the afternoon heat.'

Eagerly, she gestured Cecil forward to her seat. 'I am glad you have returned to us, Cecil. I missed the wise counsel of my treasurer this past week. You have always been a true and loyal friend to your queen.' Deliberately intending to sting Robert, she smiled into the silence that followed, satisfied that her barbs were hitting home. 'How is your wife? Is your son Thomas here with you for his knighthood?'

'Indeed, Your Majesty. He is preparing himself for tomorrow's ceremony. And Mildred is in much better health, I thank you, though I fear she found the journey up here a little wearing.'

'Well, I shall be glad to honour your son tomorrow. He has done excellent service to his country, it is a pleasure to have such men about me. But where is Signor Massetti, where is Philip Sidney?'

Still furious with Robert, Elizabeth ignored his bruising stare and waved her fan, summoning the young Massetti to her left side and Philip Sidney to her right.

Massetti came wreathed in smiles, a swift Italian compliment ready on his lips, and she motioned him to kneel beside her. It entertained her to have Walsingham's new dog by her side, if only to see her spymaster frown at their extravagant conversation.

Lean, muscular and imposing in a silver-sable doublet and hose, Philip bowed and approached his queen with only the tiniest hint of a smile. It was clear he knew which way the wind blew, clever, discreet boy that he was. She took his hand in hers and patted it, fixing her gaze on his handsome young face as though there were no other man worth speaking to.

'Come, Pip, sit beside me a while. You know how I love to hear you tease the meaning out of everything.' She laughed, and made sure her laughter was heard by everyone on the dais. 'What did you think of the newly wedded couple there? I have been told you are quite the philosopher these days. Tell me, is virtue more important in a bride than beauty?'

Young Philip Sidney answered her questions with studied seriousness, launching into an intellectual debate on the comparison of virtue with beauty. Yet although Elizabeth smiled and nodded in all the right places, her attention was busy elsewhere. Her gaze followed the stiff back of her favourite as he stepped down from the dais and strode away into the castle.

She was incredulous, then suddenly furious again. How dare her host walk away before being dismissed? Robert had left the royal presence without asking permission, without so much as the respectful bow due to his queen. Was this to punish her for calling Massetti and young Pip Sidney to her side instead of him? She would grant him a peevish dislike of the smooth-cheeked Italian newcomer, but to become enraged that she had favoured his own nephew . . .

Oh, such boyish jealousy did not become an earl.

Pleased and piqued at the same time by his arrogant behaviour, Elizabeth considered sending after him to return to the dais, to humiliate him in revenge for this travesty of a bridal. But then she caught Cecil's eye.

No, her cautious-minded secretary was right. Better to chastise Robert in private, where heated words could be more easily exchanged without fear of being overheard. Besides, to call further attention to their quarrel now might be to suggest some odious comparison between herself and that ancient, toothless bride – a comparison she wished to avoid.

As Robert was about to pass through the shaded gateway into Kenilworth's outer court, she saw him halt, suddenly bending to speak to the young Moorish girl, Lucy. It was only the briefest of exchanges, just long enough to whisper a few words in her ear. Then he was gone, striding away beneath the shadowy arch of the gate.

'No, don't stop,' Elizabeth insisted, turning to smile flatteringly at Pip Sidney. He had paused in his speech, looking hurt that she had not replied to a question. 'I am all ears, my young Socrates.'

# Thirty-nine

LUCY SHIELDED HER EYES TO LOOK UP AT THE QUEEN, SEATED UNDER her gold canopy high on the wooden dais. She felt ridiculously hot in the stiff ruff and heavy-skirted gown they had given her to dance in, the thick row of stitches itchy where it had been altered to fit her broader shoulders. The court gown might be expensively embroidered, with a fine lace trim fit for a proper lady, but it was not as comfortable as the simple gowns she had brought from London. If it had not been so warm when she rose that morning, she would have worn a shift dress underneath. But after yesterday's thunderstorms, this fresh heat was almost unbearable, the wide blue sky above the tiltyard dazzling, and her gown was so tight at the waist she could hardly breathe. To have put more layers on underneath would have been to invite the embarrassment of a fainting fit, and she could tell from the Queen's sharp stare that such weakness would not go unnoticed.

The tilt games finally came to an end, with the victor being crowned with laurels by the Queen herself, and after a short pause a simple country dance began.

Lucy watched the dancers with a thundering heart, constantly dwelling on her own trial to come, her palms moist with sweat as she clapped to the beat. She had been told to change her gown and attend the Queen after Mass. The thought of having to dance before so many courtiers and commoners made her stomach knot with terror. Even though she had foolishly hoped to be called up

273

on to the dais to perform again before the Queen and court, she feared it almost as much as death itself.

Glancing about her, she caught a glimpse of Tom's dark head and leather-clad back near the gateway into the outer court. He was leading a bay horse slowly back towards the stables; it appeared to be lame. As she stared, desperate for him to turn round and see her, Tom glanced back over his shoulder for a brief moment, as though he had felt the touch of her gaze. But the crowd was dense about the Queen's dais and she knew herself to be invisible. Then Tom turned away into the outer court. He could not have seen her. Nonetheless, Lucy felt a new confidence at the sight of him and straightened, shaking out her gown.

The dance finished, and the Queen called her name.

Stepping lightly out of the crowd, Lucy climbed the steps on to the covered royal dais, not entirely displeased by the way the courtiers parted to let her through, some of them whispering about her, staring greedily at this strange new favourite of the Queen.

'Your Majesty?'

She sank into a low curtsey under the cool of the shaded canopy, listening to the click and rustle of the courtiers' feathered fans, and remained there until the Queen told her to rise. Indeed, she did not wish to look Her Majesty in the eye.

Her heart sickened, waiting for what she felt must be the inevitable question. If asked, she must either tell the truth and betray the charming Lord Leicester, or lie and betray her queen. *But which should it be?* His lordship had spoken to her as he left the tiltyard, and begged her not to tell the Queen of his secret meeting with Lettice.

'I'm told you have prepared a new dance for us, child.'

The Queen was watching her closely, her cheeks flushed even under the white foundation she always wore, a slightly wild look to her face. Her red wig had been dressed simply with a single circlet of gold, echoed by a gold chain about her waist from which an elaborate gold and ruby pendant hung.

'Yes, Your Majesty.'

'Show us then. We have had enough of country dancing today and would like to see something with a little more skill. And mind you do not mar your steps, Lucy Morgan, for I shall be watching closely and am accounted a good judge in such matters.'

Her voice was shrill; the Queen was angry about something, Lucy realized with a terrible thrill of fear. If she were to ask now . . .

But to Lucy's immense relief she did not ask. Instead, the Queen sank back against her cushions as though exhausted and gestured heavily to someone out of sight. There was a series of staccato commands from the captain of the royal guard, the noise of shuffling feet, and Lucy saw that a space was being cleared for her on the dusty ground of the tiltyard.

A space in which to dance.

She descended from the platform and stood, waiting for the castle musicians to assemble before the Queen: drums, pipes, shawms, hautboys, and an ancient hurdy-gurdy with a wooden crank. One of the men spoke to her and she answered him without thinking, her lips numb and her eyes burning, her whole body on fire yet ice-cold at the same time, moving without awareness. She had chosen an old French lament for this dance, and had worked on the steps on her own in the mornings before anyone else was awake, humming the tune as well as she could recall it. Now she would have the musicians to guide her, but an audience too, and every opportunity to stumble or make a mistake. But it was too late to draw back now.

Someone rapped out the beat, slow and sombre against the wooden frame of a tambour, then the music began. Lucy turned in the dance, her body responding instinctively, sweeping her feet one way and then another across the dusty ground, bending her waist to the haunting lilt and surge of the hurdy-gurdy.

Here, she could be herself, without fear and with only the music for company.

Sunshine burned on her closed lids. Opening them, she danced on, dazzled but alive. Her hands strong, graceful. Her feet pointed thus. Immaculate. The ring of their faces blurred slowly. A tree, shaken: white petals, blossom drifting on the air. Lucy turned, arms wide and spinning, into the last movement.

After the music had finished, she dropped, trembling, into a curtsey below the Queen.

'Rise.'

Lucy straightened, listening to the spontaneous applause and foot-stamping of her audience. She found courage in their approval, eager to hear it, taking it as her due. Was it sinful to seek applause for her work, for these public performances? She had been hidden at the back for so long, unseen and unheard, that listening to their applause was like coming alive again, being born of a new mother. Perhaps, returning to hot, dirty London at summer's end, she would be forgotten, sent back to the chorus by a furious Mistress Hibbert, outraged at her presumption in dancing and singing for the Queen without her permission. Then Lucy might wish she had taken less pleasure in her own skill, finding herself invisible once more, stuck at the back in a coarse gown and cheap shoes.

The Queen had risen too, descending the steps from the dais. Her ladies hurried after her, catching and lifting her gold train so it would not be ruined in the dust. She paused before Lucy. At her back, Walsingham waited in silence.

Queen Elizabeth's eyes glittered, searching her face, then she bent her head, her words meant only for Lucy's ears.

'That matter of which I spoke to you lately in the gardens,' she whispered. 'Have you any news?'

Lucy quaked inwardly. Her lips opened, trying to form an answer, but her mouth was too dry to make a sound.

This close, the cloying scent of the Queen's rosewater mixed unpleasantly with the odours of overheated flesh under the vast, gilt-edged ruff and jewelled, golden gown. Lucy stared at the sheer intricacy of the ruff, and told herself not to faint.

The Queen frowned, drawing back slightly to look at her face, as though she already knew the truth and only needed Lucy to confirm it. Lucy tried but could not raise her eyes to meet the Queen's. The desire to speak, to blurt out every tiny detail she knew and leave nothing unsaid, was almost overwhelming; it twisted and writhed in her gut, like a serpent about to bite its way out through her belly.

'Speak,' the Queen insisted, her impatience unmistakable. 'What have you discovered?' Her voice dropped to a hiss. 'Have there been any *letters*?'

'N-not yet, Your Majesty,' Lucy managed, stammering. She could only curtsey again as the Queen swept past in a rustle of gold cloth, an overpowering smell of lavender wafting from the pomander hung about her neck.

Fumbling to cross herself and ward off any evil she might have invoked, Lucy waited in silence, head bent to hide the fear in her eyes. The rest of the court streamed past, following the Queen's party back into the outer court.

No, she had not lied. Nor yet had she told the Queen the whole truth. It was a lie by omission. A lie of conscience. She had concealed what she knew in order to protect his lordship, who had been kind to her and given her this chance to perform before the court. But she did not know how much longer she could continue to tell these lies and half-truths to the Queen before her disobedience was found out and punished.

Master Goodluck might make his living by deception, and find it no great work to conceal his heart. Yet the truth had always been written clear in Lucy's face for all to read. To unlearn honesty was the hardest thing in the world.

# Forty

THE BENCHES IN THE GREAT HALL HAD BEEN PUSHED BACK TO ALLOW more space for those wishing to be present at the knighting ceremony. With the courtiers standing about in their rich costumes and fancy hose, and two brightly plumaged birds perched in a hanging cage, and sunlight streaming in through the high arched windows, the place had the air of a holy day street pageant, a brilliant tableau of characters and strange, exotic creatures from a world beyond the everyday.

Lost in a wave of nostalgia, Goodluck remembered a certain player whose clear delivery and impressive strutting had thrilled him as a boy. The man had inspired him to make his living the same way – though fate had intervened, of course, prompting him into the greater thrill of espionage.

'Make way there!' someone called out, knocking against him in passing. A stiff-backed young man carrying a velvet brocade cushion before him, on which had been laid an ornamental sword, jolted Goodluck back to the moment, to the ceremony ahead, and the risk he ran by being here.

Still standing in the doorway at the rear of the hall, he shrank back into his hood and searched the faces of the courtiers for the man he had come to see. It was important that he was not too conspicuous. He had stolen this suit of blue livery so he might pass for one of Leicester's men, but any of the earl's officials would know him at once for an imposter.

At last he caught sight of Walsingham, standing discreetly behind a row of courtiers to the right of the Queen, apparently absorbed in the proceedings but in fact searching the room in much the same way as Goodluck himself.

Their eyes met for a few brief seconds, and Walsingham stiffened. Then he nodded, almost imperceptibly, and Goodluck slipped out of the great hall and made his way down the stairs to the next floor. Here, he was away from the music and the calling out of names of those to be honoured, and the armed guards patrolling the place who might have asked awkward questions if he had lurked in the doorway any longer.

There was a small communal privy on this floor. Goodluck had never been inside, but he could tell the function of the room by its smell as he approached. A courtier came out, hurriedly adjusting his hose before taking the stairs back up to the hall two at a time. Goodluck stood at the door a moment, listening until he heard the sound of someone quietly descending from upstairs, then slipped inside.

The privy was windowless, very close and hot. There were three narrow cubicles with doors, and an open area for pissing – a shallow, rancid gutter set into the floor sloped away into a chute to the gong farm, presumably for use when the weather was too poor to venture outside in the fresh air. He glanced into a cubicle and saw that the original stone seat had been 'improved' with a shiny new wooden frame. In the stifling heat, the smell from the chute below was revolting, and Goodluck's nose twitched in protest. But at least it meant few people would care to linger in such a place, unless they had come for the obvious.

Thankfully, he did not have to wait long. The door creaked a moment later and Walsingham entered, a look of mild distaste on his face. He hesitated, glanced at the three closed cubicle doors, and raised thin, dark eyebrows in a silent query.

'We're alone,' Goodluck supplied.

'I cannot be long here. Lord Burghley's son is to be knighted this morning and my absence will be noted. Besides, his wife has never been one of Her Majesty's favourites, so I may be called upon to smooth ruffled feathers before the end of the day.'

'I'm sorry not to have sent a message, sir, but I couldn't trust the new code you sent. Not for this.'

Walsingham raised a fragrant pomander to his nose, sniffed at it delicately, then let it fall again on the chain about his neck.

'Go on,' he murmured.

'Do you recall the steward's assistant, Malcolm Drury, the man who drowned? I believe the Italian may be in possession of one of his keys—'

'This is old news, surely?'

'Sir,' Goodluck inclined his head respectfully, 'I was mistaken there. I thought at first it meant nothing, that holding keys to the inner court would be a useless advantage, since they would inevitably fail to get past the guards posted at every entrance. But there is another possibility I hadn't considered.'

Walsingham looked at him enquiringly, and raised the pomander to his nose again. 'I do not consider myself an impatient man. But the privy is perhaps not the best of places for a protracted conversation.'

'Briefly, sir, there's a key on the missing set that opens an underground storage room to the north-west of the Queen's apartments. It fell out of use about eight years ago, and I've been told it's kept permanently locked now. But there may be a way to access the new state apartments through a roof hatch that leads up into the storage room above.'

'And you believe the Queen's enemies hold the key to this chamber?'

Goodluck nodded. He felt the blood beating in his throat, his head light, and put a hand on the wall to steady himself. He knew instinctively that the older man was not going to listen. That nothing he said would make any difference. Yet still he had to make the attempt. 'For all we know, the Queen's Majesty is in greater danger with every night that we delay. I very much fear that we have been watching the wrong people. I have not yet established who is pulling Massetti's strings, and the bear-tamer has proved difficult to watch. He is too good at slipping away from those who follow him.' Goodluck shook his head. 'Sir, we must act now.'

'And by act, you mean . . . ?'

'Make arrests. Starting with Massetti and the bear-tamer, and any other Italians with whom he may have made contact since arriving here.' Determined to state his case fully, Goodluck added, 'The dead man they dragged from the mere – I smelt something odd on his breath. I didn't connect the two at the time, but there was a vial of colourless liquid in Massetti's room with the same sickly odour to it. I think the man was poisoned by Massetti and then dumped in the mere to make it look like a drowning.'

'Poisoned by *Massetti*? Let me be clear, my friend. Even if Petruccio Massetti is involved in this latest plot, which I find hard to credit, it is not in him to act so violently. Do not forget how well I know this young man. From what you say, some Catholic sympathizer at the English court may have attempted to recruit him. Or made some overture of friendliness towards him, hoping to turn him against the Queen. No, arresting Massetti and his associates is not the course we should follow. We must watch and wait, in the hope that a greater man is hooked on this particular line. Besides, Her Majesty is concerned that even the hint of a new Catholic plot may precipitate some fresh taste for sedition among our secret Papists here in England. Which it certainly would, of course.'

Francis Walsingham moved to the wall where the stinking gutter ran to the chute, tugged at his hose and began to urinate.

'You disagree with my decision?' he asked idly, not looking at Goodluck. 'Well, no doubt you have reason to do so. The Queen's life is in danger and her would-be assassins rub shoulders with us here in this castle, a stronghold intended to keep out her enemies, not pamper them with soft beds and fine wines. But nothing is as simple as it appears, my good friend. By making these arrests now, we remove the body of the threat but not the head, and it will merely return in a new and perhaps more deadly form.'

Frustrated though he was, Goodluck had to concede that Walsingham was right. There was a longer game to play than this one, a summer plot too swiftly brought to an end by arresting Massetti. Yet the threat to the Queen remained, and it was Goodluck's difficult business to ensure that the assassin himself – whoever he was, and wherever he was hiding – could not reach his target. Otherwise everything he and the others had done here at Kenilworth, the risks they had run, would have been in vain.

'What now, then?'

There was a faint sound outside the door, barely audible. Both men fell silent.

Had they been overheard?

Walsingham turned on his heel and left the privy without another word, the scented pomander raised once more to his nose.

Goodluck squeezed into one of the hot, dirty cubicles and closed the door with a noisy clatter, listening to hear if anyone else had entered the room. Sweat rolled down his back in the tight blue livery as he waited. But there was no further sound from outside and, after a few more minutes, he slipped out and down a narrow set of back stairs to the lawn behind the great hall.

His heart was racing as he burst out into the sunlight, gasping at fresh air.

He leaned on the wall for a moment, suddenly sickened, possibly from the relentless heat and stench of the privy. But deep down he knew it was fear, and despised his own weakness.

Goodluck could not help but think this assignment had the stink of disaster about it. His meeting with Walsingham had been not only risky but inconclusive. Walsingham's affection for the young Italian must be clouding his judgement. He was widely considered the most ruthless man in England, yet he would not have Massetti touched – and why? Because Massetti had once saved his family from a bloody end. What other explanation could there be? Unless it was indeed true that Walsingham was involved in a deeper game, seeking to discover the name of some high-ranking traitor at the English court by leaving Massetti to play out his part undisturbed.

Not that Massetti appeared to be anything but a pawn, a decoy, a dupe who had mistaken his role in this conspiracy. Massetti was clearly the man they were supposed to be watching – no doubt while the true assassin made his way by some secret means into the Queen's apartments and killed her without a single guard raising the alarm.

And if this true assassin should succeed?

If the Queen were to be assassinated in the safety of her own rooms, while they had full knowledge of this plot and knew even the whereabouts of some of its key conspirators, Goodluck might as well hang himself now from the nearest roof beam and have done with it.

Straightening, he hurried down a further flight of steep steps and through a cool, dark archway towards the lakeside. He had an urge to kneel down at the water's edge and splash his face, wash away the stench of failure. With his gaze fixed on the glint of sunlit water ahead, he almost did not see the dark shadows passing across the mouth of the passage.

Young, slim-hipped shadows in green livery, cracking jokes in Italian, laughed in the fresh sunshine, arms linked warmly about each other's waists.

As Goodluck emerged from the passageway, one darted ahead of the others and threw herself in a rolling cartwheel across the grass. A burst of laughter followed. Then she rose to her feet and, clear as a warning bell across open fields, called out a name that froze Goodluck where he stood, his heart suddenly a stone.

'Alfonso!'

One of the Florentine acrobats, a young man with a thin curling moustache and lazy smile, turned to give his friends a mocking little bow before he too launched himself into a cartwheel, knifing through the sunlit air.

# Forty-one

LUCY CLIMBED THE STAIRS TO THE ROYAL APARTMENTS, THE STONE walls lit by warm patches of sunlight at every turn. A serving girl ran past her in tears on the first-floor landing, almost tripping down the stairs in her haste to escape. From above, the sound of the Queen's voice raised in anger made her pause, gripping the rope set into the wall to aid her ascent. If she had not been summoned to attend the Queen for luncheon and then at the hunt, she would have turned round and made her way out to the Brays, where the smoke from the camp fires would leave her eyes smarting but at least she would be free and unwatched. The stuffy, closeted atmosphere of the Queen's apartments these past few days had felt like a prison, with her smallest misstep noted and censured. More accustomed to the homely, ramshackle chaos of the domestic staff quarters in London, Lucy found herself almost hating the propriety and hush of the Privy Chamber at Kenilworth.

A burly guard was coming down the stairs, broad-shouldered and barrel-chested, taking up almost all the narrow space. As he descended, he was whistling a tune which she recognized as a ribald soldiers' song about the Queen herself. And in the royal apartments too!

Flattening herself against the wall so this insolent guard could pass, Lucy glanced up to find dark, twinkling eyes and an unmistakable beard.

'Master Goodluck!'

'Hush!' Goodluck lifted her hand to his lips, and she could not help smiling at his mock-gallantry. 'Don't give me away. I make a fine soldier, don't you think?'

He was wearing the badged livery of Leicester's men, the blue doublet straining across his large body. She stared, perplexed. 'Yes, indeed. But how did you—?'

'It helps, when searching a place, to make yourself appear to belong there.'

'You've been searching the Queen's apartments?'

'Not her rooms, but the building itself.' He shot her a smile, then glanced over his shoulder to reassure himself that he was not being followed. 'Lord Leicester swears there are no secret passages into this building other than the ones we are already aware of, but I like to make sure of such things myself. Though discreetly, of course, to avoid scattering the pigeons.' He indicated the blue livery. 'Hence this rather unflattering coat.'

'But if you are caught?'

'Then I will spend a few hours languishing in his lordship's dungeons until someone comes to release me.'

'Oh, Goodluck,' she moaned, leaning her head against his broad chest. The steady beat of his heart went some way to comfort her, but she was still afraid for his safety. 'Why do this dangerous work?'

'Why, because there is no one else foolish enough to do it for me,' he replied, his voice level and amused. Gently, he raised her chin and looked down into her face. 'And you, my little songbird, how is the Queen treating you? Are you still happy at court now that every eye is upon you?'

She grimaced at the difficult question – or rather its answer – then wished she had not, seeing how seriously Master Goodluck watched her.

'It is hard sometimes,' she admitted in a small voice. Then she managed a smile of enthusiasm. 'But I love to entertain the Queen, and now Lord Robert has written a song for Her Majesty and I am to perform it before the court.'

'Lord Robert?' he repeated, his brows raised.

Realizing her slip too late, she rushed to correct herself. 'Lord

Leicester, I meant to say,' she stammered, but knew her guardian would not let it go so easily.

'Well, now.' His smile was dry, and not altogether kind. 'Making friends in high places, I see.'

'His lordship told me to call him that,' Lucy tried to explain, not liking the way Master Goodluck had drawn away from her, a strange and hurtful distance in his face. 'But I see now that it would be a mistake. The Queen would not like it.'

'I'm glad you have the sense to see *that*, at least.'

As he turned to descend the steep stairs, Lucy caught at his arm. 'Wait, I've just remembered something you should know. I saw a man a few nights back, I think it was the bear-tamer you've been watching. He seemed to be meeting another man, over by the Watergate Tower.'

'Did you know this other man?'

'It was too dark to see his face clearly,' Lucy admitted, then caught her lip between her teeth, worrying at it. 'Tom said something about a man who was found drowned. One of Leicester's men. Could the two be connected, do you think?'

'Perhaps.'

It was only one word, and lightly spoken too, but Goodluck was frowning and Lucy felt suddenly alarmed. Was the threat to the Queen's safety so very serious? She clutched at his sleeve. 'You don't think these conspirators could reach the Queen, do you? With Leicester's men everywhere, and her own guards at her door, how could anyone come at her without being caught?'

'I don't think they could get past the guards, no. But there are other ways into the castle. Unguarded ways. I was just looking into it. There's a disused storeroom between the Queen's apartments and the old hall, and it's possible someone could get in through that. But it's kept locked.'

'So it's safe?'

Goodluck hesitated, seeming to think aloud. 'The key's missing. It could have been on the dead man. But it's not an easy way in. It's more likely they would try to strike while the Queen is on the move, perhaps out hunting. That's where their best opening would be.'

For a moment, Lucy wished she knew nothing about this Catholic plot, that she was as innocent as when she had arrived in Kenilworth and able to sleep easily at night. 'Promise me you'll be careful? I couldn't bear to lose you. These men are trained assassins. They're *dangerous*.'

'So am I, Lucy.' Goodluck's smile was far from reassuring; for a few seconds, she looked into those cold dark eyes and was almost frightened of the man who had raised her. 'Now you'd best go about your work and stop interfering in matters that do not concern you. I heard the Queen shouting for you earlier. I don't think you should keep Her Majesty waiting. I've known too many shrews not to recognize the ugly mood she's in.'

'Everyone shouts at me these days,' Lucy muttered. She picked up her skirts obediently enough and began to climb the stairs to the state apartments.

'What do you mean by that?'

Turning, she saw Goodluck still there on the winding stair, staring up after her, a searching look in his eyes.

'Nothing,' she said hurriedly, then realized that a man like Master Goodluck would never be satisfied with such an empty reply.

It made her shudder to think how he must extract the truth from those unwilling to answer his questions. No wonder he had hidden his true profession from her while she was a child; it was not a comfortable thing to look at the man she considered her father and know that he was a spy, trained to watch others in secret, to interrogate, to find answers – and to kill.

'Well, almost nothing.' She shrugged, wishing to make light of the incident. 'I quarrelled with Tom.'

Goodluck frowned. 'Quarrelled?'

'He thought . . .' Lucy found herself blushing fiercely. She could not bear for him to know *this*. It was too intimate, too humiliating. 'Tom misunderstood our friendship, and we had a few sharp words over it, that's all.'

Goodluck must have seen it in her eyes, his stare piercing through to the truth even in the dimly lit stairway.

'Tom tried to seduce you?'

'No!' Lucy felt herself blush harder still, and knew that such awkwardness gave her away.

Why must she always be such a knock-kneed child with him? The man was no longer her guardian. She was a woman now, with work at court, even if she was still unmarried. Surely it was time she outgrew this foolish deference towards Goodluck and made her own decisions, unhindered by his over-strict opinions on how a young woman should act?

Master Goodluck made as if to come after her, but she shook her head, holding him at arm's length.

'What I mean is, I was an idiot and gave Tom good cause to think he could kiss me, and then I . . . I changed my mind. It was my fault, not his, and we have since made a peace together, of sorts.' Lucy managed a smile, seeing the anger in his face. 'It was a foolish thing, nothing of any moment. I beg you would forget it.'

But she could see that Goodluck would neither forget nor forgive. His dark eyes burned with fury, however tightly controlled, and his hand had clenched into a fist. Sometimes it was almost as though he considered himself her true father and therefore guardian of her morals even now, when she was old enough to choose whomever she liked to take as a lover. Though indeed she had no intention of behaving as loosely and recklessly as most of the other girls in the entertainers' troupe; let them lose their innocence, and enjoy themselves at night down in the kitchens or in the servants' halls. She would keep herself chaste until her wedding night, just as she had promised Queen Elizabeth.

None of it was Goodluck's business, though. She loved him dearly, and trembled to think of the danger he put himself in daily for England's protection, yet she was no longer his charge and he must be made to see it.

'Though if I were to take Tom into my bed,' she added, her voice shaking despite her resolve to be frank with him, 'it would not be your concern. I am old enough now to take a lover if I choose.'

Then she turned, without a curtsey or even a glance at his face to gauge his reaction, and hurried up the last few turns of the stair to the royal apartments. Behind her, on the dark steps, Lucy could feel the weight of Goodluck's eyes watching her until she was safely out of sight.

# Forty-two

AFTER CHECKING THE QUEEN'S ROOMS WERE SECURE, GOODLUCK returned to see Twist and the others. He made hurried enquiries, and the answers he received alarmed him. No, their men had never seen the Florentine acrobats anywhere near the bear-tamer. But no matter, for the troupe had dismantled their tent and packed up that very hour, and were reputed to be on their way further up the country. Sos had seen their cart rumble out of the north gate, carrying all their goods and supplies for the road, with the green-liveried acrobats walking behind, arm in arm.

Catching up with their slow cart, Goodluck was not surprised to see the troupe turn off the road a few miles from Kenilworth. After some muttered deliberation under the trees, they left their cart under cover and doubled back cross-country through the forest, following the line of the castle battlements whenever it became visible in the distance.

Now the troupe appeared to have come to a halt in the sun-dappled clearing ahead, and were speaking to each other in lowered voices. Goodluck could make out the odd word, but had little chance of hearing well enough to decipher their rapid Italian. Keeping well under cover, he crept from tree to tree, careful not to crack twigs underfoot, glad now that he had snatched up a mud-brown hooded cloak on his way out of the tent. It usefully hid the blue livery he had adopted in order to search the state apartments, satisfying himself that none of the would-be assassins had already entered the building and were concealed there.

Goodluck leaned against the trunk of a sturdy old oak, hidden from sight but still within earshot of the troupe of acrobats. He surveyed them as they went quietly about their business, opening packs and sharing out the goods they had brought with them into the forest.

He thought back to his conversation with Lucy. What in heaven had she meant by that last remark?

She was growing into a beautiful and talented young woman; indeed, she had altered and grown in some indefinable way even during the ten days or so since her arrival in the Queen's train. Truth was, she was no longer his ward, and he could not hope to control her decisions now. But he loathed this corrosive suspicion that the black groom had raped her – or, at the very least, had tried to seduce her, still an innocent girl.

At the very thought of young Tom hurting Lucy, a mindless fury rose inside him, as though he wanted nothing better than to snap the boy's neck.

There had been something so unhappy in her eyes on the stairs ... a look that had reminded him of her long-dead mother. Another Moorish beauty, vulnerable to a certain kind of man.

Yet like must incline to like, and he could not prevent his Lucy from growing up and becoming a woman. Even if it pained him to think of her being hurt or betrayed.

He did not trust that boy. But then, he never entirely trusted anyone.

Goodluck froze, as did the Florentines in the clearing, hearing a sound. Someone was approaching through the trees. Not from behind him, thank God, but from the opposite direction. He waited in silence, breath held, as did the men he was watching, all of them tense and keen to see who it was.

Then one of the acrobats – a slant-eyed woman, dark-faced and slender – gave a little cry and launched herself forward.

'Be quiet!' one of the others admonished her, but the woman paid no attention, hurtling towards the hooded and bearded man who had just walked into the clearing, throwing herself on him. They embraced passionately, with many exaggerated kisses.

Though not without some difficulty, Goodluck noted, as the man was holding a chain in his hand, at the end of which lurked a great black bear.

The bear reared up and was jerked back to the earth with one sharp tug.

It sat back with a lurch, groaning loudly, and raised its black front paws as though in protest.

A female bear, Lucy had said, recounting its unprovoked charge against her outside the stables. Perhaps the animal was jealous of the slant-eyed acrobat, without a doubt the man's lover.

They were organizing themselves now, weaving skilfully about each other as they worked, speaking in quiet voices. One man was directing the slant-eyed woman in some complicated action, another handing her a knife, which she slipped daintily between her teeth, clamping down hard on the blade. An older woman was examining the bear. The animal was kept on a short leash during this, its front paws raised, a stick held threateningly in front of its face. No one spoke above a murmur, as though aware they might at any moment be observed.

Frowning, Goodluck considered whether he might move any closer without being discovered. As it stood, he could barely catch a word of their conversation. Yet one thing was clear to him: these people were highly trained, used to working together, some of them perhaps even experienced in the art of assassination. They would not easily be drawn into making a mistake that could expose their plot – or the nobleman behind it. For it was certain that Massetti could not be the sole backer of their scheme. Experienced teams like this tended not to work in pursuit of a cause; in most cases, they were mercenaries. Only a large amount of gold or other enticements could have hired such skill, and a man like Massetti was not wealthy enough to have brought so many across Europe on his own coin.

There was some earnest discussion now among the acrobats, then the bear-tamer tapped the bear with his stout knotty stick and muttered some command under his breath. As the shaggy creature reared up, he turned and took up a crouching position behind it.

Through all this preparation, the slant-eyed woman had taken a few steps back and dropped her cloak to the ground. Beneath it she wore a loose dark tunic top and tight-fitting men's hose, closely gartered. She herself was of a slender build, her breasts barely noticeable, black hair cut short as a boy's; the heavy fringe almost met the dark of her straight, frowning brows, giving her an Egyptian air.

She kicked off her shoes and stood barefoot, the knife still held between her teeth.

'Hey-up!' shouted one of the men.

The bear was standing straight now, erect as any man, both front paws outstretched, its back turned on the troupe.

Bouncing off bare toes, the woman ran forward and leapt forcefully on to the cupped hands of the crouching bear-tamer, using his strength to vault up into empty air.

Twisting in a somersault, she landed on the bear's back. She grasped a few handfuls of black fur and stood on the animal's broad shoulders, her thin arms stretched out for balance, the knife still clamped between her teeth. The bear swayed slightly at the impact – though not with surprise, it seemed to Goodluck – and nearly fell. But the bear-tamer, via a series of guttural cries, tuts of his tongue and taps with his stick, managed to keep the animal from sinking back to its more natural four-legged stance.

On the bear's high back, the woman stood considerably higher than the lowest branches of the oaks around them. Indeed, she now stood at twice the height of a man. With grudging admiration, Goodluck doubted he had ever seen a more impressive somersault, given the short distance she had taken to achieve that speed and power.

Yet why bother with such a trick? To vault the guarded mereside wall below the Queen's apartments?

If that were indeed the plan, how did the others in the troupe intend to get over? By using a rope, in plain sight of the guards who would be posted there at all hours?

No, such a plan would be risky and over-elaborate.

Goodluck regarded the woman steadily. There was a surprising strength in those legs, and her acrobat's sense of balance held her steady on the bear's shoulders as the animal swayed forward and back in response to muttered commands.

For several minutes, a low rumbling sound had been growing steadily louder at Goodluck's back. Thinking it the wheels of some rough trader's cart on the nearby road to the castle, he had ignored it. Now he realized his mistake and turned his head in consternation, hearing the thud of hoofbeats and seeing the flash of gold and silver through the trees.

The royal hunting party!

The road from the castle must run parallel to his hiding place, he realized. He had thought today's hunt would pass out in the other direction, towards the Chase. But his luck must have changed. For although the riders were at a safe distance, almost invisible through these densely crowded trees, the rehearsing acrobats would be bound to look in his direction as the hunt passed and it was too late for him to seek better cover.

He flattened himself against the creeper-thick oak and held his breath, listening for any sign that he had been spotted by the Italians.

None came, and after a moment the Queen's hunting party had passed on. The welter of yelps from the pursuing hounds faded into the distance as they dropped further into the wooded valley.

For another few moments Goodluck waited in silence, the trunk against his back, staring at the green forest.

Then slowly, with the utmost care, he turned his head – to find the blade of a knife six inches from his eyes, and the unsmiling, dark-eyed face of an Italian.

# Forty-three

IT WAS ALMOST TWILIGHT WHEN LUCY WOKE. SHE REALIZED WITH A tremor of fear that her 'short rest' had turned into several hours' sleep. She had only put her head to the mattress for a brief spell, overwhelmed by exhaustion after days of late nights and early mornings, attending the Queen, learning the words of the song Leicester had set her to perform, and trying to avoid drawing attention to herself in case it led to some betrayal of his lordship's faith in her.

How late was it? Where was everyone? Had she missed the hunt?

Groggily, she stumbled out of bed and dressed in the half-light, the stiff fastenings of the unfamiliar court gown almost defeating her. One of the seamstresses had helped her to narrow the waist, let out for some larger woman in the past, but the task had been performed too well and now she could barely move. Lord Robert had procured it for her, saying she must look 'at her finest' tonight, when she was due to sing his love song before the Queen and court. If she was not too late . . .

Why had no one woken her?

Her heart juddered in her chest at the thought of missing her performance before the Queen. And tonight of all nights. Leicester would be furious with her, and rightly so. There were to be fireworks, and a water battle out on the mere, with vast fantastical creatures from legend – some of which she had seen being prepared that afternoon, the enormous creations dragged on rollers down to the lakeside and rowed out to the central raft.

Peering out of the window, she could see only the Brays' side of the mere, barely visible in the warm, smoky twilight, but she could hear distant shouts just north of the castle and knew the evening's entertainments were still being prepared out on the lake. So it could not be too late. Nonetheless, if she did not hurry, she would be unable to join the Queen's ladies for the procession out to the lake, and for that she would be in serious trouble.

Hurriedly, she smoothed out the thick, heavy folds of the gold-embroidered underskirt, and wished again that she had someone to help her; there was still the extravagant white ruff to attach. 'I want you to look like an angel from heaven,' his lordship had told her, and she knew she must not disappoint him. An angel with sore fingers, she thought. Attaching the ruff was a fiddly business and by the time Lucy had slipped on her tight white and gold shoes, donated to her by the beautiful Lady Helena herself, the women's quarters were so dark she could barely see her way to the door. But at least the corridors in this wing were well lit with torches, so she was able to find her way across the building to where the ladies of the court would be assembled – if they had not left yet.

'Lucy!'

She turned, fearing a reprimand for her lateness. But it was only Catherine, her friend from Norfolk, who had run up behind her in the flickering torchlight. They had been close before arriving at Kenilworth, where it seemed to Lucy that she had been separated from almost everyone she knew and made to live among women who were her social betters. Since moving into the inner court, she had felt too nervous to speak or even take her fair share of food at mealtimes, in case her behaviour was considered impertinent. So she greeted Catherine with relief, glad to see a friendly face.

'Catherine,' she said, and hugged her. 'I'm late. Are you coming on the procession to the lake?'

The younger girl shook her head. 'I've been sick. I'm to watch from the windows with the other servants.'

'I'm sorry, I didn't know you had been sick.' Lucy stared at her friend's pale face, exasperated. If only she had time to talk properly. Concerned, she picked up her heavy skirts to ascend the staircase to the royal apartments. 'Will you walk with me, Catherine? I was told to attend the Privy Chamber before the procession began. I only hope the court hasn't left yet.'

'No, the Queen is still in her rooms. She's been there since they returned from the hunt. And in a fine old temper, they say.'

Lucy bit her lip. 'I was supposed to ride out to hunt today. I hope no one missed me. I was stupid and lay down to rest, but I fell asleep and almost didn't wake up in time to dress. I was so exhausted. And I've hardly seen you these past few weeks.'

'You must be happy, though.'

'What do you mean?'

'Being the Queen's new favourite?' Catherine flushed, looking away. 'It's what you always wanted, isn't it? To sing before the Queen? The others are saying you'll never return to the troupe, not with Lord Leicester looking out for you. He'll be the new king, you know. They are to be married come autumn.'

'*What?*'

Lucy could not believe what she was hearing. She had grown so used to the idea of secrecy, that everything must be whispered for fear of being overheard, it shocked her to hear such things spoken out loud in the open corridor. Yet Catherine did not look disturbed, her face quite innocent. It would seem that the whole court knew about Leicester and Her Majesty.

'Oh quick!' Catherine grabbed her elbow, pointing hurriedly ahead as the door to the state apartments opened and the two guards at the entrance stood to attention. 'Look, the court must be moving down to the lakeside. You'd better hurry.'

Her friend had turned to descend the stairs, not daring to block the way. 'Go on, you don't want to get into trouble.'

Reluctantly, Lucy ran up the last few steps to join the crowd now thronging outside the Queen's apartments. It was simple to slip into the procession at the back, dropping a low curtsey to Lord Leicester as he passed, though she felt a little unnerved by the hard glance he threw her. He must have noticed her tardiness. Unless she had displeased him in some other way?

It still weighed heavily on her mind that she had promised to report back to the Queen on any messages Leicester had sent to the Countess of Essex, and Lucy did not know how long she could avoid doing so without having to lie outright. And that was not only a sin, but treason, surely? To lie to the Queen would be to risk her own neck, a thought which left her pale and trembling, wishing she could ask Master Goodluck for his advice.

But Goodluck was nowhere to be seen, however much she scoured the massed crowds for his bearded, smiling face. No doubt her former guardian was still angry with her for daring to speak so plainly. Her heart sank as she realized he had not come to watch her perform. What had possessed her to make an enemy of her dearest, oldest friend?

Down at the lakeside, a huge tented pavilion, open on three sides and illuminated by many candles, had been prepared for the Queen in case of rain. For although the days continued hot and sunny, a summer storm had been predicted by the groundsmen. It was clear that Leicester was taking no chances with this very special evening's entertainments. The main body of the court was ushered under the tented roof, and a raised throne-like seat had been set for the Queen, with cushioned benches below for her ladies and chief courtiers. Unseen in the darkness, musicians positioned out on the lake were already playing a popular French melody as they arrived, while servants were sent to thread their way between the courtiers with spiced wine and trays of sugared fruits.

Hovering outside the pavilion, desperate not to be noticed by the Queen, Lucy caught a sudden glimpse of the lute player appointed to accompany her singing, and her insides knotted with fear.

She felt sick, and took up a cup of wine from the passing tray, hoping to steady her nerves with its spicy warmth.

'Are you ready to sing for Her Majesty, Lucy Morgan?'

Her hand shook, spilling the wine and nearly soiling her new gold and white gown. 'Your lordship,' she stammered, curtseying awkwardly, the cup still held out to one side, dripping like blood over her fingers. Lord Robert took the cup from her gently, handing it to a servant, and she realized he was waiting for her reply. 'Yes, if you please.'

'You will not forget the words? And your heart – it will *feel* each word, press it home to the melody?'

'Yes, your lordship.'

Leicester laid a hand on her shoulder, his voice strained. 'I need this, Lucy. Woo the Queen for me tonight with your song.' She glanced up, finding his eyes dark and intense. 'All is not well between us.'

Silently, she nodded, and the earl's hand fell away.

A path had been cleared for her through the crowd. She stepped lightly forward, feeling empty, thin as air, her face drained of blood. Between the pavilion and the mere, a small wooden platform had been pushed into place, draped with white silk. There, the lute player sat waiting for her, his face sombre in the flickering torchlight. Lucy climbed the three steps up on to the dais, feeling as if she were going to her execution. She stood facing the court, trying not to look directly at the Queen, though she felt the burden of that sharp gaze on her face and shivered. The heat of the summer's evening was stifling, and yet still she shivered.

'Your Majesty,' she began, and found her voice barely audible above the great hum of the crowd. She cleared her throat and started afresh. 'If it please Your Majesty, I am to sing a song for you of Lord Leicester's own composition. Though first I am instructed to ask if you are willing to hear it, Your Majesty?'

The Queen looked at Lord Robert, a long assessing look, while the court held its breath and Lucy stood in full view of everyone, her fingers plucking at her gown. Then the Queen nodded, her white face still and emotionless above her broad ruff.

'Let us hear this song of Leicester's.'

Master Oldham strummed the heart-catching opening chords on his lute, and Lucy opened her mouth to draw breath. After that, she remembered nothing but the smell of torches, guttering and flaming, and the silence all about her, until the last throbbing line of the song died away.

The applause came as a shock, almost a knife to her throat, startling her out of her daze. She gasped, and realized that her trial was over, the song was done, and she had not forgotten any of the words nor missed a note as she had feared. Suddenly, like surfacing from icy water, she became aware once more of the dozens of curious eyes watching her, and then she saw Leicester, a smile on his face, whisper something into the ear of his betrothed.

The Queen gestured him to stand back, and summoned Lucy with a brief tilt of her head. 'Come!'

Sinking on to her knees in a deep obeisance before her, Lucy remained in that position while Her Majesty leaned forward to question her. To her surprise, the Queen's voice trembled slightly.

'You sang well.'

She clicked her fingers, and a pretty young page boy came forward with his head bowed, carrying a small wooden chest, its lid thrown open. The Queen glanced inside the chest – almost idly, it seemed to Lucy – then drew out a delicate gold necklace, adorned with a large, single pearl. This she threw to Lucy, who fumbled to catch it, almost dropping the lavish gift in her astonishment and dread. The pearl lay cool in her palm, worth perhaps a thousand times more than most performers earned in a lifetime.

'Thank you, Your Majesty,' she managed, 'though truly I do not deserve such generosity.'

'That, we shall see,' the Queen replied in a dry voice. 'Now come closer. Here, at my feet.'

She waited while Lucy rose and approached the foot of her high-backed cushioned seat, dropping into a curtsey.

'Do you have anything you wish to tell me, child?'

So the moment had come at last, here in front of the whole court, and with Lord Leicester listening!

Her heart hammered violently against her ribs and she heard herself stammer in reply, 'No, Your Majesty. Forgive me.'

There was a horrible pause. Then the Queen's voice softened, almost indulgent. 'Come, child, it is not a difficult matter. You may rise and whisper in my ear if you are afraid to speak in front of all this crowd.'

'I . . . I have nothing to say, Your Majesty. I most humbly beg Your Majesty's pardon.'

'Nothing?'

Somewhere behind her on the lake the first fireworks shot up with a violent, resounding crack. The crowd gasped and several of the Queen's ladies clapped their hands in delight. The evening's entertainments had begun, perhaps at some unseen signal from Leicester. No doubt he thought a distraction would save them both from this interrogation, but it seemed he had underestimated the Queen's persistence.

'Nothing?' she repeated.

Another firework exploded overhead, blood red, and the royal pavilion was lit up for a moment by its passage, every face seemingly turned up to stare at the night sky.

Lucy heard the fury in the Queen's voice but still did not dare speak the truth. To do so would almost certainly condemn both his lordship and the Countess of Essex to death. The weight of that knowledge was an iron band across her shoulders.

She bowed her head, almost sobbing out her wicked denial. 'I know nothing, Your Majesty.'

The fierce slap that followed caught her by surprise. Lucy fell sprawling, and knocked her head painfully against the wooden dais. A gasp went up around the court, but just as swiftly the courtiers' faces turned upwards to watch the dazzling streaks of the fireworks, not daring to anger the Queen by staring. A shout of 'For England and Her Majesty, Queen Elizabeth!' rang out across the lake, and the water battle commenced with a series of explosions, a deafening roar of cannon fire and the drifting, acrid smell of smoke.

And above the noise of the water battle she heard the Queen's command, 'Get out of my sight, ungrateful whelp!'

One of the older courtiers helped Lucy discreetly to her feet, his face not unkind, then turned back to the spectacle. Terrified, she slipped the necklace about her throat with trembling hands, concealing the expensive pearl beneath her high-necked bodice, then curtseyed low to the Queen and backed away into the shadows.

Far from the circle of torches by the bridge over the lake, it was possible to mix unnoticed with the crowd, most of whom were too busy admiring the flashes and furore of the water battle to glance at the black girl passing among them, head bent to hide the blood trickling down her face.

A great 'Ooohhh!' went up from the common people pressing

hard against her back and shoulders, followed by an ecstatic cry of 'Triton! Triton!'

There was blood in her mouth, a warm sour taste. But at least her head was still on her shoulders. She could hardly hear the bang and crack of the fireworks over the lake for the thundering of her heart.

She had sung for the Queen, as his lordship had insisted she must. Now all she wanted was to escape this noise and merry hell, and find somewhere quiet, some secret hideaway where no one could witness her shame and disgrace. The faces about her swam. Where was Goodluck?

# Forty-four

ELIZABETH SAT STRAIGHT-BACKED, CLUTCHING THE ARMS OF HER seat, shaking with fury. Damn that girl! Impudent dark eyes staring up out of her black face, like the Devil himself, mocking her failures. The fireworks shooting over the lake in fiery streaks dazzled the Queen's eyes, but she refused to lower her head, staring blindly ahead so the courtiers nearest her would not see her defeated. The people shouted 'Triton! Triton!' and she saw the vast weed-covered creature approach the bridge where they sat, lifting his trident and calling aloud to her. Beneath the seated Triton swam a great false mermaid dressed with shining scales, glinting in the torchlight. It must have taken many months to create, and on any other day would have been a cause of great delight and admiration for her. Yet tonight she could hardly bear to look at it, her face set like stone.

Robert bent to her ear again, his voice low and urgent. Elizabeth dismissed him with an angry gesture. He wanted to know how she had received his song. His song!

The other courtiers knew something was amiss, and some were staring covertly. She could see the gleam of their curious eyes, while others carefully avoided the swivel of her Gorgon's stare. She was suddenly, forcibly, reminded of the court's careful, politic silences whenever her late father had lost his temper, and knew a gnawing sense of despair.

Did they see her as no better than tyrannical old King Henry, her temper just as dangerous and incontinent when crossed?

She had struck the Moorish girl, but that was nothing. Lucy Morgan was a servant, and her refusal to speak, to admit a role in carrying messages between Robert and Lettice, had infuriated her. Walsingham had told her everything, had exposed their secret meetings, the part Lucy Morgan had played in bringing them together. He had been more than generous in doing so, for she knew it pained him to speak ill of Lettice. No, the truth could not be hidden so easily. Foolish, wicked child, to defy her queen. She had deserved her public disgrace, to be slapped down and sent away. But this terrible desire to call for her soldiers, to have Robert and Lettice arrested and placed under close guard until she could manage their executions . . .

*In God's name, I must not act rashly.*

Elizabeth's fingers bit into the arms of her seat and she rocked forward, staring wide-eyed at the spectacle out on the lake, pretending an interest she did not feel as Triton sped across the waters, riding his giant mermaid. But she was oddly satisfied to realize how much Robert had spent to put on this show for her, digging so deep into his private coffers he must have all but beggared himself. And for what?

She would not marry him. Nor would he understand her reasons. First, that he was unfaithful. Yes, all men betrayed their wives, she knew that as well as any other woman – and kings more than most. But with Lettice? Her own cousin, strikingly like her younger self, still strong and vivacious, still capable of bearing children. Her gorge rose at the thought of them together.

The bleeding and the pain. She forced herself to dwell on that instead. It was God's sign that she should not become a wife. To bleed so heavily after each night spent with her husband would weaken her, even leave her close to death if it continued.

She summoned Helena to her side. 'Where is Lady Essex?'

'She is still abed, Your Majesty.'

'Still?' Elizabeth's eyes narrowed suspiciously on the younger woman's face, whose beauty seemed almost a conspiracy of nature – her perfectly smooth, white complexion made even more striking by a mass of red curls. 'The countess seemed to be recovering from her sickness when last I saw her. Has she been seen by a physician? What ails my cousin?'

The beautiful Helena looked frightened. Her voice dropped to a discreet whisper, barely audible over the crash of the water battle behind her. 'Your Majesty, nobody seems to know. Though some believe . . .'

'Well? Speak up!'

'The physician claims she must have eaten something bad, Your Majesty. That she may have been *poisoned*.'

Heads had turned now, and Elizabeth felt the strength of the court's interest, their eyes on her face, watchful and intrigued. A delicate flush rose in her cheeks as she stared at her Swedish-born lady-in-waiting. 'What nonsense!' she rapped out. But she could not hide her discomfort. If Lettice were to die now, with this talk of poison in the air, the whispers would say it had been done on Elizabeth's account. That she had ordered her own cousin's death, as punishment for this clandestine affair with Robert. Or to remove the threat of Lettice's beauty.

She caught a sudden movement at her shoulder, and turned to see Robert staring at Helena too. He was pale, a haunted look in his eyes. For an awful moment she could not help but remember his wife, the sickly Amy Robsart, whom she had always despised and forbidden him to bring to court – she too had died under mysterious circumstances, and the tongues at court had wagged for months, blaming her for the woman's death.

'Have the physician give me his report directly,' she said, dismissing Helena with an irritable nod, though she knew she ought not to take it out on the Swedish girl. She, at least, was a respectable widow, and sworn to chastity at her queen's side once again, for all her beauty and passion.

As soon as Helena had withdrawn, Robert was there at her side, bowing so low he might as well have been on his knees, his hand clutching at her own.

She did not attempt to pull away, but her hostile look and unfriendly silence sent out a message only a fool could fail to understand. Only a fool, or a man so blindly pursuing his own ambition that he could no longer read the signs.

Robert drew her hand to his lips and kissed it warmly, lingering over her long jewelled fingers. She fought not to remember him inside her, moving urgently with the sharp pleasure of their coupling, but her cheeks flared with the memory.

'Lord Leicester?'

'I am sorry Lucy Morgan angered you.' His voice was ragged. 'But do these poor entertainments please you, Your Majesty? And the song the Moorish girl sang for you tonight . . . I know you are a woman of deep feeling. Did my words reach your heart?'

All of a sudden, her body weakened and she became inexplicably wretched. Tears filled her eyes and she stared at Robert longingly, his broad shoulders, his still handsome face, roughened from riding out in the summer heat, and his mouth hard, not easily given to compromise. Why could her sweet Robin not become her husband, the bridegroom she had always dreamed of?

Because she was the Queen, and it was too late to say yes to him now. She could never share her throne. Nor could she allow herself to become a poor womanly fool like her sister Mary, forever bleeding, and watching herself for the signs of a child, and suffering when they failed to come.

'As always, you have my admiration for your efforts, Lord Robert,' she managed out loud. Then she dropped her voice: 'I am sorry I had to forbid you my chamber but I was not well.'

'I only wished to bring you comfort.'

'I know it.' She struggled to find the words. 'But even your company could not have done me any good. This sickness, this thing that dogs me, is between me and God alone.'

There were lines etched in his forehead, beside his eyes, his oddly sombre mouth. 'Your Majesty,' he began haltingly, 'may I beg you . . .'

She encouraged him to go on, smiling, though her heart sank. She knew what was ahead.

'Make our good news public,' he whispered, raising her hand once more to his lips. This time his kiss was dry, and his lips trembled against her white skin. 'Allow me to announce our betrothal to the court and set a date with the Privy Council for our marriage.'

'I cannot.'

'Your Majesty, I had your promise on this.'

'You must not ask me again.' She pulled her hand away, and her voice grew hard, strengthened by anger. Robert was not a man of weak intellect. He must be made to understand why he could not hope for more. That what they had enjoyed in secret was all that could ever happen between them. 'I gave you no such promise, my lord. There is nothing to announce.'

Robert rose and stared down into her face.

She avoided that accusing gaze. Oh, let him stare, let him brood and consider rebellion. He might be one of the most powerful men in England but he was still her subject; he had no power beyond what she had already given him. Yes, she had made a promise, of sorts. But what a woman might whisper to a man in passion was no binding oath but merely the words of love. A foolish, undisciplined love at that.

Robert knew all this as well as she did. To pretend otherwise was simply political coercion. And she would not be coerced.

He drew breath, and she heard the anger in his voice. 'Then do I have permission to leave your presence, Your Majesty? There are a few pressing matters to which I must attend. I will return before the battle has finished.'

Robert wanted to go to *her*, that much was written clear in his face; to run to Lettice's bedside and see how the adulterous she-wolf was. The impulse to scream 'No!' warred in her chest with a violent desire never to see him or his rutting bitch again. Though to allow them both to quit the court could be dangerous. It should not be forgotten that an alliance between her cousin and Leicester, however adulterous, might in time constitute a threat to her throne.

'You may leave us,' Elizabeth coldly agreed, returning her gaze to the spectacular battle on the lake, not even waiting to see her lover go. Should he, or the Countess of Essex, be suspected of making the slightest move against her person, by letter or by deed, she would issue warrants for their joint arrest, trial and execution. However much agony one of those deaths, at least, must cause her.

# Forty-five

'DOWN! STAY DOWN!'

A booted foot was shoved hard into Goodluck's back. He exhaled with the sharp pain, and collapsed on to his knees in the wet mud. At least his blindfold had been removed. He kept his head low, in response to another harshly barked command in broken English, but glanced swiftly about as soon as the man behind him had moved out of kicking range. They were still in the woods, but further in now, somewhere to the north-east of the castle by his somewhat hazy calculations, and had halted their march beside a pool fed by a narrow stream. They had been walking maybe an hour, but could not have gone far from the castle walls, for it had been a slow progress even without the bear. The shambling creature had been led away on a rope by one of the other men before they started out, after a brief, muttered discussion between him and the bear-tamer.

Had the discovery of Goodluck's presence in the woods ruined the timing of their attack? He fervently hoped so.

While he still could, he would attempt to delay their planned assassination of Queen Elizabeth. He had already stumbled over every tree root or jutting rock along the way, loudly and apologetically blaming his blindfold.

Goodluck straightened his aching back, drawing some strength from the fact that he was still alive. His wrists were bound behind his back, but the Italians had grown tired of his repeated falls and had now removed his blindfold, for which he was grateful, even if it suggested they planned to kill him soon.

With a start, he recognized the cloaked man, torch in hand, who had been waiting for them near the stream and now came forward from his hiding place behind the trees.

Massetti handed his flaming torch to one of the men and threw back his hood. His handsome face was strained, yet he smiled politely enough at his co-conspirators.

The young Italian held out his hands to the leader of the troupe with an eloquent greeting in his own language, adding swiftly, 'I'm sorry I couldn't come sooner. It's been very difficult to get away, Walsingham's spies watch me so closely.' His smile faltered as he looked down at Goodluck's kneeling, bound figure. 'What is this?'

'We caught this one spying on us. He pretends to be one of Leicester's men, with this badge and the blue livery he wears. But it's more likely he's an agent of the crown. He and his friends have been camped up at the castle, watching who comes and goes. They have no subtlety, these English spies. They move about as noisily as children and think nobody notices them.'

'Is it safe to speak in front of him?'

'If we keep to Italian, yes. We were discussing his death earlier and he showed no sign of understanding. Do you know him?'

Massetti frowned. His face was troubled as he signalled the man with the torch to raise it higher. With obvious hesitancy, he stepped into the flickering circle of light to take a closer look at Goodluck's face.

'I don't think so,' he said at last. 'Perhaps I've seen him about the castle. I can't be sure. All Leicester's men look alike to me.'

'Well, no matter.' The leader of the troupe gave an eloquent shrug that left Goodluck in no doubt about his impending death. 'We'll soon find out who he is and what he knows, if anything. Then we'll kill him and hide his body here in the woods. By the time they stumble across him, the job will be done.'

Massetti shivered, and carefully averted his gaze from Goodluck's face. He looked instead at the bear-tamer, who had been standing silently all this time, arms folded across his chest. 'I got your note, but must protest against your summons here tonight. My having to slip away from the court may have roused suspicions. And why did you not reply to my last message?'

'I did not reply, my esteemed Massetti, because there could be no reply to your message except one.' The bear-tamer smiled unpleasantly. 'But I see you understand me.'

Massetti blenched and took a hasty step back. His hand went nervously to his throat, loosening the courtly ruff that must have suddenly seemed too tight. 'I have done what you asked of me. Thanks to my efforts, the Association of the Bear will soon triumph and this heretic England will return to the true faith.'

Goodluck stifled his instinctive grimace before it could be seen. *The Association of the Bear!* He had been hunting an individual by that name, and all the time the 'Bear' was a group, a determined collective that sought to remove Elizabeth from the throne.

'I have helped with your venture,' Massetti continued, glancing about the circle of faces as though seeking a friendly one. 'I paved the way for you to enter Kenilworth unchallenged, and had to face some very uncomfortable questions about my loyalty from my old master, Walsingham. He guards his virgin queen with great zeal.'

The bear-tamer spat into the stream. 'That Protestant whore!'

'Just so, just so. But you must see that as soon as . . .' Again, the young man glanced nervously at Goodluck's face, and away. 'As soon as Elizabeth is dead, suspicion must fall on me. They already know some plot exists, that was clear from Walsingham's questions. Your plan is, of course, quite miraculous, a work of true genius. And yet there is a flaw.'

'There is no flaw.'

'Not in the execution, perhaps. But afterwards, when the deed is done, it will be hard for us all to get away from Kenilworth.' Massetti gave his co-conspirators a weak smile. 'If I stay, it will be impossible for me to escape the suspicion that must fall on all foreigners at court. I will be examined again by Walsingham, followed everywhere by his servants. I may even be tortured on his intolerable rack.'

'I see what you mean.' The bear-tamer nodded, as though considering the matter seriously. 'And you feel, my good lord Massetti, that you may be unable to withstand such tortures?

That the rigours of an English interrogation may put the rest of us in jeopardy?'

'Oh, I am not such a fool as to betray my fellow countrymen. But I fear it may be difficult not to answer *any* of their questions. These men know their business.'

'As I do mine.'

'Agreed, my friend. That is why I ask, knowing how things stand with your plan, that you leave off your entry into the castle until tomorrow night. Allow me to make some excuse about my wife's health back in Italy, so that I may leave court in the morning and my involvement in this plot may not so easily be proved.' Massetti gazed around at the rest of the troupe, a falsely hearty smile on his sallow face, though his fear was palpable. 'I shall return to London at once and thence to our own country, where all those who have supported this action from the start will await your triumphant return as soldiers of the true faith.'

'Hmm. You have already expressed a concern for your wife's health, is that not so?'

Massetti frowned. 'Have I?'

'When my men paid you a visit, you were told that your wife and child might suffer if you did not keep your side of the bargain.'

'But I have k-kept my word to the Association of the Bear,' Massetti stammered. His voice rose. 'I provided false letters of passage for you through Dover Port and into this castle. I told lies to Walsingham to prevent suspicion from falling on you. And I have set everything up for the smooth running of this evening's business. The death of the steward's assistant made things difficult for me, yet I said nothing and hid the evidence for you. I have been a good friend to you and your patron in this business.'

Patron?

So there might yet be a nobleman at Elizabeth's court pulling the strings behind this Association of the Bear, just as Walsingham suspected. But who?

Goodluck listened to their exchange with what he hoped was a dumb expression; they must not know he could understand every word. Though much was still unclear to him. The central stairs to the Queen's apartments would be guarded too heavily for such a small group to prevail, even if they charged it en masse. Goodluck wondered which of the castle guards had been prevailed upon to take a bribe from the Italians, and how such a thing could have been achieved among hand-picked men. Were covert Catholics even more deeply embedded in England than Walsingham feared?

'Yes, all that is true.' The bear-tamer held out his right hand to Massetti, who shook it uncertainly. 'You have mostly done what we asked of you, Massetti, and because of that you will not suffer unduly. Nor will your family be touched. Have no fear on that score, whatever threats you may have heard from us before. But we must enter the castle tonight, the plan is already in motion.'

'Not . . . Not suffer? I do not understand.'

'I am truly sorry, my friend. If it is any consolation, Catholics everywhere will thank you for your loyal service in this matter. Perhaps even the Holy Father himself will spare a moment to pray for your soul. But you must realize that we cannot leave you behind to provide answers under torture that might embarrass our masters. That was never their intention. We are sent here merely to ensure that England returns to the Catholic faith it held under Queen Mary – a wish, indeed, that both you and your family have always shared.' As Massetti backed away, a look of horror dawning on his face, the bear-tamer nodded to the slant-eyed woman behind him. 'Do it.'

Realizing too late the fate that lay in store for him, Massetti turned and fled.

He got fewer than a hundred paces before the woman, darting over the woodland floor like a shadow across the face of the sun, caught up with him and leapt on his back.

With skilful speed, she yanked his head back by his short dark hair and dragged a shining blade across his exposed throat, so the blood spurted scarlet over the white ruff.

Massetti tried to shriek, but by then he could make only a horrible bubbling sound; the woman relinquished her hold, dropping back lightly to the ground. Massetti staggered on a few feet, trying to contain the blood jetting from his throat. Then he fell, face down, into the dirt.

By the light of a guttering torch, Goodluck watched the dying man's last feeble jerks, then looked up as a shadow fell over him.

It was the slant-eyed woman, staring down at him, the blood-stained knife held loose by her side. He had thought her attractive before. Close up though, there was something cold and inhuman about her dark, almond-shaped eyes, the straight line of her mouth.

'Madam?'

Goodluck met her steady gaze with a nod of acknowledgement for her skill.

A little politeness might smooth the way ahead. Knowing it was his turn to be dispatched, the best he could hope for was as swift a death as the one Massetti had so thanklessly received.

'Wait,' the bear-tamer said, staying her hand. 'There isn't time. This one must be questioned before he is killed. Let us go back to the castle and leave him to Alfonso.' He turned away, and there was a note in his voice which chilled Goodluck's blood. 'Alfonso, you know what to do.'

# Forty-six

'LUCY MORGAN?'

Wearily, Lucy sat up. She wiped her damp eyes on her gold-embroidered sleeve, and wondered when they would come to strip the fine garment from her back.

It was young Will Shakespeare, his pale, freckled face filled with consternation.

'Hello, Will,' she whispered, managing a crooked smile. 'Come to see the battle on the lake?'

'You're hurt,' the boy said, ignoring her question. He held out a small, grubby handkerchief.

She glanced down at her gown, following his gaze, and drew a sharp breath. She had forgotten she was bleeding and had wiped her damp face with her beautiful sleeve – which was now streaked with brownish-red blood. Oh, she would catch a second whipping for sure now, on top of all her other woes.

But she was not safe here. The crowd was but a few feet away from where she had sat down in the shadows, hoping not to be seen, and for all she knew there were hostile eyes watching her at this very moment.

Trying not to let her despair show, she marshalled her strength and got to her feet. Will supported her, and she looked down into his sweet face.

'Thank you. You're an angel.'

'No, mistress,' he replied, without even stopping to think, 'you are an angel, as strong and proud as the cherubim who guard the entrance to Eden.'

She could not help but laugh at his serious tone, the boy was in such earnest. 'If I am an angel, Will, I must be a fallen one. Fallen from grace with Her Majesty.'

Gingerly, she put a hand to her temple and felt a weeping gash, her fingertips reddened with fresh blood as she drew them away. She must have reopened the wound from her fall.

'The Queen struck me for disobedience, Will,' she whispered, staring down at her fingers. 'I deserved that punishment. I expect I shall be whipped too and turned away from the court. Perhaps even imprisoned. But I could not speak the truth without condemning someone else. Do you understand?'

Will's face was solemn. 'I saw what happened, mistress. But I could not hear what the Queen said.'

She gave a little sob. 'It was not my fault. I did not ask to carry those messages, nor to help her ladyship . . .' She pulled herself up short, seeing his frown. 'No matter. What's done is done. All I can do now is bear whatever punishment I am given as best I can.'

The boy nodded. Over their heads a bright firework popped with an almighty crack. Lucy shrank nervously from the sound, hands clamped over her ears.

Will tugged at her sleeve. 'If you are afraid, let's go back into the outer court,' he suggested, raising his voice above the sound of another cannon shot, fired over the lake. The boy's eyes glistened as he stared at the smoke drifting above the mock-battle. Then he turned back to her with resolution in his voice. 'Follow me. I know a short cut.'

She jumped up and ran after him as he ducked below the arms of the crowd and began to thread a path away from the lake.

'No, wait,' she said breathlessly, catching up with the lad. 'I need to find my friend, Master Goodluck. Do you know him? He's one of the players from London, a great fellow with a beard.'

Will frowned and shook his head.

A moment later, Lucy saw Master Twist through the crowd, his head turning from side to side as though he too were searching for someone. Perhaps Goodluck? She called his name but her cry was lost in a great thundering volley of charges in the water battle.

Hurriedly signalling Will to follow, she pushed sideways through the massed crowd of people, ignoring their angry protests and sharp pinches, until she came to Master Twist's side.

'Master Twist,' she gasped. She saw his surprised look, the way his gaze moved straight to the gash on her forehead. She did not explain the wound but nonetheless felt herself blush with shame. It was as though she had been publicly marked for her disobedience to the Queen. 'I've been looking for Goodluck. Is he not with you?'

'We've been looking for him too. No one's seen him for some hours. We're getting worried.'

She stared, hearing the undisguised concern in Twist's voice. 'What do you mean? You think something's happened to Goodluck?'

'Sos saw him leaving the castle by the north gate. Some of the Italian performers packed up and left this morning, and Goodluck must have decided to follow their trail.' He frowned heavily. 'That was in the mid-afternoon. The Queen's hunting party went out at five and was back by eight. We expected Goodluck to follow the hunt back in, for they must have taken the same road, but he never returned.'

Her stomach wrenched with sudden fear. Not returned? The possibility that her guardian was dead flew across her mind like a frightened bird, and she stilled it, unable to think such a thought without collapsing. There could be a thousand other reasons why he had not been seen.

'Then we must find him,' she said decisively.

'That's what I've been trying to do,' Twist said, a dry note in his voice, and again his gaze lifted to the cut on her temple. 'That looks bad. How did you—?'

'It's not important.'

'Well, we must begin a search. Goodluck may be dead, or our acrobatic friends may have taken him prisoner, but we need to be sure either way. We've been watching both the north and south gates since Goodluck left, and none of the Italians have returned. So if they have him, they must have taken him to some safe place outside the castle walls, perhaps to interrogate him.'

Will interrupted them, his high voice as yet unbroken. 'What about the Brays? Father and I came that way tonight. There are many good hiding places there.'

Twist looked down at him, his brows raised, as though only just registering the presence of the boy. 'Yes, that's an excellent thought,' he agreed, rather too readily, and Lucy sensed that Twist was trying to get rid of them. 'Why don't you and Lucy start your search out in the Brays? Only be careful and keep your wits about you. These men are dangerous. I will follow on when I can. First, I need to find Walsingham's man. His master must hear of Goodluck's disappearance, and tonight.'

Leaving him, Lucy elbowed her way through the crowd with young Will at her back. In the heaving press of flesh about them, she felt his fingers clutching at her skirts, uncertain, anchoring himself to her. They passed through the gate unchallenged – even the guards seemed absorbed by the sea-battle out on the lake, with its fire-monsters and galleons and vast, dancing lights – and hurried across the half-empty outer court. Most of those living in tents there had gone outside to watch the battle on the mere, and those in the great buildings above the court were no doubt watching from the windows on the other side. Soon, though, the battle would be over, and the excited crowds would return to swell the outer court and the smoky alleys of the Brays. Once that happened, their chances of finding Goodluck would be reduced almost to nil.

As they drew level with the tall, elegant buildings of the state apartments, every window glittering with candlelight in antici-pation of the court's return, Lucy began to feel nervous, her stomach unsettled.

As she hesitated, a doubt stirring in her heart, Will gestured impatiently towards the Brays. 'Mistress, we need to find Master Goodluck. That's what the other man said.'

'John Twist,' she muttered. 'Yes, I know what he said.'

She stood hesitantly, gazing about herself in the darkness of the outer court. What should she do?

If only she had Goodluck to advise her . . .

The ancient gate to the tiltyard and the Brays stood ahead of them, its narrow entrance barely a cart's width in size. To their right stood the new, brightly lit royal apartments. To her left she could see the wide-open double doors to Leicester's enormous stables, and outside it, dozens of horses, muddy and exhausted from the hunt, still being rubbed down and watered by the stable boys.

*Tom.*

Due in part to Leicester's abrupt summons to the music room, she and Tom had parted on poor terms, their argument of the other night still not forgotten. But what other choice did she have but to ask for Tom's help in finding Goodluck? Her guardian was the man they needed tonight, she sensed that instinctively. Yet she and Will could not hope to find him on their own. Besides, if there was some plot in hand to murder the Queen of England and she did nothing to forestall it, she would be little better than an assassin herself.

That thought chilled her, and she seized Will's warm hand. 'Come, young Master Shakespeare,' she said boldly, hoping fervently that she was not mistaken in her trust, 'I know a friend who will help us find him.'

The men stared to see a woman entering the stables, and a young black woman at that. Several turned and stopped their work to look her up and down, one of them making a ribald comment that left Will flushed and angry, ready to do battle on her account. She hushed him, and asked in a clear voice where she could find Tom.

This request silenced the laughter, and one of the older men pointed them further down to the right. 'He'll be with the Queen's own horses,' he volunteered in a thick Warwickshire accent, but his eyes were not friendly. 'Who's the lad?'

Lucy ignored him, but gripped Will's hand more tightly. 'This way,' she murmured, with more confidence than she felt.

'He's not *her* son, that's for sure,' one of the others called out, and the laughter started again, louder now.

Will said nothing, seeing the tension in her face, but as soon as they were out of earshot he whispered fiercely, 'How dare they! If I was a year older . . .'

She smiled, and shook her head. Then her face brightened, for she had seen Tom. Yet still she hung back, for Tom was holding his cap in his hand, speaking respectfully to a portly man in a rust-red doublet, clearly his master. The man moved on and paused before them, staring from Lucy to Will as if he would stop and question their presence there. Lucy swept him a low curtsey and the man seemed to think better of it, nodding as he passed. Perhaps the extravagant gold and white court gown had changed his mind.

Tom straightened from his work, frowning. 'Lucy?' He glanced at the boy, then back at her. His eyes focused on the cut on her forehead. 'Is something wrong?'

Much to her shame, at this innocent enquiry she burst into tears, quite unable to speak. There was the briefest of hesitations, then his strong arms closed about her, his voice in her ear, deep and familiar, offering her comfort. She dropped Will's hand and embraced Tom, so relieved to see him that her whole body was trembling.

'How did you hurt yourself?' he asked, pulling back to look again at the cut.

'I angered the Queen. She hit me.'

He was silent, and she could feel his tension. 'You did not sing well enough to please her?'

She closed her eyes. 'No,' she whispered. 'Hush, it doesn't matter. Listen, Master Goodluck is missing. You remember what I told you, that he was here to keep the Queen safe? I think the conspirators may have taken him. The same men who killed that steward of Leicester's.'

'What?'

'I think Master Goodluck may have discovered what they are planning.' She hung on his sleeve, pleading with him. 'Tom, I would not ask if I did not need your help. I'm so afraid. His life may be in danger.'

She had half expected him to argue with her, to persuade her not to be so foolish and to wait for Goodluck to reappear. Instead, Tom reached for his jacket, which lay on a heap of straw. Beneath it was a sheathed dagger. He threw the jacket aside and shoved the dagger into his belt, his face hard.

'We'd best hurry.' Tom ruffled Will's hair as he passed, and earned a hesitant smile from the boy. 'Where shall we look for him first, then?'

# Forty-seven

LETTICE LAY IN A NEAR-STUPOR, TOO HOT FOR THE THICK, RICHLY embroidered covers they had given her, her eyelids barely able to stay open for more than a few seconds at a time. Some kind of summer storm was raging in the darkness outside her window, but she did not have enough energy to rise from her bed and stagger across to look out at the sky. Instead, she lay in a sweat-drenched, mumbling slumber and listened, wondering how long it would be before she died. Or perhaps she was already dead, and this was hell. From beyond the thick walls of the castle, she heard terrible cracks of thunder, accompanied by lightning that seared the back of her eyeballs with white light, and sometimes the whole room shook as though Kenilworth Castle were under attack.

The physician had come to visit her just after dawn. It had been a long night of cramping, and the bleeding had been severe. She remembered his visit clearly, for he alone had understood her ailment. The women had clucked about her stained bed, and offered herbal remedies and warm spiced wine, and even prayed over her – as though God would wish to keep such a wretched creature alive. But the physician had come and shooed them out, like hens.

He had stood in silence, his finger at her throat, as though the over-rapid beat of her heart could reveal the true extent of her evil. Then he asked two or three questions, which she answered from between numb lips, eager now for death to take her. Reaching into his medicine chest, he withdrew a narrow vial of some greenish liquid and forced her to drink it. The taste was horrible, but she swallowed every last drop, hoping it might hasten her death. He raised her bloodstained shift, groped between her legs, and said the baby was gone.

With a grim face, the physician called for the women to return. He demanded that they change the bedding and put down fresh rushes around her mattress, and burn a sweet-scented candle to freshen the air. And since then she had slept more comfortably, and the pain had slowly eased.

Now she just felt limp and sleepy, her eyelids leaden. Heat burned in her cheeks as though she still had a fever.

The door creaked open, and she saw the torches outside in the corridor through the sudden gap. Someone came in and shut the door with a quiet hand, then hesitated before approaching the mattress where she lay, still uncovered, too hot and exhausted to move.

Was she to be murdered in her bed?

The thought of her death did not alarm, though she felt a pang of remorse, knowing she would never see her pretty, soft-cheeked children again. But perhaps, with her passing, they might be allowed to bury her shame with her body, and live to marry well and be useful to the throne. Besides, it was better she should die now than live defamed and in exile, far from the English court.

Still, her body disagreed with the equanimity of her mind. As her assassin sat beside her on the mattress, her mouth let out a feeble cry and her hands fluttered up to save herself.

It was a man. She knew his smell, the scent of leather and horses . . .

'Robert!'

'Hush,' he said swiftly, grasping her hands and pressing them gently. 'You are sick. Very sick. Do not attempt to speak.'

'The child is dead.'

'I know.' He leaned over and kissed her on the forehead. 'I spoke to the physician just now, before I came in. He says the worst is over. Do you hear me, my beloved? You will be well again.'

Her mind burned with confusion. Was she imagining his visit, the touch of his cool lips on her face?

'I'm sorry,' she managed.

He said nothing, and again she dreamed herself back into her nightmare, with the assassin creeping slowly through the room. At any moment his hand might descend on her mouth, to crush the life out of her frail body and leave only this husk for her husband.

Sighing, she turned her face into the pillow. What did it matter? She was tired of life, of men. Only the thought of her children still had the power to animate her.

'Ask my children to forgive me,' she said, her voice muffled against the covers, 'and kiss them goodbye for me.'

'No, no!' Robert was kneeling beside the bed, his face close to hers. His hands shook her, disturbing the deadly slumber into which she so desired to slip. 'Stay awake, Lettice! Open your eyes, my love, my little love!'

What had he called her?

She forced her eyelids open and stared at him by candlelight. He was so close, she could see the soft hazel flecks in his dark, dark eyes. She reached out to stroke his cheek. 'Robert,' she whispered, her quiet words meant only for him. 'You should not come here. I am cursed. If the Queen should hear of your visit—'

'Damn the bitch, I'm done with her,' he replied in a low, shaking voice. 'She has played me long enough. Your husband cannot live for ever. And when he dies, you and I shall be wed.'

'He will outlive me, I fear.'

'No, he will not,' Robert stated, without any hesitation. 'Even if I have to see to that myself.'

Her breath strangled in her throat and Lettice felt herself faint, the world slipping away into an odd, rushing paleness. When she came to again, opening her lids to a dim, candlelit chamber and her lover's strong arms supporting her, she raised her gaze to his handsome face and found nothing but love there, glowing fierce and true in the darkness.

'I love you,' she managed weakly, knowing she would die happy now, with those words on her lips.

Robert smiled, and bent to kiss her.

'And I love you,' he whispered. His voice grew harder, clearer. 'But you must shake off this sickness, Lettice. The Queen shall not dictate who I am to woo or wed, and if your husband returns from Ireland you will need all your strength to face him.'

# Forty-eight

LUCY GAZED UP AT THE TALL, BRILLIANTLY LIT WINDOWS OF THE Queen's state apartments high above, and shivered.

The fireworks were long since finished, a chill northerly wind had begun to blow, and the sloping castle grounds stood dark and hostile at the mereside wall. The Queen would have retired to bed in her royal chambers by now, accompanied only by one or two of her women, and although her personal guards would be on the doors, they were unlikely to know that conspirators against Her Majesty might be attempting to gain entry to the castle that very night.

Lucy had no cloak and was still wearing her court slippers, too fine and thin-soled for wandering about this rough, nettled slope between the castle and the outer walls. But there had been no time to change her gown or shoes, or even slip a pair of wooden pattens over them to protect them from the dirt. Instead, she wrapped her arms about her chest for warmth and hoped she had not drawn Tom and poor young Will out into the dark on a fool's errand.

'Come on,' Tom murmured in her ear. 'There's no sign of Master Goodluck here. We should try further out, beyond the tiltyard.'

She hesitated, agreeing with Tom yet somehow unwilling to move on. She stared up towards the Queen's apartments as though the answer might lie there. The gate in the mereside wall was guarded. She could see the broad bulk of the guard even from this distance, and knew that many more must stand at arms inside the towers beyond. Her Majesty was well protected. So why were the hairs standing up on the back of her neck, her belly aching with an unexplained fear?

The dark slope above, which led over rough ground to the gate in the mereside wall, did not look inviting. Indeed, she would never have countenanced taking such a route without Tom at her side to protect her. Yet that was the way they ought to take tonight, she felt it in her bones.

'Goodluck told me about a room beyond that gate,' she said, pointing. 'A locked room, and the key gone missing. He thought it was important but he was not sure how it could be useful to the assassins. Tom, what if they have the key to that room and are able to get through the gate?'

'But it's guarded, look.'

'Guards can be killed,' she whispered, shivering. 'Or bribed. It's worth a look, at least.'

Tom held her eyes deliberately a moment, then nodded. 'If you believe we should climb up there and watch the gate rather than keep looking for your guardian, then that's exactly what we shall do.'

'Thank you.'

Belatedly, Lucy thought to leave the boy behind as lookout. He was too young and soft-faced to help defend the Queen. Besides, if anything happened to him, how would she face his father, who might even now be scouring the lakeside for him?

'Will you stay here for us, Will,' she asked, indicating a dip in the bank where he could sit, 'and whistle a loud warning if you see anyone coming this way?'

'If you are right, it would be better to send him away altogether,' Tom muttered, still staring into the darkness, his words intended only for her. 'As soon as they realize he's a look-out, they'll slit the boy's throat.'

Such a grim possibility had not occurred to her.

Tight-chested, she took young Will by the hand and tried to smile encouragingly. 'Indeed, dearest, if you could . . . If you are able to find Master Twist and tell him where we are, that would be the most help to us now.'

Will looked sulky at this suggestion and glanced at Tom over her shoulder, as though suspicious that he was behind this request. 'Leave you? But what if you are attacked? You may need me.' Stoutly, the boy stuck out his chest. 'I'm stronger than I look.'

'I know, and I do need you, Will. But someone has to fetch Master Twist and his friends.' She added a hint of urgency. 'Find them as quickly as you can and bring them to us here, below the royal apartments.'

'You'll wait for me to return?'

She shook her head, though wishing secretly that they *could* wait for the others to arrive. The thought of what might lie in store for them was terrifying.

'We must go on. The Queen may be in danger.'

Once the boy had gone, scampering away across the outer court with the effortless speed of the young, Lucy turned and began to follow Tom up the steep bank. She slipped a little on the loose soil, holding up her white and gold skirts. It was growing colder now and the tall trees around them, their branches heavy with summer green, rustled menacingly in the dark. 'Maybe Will's right,' she called out after him as they climbed. 'We could wait here until Goodluck's men come to help us. What good can we do, after all, just the two of us?'

But Tom was not listening. A cry of 'Fire! Fire!' had risen above them at the base of the Queen's apartments. A muffled alarm bell began to clang somewhere inside the castle. Soon after, two men came running with sloshing buckets from Mortimer's Tower, the nearest waterside defences. The guard must have unlocked the gate to allow them entry, for they passed through un-challenged; now the gate stood wide open, and the guard too had disappeared, leaving his post unattended.

'Tom!' she cried, clutching at his arm.

'I see them,' he said grimly, for as they had paused in their steep ascent to the wall, three dark figures had slipped through the undefended gate, the largest of the three shambling along on all fours, beast-like, a chain about its neck.

'The bear and his tamer!'

Suddenly, Lucy came to a halt. She leaned forward from the waist, out of breath, not wanting to go on.

'Those men . . .' For the love of God, she could barely speak. 'They are the assassins, I know it for sure now. Tom, we must fetch help. Master Goodluck—'

'May be dead for all we know.' Tom shook his head and motioned her to keep climbing. After a moment, she followed him up the rough slope towards the open gate, protesting urgently, but Tom did not seem to hear her. He turned near the top, a light in his eyes. 'It's too late now to fetch help. Besides, young Will has gone to tell Master Twist where we are. We must follow those men and stop them before they reach the Queen.'

'You and I alone?'

'Yes, but with God on our side,' he reminded her, reaching for her hand. His fingers found hers in the darkness and squeezed them gently. 'Whatever name you give your God, Lucy, pray to him now for the strength and courage to go on. What, would you leave your duty undone out of fear?'

Struck by his words, she shook her head slowly.

'Then come through the gate with me,' he urged her, and helped Lucy up the last few feet. Hand in hand, they came to the high wall that stood between the inner and outer courts, and hurried through the unguarded gate. 'We may be the only ones who saw them, who know the assassins are inside the castle. They may already have found their way to the Queen. You think any of those will help us?'

He pointed at the wide-open door to the storeroom from which a thick, stinking smoke was already pouring. Through the livid red glow from the flames inside, she could make out the silhouettes of men running back and forth, no doubt attempting to move the most precious of the Queen's belongings before they caught fire. A shout for 'Water!' had gone up along the wall defences and the alarm bell was now tolling in earnest, waking those who had already retired for the night.

She knew what Tom meant, watching that chaotic scene. Which of those guards, frightened out of their wits by the con- sequences of a fire in Her Majesty's storeroom, would spare a few minutes to search along the base of the castle for . . . what? A wandering bear and his tamer? An assassin whose face no one had ever seen?

'No,' she whispered in agreement, and turned to climb higher into darkness.

One hand resting on the knife at his belt, Tom pushed his way through the bushes with Lucy struggling along behind him, vicious holly branches snagging on her embroidered sleeves and skirts. A gust of wind made the foliage shake and rustle ominously, and for a moment she feared that someone was in there, watching from behind the thick, impenetrable branches.

Tom uttered a strong oath, staring through the windy dark. He lifted his arm and pointed ahead to a low, rectangular blackness outlined against the red sandstone of the castle walls.

'Look!'

'What is it?' She came level with him, frowning as she tried to make out what he had seen. 'Is that a door?'

He grabbed her arm as she went to pass him, and shook his head. 'Wait, there may be someone on the other side.'

'Now who's afraid?'

He stood a moment, as though trying to balance different paths in his head, then drew the dagger from his belt.

'I want you to stay here until the others arrive,' he said, his voice firm. 'I'm going through that door to see where it leads.'

'What, stay here and get my throat cut too?'

'Come with me then,' he agreed reluctantly, weighing the brutal-looking dagger on his palm. 'Keep close behind me, and if I shout, run.'

He pushed at the thick, black-studded door in the castle wall and it opened easily, left unlocked by whoever had entered earlier. Over his shoulder, Lucy could see nothing at first but darkness, then a faint glimmer of light at the far end of the chamber. Bending as low as she could manage, she slipped after Tom through the narrow doorway and into the room beyond. A small lantern had been set in an alcove, by whose light she could just make out an opening in the ceiling high above them, and the ghostly glimmer of a rope dangling from its dark hole.

Jumping down from the threshold, which was set higher than the chamber itself, she bumped up against Tom's rigid form.

Caught off balance, Lucy stumbled sideways and almost fell

over a heap of empty storage chests lying scattered across the earthen floor; the wood was so rotten, she put her foot straight through one of them, crying aloud at the pain in her ankle.

A furious roar from the shadows made her straighten.

'Lucy, get out of here!'

At Tom's warning shout, she jerked her foot free in sudden alarm and staggered backwards into the damp, lichened wall. Ahead of them in the chamber was a roaring black mass which blocked out the meagre light thrown by the lantern. For a moment she stared up at the monster, wide-eyed, so terrified she could hardly breathe.

'Holy Mother, defend us!' she whispered under her breath, and crossed herself.

It was only as the demon moved, rearing up and extending dangerously claw-tipped paws, that she realized what it was – no creature of childhood nightmares, but the Italian's performing bear.

Tom ran forward with a shout, feinting with his dagger and whirling about the bear's bulky figure, no doubt trying to draw the animal away from her. The black bear turned, swiping at Tom and giving another infuriated roar.

Suddenly, a swarthy face appeared at the opening in the ceiling. Staring up, she recognized the bear-tamer. Without hesitation, the bearded man swung down the rope and landed with a thud on the earthen floor.

With her back still against the wall, Lucy cried out a warning to Tom, who was engaged in a deadly game of tag with the bear. But before Tom could create any space between himself and the bear's claws, the Italian drew a curved dagger from inside the folds of his cloak and leapt towards him.

'Run for the guards!' Tom shouted across at her as he lunged, making the bearded Italian dance swiftly backwards.

Lucy glanced back at the narrow doorway, a smoky glimmer of light just visible on the grassy bank outside. Then she looked up at the black opening in the ceiling with its sturdy rope still dangling just short of the ground. The bear-tamer must have stayed behind to guard the escape route. Which meant someone else was the assassin – and was already up there, in the royal apartments. No doubt undetected, thanks to the fire that had been deliberately set in the Queen's storeroom.

Not stopping to consider what she was about to do, Lucy ran forward and made a grab for the rope. She missed it and gave a despairing cry, stumbling and falling to her knees.

Frowning, the swarthy Italian turned to stare at her.

Tom instantly lunged again, catching the man off-guard and slashing through his cloak.

Lucy backed up a few steps, tucked her skirts up under the belted waist of her gown, then leapt again, aiming higher than before. This time she caught the rope and dragged herself upwards, remembering how to pull her own weight, hand over hand, until her feet were gripping the rope too and she could shinny upwards. It hurt terribly, her palms stinging at the un-accustomed roughness of the rope, her shoulders almost wrenched out of their sockets at each pull, but she fixed her eyes on the dark opening above and kept climbing.

From the darkness below, Lucy heard the bear roar in fury again and then Tom cry out, swearing violently.

Her heart nearly burst at his cry. Had Tom been wounded?

She dared not stop and look back. Reaching the hatch in the roof, Lucy angled one knee and wedged it inside the dusty frame. Swinging her other leg up with a terrible ripping sound as the gold-embroidered skirt tore, she dragged herself on to the wooden floor beyond and lay there a moment, panting with exertion.

Forcing herself to sit up, Lucy stared breathlessly about the small, darkened room. It was another windowless storage chamber, containing what appeared to be chests and wooden barrels at floor level and stacks of woollen blankets on shelves. The door was only a few feet away, standing slightly ajar, and through it she could see torchlight.

She leaned back over the opening and called Tom's name, her voice oddly hoarse, echoing about the walls.

There was no reply. She stared hard a moment longer, but could see only the faintest glimmer of movement in the heavy shadows below. Then she remembered her mission.

The Queen! She must alert the guards!

Lucy staggered to the door in her torn gown, heart pounding, arms and legs aching fiercely from the climb, and yanked it wide. A dark narrow corridor led away from the room, ending in a blank wall with one heavily studded door. She found it unlocked and opened it into another dark storage area, this time so cluttered with boxes and chests piled to the ceiling, she had to clamber about their teetering stacks to reach the curtained opening in the opposite wall. The curtain had been pulled slightly to one side, and through it she could see brighter torchlight, the gleaming polished wood of the Queen's building.

Hesitating behind the curtain, she heard shouts of 'Fire!' and 'Water!' in the distance, the voices too far off to be of any help. She must go on alone.

Lucy drew a shaky breath, then forced herself to creep past the curtain and out into the light.

On the landing outside the royal chambers, a few feet apart in the flickering torchlight, lay the bodies of two guards, one slumped against the wall with a great gash in his throat, the other with his head at an odd angle, his neck clearly broken.

Beyond them, the double doors to the Presence Chamber stood wide open and undefended.

Holding her breath, Lucy stooped to pluck the young man's knife from his belt, ignoring the blood that dribbled over her fingers. Then, on silent feet, she stepped over the other body and entered the Queen's apartments.

# Forty-nine

THE LAST TORCH HAD GUTTERED AND BEEN THROWN INTO THE stream beside him. The acrid taste of its smoky remains was still in his mouth as Goodluck emerged from the water, gasping like a landed fish. He was almost grateful for the searing pain in his lungs, the way his mouth sucked on the air like a crazed baby at the breast, unable to do anything but make this rasping sound. At least this way he had no time for thought, except the most basic: *survival*.

Such a sharp focus brought complications of its own, however. The easiest thing would be to spill everything he knew, hoping for a quick death. But England demanded more loyalty from him than that, and he had his pride.

'Why do you watch?' The questions came in rapid, broken English, one after the other, hoping to confuse him. 'What is your master? Your name, who is it?'

Goodluck choked, still gargling in the back of his throat, and spat out a mouthful of water that wet the young Italian's shirt.

Alfonso – as the bear-tamer had called him – swore fiercely in his own tongue. With an iron hand, he pushed Goodluck head first back into the chill stream and held him there.

Goodluck struggled to remain calm, not to fight the water that swirled about him, coldly filling every orifice and threatening to overwhelm him. Soon, he would no longer be able to refuse to answer. Everyone had their limits and his were fast approaching. Blotting out the truth, he concentrated on the questions he could most innocently answer, reciting them in his mind, knowing that soon he would have to speak.

'Your name, who is it?'

*Goodluck, my name is Goodluck.*

Once a person yields to torture and begins to speak, giving his name and his barest details, that is when the one interrogating him should press the hardest, for it is then that a man is most likely to betray himself and his friends.

'Your master?'

*Robert Dudley, Earl of Leicester.*

Mentally, he shied away from the name of his true master. Walsingham. He must not even think of it. He was from Warwickshire, not London. He was one of Leicester's men, a simple soldier from a quiet Warwickshire village. A son of the soil. His parents had worked all their lives in the fields. This was all a terrible mistake. He was no spy.

'Why do you watch?'

*I came into the forest to relieve myself and heard a strange beast. I was curious. Then I saw—*

The hand gripped his hair, dragging him back into a thick, lung-scraping darkness, and the relentless battering of questions.

'Who are you?'

'Goodluck,' he managed, through a mouthful of weed-infested stream water, resisting the urge to retch. 'Goodluck.'

Again, a throaty voice cried out, 'It is the same answer. Put him back in!'

Oh, she was not stupid either, the woman who had stayed behind to help Alfonso with the interrogation. She was nothing like the one with the knife. But just as vicious, an older, round-hipped creature nearing her thirtieth year whose stony eyes and uncouth tongue made her feminine curves uninviting.

Thrusting her foot down on the back of his head, the hoarse-voiced woman shoved Goodluck into the dark water almost up to his chest.

He thrashed about, too tired to act the hero, becoming readier to talk. But he could not betray his friends. Better to let them drown him first. Though the two of them would have their fill of pleasure before killing him.

His eyes bulged. He felt pressure mount behind them, as though they were being pushed out from inside his skull. His throat was tight, his lungs burning. He longed to open his mouth, to let the water rush in. He could not resist any longer. He had no name, no mind, only this need to breathe. His jaw flew open like a released spring and he gulped, sucking in death, drinking the cold stream, even while his chest popped and his limbs jangled, his body violent in its reaction.

The woman removed her foot and he bobbed back up beneath her, like a cork on a piece of netting. Thankful to be alive, he gasped at the air and immediately vomited into the stream – no holding it back this time. The woman laughed, moved away, made a few disparaging remarks in Italian about Goodluck's virility.

'Why do your people watch us?' she demanded. 'Speak, and save yourself!'

He fought with the sweet, alluring impulse to tell these two everything he knew, to void himself of all those secret, hidden facts they sought – his true name, his master's name, the places where he had spied that year, the names of all the men he had ever worked with.

'I came into the forest . . . when I heard—'

'Lies, mere stories!' the woman hissed. 'Do not trust him, look at his eyes. He knows more than he is saying, this one. It's time to cut him, Alfonso. Cut him until he talks.'

Goodluck received a violent kick from behind and would have tumbled again, hands still bound behind his back, head first into the stream – except that his shoulder caught the bank and flipped him sideways on to a sharp rock. He fell awkwardly, half turned on his back to stare up at the stars through the leafy branches overhead.

Then he heard a splash.

Alfonso swore under his breath and knelt beside him on the muddy bank, reaching out awkwardly into the water.

The clumsy young fool had dropped something.

With an effort, Goodluck lowered his gaze to examine the curl of the young man's beard, the paleness of his skin emphasized by dark eyes and hair. For a moment, he found himself thinking of Lucy, her coarse black hair always tucked inside a demure hood these days, and remembered her as a young girl, running free in his sister's garden, her unbound hair wild as a holly bush about her head. How she had laughed as he chased her.

Regret filled him, swelling his chest with unshed tears. He had hoped to see Lucy married to a good man and know her happy and content, to do a father's duty by the girl. Instead, he would die tonight at this young fool's hands, and never meet her children.

His wrists, playing the rope against the sharp rock beneath him, seemed a little wider apart now, no longer bound so tightly.

Then Alfonso was leaning back on his knees, turning towards him again, lips curved in a cold smile. In his hand, a treacherous-looking knife dripped, gleaming in the starlight.

'Now to finish this.'

# Fifty

ELIZABETH KNELT AT HER PRAYERS, HEAD BENT, HANDS CLASPED before her. To her right, Lady Mary sighed deeply, and young Swedish-born Helena, never one for lengthy devotions, fidgeted to her left. Elizabeth herself was not over-keen on too long a communication with the Lord but she was not yet ready to lie down. Indeed, she feared a long night of restlessness lay ahead; her mind was too busy for sleep, incessantly working over the problems of the day even while she was readied for bed. Her ladies had slipped a nightgown over her head, brushed her wig until it shone, and cleansed the whitening paint from her face and throat.

Outside the high leaded windows, the wind had begun to howl about the castle, growing stronger every minute. She could hear distant shouts and the sound of a bell tolling somewhere below in the castle grounds.

Elizabeth shivered in a sudden chill draught. Her undressing had taken nearly two exhausting hours. The heavy gown required several women to unfasten and remove each separate piece, and then her pearl-laden wig had refused to be parted from the supports holding her vast, perfectly white, angel-wing ruff in place. She wished that her women had at least thought to cover her head with a cap before prayers.

Discreetly, Elizabeth opened her eyes and peered about herself. The lacy white cap lay on the bed, only a few feet away, waiting for her to finish her devotions.

'Lady Mary,' she murmured, eyes closed once more, hands still clasped as though in prayer, 'my cap.'

There was a rustle to her right, the sound of slippered feet on creaking floorboards, then soft hands were fitting the lacy cap to her head, gently tying the white ribbons in a bow beneath her chin.

'Your Majesty,' Lady Mary whispered with her habitual deference, and sank back to her knees behind her.

No sooner had Elizabeth begun to brood on the unsatisfactory events at the lakeside, that wicked Moorish girl's refusal to obey her, than a crash and a muffled cry from the Privy Chamber brought her head up again, hands falling to her sides.

Mary and Helena had leapt to their feet immediately, taking up flanking positions to protect the Queen. Though what they thought they could do against an attacker, she could not conceive.

Elizabeth signalled the two ladies to help her up, then placed a finger on her lips and gestured Helena cautiously to investigate.

The younger woman hesitated at the thick, studded door, listening to the sounds of struggle behind it, then called out in an uncertain voice, 'Master of the Guard?'

There was no reply.

'Is the chamber door locked?' Elizabeth demanded.

Lady Mary shook her head. She fumbled at her belt and held up the key. 'We lock the door only when you are abed, Your Majesty,' she replied in a whisper.

'Lock it now.'

Mary nodded, and hurried to secure the door to the Privy Chamber.

Before she could reach it, the door was flung open, and a short, dark-robed figure stood on the threshold. Grim-faced, this creature stared wildly into the chamber, then began to advance on the three of them, bearing a long unsheathed dagger still shiny with the blood of its previous victims.

Lady Helena cried for the guards to come quickly, her back straight, anger shaking in her voice.

Elizabeth stood silent. She could have told her lady-in-waiting that the men on guard outside her doors were already dead, otherwise this assassin would never have penetrated so far into the state apartments.

Lady Mary stepped in front of the Queen. Her jewelled fingers trembled as they groped for the cross about her neck. Nonetheless, she demonstrated a stalwart composure in the face of death.

She raised her chin. 'You shall not pass, villain. This is the Queen's bedchamber.'

The dark-eyed assassin stopped and studied each of them in turn, as though trying to decide which of these women, all in lace nightgowns and caps, was the Queen of England.

It was only then that Elizabeth realized her would-be murderer, despite the bloodstained dagger and the masculine attire, was a woman.

Outrage and fury reared inside her and she cried out, 'Don't dare to come a step closer, you foul disgrace to the female sex!'

The woman, if she deserved such a description, bared her teeth in a grin and shifted her knife to the other hand, her dark eyes fixed on Lady Mary.

Helena, resourceful as ever, had come up behind Elizabeth with a fur-lined mantle, and now made a show of draping this ceremonially over her shoulders. 'I've opened the passage at the back of the room,' she whispered in her ear, shocking Elizabeth with her knowledge of the secret door through which Robert had often entered and left her bedchamber. 'Mary and I will charge her, and you must—'

'Your Majesty!'

Another woman had come staggering through the doorway, also brandishing a knife and with blood pouring from a deep gash across her cheek.

It was Lucy Morgan.

'Your guards are dead,' Lucy gasped. 'I'm sorry, Your Majesty. I tried to stop her but she was too strong for me.'

With a hiss of frustration, the woman turned and lunged at Lucy with the knife. It seemed certain that she would kill her. Yet somehow Lucy managed to evade the assassin's blade. One moment she was leaning in the doorway, as though near to collapse, and the next she was several inches away, astonishingly light on her feet. The killer lunged again, and Lucy's sleeve ripped loudly. But again she moved so swiftly, as though dancing for the

Queen, the assassin was unable to catch her. The next time, however, Lucy was less lucky. The knife made contact with the sleeved shoulder of her gown, ripping the stitches and slicing through to the skin beneath.

Lucy cried out in pain and dismay, dropping her knife, and stumbled to her knees as a red stain began to spread across her shoulder.

The assassin turned her back on Lucy, indicating with a contemptuous gesture how little of a threat she considered the girl. Assessing Elizabeth again through dark, narrowed eyes, she gripped the long dagger more tightly and crouched as though about to spring.

Lady Mary spread her arms wide. 'You must kill me first,' she insisted, her voice rising on a note of hysteria. 'And I will not make it easy for you.'

'If that is your wish.'

As the assassin trod purposefully towards Mary, Lucy Morgan lurched to her feet and threw herself violently at the woman, knocking her off balance and sending both of them sprawling across the floor. The dagger spun out of the assassin's hand, clattering against a cabinet. A large gilt candlestick toppled at the impact and the burning candle fell on to the woollen rug beneath, setting it on fire.

Helena grabbed at the skirt of her nightgown and hurried past the struggling women on the floor to seize the fallen candlestick. But she was too late. Flame had already licked along the rug towards the heavily embroidered bed hangings, crackling ominously. Now smoke billowed upwards, shrouding everything in grey.

'To me, Your Majesty!' Lady Mary bustled Elizabeth to safety at the back of the room, a martial light in her usually sombre eyes. 'Pray do not fear. Lady Helena and I, we shall not allow harm to come to you.'

Smoke and the stench of burning wool swamped the Royal Bedchamber, and Elizabeth found herself coughing violently, barely able to breathe. Mary dragged the lacy cap from her own head and handed it across so that Elizabeth could cover her mouth. Helena was attempting to stamp out the fire with only her slippered feet, the poor brave girl, and shouting, 'Alarm! Alarm! Rouse the castle!'

The assassin kicked Lucy Morgan away and rose to her knees, groping now for the dagger. There was a cold fury in her eyes.

'You will die, Elizabeth, bastard whore of England,' she hissed in Italian. Her fingers closed around the dagger's slim handle, and a note of triumph crept into her voice. 'God guides my hand tonight. See, here is your death.'

Behind her, a bright flash of gold descended through the smoky air, and the assassin fell, her eyes wide with surprise.

Lady Helena stood over the motionless body and studied the bloodied candlestick in her hand as though she had never seen it before. She gazed on the assassin, then lifted a stunned gaze to Elizabeth's face.

'I think she's dead, Your Majesty.'

Elizabeth allowed Lady Mary to lead her past the crumpled body of the assassin and into the Privy Chamber. That broad, high-ceilinged room was less smoky than her own chamber. She was able to lower the cap from her mouth and breathe clean air again. By whose treachery had this Italian assassin been permitted to enter her state apartments? The traitor's head must be placed on a pike before the castle gate, she thought.

But even as she considered that prospect with pleasure, Elizabeth knew she did not wish the world to know how vulnerable she still was to attack.

Again, yet again!

Then Robin was suddenly there in the room, pale-faced. He knelt before Elizabeth, clasping her hands, and begged her to forgive him for not preventing the assassin's attack.

'Your Majesty, I would not have had this happen for the world. We have caught some of the conspirators, and riders have been sent after those who escaped. They will pay for this venture with torture and death, they and any here who are found to have helped them.' Her favourite held her hand tightly in his grasp, not letting her pull away, pressing warm lips to her skin. 'I will see each of these dogs run to ground and torn apart for this treachery.'

'Tear them apart if you wish, but I will not have this spoken of abroad,' Elizabeth insisted. 'We will give the Catholics fresh hope if we let them know how close that creature came to killing me.'

As a thick noxious smoke continued to billow out from her ruined bedchamber, Elizabeth found herself being ushered away from the royal apartments by a flock of her white-gowned ladies – surrounded now by burly guards at arms – to a hastily prepared chamber. A flagon of wine was set out for her, and there was clean linen on the simple bed.

'Where is Lucy Morgan?' she thought to ask wearily as her ladies ushered her into a fresh nightgown, but nobody seemed to know. She told Lady Mary to set her chair by the window, and sat there, her nerves a-jangle, knowing she could not sleep. 'Was she badly hurt? The girl showed great courage tonight. She should be rewarded.'

Helena curtseyed, offering her a drink of wine. 'Should I send for Lucy Morgan, Your Majesty?'

'Tomorrow will be soon enough. Let her hurts be tended first. Tonight I must see Walsingham. Though I imagine he is already on his way up.' She smiled at Helena. 'But you too were courageous, Helena. I owe you my life. It shall not be forgotten.'

'I did nothing but my duty to Your Majesty,' Helena said humbly, and backed away with her head lowered.

'Indeed.' Elizabeth's smile faded. She stared down into her cup of wine. 'I fear not all my subjects are so loyal, Helena.'

# Fifty-one

LUCY, COUGHING AND BARELY ABLE TO SEE FOR THE SMOKE, ROLLED
from her back on to her hands and knees.

The assassin lay nearby in a dark pool of blood, gazing directly
at her through the greedy flickering of flame, slack mouth turned
down at the corners.

Lucy stared, shivering at the sight of her deadly enemy, every
muscle in her body tensed for another fight. Then, belatedly, she
saw the dull sheen across those eyes and realized the woman was
already dead. She was glad then, remembering their struggle in
the antechamber, how she had tried to disarm the hooded
assassin, only for the hood to fall back and reveal her smooth
dark hair.

A woman!

That instant of disbelief had almost cost Lucy her life. She knelt
up, feeling shakily for the wound in her shoulder. Thankfully, it
was not as grave as she had feared. There was hardly any blood,
just a sharp, wrenching pain that left her wincing as she staggered
to her feet.

A hubbub of urgent voices came from the Privy Chamber, the
sound of running feet.

'Your Majesty?'

Painfully, holding on to the wall for support, Lucy made her
slow way to the door.

A handful of guards appeared in the doorway, barely noticing her. On the shouted order of their captain, they seized the assassin's corpse without ceremony and began to half drag, half carry it away. The woman's head lolled unpleasantly to one side, leaving a trail of blood across the rushes, mouth gaping open now, eyes still staring.

As Lucy watched this horrible spectacle, her legs trembling, one of the guards, a burly fellow wearing Leicester's badge, grasped her by the shoulder and pushed her roughly to one side.

'Out of the way, girl!'

'Please, where is the Queen?'

'What is it to you?' The man spun on his heel and stared down at her, his eyes narrowed. She had a sudden memory of the guard who had left the gate in the wall undefended, his bulky form swimming up out of the darkness in her mind. This one leaned closer, his reeking breath hot on her face. 'Mind your own business, girl, and get back to the servants' quarters. There's no place here for the likes of you.'

'Blount!'

Surly-faced, the guard turned away, sketched a half-salute to the captain who had challenged him, and hurried out in the wake of those carrying the corpse.

Briefly, the captain also looked her up and down, noting her bloodied gown, suspicion flickering in his face. Then, with some reluctance, he nodded for her to follow the others.

'Better take yourself downstairs and get those hurts seen to. Don't think about wandering off though. You may be wanted for questioning, so stay in the women's quarters until you're sent for.' He added brusquely, seeing her hesitation, 'Well, do as you're told, girl. If you've nothing to hide, no one will harm you.'

It seemed Lucy had no choice but to follow the slowly empty-ing crowd through the doors of the Presence Chamber and out on to the landing beyond, clasping her shoulder to lessen the pain. The Queen was nowhere to be seen, nor any of her chamberers and ladies-in-waiting. Some of the courtiers who had come to gawp at the commotion were still in bedgowns and nightcaps, shivering in the sharp draught from the stairway.

Lucy slipped unnoticed between the muttering courtiers, yet she did not take the stairs down to the next floor as she had been ordered. Instead she found herself following her route back along the narrow corridor to the darkened storeroom, whose door still stood ajar, and the gaping hole in the floor. That was where she had last seen Tom, holding back the bear and his tamer while she climbed the rope.

Kneeling on the lip of the hole, she leaned forward and stared down into terrifying blackness.

'Tom?' she whispered. The sound of his name echoed about the damp walls below.

Lucy knew what she must do, but did not want to do it. She was wounded, her head ached fit to burst, and she was scared. What would she find down there? The dead body of her friend? The black bear with its lethal claws and teeth? Or perhaps a handful of the assassin's countrymen, waiting for their friend to make her escape?

Lucy tucked up her skirts, groped for the rope that she knew must still hang there, swung both legs over the edge of the hole and let herself down into darkness.

The bear lay on its back just below the castle wall, stiffening already into death with wounds to its throat and belly, black blood seeping into the soil. She stared at its vast corpse a moment, then swallowed her sickness and stumbled on, fearing what lay ahead. She found Tom about a hundred yards further down the rough slope, half hidden behind an ancient oak stump. She knew he was dead as soon as she saw him, his dark mass spreadeagled in the starlit grasses, yet allowed herself to hope for a moment that she was mistaken.

'Oh Tom,' she managed under her breath, gently lifting his head into her lap to cradle it.

Leaning closer, she saw the blood congealed on his shirt, and the deep, ragged gashes to his chest which had drained his life away. He must have tried to crawl on after killing the bear, brave to the end, perhaps thinking to raise the alarm at the gate below. He had died in the attempt.

Tears choked her and for a while she could only repeat his name, rocking back and forth. 'Tom, Tom.'

There was a shout from below. One of the guards must have

seen her. With hoarse cries, a line of bobbing torches began to ascend the slope, then she was surrounded, the smoky light illuminating Tom's face, the proud jut of his chin, his eyes closed. Were it not for the blood smeared across one cheek, he might have been sleeping. There were mutters of recognition from some of Leicester's men, and one tried to lay his jacket over Tom's face, hiding him for ever.

She wept then, bitterly, fearing they might handle his body roughly, just as the guards had handled the assassin in the Queen's chamber. She refused to let them cover him.

'Leave me,' she told them. 'I will look after him.'

One of the men bent to drag her away and she resisted fiercely. 'No! I must stay with him. This is my fault. Tom would still be alive if I had not asked him to come with me tonight.'

Fresh cries brought new men up the slope to where she knelt, protecting Tom with her body.

Through the stinking smoke from the torches, she recognized one of Goodluck's men among the newcomers, and called out to him in relief. 'Master Twist! Tell them to leave him. This is all my doing. I must be allowed to . . . to clean his wounds before . . . before . . .'

Master Twist knelt beside her and looked carefully from her face to Tom's, then shook his head. 'You must leave him to these men now, Lucy. He is one of theirs. They know what to do.'

'I will not let them touch him!'

'You must,' he insisted, then lifted her away from Tom, pulling her damp face into his shoulder. 'Hush. Come now, there is some-one here who has been most anxious to see you safe. And then you must have your own hurts tended.'

She saw Will standing behind him, his face pinched and white in the torchlight, more like a wraith than a living boy, and her heart flooded with guilt. In her grief and pain, she had forgotten about the child.

He was staring down at Tom's body in a kind of trance, his eyes wide and fixed.

'Don't look,' she whispered, hugging him. 'You should not be here. Where is your father?'

'Below at the gate. He is waiting for me.'

'Then you must go to him at once. He will be worried. Come, I'll walk down with you. The castle is not safe tonight. There . . . there are murderers walking free here.'

'Not for long,' Twist muttered, his face grim.

With one arm about her waist, Twist led her and Will down the dark slope, away from the man who had helped to save the Queen's life, his body stiffening on the cold ground. Bitterly, Lucy wondered if the Queen would ever know his name or be told of his fate. She must ensure that the Queen was informed, even if that meant braving the royal presence again, knowing how much she had displeased Her Majesty. Better to face punishment and disgrace for failing to obey the Queen than allow Tom's sacrifice to go unspoken.

'Where is Goodluck? Did you find him?' she asked Twist quietly, not wishing to alarm the boy any further. Young Will seemed to have fallen into a reverie, his face distracted.

'No one seems to know,' Twist replied. He said nothing more for a moment, then added in her ear, 'Best to prepare yourself for the worst. If Goodluck was still alive, he would surely be here with us now. This has been a dark night's work.'

Lucy nodded, though her heart bled at the news.

First Tom, then Goodluck.

She did not want Will to see her distress. Kneeling hurriedly at his side, she kissed him on the cheek. 'Farewell,' she said, and put the boy into the hands of his waiting father.

'Farewell, Lucy Morgan!' Will called back over his shoulder. 'Until we meet again!'

Once they were both safely out of sight, Lucy turned away and hid her face in her hands.

# Epilogue

*Richmond Palace, south-west of London, autumn 1575*

THE CROWD BEGAN TO CHEER AND WAVE FLAGS AS THE PROCESSION rounded the bend and the gold and white vision of the Queen once more approached the vast gates of Richmond Palace. It was still warm for early autumn but a cooling breeze from the river kept the courtiers from overheating in their stiffened silks, brocades and jewel-studded velvet jackets. Somewhere behind the high palace walls a chorus of trumpets sounded, startling birds to rise from the banks of the River Thames. The familiar stench of the river mud was dulled now that high summer was long past and the court had not been in residence for many months.

Two well-scrubbed small children ran out of the crowd with bunches of wild flowers and presented them to the Queen.

As she bent to receive them, exchanging a few words with the children, voices on both sides of the crowd-lined thoroughfare called out, 'Welcome back, Your Majesty!' and 'God bless Your Majesty!' and 'God save our Good Queen Bess!'

Lucy, riding a short distance behind the Queen's party, no longer had to remember Tom's advice to keep her hands low and the reins short whenever the crowd pressed too near, for it came naturally to her now.

Faces from the crowd stared up at her, some mean-eyed and

suspicious, others openly admiring of her skin, so black against the white of her cloak. 'Look at the Moor!' one intrepid woman shouted, and the crowd there took up the cry, swelling forward to see 'the Moorish girl!'

Within a few minutes, the guards had to ride close and drive back the people with their pikes, while flowers and insults alike rained down on Lucy's head. The crowd's attention was terrifying, their faces lifting and rolling like a wave of the sea. Once, she would have died of fright, listening to their shouts. Now, all she could think of was how the guards at Kenilworth had dragged her to the back, out of sight of the entry procession, for fear the colour of her skin would frighten the Queen.

Just ahead, Lord Robert turned to glance at her, his dark eyes restless, a stormy look about his face. It was common knowledge that the Queen had forbidden the Countess of Essex to follow the progress back to London. It was said that Lettice had been ordered to spend time at home with her children and her husband, recently returned from Ireland, and his lordship was in a fine temper over that.

Of course, nobody was talking about their affair. Yet everybody knew. Lucy was still unsure how two contraries could be true at the same time, though it was not the only instance of such doubleness. It was an open secret at court that the Queen was no 'virgin', yet to speak such a treasonous thought aloud would be to ask for an agonizing death.

Nonetheless, she risked a brief smile for his lordship's benefit, then discreetly lowered her gaze to her horse's plaited mane. Falling into a kind of daydream, she had a sudden memory of a gentle afternoon on the woodland paths at Kenilworth, riding under the trees with Tom, his hand clutching at her bridle – she could not remember if it was because she had nearly fallen, or whether the horse had startled at something and tried to bolt – and this simple realization left her half in tears, biting at her lip. Already her memory of those long sultry days at Kenilworth was fading, his beautiful smile, his lithe black body, the grace with which he had held himself.

*Tom.*

Coming level with the gates, Lucy found herself caught in a

melee. The crowd pressed in hard, shoving this way and that. The reason was simple enough. The road narrowed here, with double guards on either side to prevent the commoners from entering the palace, and the courtiers on horseback could only pass through the gates two or three abreast.

Falling in beside two older courtiers, their lined faces showing their exhaustion, Lucy sat waiting her turn in silence.

She felt a sudden tug on her reins, and glanced down.

'Penny for a sick beggar?' the man cried in a hoarse, cracked voice. His face was blackened with dirt, his eyes bloodshot. 'Save you, mistress, have you a penny to spare for your old father here?'

One of the courtiers in front turned round, his face wrinkled in disgust at the smell, and lifted his whip. 'Get away from the lady, sirrah!'

'No, please,' Lucy said at once, horrified by the threat of brutality. 'Forgive me, sir, but I do have a penny for him. He is old and almost blind, do you see?'

'He is not a day older than I am,' the courtier spat, but spurred his horse forward, leaving her beside the palace gates with the beggar clutching at her gown.

She fumbled for her purse, hidden among the folds of her skirts, and extracted several coins.

'Just one, Lucy,' the beggar hissed. 'Are you trying to make them suspicious?'

Lucy's whole body jerked in shock as she stared down into the dark, watchful eyes of Master Goodluck. She nearly cried his name aloud but Goodluck laid a warning finger on his lips.

'Goodluck,' she breathed, but said no more at his furious shake of the head. He was in disguise, for some reason she could only guess at, and she might endanger his life by betraying that she knew him.

Correcting her mistake, Lucy made a great show of dropping one slightly bent penny into his trembling, outstretched palm.

'One penny, old father,' she said clearly. Then she bent further towards him with a little cry of disgust, pretending to brush her gown clean where he had touched it. Her voice dropped almost to nothing. 'I thought you were dead!'

'It takes more than that to dispatch me.'

Some men in the crowd jostled past him and Goodluck made a noisy show of dropping the coin into his belt pouch, hoarsely crying aloud his thanks.

'I leave for the coast tonight, but I had to see you first.'

Anxious at once, Lucy searched Goodluck's face for signs of trouble. 'Why?'

Under the grime, his blackened mouth cracked into a smile that revealed strong white teeth. 'Because you are my sweet Lucy Morgan and I wish to take the memory of your face on the road with me.'

'Oh, you fool!'

'Hush!' he cautioned her. He was still smiling, but she could hear disappointment in his voice, and a little disapproval too. 'I hadn't expected to find you such a great lady. With rings on your fingers and bells on your toes. This gown alone must have cost the Queen's coffers dearly.' He glanced at the fading scar on her cheek, where the assassin's knife had gashed her. 'I thought that business at Kenilworth would have scarred you for ever. Yet you are as beautiful as ever you were. And you ride close to Her Majesty.'

'I have to ride close at hand,' she whispered defensively. 'The Queen likes me to sing to her sometimes on the road.'

'My little songbird.' His mouth twisted in a brief smile. 'Listen quickly now, Lucy. If I don't come back to see you within a year, never mention me again. Pretend not to know my name. It will be safer that way.'

She stared, aghast. 'Why would you not come back?'

'Just remember what I've said.'

'How could I ever pretend not to know you? You are my guardian.'

'Not any more. Besides, a dead spy is an embarrassment to his country and best forgotten. Look what happened to young Massetti. Buried in an unmarked pit somewhere, and not a word home to say how he met his end. Even your friend Tom.' He paused. 'He was a brave lad.'

Tears filled her eyes and she found she could not speak.

Someone jostled him from behind, and Goodluck drew down his hood, so that all she could see of his face was his unsmiling mouth and the beard below.

'Farewell then, young mistress.' His voice was that of the old beggar once more, hoarse and breaking. 'God bless you!'

Forgetting all Tom's careful advice, Lucy fumbled and dropped the reins. By the time she recovered them, her impatient horse had squeezed through the palace gates and her own dear Master Goodluck was gone, lost behind her in a blur of faces and waving flags.

She cried out in frustration and despair, her voice swallowed up in a sudden, frantic cheering as Queen Elizabeth, having now reached the grand pillared entrance to Richmond Palace, began to dismount from her horse. The crowd was in a fever of excitement now, and more guards poured out of the palace barracks to contain the thronged masses at the gates.

It was all Lucy could do not to weep openly.

Recovering herself, she sat straight-backed, head high, as stiff in the saddle as the Queen herself. She would not permit any of the courtiers to see her cry and to despise her for such a sign of weakness. This was her chance to rise in the world, to shine, and she must not cast it aside for any man. Besides, she could draw some comfort from the knowledge that Master Goodluck was not dead, as she had feared. There was still the chance that she might see him again, one day.

# *Author's Note*

It is only half an hour's drive from my Warwickshire home to Kenilworth Castle, once a great English fortress, now lying in partial ruins. It was on regular visits to the castle, maintained by English Heritage and a favourite outing for our kids, that I first conceived the idea of setting a historical novel there during the time of Elizabeth I's visit in 1575. Queen Elizabeth liked to escape the stinking cesspits of the city during the summer months and tour the countryside 'on progress', with her court in attendance, visiting the grander homes of her subjects. These passing visits were often so lavish, the cost of accommodating and feeding the Queen and her vast entourage falling entirely on the host, they left many courtiers destitute. Even the wealthy Robert Dudley, Earl of Leicester, spent the rest of his life trying to recover from the nineteen-day extravaganza laid on for his queen in 1575. There can be little doubt he had hoped to recoup his loss that summer in daring style – by finally persuading Elizabeth to marry him.

Gossip during Elizabeth's reign constantly linked these two, claiming clandestine meetings between the 'Virgin' Queen and her 'Robin', as she affectionately dubbed Robert Dudley, and even a number of secret children, presumably born and spirited away at dead of night. Despite the frivolous nature of such rumours, a letter from the long-dead Leicester was found in a bedside chest after Elizabeth died, with 'His last letter' written across it in her own hand, a keepsake which suggests more than mere affection for a favourite courtier.

So why would Queen Elizabeth choose not to marry Robert Dudley if she loved him, particularly after promoting him to the title of earl, so much closer to her own rank? Theories abound, from the pragmatic one of wishing to retain control over her throne to the fascinating suggestion that she was in some way physically abnormal, i.e. incapable either of normal sexual intercourse or reproduction. The simplest explanation may be that Elizabeth, having had ample opportunity in her youth to witness the devastating effect of marriage on women, with both her mother and stepmother executed by a lascivious husband, chose to rule England alone despite the enormous pressure on her to marry. Yet there always remained rumours that the Queen was barren, or suffered from some mysterious gynaecological complaint – though discreet examinations carried out on behalf of foreign suitors appear to have been inconclusive.

Elizabeth's chief rival for Leicester's affections in 1575 was the fertile and red-haired Lettice Knollys, another of the Boleyn family from which Elizabeth also sprang on her mother's side, famed for their charm and beauty. It was whispered that Anne Boleyn's sister Mary had fallen under Henry VIII's roving eye, and been married off to the discreet William Carey before her pregnancy was too apparent. If so, her granddaughter Lettice might have considered she had almost as much of a claim to the throne as her cousin Elizabeth, since both Elizabeth and her own mother, Catherine Carey, would have been 'bastards' descended from the late King. (Elizabeth was declared illegitimate following her mother's execution in 1536; that ruling was never lifted, even after she was returned to the line of succession.)

Some historians consider Elizabeth to have been unaware of Leicester's rekindled interest in the beautiful Countess of Essex, but this seems unlikely. The two had enjoyed a brief fling ten years before, at which time Elizabeth had angrily warned Leicester away from her younger cousin, and in the claustrophobic atmosphere of the court, with its many observers and informants, the Queen could hardly have remained ignorant of their renewed affair for long. After all, it was only just prior to this that Leicester may have married one of her other ladies-in-waiting, Lady Douglas Sheffield, in a secret ceremony which he later vehemently denied – though Lady Sheffield produced a son in 1574 whom Dudley acknowledged in his will.

In 1575, Lettice Knollys was wife to the Earl of Essex, a strict military man who was away subduing the Irish, and mother to his children. The earl openly quarrelled with his wife on his return in November of that year, presumably over her affair with Leicester, and died soon after going back to Ireland during what may have been an outbreak of dysentery. There is no hard evidence that Essex was poisoned, but there was open enmity between the two men, not least thanks to the gleeful rumour that Lettice had already borne several children to the indefatigable Leicester, whose illegitimate offspring must by now have been littering the back streets of England. Whatever caused it, Essex's death cleared the way for Robert Dudley to marry his widow in a secret ceremony at Kenilworth in 1578. One can only imagine Elizabeth's reaction, first on discovering this betrayal, and later, when Lettice gave birth to a healthy baby boy.

In this retelling of Elizabeth's visit to Kenilworth, I have drawn extensively on *Robert Laneham's Letter*, a document published soon after the royal visit in 1575, perhaps as a paid exercise in propaganda. In this journal, Laneham describes both Kenilworth Castle and Leicester's extravagant festivities in meticulous detail, including the many hunting expeditions enjoyed by the Queen whenever the weather was favourable. But Robert Laneham would not, of course, have been privy to intimate goings-on in the fabulously furnished state apartments, built specially for Elizabeth's visit. My own frequent visits to Kenilworth Castle, though it is much changed since Tudor times, have aided me in imagining the carnivalesque atmosphere it must have possessed that scorching hot summer, with as many as 300 cartloads of workers and courtly hangers-on housed about the castle and its environs, plus a steady stream of local visitors to the 'spectacles' laid on as entertainment. And in common with many historians and literary commentators, I have envisioned the young Will Shakespeare, then a boy of eleven, travelling from the small market town of Stratford to see the Queen and her glamorous court at Kenilworth.

Which brings me to Lucy Morgan. That such a person existed, and may have been one of Queen Elizabeth's small army of attendants in the years following the festivities at Kenilworth, is attested by court records. The name Lucy Morgan appears several times between 1579 and 1581 in both the Egerton Manuscript* and the Public Records Office. She is noted chiefly as having received gifts of clothing from the Queen's 'Great Wardrobe' – on one notable occasion, 'six yards of russet Satin and two yards of black velvet', a lavish gift at a court where ladies-in-waiting dressed in black and white, and were not supposed to outshine their queen. There is also mention of a generous six shillings eight pence in Sir Thomas Heneage's office book in 1582, given as a traditional New Year's Day gift to a 'Mistress Morgan's servant', a sure sign that Lucy Morgan herself enjoyed 'bouge of court' or free board and lodging courtesy of the Queen, most probably in the capacity of lady-in-waiting to Her Majesty.

As for Lucy Morgan's African descent, some historians have linked this privileged Elizabethan lady-in-waiting with a later 'Black Luce' or 'Negra Lucia' living in Clerkenwell, courtesy of informal letters and reports written at the time. The Lay Subsidy Roll would seem to support this conjecture, showing a 'Lucy Morgan' living in that area in 1600, and Leslie Hotson makes an interesting case for these being one and the same person in his Shakespearean study, *Mr W.H.* But the character of Lucy Morgan as drawn in this book remains my own creation, albeit with links to her shadowy namesakes in the past.

Were there black performers at the court of Elizabeth I? Absolutely, and a painting by Marcus Gheeraerts the Elder from 1575 proves it, depicting black musicians and entertainers performing before the Queen. Indeed, due in part to the newly flourishing slave trade, there was a growing black population in England during the later Elizabethan era. Religious belief was a vital element in determining how easy life would be for these early black settlers. A rapid conversion to Christianity, which enforced the adoption of a Christian name, eased integration and enabled

* British Museum Egerton Manuscript 2806, ff. 148, 152v, 167v.

immigrants to avoid cruel penalties – including imprisonment and execution – for religious non-observance. These converts would not have retained their original names after baptism, making it hard to tell from official records just how many settled here in Britain during the sixteenth and seventeenth centuries. Their social status was also uncertain, following a famous test case in 1569 which apparently gave us the following judgement on slavery: that 'England was too pure an Air for slaves to breathe in'. To add to this confusion, parish records of the time either simply noted their colour – as if this alone was an indication of status – or intriguingly described black people as 'servants' rather than slaves. So the fictional Tom Black in this story loses his African name to become 'English' and reinvent himself as one of Leicester's head grooms – a free man, if still in service – and such a radical change of identity was by no means unusual.*

The character of Master Goodluck is based on the model of the Tudor theatrical spy, familiar to us from the story of the play-wright Christopher Marlowe, who may have been secretly working for the government at the time of his murder in 1593. The best of these spies were probably intelligent, highly educated and inventive men, gifted in languages, yet also mavericks and loners, choosing to lead dangerous and unconventional lives. Masters of disguise, trained in the ways of codes and ciphers, such men would have moved regularly between a dubious existence on the fringes of the court and the dangerous back streets of Europe. Although the name Goodluck appears in parish records of Tudor London, my character here is entirely fictional, the younger son of a disgraced gentleman, forced to make a living from his wits under an assumed name. The need for such versatile men in and around the English court was a daily reality during Elizabeth's reign.

Indeed, it is likely there were far more plots against the Protestant Queen's life than we have evidence for. Some of these, like the 1577 conspiracy planned by Don John of Austria, would

---

* Peter D. Fraser's essay 'The Status of Africans in England', in *From Strangers to Citizens* (Sussex Academic Press, 2001) edited by Charles Littleton and Randolph Vigne, makes an excellent introduction to this fascinating topic.

have been thwarted at an early stage by the ever-watchful Francis Walsingham, not only Elizabeth's principal secretary by this stage but her spymaster too. Walsingham ran a comprehensive network of spies both at home and abroad, their covert activities often funded out of his own pocket. The reason for such a network is clear. Catholic nations like Italy provided no end of zealous would-be assassins and plotters, the most famous of whom was Roberto Ridolfi, a Florentine double agent whose daring 1571 plot to overthrow Elizabeth led to the execution for treason of her cousin, the popular Duke of Norfolk, and would have done nothing for Elizabeth's sense of security.

The plot against Elizabeth during her stay at Kenilworth is, of course, pure invention. It was inspired in part by Robert Laneham's mention of a travelling Italian acrobat so flexible he seemed to have no backbone but 'a line like a Lute string'. This gave me my troupe of Florentine acrobats. There is also a curiously detailed account in Laneham's letter of the Queen's horse being startled in the woods by a Savage Man – another of Leicester's play-actors – a minor incident which seemed to alarm everyone present to a surprising degree. This is suggestive of a general uneasiness around Elizabeth's personal safety when out in public, and indicates that assassination was still considered a real and present danger. So it is not unlikely that there were a number of plots against the Queen during the mid-years of her reign, and that some were hushed up to prevent what might now be termed 'copy-cat' conspiracies.

In imagining the particulars of my Italian plot, I have taken certain liberties with the geography of the castle and its environs. The castle was reduced to ruins during the later civil war, to prevent it being used as a stronghold, so what we know of its infrastructure is based on a combination of old maps and drawings, a few preserved documents, and architectural conjecture. Many of the places mentioned can still be seen today, including the strongroom below the Queen's apartments where her most precious possessions would have been stored, which now stands open to the elements. Others are based on guesswork and imagination, such as the medieval roof hatch used by the acrobats to gain access to the Queen. The room itself exists, but the ceiling is long gone. Equally, some events mentioned in Robert Laneham's letter have shifted to other locations about the castle, for the exigencies of the plot. I have also, in consultation with experts at Kenilworth Castle, used a pinch of imagination when describing the duties of some of Leicester's staff, such as the fictional Caradoc, one of the steward's assistants, and Tom Black himself.

Writing this novel has been the achievement of a personal dream. I fell in love with history at school, flirted with it at university while studying Elizabethan and Jacobean playwrights, and have now committed some of that love affair to paper. The past is not always so very different from our own age, after all. Although my Lucy Morgan is a partly imagined character, a woman who existed in official records (though perhaps not as I have depicted her), she represents a type of brave, aspirational and passionate young woman familiar to us today, a character whose talents and shining personality raise her from poverty and obscurity to the Tudor version of celebrity.

*Victoria Lamb*
*Warwickshire, August 2011*

# Select Bibliography

I consulted a wide range of books, papers and pamphlets during the writing of this novel. The titles that follow are those to which I owe the greatest debt, with my personal triumvirate consisting of Robert Hutchinson's masterly portrait of Walsingham and his secret network of spies, *Elizabeth's Spy Master*, the marvellously detailed account of Elizabeth I's visit to Kenilworth, *Robert Laneham's Letter*, for which Tudor historians must be forever grateful, and *Elizabeth's Women: The Hidden Story of the Virgin Queen* by the talented and insightful Tracy Borman.

I am also deeply obliged to Peter D. Fraser for his essay 'The Status of Africans in England', in *From Strangers to Citizens*, pp. 254–60, and to Kathy Lynn Emerson, for her *Who's Who in Tudor Women* (http://www.kateemersonhistoricals.com/ TudorWomenIndex.htm), an online addition to *Wives and Daughters, The Women of Sixteenth-Century England* (Whitston Publishing Company, 1984).

The song 'Ah, Robin' is by William Cornysh (d. 1523).

The editions cited below are those consulted, even where earlier or revised editions exist.

Archer, Jayne and Goldring, Elizabeth and Knight, Sarah (eds.), *Portraiture, Patronage, and the Progresses*, Oxford University Press, 2007

Arnold, Janet (ed.), *Lost From Her Majesties Back*, The Costume Society, 1980

Borman, Tracy, *Elizabeth's Women: The Hidden Story of the Virgin Queen*, Jonathan Cape, 2009

Drew, John Henry, *Kenilworth: a Manor of the King*, Pleasaunce Press, 1971

Furnival, F. J. (ed.), *Robert Laneham's Letter: Describing a part of the Entertainment unto Queen Elizabeth at the Castle of Kenilworth in 1575*, Chatto, 1907

Gristwood, Sarah, *Elizabeth and Leicester*, Bantam 2007

Haigh, Christopher, *Elizabeth I*, Longman, 1988

Hotson, Leslie, *Mr W.H.*, Hart-Davis, 1964

Hutchinson, Robert, *Elizabeth's Spy Master: Francis Walsingham and the Secret War that Saved England*, Weidenfeld and Nicolson, 2006

Jenkins, Elizabeth, *Elizabeth and Leicester*, Phoenix Press, 2002

Jones, Philippa, *Elizabeth Virgin Queen?*, New Holland Publishers, 2010

Levin, Carole, *The Heart and Stomach of a King: Elizabeth I and the politics of sex and power*, University of Pennsylvania Press, 1994

Littleton, Charles and Vigne, Randolph (eds.), *From Strangers to Citizens: the integration of immigrant communities in Britain, Ireland and colonial America, 1550–1750*, Sussex Academic Press, 2001

Malcolm-Davies, Jane and Mikhalia, Ninya, *The Tudor Tailor*, Anova, 2006

Martyn, Trea, *Elizabeth in the Garden*, Faber, 2008

Neale, J. E., *Queen Elizabeth I*, Penguin, 1990

Palliser, David Michael, *The Age of Elizabeth: England under the late Tudors 1547–1603*, 2nd ed., Longman, 1992

Strong, Roy, *The Cult of Elizabeth: Elizabethan Portraiture and Pageantry*, Thames and Hudson, 1977

Weir, Alison, *Elizabeth the Queen*, Vintage, 1998

# Acknowledgements

I dedicate this novel to the memory of my mother, the romantic novelist Charlotte Lamb, whose pen-name I have adopted in tribute to an amazing global career which encompassed both historical and contemporary bestselling fiction over a thirty-year span. I'm sure my mother would have read *The Queen's Secret* avidly, and then told me precisely what was wrong with it.

My grateful thanks go to my agent, Luigi Bonomi, whose warmth and helpful advice has been such a boon to me, and to Selina Walker, Jess Thomas and all the team at Transworld for their belief in this book.

While researching *The Queen's Secret*, I drew on a number of sources for the character of Lucy Morgan, including Leslie Hotson's *Mr W.H.* and Kathy Lynn Emerson's *Who's Who in Tudor Women*. For these, and for Kathy Lynn Emerson's help in tracking down various elusive citations, I am extremely grateful, as I am for Trea Martyn's helpful responses to my queries concerning the Elizabethan gardens at Kenilworth. I would also like to extend my thanks to staff at both the Bodleian Library, Oxford, and Warwick University Library for their support in accessing relevant texts.

Thanks also to the English Heritage staff at Kenilworth Castle who have made me welcome during countless visits over the past two years, especially Stefanie Van Stokkom for her patience and historical expertise. Any liberties I may have taken with events and geography are despite her very useful advice, not because of it.

I also wish to mention Summersault, a jazz café-restaurant in Rugby, where much of this novel was written. Many thanks for not turfing me off my favourite table once my coffee was cold.

And I reserve a special mention for the Romantic Novelists' Association, whose glittering parties and camaraderie are second to none.

Lastly, I acknowledge the loving support – and occasional acceptance of washing-up duties – of my husband, Steve. *Sine qua non.*